T0267764

# THE LONG RUN

# JAMES ACKER

ISBN-13: 978-1-335-42862-2

The Long Run

For questions and comments about the quality of this book, please contact us
at CustomerService@Harlequin.com.

Inkyard Press
22 Adelaide St. West, 41st Floor
Toronto, Ontario M5H 4E3, Canada
www.InkyardPress.com

**Printed in U.S.A.**

To Wes. A place to rest my head.

And to Jersey. You know what you did.

# summer

*Even on the most beautiful days in the whole year—the days when summer is changing into autumn—the crickets spread the rumor of sadness and change.*

*—E.B.  White*

# bash

*aug. 17*

*mood*

I was behind the diner. I was sweating. I was thirteen minutes into my one break of the day and Matty wouldn't shut the fuck up.

"You see table five?"

"Mm. The Cinnaminson kids?"

"Yeah. They were talking shit. Laughing and shit."

"'Bout you?"

"'Bout you."

I didn't care. I didn't care what the Cinnaminson track captains had to say. I didn't care what my good friend Matty had to say. It was the hottest day in a month of hot days, and I guess I just didn't care.

I sucked my teeth and ate my eggs.

"Cinnaminson kids ain't shit."

Matty paced around the dumpsters and I could tell I was disappointing him. He wanted me to take the bait, get angry too. He wanted me to cut my lunch short, storm back through those diner doors and knock some second-string relay meathead's dick in the dirt. Personally, I just wanted to finish my eggs.

"You don't wanna know what they were saying about you?"

"Nope."

"Really? 'Cause I'd wanna know."

"I'm set."

Matty rolled his eyes and kicked at the chain-link fence.

"They think 'cause they took State over us one fucking season, they can talk shit all they want. Eat lunch any place they want."

"Matty. Chill."

"Like, we work here, man. This is our job, Villeda, they wanna fuck with us? With you?"

"It's just talk, dude, don't—"

"You just gonna let them call Bash the Flash a bitch?"

I sighed into my burnt plate of scrambled eggs. This wasn't a problem that would go away. Matty or the Cinnaminson captains. This heat. I squinted up from my milk crate.

"Can I finish my break first?"

The sun had a bad habit of hitting hardest the second I went on breaks. Made the back of the Rte. 130 Diner a hard place to relax. That's Jersey summers though. They begin and end with a heat wave. I could barely catch Matty's smirk through all the glare.

"Fine. Enjoy your eggs. Bitch."

He slipped through the back door, presumably to find someone else to talk at, and I breathed. That screen door slapped shut and the relief was instant. I was alone. Just me. And my dumpster. My eggs. Just the sun and the heat and this feeling and me for the last three minutes of my break.

I don't know when summer decided to suck but here we are. And the sad thing is that I used to love summer. I mean, duh, every kid loves summer but, for real. Summer was my jam once upon a time. We were tight, went way back. I loved everything about summer. No school, no church, no homework, all my friends, all the swimming, all of it. But lately, I've only been swimming to condition for cross-country. And all my free time goes to extra shifts at the diner. And I kind of hate my friends. Then again, these are all things I've brought on myself. So maybe it's me. Maybe I killed summer. Stabbed my oldest friend right in the back.

It should be said that summer did nothing wrong. This particular summer's just sucked ass. Every day, something new is wrong. There've been a couple of things wrong with today and it's barely past noon. For one, the air-conditioning unit broke in the diner and we're about three weeks deep on this heat wave. The local news said the wave is breaking New Jersey records, so congrats, I guess? It got so bad today we ran out of ice and there were customers leaving mid-meal. Had to deal with two unpaid tickets by the end of the breakfast rush. Plus, my boss has been up my ass because he assumes I know how to fix shit like air conditioners. Avi is always asking me or Matty to check on the breakers or look at his shitty car, like busboys should double as a pit crew. He's bold like that. Presumptuous. Like, he chewed me out this morning for not "smiling right." I'm sorry, but what the hell does that even mean? I should be doing a song and dance while I wipe down tables at the ass-crack of dawn? Maybe stop counting my tips every close, I'll give you a fucking grin.

*"Jesus."*

I was getting too hot. I took a long breath and leaned back against the brick of the diner. It helped a little. I checked my phone. Two minutes left. I started eating quicker.

Thing is, I should've been home by then. Two new kids called out 'cause of the heat, all last minute and shit, turned my opening shift into a full double on the hottest day in decades. Had to steal myself a little minibreak around ten just to cool off. Hid my ass in the walk-in and just waited. Sat on a bag of frozen fries. Sipped a coffee. Stared at my breath. And that was the best part of my day. Which is sad.

Cansado.

Before my mom died, she gave my stepdad a big box of gifts for me. He keeps them in this storage unit at his warehouse and brings me one every Christmas or birthday. They range from stocking-stuffers to books to handwritten notes. Nothing too fancy but I like it that way. So, when I turned eighteen a few weeks ago I pulled a Spanish word-a-day calendar from her pile. It was an inside joke between us because I never had any interest in learning the language. My dad left us when I was eight and, in my head, not learning his language was a great *Fuck You* to his sorry ass. Mom said I'd regret not learning it one day. Hence, el calendario. As a concession to her, I try to work the day's word into my life. Some have been easier than others. Today was cansado.

Cansado, cansado, cansado. It was love at first sight, man. I love *cansado* because it finally puts into words what I've been feeling all summer.

*CANSADO (adjective)*
*Tired*
*Weary*
*Miserable*

All tied up in one word. I've been chewing over *cansado* all day, even in the freezer. Trying it out loud. Tasting it. Cansado. 'Cause *sad* wouldn't cut it. It wasn't like I was depressed or nothing. The internet says *depressed* is when you can't feel anything and that wasn't me. I was feeling a lot of things. I just didn't like any of the feelings. But cansado? *Tired. Weary. Miserable.* Fit me like a trusty pair of jeans.

Why was I tired? If I wasn't clear before, I've been working opening shifts and the occasional double six days a week this entire summer. Throw that on top of the long-distance regimen my coach put me on to prep for cross-country and I'm surprised my body hasn't forced itself into hibernation mode.

As for weary? Now, I see tired and weary as two separate, distinct feelings. I'm tired because I've been running hot (literally and figuratively) for three months now. I'm weary for other reasons. Customers who skip out on their bill make me tired. Avi side-eying my tips 'cause he thinks I'm pocketing from the register makes me tired. People I don't care about make me tired. It's the other people making me weary. My "friends."

I use quotes because if I was drawing up my will, I'd maybe call two people in my life an actual friend. I don't give out the word easy. It's not that I'm not liked—the opposite, actually. I am a well-regarded individual. Even got myself a nickname. *Bash the Flash.* Fastest legs in the Tri-State. I don't call myself that, but people like to talk.

Ask around about me and you'll hear a lot of differing opinions.

"Bash? Bash the Flash? He's chill."

"He's loud."

"He's cocky."

"He's sweet."

"He's Mexican."

"He's Black."

"He's funny."

"He's quiet."

I'm a lot of different things to a lot of different people but the feedback's mostly all positive. The only thing everyone in my school seems to agree on is that I am "the best."

I hear this all the time. It seems like a compliment, I get that, but what it really means is that I have to be a chill, loud, cocky, sweet, Mexican, Black, funny, quiet guy depending on whoever's in my face. And because I'm *the best*, people are always in my face. The problem with being *the best* is everyone wants to find out why. The problem with being *the best* is you gotta prove it every day. To people you don't know. Or like. That's what makes me weary. All these people of mine thinking I'm *the best*.

So, why was I miserable?

Because I love being the best.

*Bash the Flash.*

I don't know when it started but I have this itchy need to be great at shit. I guess it's a competition thing. Probably why I'm such a good runner. It's not like I get off on being better than people. It's really not that. I just always want to be improving. It's a competition with myself. I think that's why I've been so distant with people this summer. I didn't have a great junior year. My grades were fine, my times were okay, but I just started to get sick of people. I used to be better at the juggling part of school but by March I stopped seeing the point. So, on the last day of classes, I made a deal with myself to focus on myself. Improve my times. Make some good money for the Rutgers fund. Figure myself out a bit. Maybe that's why summer's sucked so much. Too much myself. I don't know about myself. I don't really know what he wants.

On the Fourth of July a few weeks ago, after I left Matty's **USAAAAAAY** party early, I ended up drunk at Zelley Park. I was sitting on the top of this metal slide I used to love as a kid and I asked myself a simple question.

"Hey. Bash. Whatchu want?"

And I just sat there like a jerk waiting for a response. I didn't have one. 'Cause I didn't know.

I banged my head against the brick of the diner and checked my phone again. One minute left. I'd say a minute and some wiggle room but Avi has a sixth sense for when our breaks are up. To his credit, Avi's good enough to let staff eat free as long as we stick to basics and don't do it where anyone can see us. My current hideaway is this nice nook between the recycling dumpster and a stack of milk crates/chairs. When I started my break, the dumpster was giving me the perfect amount of shade but it didn't last for long. Never did. The sun had better places to be.

I squinted up at the big fireball glaring down at me from the sky.

*"...Fuck you."*

The sun had no response. Coward.

It took a second to blink the shine out of my eyes. After a few good rubs, my vision came back and I could focus on what was in front of me.

Who.

So, the back of the diner looks out onto this strip mall parking lot. It's mostly boarded-up businesses, Korean takeout, and this one exotic pet store I have heavy theories is a front for the New Jersey mafia. The lot is usually pretty vacant which makes my dumpster lunch bubble the perfect getaway. I could just breathe there. Not have to be someone. Not have to be.

So, yeah, I was a little pissed to see Sandro Miceli waving at me.

He was a good stretch from the diner but, even with the sun in my eyes, I could still make him out through the chain-link. I don't know the guy all that well but he's pretty distinguishable. For starters, he's giant. Biggest kid in my grade by a good three inches. The track guys call him the *Italian Yeti.* Tall and hairy. Dude looked like a fucking tree out there in the parking lot, waving a branch for absolutely no one. He had this bright neon green cast on his leg and some of the tallest crutches I'd ever seen wedged under his arms. The guy looked ridiculous. I don't know how he managed to break his leg but you'd think a person with his injury would be in the shade or in a car or, God forbid, not waving at me across a hot blacktop like a fucking goon.

I took out my phone and pretended to text. Acted like I didn't see his wave. It wasn't like I didn't know the dude. I was a track captain, he was a field captain. We went to the same school, similar parties, it wasn't like we were strangers. But I still had half a plate of ketchup/eggs to scarf down in my remaining seconds of break and I was going to finish them in peace, damn it.

When I eventually looked up, Sandro Miceli was gone. For a moment, I wondered how long the Italian Yeti must've been waving before he realized I wasn't a guy you wave to.

I checked my phone. I'd gone a minute over break and no one had come to tear my head off. Huh. Little victories.

*"VILLEDA!"*

I heard the sound of chain-link before I saw Matty climbing up the fence. He was running away from the two Cinnaminson guys I'd seated right before going on break. I was catching them midfight but the trio had already managed to give each other two bloody noses and a torn shirt.

God fucking damn it.

The bigger guy pulled Matty off the fence and sent him cracking onto the pavement. Before either could lay into him too much, there I was breaking a milk crate on the big boy's back. A cheap shot, sure, but I was tired.

The guy crumpled to the ground and Matty screamed in his face.

"YEAH, MOTHERFUCKER, YEAH!"

Then everyone was up again and I guess we were fighting. It wasn't the first time I'd fought at Matty's side. It wasn't the first time it was all Matty's fault. But if I'd learned anything in my four-year friendship with Mateo Silva, it was that some people just needed to get punched in the face.

*"FUCK YOU!"*

*"PIECE OF SHIT!"*

*"FUCKING FAGGOT!"*

*"HIJO DE PUTA!"*

*"CINNAMINSON SUCKS ASS!"*

Matty was back on the ground with the smaller guy, rolling around, pushing faces and scratching elbows, and I had my guy up against the chain-link. I'd just whacked the dude upside the head, rocking his ear in the perfectly worst way, when I thought about what Avi had said to me maybe an hour ago. How I just couldn't seem to *smile right.*

*"Don't look so miserable all the time, Villeda! You're young! It's summer! Cheer the fuck up!"*

And, you know? I had to give him that. 'Cause the man was exactly right. I was young. It was summer. I should've been having the time of my fucking life.

I felt a fist crack against my jaw and knew I'd be losing a tooth. With blood in my mouth and another five hours left in my shift, I declared summer officially dead. Pulled the plug. Called it.

**Time of Death: 1:33 p.m., August 17.**

# sandro

*AUGUST 17*

### *MY HAIRY ASS*

Look. I'll say it. Dudes look real ugly when they fight. I'm not even talking from some judgment place here, their faces just look mad unattractive when they're really in it. It's not like the movies, no one comes out looking like a cool action star when they're throwing or getting thrown. God's honest, it looks like they're trying to take a shit. No other way around it. Most guys look like they're white knuckling their way through a real bowl buster.

All this to say, Bash Villeda looked real ugly today.

I was watching the guy land the third in a three-punch combo on a Cinnaminson track captain and it truly looked like he was about to drop a load right there in the parking lot. His technique was A1, no surprise for Moorestown Athletics' golden child, but his face was all *"Oh, God, this one might split me in half."* The clenched anger. A shameful determination. An ugly need to win. Such a different face from that one I was just waving to minutes ago. That mopey guy sitting alone by the dumpster ignoring my ass looked way different. That was a guy I could maybe feel sorry for. That wasn't *Bash the Flash.*

And wouldn't you know it, the second I considered tagging in and paying it forward, the Flash took a sucker punch to the chops and dropped to the ground. Like a sack of potatoes. You hate to see it.

I just sighed.

"…Anywho."

I kicked up my crutches and moseyed on along the blacktop, limping away from the sounds of fists on ribs and dicks on display. It's not that I couldn't help my Moorestown brothers defend our track-and-field team's honor. I'm bigger than anyone in that dogpile, Cinnaminson or otherwise, and I know my way around a punch. But I had places to be and a cast on my leg and, most importantly, I did not want to. There's no chance in God's green hell that either of those track a-holes would join a fight for my sake, so why should I return the favor? I mean, I'm not a petty person but maybe when a guy waves to you, maybe if you do the courteous thing and wave back, maybe *then* you can expect some backup in your little brodown throwdown, but for now? On this particular summer day? This field captain's got better places to be.

Namely: Dr. Harriet Kizer and her humble medical practice.

The Miceli family has been trusting Dr. K since before I was born and, truly, I could not tell you why. There's nothing particularly charming about the good doctor, her office smells as old as it looks, and the strip mall by the highway's got to be the least convenient location in town. All this to say, the doc's not my favorite hangout spot. Usually.

Today, though, I was actually rootin' and tootin' to schlep all the way across town. I didn't mind braving the sun and the elements and the swamp-ass this particularly sweltering day. Because today was August 17 and, according to the calendar I'd been obsessively tracking all summer, August 17 was Cast Day. That's right. After an endless summer of sweating and itching and schlepping, this big green asshole on my foot was finally coming off.

Good fucking riddance.

Once the rotating blade settled and the cast was off, I couldn't stop staring at my newly bare foot in the mirror. My legs were dangling off the exam table, just touching the floor, and I could see that this new tan line was going to be a problem. My healthy foot was proper tan. A summer of sun on the Atlantic City boardwalk got it nice and toasted and my leg hair looked dark and lush. The other foot, however, looked like a newborn bird. Darth Vader under his helmet. A testicle. All pink and shriveled.

Hm. A problem, indeed.

I diverted my mind away from my testicular foot and turned my attention to the waxy paper they always have on those exam tables. Like wrapping paper for your ass. I wiggled around a little, enjoying the crunch.

"Hey, where do you buy this?"

I looked up to confirm that the doctor who's known me since I was a newborn was, in fact, ignoring me. That's fine. I'm used to it. My brain quickly shifted gears.

"Oh! Hey, Dr. K? So, I was reading online that there's this pill or something, like a vitamin or whatever, that can slow hair growth. You know anything 'bout that? Or something like that?"

"Oh, I bet."

I couldn't tell if she was listening but I didn't know who else to ask about this. Worth a shot, right?

"Yeah, 'cause, like, I like the scruff and no one else in my grade can really grow much of anything. Like, my brothers couldn't at my age. But... I don't know. It's just...it's a lot sometimes?"

"Mm. I'd imagine."

"So maybe if there's something I could take or, like, something I could do to make it stop growing so much? Not stop growing altogether but...you know, maybe just let me catch up a bit?"

"Oh, I hear ya."

My newly hatched foot twitched.

*Do you? Do you hear me?*

I could've self-immolated and received the same responses. It's my own fault for bothering to ask. Bothering to engage. Bothering. That's what happens when you stick your neck out. Someone's always there to trip over it. My eyes made their way back to the mirror. My hairy feet. My hairy legs. My hairy neck.

I sighed. "Hairy, hairy boy."

So, I know what you're thinking and, no, I don't have

much hair on my ass. Like, honestly, it's nearly hairless. *Next to* hairless. There's an understandable, lightly colored fuzz but it's nothing like my face, chest, pits, or legs. I feel the need to clarify this because, looking at me, one would assume it's a full forest down there. But it's truly not. I promise. I just get insecure sometimes 'cause, like, I get it. I am a hairy person. If you were to break me down into adjectives, *hairy* would make the top ten. Top five, I'll be fair.

The topic of hair has really been weighing on me lately for a few reasons. Two, to be specific. The first being that Jersey's currently on fire. This heat wave compounded with the nifty inconvenience of the cast on my leg means that I've been 98 percent sweat all June, July, and Augie Doggie. I haven't gone twenty-four hours without a midday shower and tank-top swap and my hair is only making things worse. It's dark and traps heat and most days I consider shaving myself clean if I weren't so terrified it'd all grow back thicker and in greater numbers.

The second reason for my hair fixation is my shoulders. For context, I've got *great* shoulders. Everyone says so. I don't know the difference between *great* shoulders and average or subpar shoulders, but apparently I've been blessed with a certain broadness that according to my father, brothers, and doctor would be "great for football" and "wasted on your dumb ass." I don't take pride in much but, hey, I got good shoulders. They make me an excellent shot-putter and I can fill out a sport coat nicely. All this to say, my beautiful, perfect, God-given shoulders are under siege.

I get having a hairy face. It's actually nice 'cause no one else in my grade can grow much at all. The chest is kind of cool too. And I understood when I got pit hair. That's life. And I knew to expect all the forestation on my crotch. I even got over my hairy feet. Qué será, Quesarito. But I am now getting hair all over my fucking shoulders and, I tell you, the line has been crossed. Because if I'm not in school, church, or Antarctica, I'm wearing a tank top. They're my default. My comfort zone. I keep my pits trimmed and apply the appropriate amount of sunblock. But how in the living fuck do I adapt to hairy shoulders? Now even my favorite tanks just expose me further to the world as *Sandro Miceli: Italian Yeti*. I was plucking the shoulder hairs at first but this doesn't seem like a problem that's pluckable. I had a dream I hit big money on *Jeopardy* and spent my winnings on laser hair removal but I can't bank on that happening. So, it's been tough.

"Mr. Miceli?"

"Hm?"

Dr. Kizer poked her head back into the exam room.

"Can you stay one more minute?"

I had errands to run and crutches to burn but one more minute couldn't hurt.

"Sure thing, Doc."

She gave me the same kind of frantic thumbs-up/run away combo Ma gives me on her busier days. Maybe Dr. K's schedule's as packed as my mother's. See, Ma loads her days from sunup to sundown. Her life is a series of thirty-minute increments and checks off a list. The woman's unofficial mascot is the Energizer Bunny and it's hard to get her to sit down for long before she's off to the new problem. Honestly, I was baffled that she had the mental real estate to remember today was Cast Day. At breakfast, I was making my nieces

and nephew eggs, trying to hear the weather report over my
family's morning screaming, when Ma pointed at the kitchen
calendar and hollered over to me.

"Oho! You excited to return that slipper?"

I laughed her off. It was an obvious question with an obvious answer but that's not why I laughed. See, I have this secret competition going between my mother and father and,
with that simple query, Claudia Miceli ended her champion
streak for the longest amount of time not speaking to me di-
rectly. My dad broke his five-day streak two nights ago when
he told me to "get the fuck out" of the TV room so he could
watch *Bones*. But with the slipper remark, Ma now holds the
belt with a record-breaking twelve days of not speaking to me.

My keeping track isn't some self-pitying thing. It's really
not. I completely understand why my parents don't talk to me
much. Between their four jobs, my two asshole deadbeat brothers, two nieces, one nephew, and our one shared bathroom,
I have a lot of family going on. The Micelis are a screaming
match in a crowded restaurant personified and the best thing
I can do to help them is take no part. I handle my own shit,
avoid my dad and brothers, and help Ma where I can. And to
her credit, I think she'd talk to me if I had something to say.
She's just busy. I get it. But for now, she holds the crown. That
cast question was the first time she'd spoken to me in over a
week. I'd say it was our first conversation in over a week, but
she didn't stick around for my answer.

If she had stuck around, I would've told her, *"No, I love
my cast. It's been pressure-cooking my foot all summer and I'm not
ready to say goodbye."* And she would've slapped the back of my
head for being a smart-ass and reminded me that it was *"your*

*own damn fault you've got the damn thing."* Which is true. I fell off my roof. Whoops. And, honestly, I'm impressed I didn't break more. I think I deserve a little credit for only shattering my foot and ankle 'cause it's a drop.

The few days following the accident might've been the first time my family's focus was on me since birth. Especially Ma. Her poor Sandro, the baby of her boys, fell off the roof trying to fix the satellite dish. All so her *NCIS* marathon would DVR correctly. A true martyr. What Ma doesn't know is that I was actually sleeping up there.

My room's in the attic. It's not as dreary as it sounds. It's insulated and shit and I can get onto the roof through the window. Whenever my brothers piss me off or my parents are fighting too loud beneath me, I'll go on the roof and cool off. Sometimes I play guitar, sometimes I chat with myself. It's nice. And it's mine.

One particular May night, when my baby niece was screaming with an ear infection, I found myself on the roof. I was strumming my guitar up at the stars, trying to sort out which ones might be planes, when I started thinking about Jackson Pasternak. We'd just had an all-grade assembly that day because someone keyed the word *FAG* into Jackson's locker. It was fucked and no one was copping to it. I don't think our class president's gay but he doesn't deserve that shit. I don't mean he'd deserve it if he were gay, I mean (a) I don't think he's gay and (b) no one deserves that shit.

Anyway, this kid behind me was whispering to his buddy the whole assembly. Halfway through I gave him a look and, surprise, surprise, it was captain of the track team and loser of today's fistfight, Mateo Silva. Matty, to someone who gives a shit. A real fucking asshole. One of the shortest guys in our grade with the biggest ego. He was giggling and whispering and I know he fucking did it. He saw me looking back at him and just gave me this bullshit kissy face. That night, up on my roof with my guitar, I went on this long train of thought where I'd confronted the dickhead after track practice. Gotten him away from Bash the Flash and his corral of sprinters and just let that fucker have it. But then the cops got involved and I had to go to court and it was a whole legal mess because I did it on school grounds and it turned into this big media circus and next thing I knew I was waking up on the ground.

My brain would only focus on my guitar at first. What was left of it, at least. My thrice-hand-me-down baby was busted to toothpicks and I almost started to cry. Then I started to suspect I might've broken my ass 'cause it was sore as hell. Weirdly, I could only feel my ass-soreness for those first few minutes which really freaked me out because there were legit bones sticking out of my foot. It was bad. But I just sat there. Surrounded by guitar parts, almost crying, my bones in the breeze. For like thirty minutes, I'd wager. I just couldn't bear to get up. Because if there was anything worse than breaking my foot open, it would've been my family's reaction. They'd pile on me like they always do.

"*Jesus Christ, Sandro.*"

"*Of course, you fell off the roof.*"

"*Are you fucking kidding me, Sandro?*"

"*Classic Sandro.*"

Classic dumb, hairy Sandro. So, I sat on the ground a little longer and thought of what my lie might be.

If you're getting the impression that my family doesn't

think much of me, I hope you'll understand why I've taken a few steps back from them. It's not that they ignore me or dislike me. It all comes from a place of love. Which, to me, makes it worse. That this is what love means to Micelis. But who doesn't have family shit? I'm not special. I'm just working with what I got. So what if my parents can go days without talking to me? So what if Ma stopped thinking about my broken foot once Raph's girlfriend got pregnant again? So what if I had to limp myself across town all summer because nobody had time to drive me anywhere? So what?

I just need to get through the next year and then I'm out of here. I can go to college and just start my life somewhere far away. Where my teachers don't automatically hate me because my older brothers gave them shit. Where I can wear a nice sweater without my dad calling me a "preppy queer." Where I can date someone. Anyone. Where I can be Sandro, not a fucking Miceli.

"Mr. Miceli?"

I snapped out of my spiraling and turned away from the mirror.

"Wassup, Doc Ock—"

I went still. "No."

"Yes."

"C'mon."

Dr. Kizer smiled up at me from the doorway.

"I'm sorry, hon. But X-rays don't lie."

The tiny woman was holding what had to be the biggest boot brace known to man, woman, or Sasquatch.

"Tell you the truth, I'm surprised we had one in your size."

"Dr. Kizer."

"I told you, Sandro, if you insisted on walking everywhere, your foot wouldn't set correctly."

*Insisted.* It felt like she'd reached into my rib cage and finger-fucked my heart. I crumpled back onto the wall.

"But...it's been all summer, Doc."

"And you just need a little more time to cook!"

Dr. Kizer leaned against the exam table. I think it was an attempt to "level" with me but it only made her look all the more pint-size by comparison.

"But I won't need the crutches anymore, right? Those are done? Right?"

Dr. Kizer gave me the same clinically apologetic smile she'd been giving me all summer. A trick she must've learned in medical school.

"Well...*walking* cast is a bit of a misnomer. Crutches are still recommended."

"Recommended?"

"We don't wanna see you limping back in here come Christmas."

For a second, I thought I could cry. But I got the tears to wait. Dr. Kizer patted my knee.

"I'm sorry, dear. I know you must be disappointed. Do you have a ride home?"

I just stared at my pruney foot in the mirror, letting her question linger. I really didn't appreciate when adults asked things they knew the answers to.

When I hobbled on my crutches back into the summer heat, I just about screamed. Half from the scorch, half because *are you fucking kidding me?* I kicked the air with my useless, broken, booted foot.

**"FUCK."**

It echoed across the empty parking lot. I took a moment to let the noise fade away.

Sorry. I'm just kind of pent-up lately. This boot news is just another tick in the increasingly shitty tally of my life. 'Cause, to answer Ma's question for real, yeah. I was really pumped to get the "slipper" off. It was just this bright green reminder that I'm a fucking idiot who fell off his roof. I thought I was done explaining what happened to people, done begging Raph to "chauffeur" me around. But nope. Because of all the walking I "chose" to do, my bones didn't set right. Super. Super fucking duper.

I limped across the parking lot and looked over to the chain-link. No one was behind the Rte. 130 Diner. No sign of a fight, save for some plastic bits from a broken milk crate. It was like nothing ever happened. It's funny how violence can pass through like that. How all that anger can come and go. Funny to see what it leaves behind.

For a moment, I thought about Bash the Flash. Well. Actually, I thought about Bash Villeda. The guy I saw sitting on that milk crate. That heavy look on his face. Before the fight. Before he was throwing punches and saying all the right tough things. And I tried to remember why I ever thought it would be a good idea to wave to him. Of course he was gonna ignore me. Guys like him only notice guys like me when we're bringing home field medals and even that doesn't save us from the jokes. All those nicknames, all in good fun. The Incredible Bulk. Queen Kong. The Italian Yeti.

And now I probably can't even compete with my fucked-up

bones. What's a teammate with a boot on his leg? What am I worth to guys like them?

I noticed a broken plate on the pavement, right around where Bash was sitting. Shards of plate and the bloody remains of some burnt-looking eggs. And I wondered if he ever got to finish his lunch. And I wondered why I might wonder something like that.

"…Anywho."

I got my crutches positioned under my pits and mentally prepped myself for the journey home. Two more miles of slogging. Three more weeks of summer. Four more months with a walking cast. And crutches. And begging. And hoping. Hoping that my bones set right this time. Hoping no one asks how I broke them. Hoping I can just get through senior year without incident.

But I'm optimistic. 'Cause if anyone can sneak his way to graduation without being noticed it's my hairy ass.

# bash

*faggy*

I was sitting in the barber chair and trying to focus on the static. My new guy had one of those little radios you hang in your shower and it was more static than music. But I needed something else to focus on.

"Shit. How'd you get that?"

The barber pointed a clipper at the bruise on my cheek. My tongue instinctively felt the sore spot in my mouth.

"Had to finish something. You know."

The guy laughed and nodded. "Oh, I know. Respect."

Whatever. He pulled out a mister and started sorting out my curls. "Damn you got a lot of head, kid."

"Been a minute."

"Need to bust out my nice clippers."

The guy was a talker, I could tell. I've never been about that.

"So. Whatchu want?"

I just wanted a haircut. Just cut my hair.

"Short on the sides? Keep it long up top?"

"I don't..."

"How do you usually wear it?"

I stared at myself in the mirror. I'd been growing my hair out all summer. I don't know if that was on purpose but it had a lot of length to it. Some height. Problem was, it never bothered me before today so I didn't know what I was supposed to be fixing. I didn't know what to say.

"I, uh... I like it long. You know?"

"Okay. So, keep it long?"

"Nah, I mean... You know."

"Shape it up? Just a trim?"

"Like..."

I tried focusing on my reflection but the dude was right there with me. Staring at me. Waiting for an answer.

"I can do whatever, kid. What do you want?"

The static on his radio was taking over the music. I couldn't focus on the question. What was the question? What did I want?

"...Just get rid of it."

He almost seemed disappointed. I just focused on the static. The buzz. The mirror.

I've got a bad face. Well, to be fair, it's my eyebrows that suck. I hate getting haircuts 'cause they just plant you in front of a mirror and, every time, all I do is stare at the fucking

things. They're bushy and close and arguably my worst fea-
ture. Or at least my most insistent. I don't know if there's such
a thing as "very insistent eyebrows" but I'm told they were my
dad's brows so maybe I was never gonna want them. I wish I
had my mom's eyebrows. They weren't a distinguishable fea-
ture of hers, but that's the point. Eyebrows should never be
the first thing you notice on a person. Del, my stepdad, says
I have my mom's eyes but it's not true. My eyes are muddy.
Swampy. Hidden under two pissed-off caterpillars. Hers were
just green. Like an island.

The radio started playing that country lady's song under
the static. Something about a kiss or a river. I think it played
a lot when I was a kid. I think I liked it.

My barber nodded over to his buddy.

"Yo, bro, turn on 99.3."

His buddy stopped sweeping hair and fiddled with the
knobs. Soon enough, the DJs over at The Buzz were arguing over if little boys should be allowed to play house and my
barber got back to shearing me. He sort of chuckled.

"Can't cut to that singsong shit. That lollipop music, you
know?"

I didn't know but I nodded anyway. Because I understood.
Man's gotta be comfortable. My hair's a big project. It gets
real thick and curly when I don't do anything to it and my
coach always gets on me about cutting it. Says I'll be faster
with short hair. I get where he's coming from but I kind of
like running with it loose. I feel like an animal or a wolf or
something. I don't know. It doesn't matter. It probably looks
better short.

"Gonna hit the sides. Tilt back?"

I nodded and tilted my head back. The barber leaned over me and put a hand on my head. Locked me in place. In this position, I could see his nipple through his tank. I tried to look away but his grip wasn't giving me many options. So, I just looked. It was just a nipple. It wasn't some secret, we all had them. But his was so dark. Like clay or redwood. There was hair too which was interesting to me for some reason. I don't know why but I've been thinking about hair a lot recently. There was sweat too. I think the guy caught me looking 'cause he smiled and laughed which seemed like a pretty stupid thing to do. I put my eyes back in my head and told myself to stop acting like a fucking asshole. One second I'm mumbling like a dickhead 'cause I don't know how I want my hair, the next I'm staring at the man's nipple? I don't know what my problem is. I'm just off. That's it. I'm just off today.

I think he had a tattoo by his nipple.

After a few minutes of keeping my eyes aggressively trained on a jar of Barbicide, the guy took a big chunk out of the back of my head. He showed it to me in the mirror, like some prized catch, and all I could think was how pissed Lucy will be when she sees me again. She loves my hair long and would hate that I didn't consult her on the cut. Only Lucy Jordan could dump a guy and still retain any input on his hairstyle. But I guess she was always a different kind of girlfriend. We only dated a few months but we've known each other all our lives. Her parents moved into the other side of my duplex before I was born. Our moms were pregnant together. Went through divorces together. Raised us, fed us, and punished us together. We're linked that way, dating or not.

I brushed a little curl out of my face and watched it fall to the floor. I guess Luce will like that my hair isn't in my face anymore. She likes my ugly brows and's always telling me that I've got a "very pretty face." Once I asked if she meant handsome and she said that I was "pretty like a painting." I don't know how I feel about that, but I guess I'll take her word. Because, with my mom gone, Lucy knows me better than anyone on earth. Which is probably why she dumped me. At least a part of it. I don't know why she dumped me exactly. Which is definitely a part of it.

If my stepdad and I ever talked, I think he'd tell me he hated what I was doing to my hair. He'll have to see the cut eventually but God knows he'd never say the words. Not much of a talker, Del. Still, I'd see it in his eyes. At his most gracious, he'd leave me with some vague comment about how much my mom loved my curls before shuffling off to work. Del works nights at the construction lot by Zelley Park and with all my day shifts this summer, we've got this whole "ships passing in the night" thing going that sorta works for me.

Thing is, I like Del. Speaking frankly, I probably love him. But the way I love my truck or my bed. Maybe that's unfair. Del's been in my life longer than not, but I don't know. We worked when I was a little kid and he was this fun young white dude but we just don't talk right anymore. It's kinda the same thing with Luce. If I think on it, Matty too. And when a guy finds he can't talk right with anyone in his life, he's gotta wonder if it's his own fault. Maybe he forgot how to talk somewhere along the way. Maybe he stayed too silent, too long and now his tongue's atrophied. Rotted away in his mouth. Or maybe he just has nothing worth saying.

"Damn, dude. You good?"

I snapped out of my stare.

"What?"

The barber was looking at me in the mirror. Half-concerned. More amused.

"You look like you want to die, bro."

A problem that's plagued me since boyhood. The second someone sits me in a chair and touches my hair, my expression sinks into something more appropriate for a funeral or the live execution of a loved one.

I just shrugged. "...That's just my face."

It only took twenty minutes and about fifty-something shrugs but I think the guy finally understood that I just wanted to zone out. He got back to it and so did I.

Thing is, I'm usually better at diagnosing my moods. It's like there's been this thorn in my chest all day. Every breath reminds me that something must be wrong but no matter how hard I dig, I can't get my finger on it.

I fiddled with a long, intact curl on my lap and thought about my mom. She did love my curls. Maybe the thorn was her. Or maybe not. Because when I go down that road, start thinking about her and how she was and all that, it's hard for me to come back. Really ruins my day in a very specific way. Whatever this feeling was, it felt different from her. This wasn't Mom-related. I'd know if it was. I know that thorn pretty well at this point.

Like, it was her birthday last Sunday. And when I woke up, I decided it could either be a terrible day and I could sulk and stew and blow up at people or I could make it nice. So, I drove our truck to our field and read our favorite book.

*Where the Red Fern Grows.* Obvious, I know, but it was the first "big boy" book she read to me growing up. Then, later that night, I added another bead to the prayer bracelet she left me with. I'm not super religious but I guess I am for her. All in all, it was a nice day. Quiet. Not a thorn.

The barber started cleaning up my neck so I looked at my lap. My finger. A little eyeball stared back up at me. A quick doodle from Lucy Jordan, not an hour ago, sponsored by Bic. If I ever got a tattoo, I think I'd let her sketch it for me. She's that kind of artist. She makes things people want to carry with them.

My heart keeps suggesting that this thorn thing's gotta be Luce-adjacent but I don't know. I mean, I do have this lingering worry that things will be weird between us. But when she caught me on our porch earlier, it felt okay. Not our best, but not as bad as I probably deserved. In a fair world, Lucy Jordan would never want to talk to me again. Because despite our being neighbors, basically sharing a bedroom wall, I hadn't exactly made myself that reachable this summer. I was moody all June, basically ignored her all July, and come August could barely so much as respond when I finally got the breakup text. Between the running and the diner and my growing allergy to talking, Lucy became an unfortunate casualty in my mission to fall off the face of the earth.

She called me out on as much today after ambushing me on our stoop. I'd just finished up my second run of the day and she was waiting on the duplex steps. Not an unusual spot for her but it had been an unusual summer. She was deep in her sketch pad when I rolled up but was all business once she locked eyes on me.

"Bash Wednesday."

"Luce Change."

"You just missed Del. Says you need to clean your room. Says it smells like ass."

I got out something like a grunt and started undoing my laces on the step below her. Like everything was normal. Like I hadn't frozen her out all summer. Like she hadn't dumped me right before my mom's birthday. But Lucy seemed game to pretend.

"You boys playing nice?"

"We're giving each other space."

"He's worried about you."

I almost laughed. If we were talking like we usually talked, I would've called Luce out on that. She was digging. Because if Del was so worried, where was he? He knows where I live. He lives there too. But instead of saying too much, I just stayed on my laces.

"He's busy. Been building condos over near Zelley all summer. He's never home."

"Rough. You still at the diner?"

"Yeah. Double shifts."

"Sounds like you're busy too."

Lucy was walking me toward something, but I was too tired to follow. My feet hurt and I was still catching my breath off my run. *Runs.* And if I let her guide my sweaty ass down that train of thought, she'd only end up telling me that she was worried too. That I was avoiding her too. That I needed to stop being a wishy-washy bitch and figure out what I want in life and talk to her for real. And she'd be right. Because

Lucy's often right. And I know she just wants to help but how about letting a guy catch his fucking breath, huh?

I'd drifted somewhere and when I came back, Lucy was drawing on my finger. The eye. It was a sickeningly realistic sketch of an eyeball, but I knew it belonged to me. She filled in a vein and sighed.

"You're shrinking, you know. Every time I see you. Little by little."

"Okay."

"Not saying anything. Just an observation."

"And I said, *okay*."

She didn't say anything to that but I could feel her stink eye. It was the same look my mom would give me whenever I'd get a little too bold at the dinner table. Lucy and my mom were always on the same page when it came to my bullshit. They had a lot in common that way. Two Black women from Jersey who loved art, loved me, and had hard rules against responding to lip. I gave it a moment and picked at some grass in my running shoe.

"...I stopped lifting. Been working on long distance. The Rutgers scout told me they like sprinters who can do both."

"Oh. So, that's where you've been all summer."

I made the choice to leave her hanging. Because I didn't want to get into how much Rutgers meant to me. I could have rules too.

After enough of my nothing, Lucy paused her doodle and really took me in. Like she was updating her image of me. She put her pen in her flannel and felt my soon-to-be-mowed curls. Her fingertips moved through the waves and, for a second, I forgot about rules. Space. For a second, I just let myself be touched. I closed my eyes and leaned into her soft hands. Her soft voice.

"It's getting long."

"Too long?"

"No such thing. It's prettier long."

"I don't wanna be pretty."

"You don't know what you want. That's kinda the problem, Seb."

Then her hands were gone. My eyes stayed closed and I heard a pen click. I heard her stand. I felt a kiss on my head and a long sigh against my hair.

"But you know that."

I thought about asking her to stay out on our porch a little longer. Just stay and keep me talking. Because if she went inside, I didn't know the next time I'd let myself talk to her. I didn't know the next time I'd let myself talk.

"Wait."

I stood up too.

"You going to Matty's thing tonight?"

Lucy laughed.

"So I can drink shit beer and watch you turn into an asshole for people we don't care about? In the woods?"

"You like the Sticks."

"It's still summer. I don't gotta be who those people expect me to be for another two weeks."

I followed her up and hung on her railing.

"…What should I tell them? *Those people.* If they ask. About us."

Lucy unlocked her door and chuckled.

"Tell'm what you want, Seb. I'm a bitch. We fought all

the time. I avoided you all summer and I never told you why. Tell'm *you* dumped *me* if you gotta." She shrugged. "Whatever. Whatever you want."

She headed inside, calling back as her front door closed. "And ice that boo-boo, pretty boy."

And she was gone. The bruise on my cheek twitched. I sat on my steps and laced right back up. I replayed our conversation, top to bottom, over my third run of the day. Lucy was spot-on, per usual. I had been avoiding her. Half 'cause I was busy but more 'cause I knew she'd smell it on me. My mission. The ocean I'd put between me and this town. All that cansado.

The problem with Luce is she knows me enough to see through my bullshit. We were just talking, perfectly calm, perfectly civil, and she still made me feel butt-ass naked. I hate that. I wear these clothes for a reason.

But Lucy's eyes weren't keeping my stomach churning. That pity in her voice didn't put this thorn in my ribs.

"Gonna have to charge you a sweeping fee, bro."

"What?"

The barber nodded around us. The floor was covered in me. Like I was a Christmas tree and the tiles were covered in my needles. It was too much. It was more than I thought I had.

My eyes moved to the mirror and I saw the finished product. What I looked like without it all. And I'll give it to him. He gave me what I asked for. I entered this shop with a head full of curls and that man got rid of them. Every single one.

"You okay, kid? I was joking about the fee."

I paid before he could brush me down or clean me up.

Cash. Let him keep the change. Didn't say a word. If I stuck around any longer, I might've said something ugly. It would've been uncalled-for and unnecessary and I would've kicked myself for the rest of the night for saying it. If I stuck around, I think I could've gotten really upset.

I stomped across the parking lot, hoodie up, got in my truck, and stared at myself in the rearview. My scalp damp. All that skin. Bald. Exposed. I looked like a fucking baby. Goddamn it, I looked like a fucking moron. A quick punch to the steering wheel and the honk came and went.

**"FUCK."**

I felt something well up in my throat. I rubbed the faint fuzz of stubble remaining across my scalp and took a long, deep breath.

*"Why did...why'd you do that, man?"*

I closed my eyes and sank into my seat. It's not that I got a bad haircut—he did a good job. I'm just not very sure that I look like myself lately. It's been getting kind of hard to tell who *myself* even is anymore but my hair's always been this hint. Something I could always agree on. Sebastian Villeda? He likes his hair. A constant. Now who was I? Some buzz-cut dickhead with a pickup truck and a thorn in his side. Ridiculous.

I peeked back in the rearview and noticed the four cases of beer hiding in my back seat. Right. Probably should've covered those better. The sight of my contraband made me finally consider the obvious. That this awful feeling in my gut, this looming exhaustion with my life, was probably coming from my most common thorn.

Matty Silva and me are boys. Have been all through high

school. I say *boys* because I always feel like I'm lying when I say *friends*. Anyone with their pulse on Moorestown High or two working eyeballs would say we are, in fact, *best* friends. We work together, hang out all the time, we're both captains of the track team. We're boys. *Matty and the Flash*. He's the one who coined my nickname. Which, I guess, is a nice summation of our relationship. He's the hype man I never hired. Always gassing me up to people. Always talking. In public, at least. We don't talk much when we're alone.

Sometimes we'll be watching a movie on his couch or be on a run and I'll get this bird's-eye view of us, how everyone else must see us. Two brown boys who can run fast and bus tables. A matching set. Very alike.

But that's all there is to us. If we're talking, the conversation's one-way. If we're laughing, it's at someone's expense. But before I can wonder if I even like my best friend, I snap back to my body and remember how Matty was there for me after my mom died. How he's had my back in fight after fight. How at least I know which Bash I have to be around him.

So, I guess we're friends. He's still a pain in my ass though. Like this morning. It was a standard opening shift of wiping down tables and eavesdropping on customers. I was busing a corner booth and dropped in on this little boy and his mom. They were sitting a few booths back, finishing up sharing a short stack. I didn't catch the context, but I could hear the mom pretty well.

"You gotta get good grades to be an astronaut."

The little boy was quieter so I had to move closer to make him out.

"Aliens don't have to go to school."

"Little man. Do you wanna be an alien or an astronaut?"

"I wanna live on the moon."

I don't know why exactly but that made me smile. Then Matty did what he always does. The second my guard was down, he popped up behind me, yanked out my headphones, and gave me a quick slap in the face.

"Caught you sleepin', bitch."

And I did what I always do and stomached it. Laughed it off. He slid into my unbused booth and I swallowed my urge to put his face through the table.

"So-ho-ho. You get shit for tonight, Bashy Boy?"

Matty's jaw always looked particularly punchable whenever he gave me new nicknames. They were different from Lucy's. Hers were funny. A running joke. Matty's always felt like a rewrite. Like *Sebastian* just didn't cut it. But I'd been on my feet for three hours and had five more to go and I didn't want to be annoyed. Because what's the point?

So I let my chill take over. "Yeah, man. We're golden."

My whole body loosened and I felt better with every shrug. It's like the monkey on my back took a smoke break and I could be cool for a little.

Matty gave me a fist bump. "That's what I like to hear. Liquor store give you any trouble?"

"Nah, they love my ass there. Got that top-shelf shit."

But that wasn't good enough for Matty. Not much was. He scoffed.

"Fucko. We don't want *top-shelf* shit. We want *Mexican* shit. Corona. Tecate. Corona *Light*. We're repping our whole country tonight, Villeda."

He was referring to the Beer Olympics. Sorry, *The Mateo*

*Silva Third Annual Beer Olympics*. It's this end-of-summer thing he's been throwing since freshman year. The track squad pairs up, picks a country to rep, and drinks to excess in the woods on the edge of town, known as the Sticks. Technically, it's a beer pong tournament but so far it's always fallen apart before the semifinals. Matty and I are favored to sweep again as Mexico but apparently now my alcohol selection wasn't to his liking. It's not like I had a lot of options. I had to *Hey, Mister* outside Delran Spirits for an hour before some college kid took pity on me, and I had limited options with my wad of ones.

But what I said was, "Yeah. I can nab more. No prob."

"Just get it to the Sticks before people show. Amanda's bringing the girls' lacrosse team and they expect to see Matty and the Flash in the finals."

"Oh. I thought this was just a track thing."

"Bashley. The Mateo Silva Third Annual Beer Olympics is about bringing people *together*. Plus, we need girls. Last year was one sweaty meathead away from a circle-jerk."

He said that a bit too loud. I checked to make sure the mom and her little boy didn't hear and moved my busing tub a booth over just to be sure.

"Field guys invited?"

"Maybe. Haven't decided."

"They're part of the team."

"They're part of *a* team."

"Coach might like it. You bridging the gap like that. Real *captain*-like."

I couldn't tell you why I was fighting for the Fieldies to join the party. I don't really know them like that. I think I just wanted to beat Matty at something and it was an argument I could win. Because the last three years of this track vs. field bullshit has always been just that. Bullshit.

Matty scratched his chin, inspired.

"Diplomacy. Very interesting."

"Just a thought. And some field guys are aight."

"Don't know about all that. But they'll bitch if I don't invite 'em again. And it's not like they'll be hard to beat. They're fat but they're lightweights. Tragic, really."

I sighed internally. We couldn't just talk about the field guys, we had to trash on them. We couldn't just talk about beer, we had to complain about it. Exhausting. Against my better judgment, I tried to pivot toward something less negative.

"Saw Sandro Miceli the other day. He seems okay."

"The Italian Yeti? Speak of the double-stuffed devil. Where?"

"Out back. Strip mall. I think he broke his leg."

"Probably tripped over himself, dumb fuck."

I gave up. It was pointless. But I did feel a responsibility to put as much space as possible between Matty's mouth and that little boy's ears so I moved to the center tables. Matty followed, right on my feet, like a shadow wearing too much body spray. He spread out on the table next to mine and inspected his neatly coifed hair in the napkin holder. After making sure each strand was in place, he zeroed in on my hair.

"You cutting that shit or what?"

"Nah, man. Girls like it long."

"Coach'll kick your ass if you roll up like that. This season's all about aerodynamics, bro."

I shrugged. "Then I'll put it in a bun."

I was so focused on not focusing on Matty, I barely noticed when I bumped into a customer. But before I could apologize, I saw her little boy. Swinging on his mom's hand, face a little messy from the pancakes. They looked just as sweet and smiley up close as they did in their booth. But before I could smile back, I heard Matty's laugh.

"Buns are faggy as fuck, man."

The monkey came in from his smoke break and found its spot on my back. Because the look on that mother's face. How quickly she got her boy away from us.

I spent a long time in the walk-in after that. A long fucking time.

I ran the tips of my fingernails across my newly bald head, avoiding making eye contact with my reflection in the rearview. Matty was a little right. Coach would be happy. And who knows? I could be more aerodynamic. And a buzz cut is a classic. A staple. It's less work than all that hair, that's for sure. Less faggy too.

I rolled my eyes at myself. *Faggy.* Like hair length has anything to do with that stuff. *Faggy* is just Matty's go-to descriptor for anything cheesy or abnormal. Like sandals or bracelets or, apparently, wanting to put your hair into a bun. He didn't mean anything about it, he was just talking shit. Matty talks shit. That's just Matty. The guy pisses me off sometimes but that's become expected. And oddly enough, I'm not pissed off right now. I wish I was pissed. I can sprint that shit off. Get in a fight or something. Nice and simple. This thing in my chest, it's something else. I don't know if it's one of my usual thorns. I think it might be something new.

I finally started the truck, hoping the AC would clear out

some of these thoughts, and blared some nice nondescript house music to get me in the "I guess I'm going to a party" mood. I kind of got lost in the beat and was about thirty over the limit by the time I entered the Orchard. Where the rich folks live. The neighborhood's essentially thirty or so identically ugly McMansions built on the remains of what used to be a really nice apple orchard and it's the best way to get to the Sticks. It's also a war zone of running toddlers, hidden cop cars, and bored housewives just dying to report boys who look like me for speeding or noise or existing. So, I turned down my music and responsibly cruised.

I was hyperaware of my driving but still nearly rolled through a stop sign. I saw it in time but Birdie's brakes aren't what they used to be. She's an old blue pickup that's been through it. My mom bought her used at sixteen and dubbed her Birdie, short for bluebird, because of her color and speed.

To be safe, I sat Birdie at the stop sign for a beat. Took in our surroundings. There were these two boys playing basketball in a driveway. The house wasn't as ostentatious as its neighbors and the kids looked like they were having fun. Actual fun. Summer fun. They looked like kids I might've been friends with. Back when I made friends. Whatever they were playing, it wasn't basketball. Not really. It looked like a game they'd made up. Something that was just theirs. And I remembered how beautiful that could be. Finding something that's just yours. Something that could only exist in the summer. Something simple and silly and the right kind of exhausting. No thorns. Just summer. And I felt a little sorry that I pulled the plug on summer so early.

I was so deep in that thought, I didn't even notice the knock on my window. The second one made me jump though. I turned to find the Italian Yeti standing at my window. Sandro Miceli. Smiling at me like a straight-up murderer. He motioned for me to roll my window down and I almost sped away. It was maybe the second time in a week this giraffe had derailed my train of thought.

But for some reason, I rolled the window down.

"Hey, Bash."

He just smiled. I didn't know what to say. "Uh… Sup, man?"

I mean, what else was I supposed to say? The guy cocked his head down the road. Toward the Sticks. "You going to this Matty thing?"

He had this tank top on that just read **ITALY**. I'd seen him wear it at practice but today it was coupled with some very short Italian-flag shorts. Three things dawned on me. First, a Fieldie was on his way to the Olympics so Matty must've taken my bait. Second, I'd completely blanked on wearing anything remotely Mexican for the third year in a row. And, lastly, Sandro Miceli had the hairiest legs I'd seen outside of a zoo. He was about an inch away from showing brain in those shorts and I had to respect the balls it took to wear them in public. So, I complimented them. The shorts, not his balls.

"…Nice shorts."

"Thanks. Nice plain white shirt."

I guess I laughed a bit at that.

He pointed at my beer cases and told me I should cover them better but I wasn't paying attention. I couldn't stop staring at his crutches. He had a fresh boot on but his crutches looked like they were nearing five hundred miles. The rubber ends were eaten up like he'd been walking all over the place, which wasn't smart. He'd graduate in that boot if he kept that up. I realized that I'd zoned out again, the fifteenth time today, only to find that he'd done the exact same thing. Only he was looking at those kids playing their own kind of basketball. And he was smiling. And I got this feeling that he had the same thought as me. At least summer wasn't dead for those boys. It was that kind of smile.

"...You wanna ride?"

# sandro

### *LOOK AT THE BALLS ON DRO*

When I got into Bash Villeda's truck, all I could think about were my balls. I love my Italy shorts dearly but, in the two years since I bought them on the Atlantic City boardwalk, both my legs and balls have grown. Before I left, my little nephew GJ told me I was one high kick away from showing the world my goods and I didn't heed his warning. But sitting shotgun in that pickup, the shitty polyester of those ten-dollar shorts riding up the upholstery, I feared my junk was a ticking time bomb.

"Windows down?"

Bash's question shook me out of my ball-fog and I nodded.

"Oh. Uh…sure."

He rolled the windows down and we both went back to staring silently ahead.

I wasn't surprised when I got the invite to the Beer Olympics. I wasn't stoked that Matty Silva was the one extending the last-minute offer but I've grown to expect the random invite here and there. See, people *love* to invite me to shit. Seriously. I'm constantly getting invited to parties I have no business attending. I nearly got shin splints last year after all the sweet sixteens I stomped my way through.

Someone once told me that I'm a "party essential." At first, I thought it was high praise. That people really enjoyed my presence. Then Syd DeStefano had this rager to celebrate getting over mono and it was the talk of homeroom come Monday. People were chatting me up, saying how wild it was and how fucked-up we all got and I just laughed and nodded along, apparently the only one who knew I was not in attendance. I'd bailed last minute due to some gas station hot dog–related food poisoning, yet Syd still thanked me for making an appearance.

It was then I realized that people liked inviting me to things but didn't really give a shit if I went. I guess because I'm quasi-friendly with everyone and because I'm loud and overall a fun guy, people considered me "essential." Like a queso fountain. Or a bouncy house. A fun thing to have but not necessarily make-or-break for your night's overall success.

That cooled me off parties this summer. I only agreed to go to the Olympics for field solidarity. Dr. Kizer's new foot prison was almost enough to keep me inside for the night, but something bigger made me follow through. Fieldies had been openly excluded from some track parties in the past, and I figured accepting a Silva olive branch was the captainly thing to do. Or maybe I just wanted to show off my favorite shorts. Maybe I'd spent enough time wallowing in my room for one summer. Or maybe I just didn't want to let the fucking boot win.

"Can you put your seat belt on?"

"What?"

I snapped back out of my stare. Bash nodded at my waist. "Your belt. People get pulled over here. And...the beer."

"Oh. Right. Click it or ticket."

"Mm."

I adjusted my sitting carefully, very mindful of my shorts, and clicked it. I waited a responsible amount of time to see if the guy's sentence fragments were going to progress into any form of polite conversation but, ten mailboxes later, decided it was a lost cause. So be it. I despise awkward silences to my core but they beat walking any further in that heat.

For the umpteenth time, my brother Raph was nowhere to be found when it came time to drive me to the party. It wasn't some great shock but, more than a ride, I guess I just wanted my family to know I had plans for the night. That I was leaving for the night to get wasted in the woods and wouldn't be doing my chores in the morning. That I might even throw up if I felt like it. That, if offered, I'd smoke weed. That, if offered, I'd have anonymous sex on the Rotary Club Nature Trail. I would've loved to tell my parents that their youngest son, Sandro, was going out for the night and he was ready to burn this town to the motherfucking ground.

But they were both at work so I just left a Post-it on the microwave. *Out late.* I guess I'm glad Raph didn't drive me.

If he had, I never would've discovered how shit Bash Villeda was at small talk.

Moorestown's premiere track captain is a well-known, well-liked luminary in our small town. He's our school's current athletic prodigy and I'm told he has a lot of top-tier scouting interest. He is biracial, has a strong jawline, and (usually) has good hair. And that's about all I know about him. If I had to guess, I met him in elementary school and in that time we've carried less than five conversations. It's not that I don't like the guy. I just don't know him. Well, I guess that's not entirely true. I know *Bash the Flash*. Everyone does.

Bash the Flash is the guy who did shrooms on the away bus and got us disqualified from the Camden Kids Fun Run. Bash the Flash is who I saw give that Cinnaminson dude some serious cauliflower ear behind a diner. The Flash is best friends with Matty Silva, noted cock, and apparently tied to his hip. I know that guy well enough. But I'd never seen him alone before. Maybe that's why I knocked on his truck window. Probably why I waved at him outside the Rte. 130 Diner too. I mean, the only reason I bothered waving was that look on his face. Same look he had sitting at that stop sign. In his truck, by the dumpster, he looked lost. Alone, the guy looked really lost.

"Love the truck."

Bash kept his eyes on the road but grunted. I couldn't tell if it was an acknowledging or a "Whatchu say?" kind of grunt so I turned the music down.

"I said I love your truck."

"…I heard you."

His eyes peeked at the volume knob. I think he was peeved

that a stranger had touched his knob. I suppose it was poor passenger etiquette.

"Oh. Sorry."

Even at the low volume, Bash never stopped nodding along to the beat.

"So. Whatchu do?" Bash glanced at my boot. I perked up. Finally. A topic.

"Oh. I broke it."

"Yeah, no shit. How?"

"Fell off my roof."

Bash had been bobbing his head to the music all drive but he went very still there. I didn't get it.

"...What?"

He just shook his head.

"Nothing."

I could see it then. In the corners of his mouth, he was trying not to laugh. I didn't know if it was at me or with me so I didn't push. He took a right at a stop sign and his big eyebrows bunched up.

"Didn't you have a green one? Like a... I don't know. A hard cast?"

I smiled. *Got him.*

"HA! You DID see me waving at you."

Bash rolled his eyes and actually smiled. "I was on my break, man, I'm not tryna talk to anyone."

"Hey, I get it. Saved me the trouble of thinking up small talk."

"See? You're welcome."

I laughed and readjusted the Velcro on my boot. "I had places to be anyway. Sorry I didn't help."

"What?"

"Help. With the fight. Looked pretty brutal."

Then Bash stopped smiling. The bruise on his cheek twitched. Whatever warming up he'd been doing, that was over. The flatness was back in his voice and he might as well have just grunted again.

"Not your fight."

His eyes stayed on the road. For the best, 'cause I was rolling mine. Say one wrong thing around these guys and it's all *humphs* and shoulder shrugs and bass in their voice. But I gotta say, my own hatred of dead air aside, Bash's silence was surprising to me. Cool guys usually play the chill card till it wears out but I always thought Bash the Flash was a real loudmouth. Always talking shit on the away bus or in the locker room. But maybe that's the Matty factor. Or, more likely, Bash wasn't talking because he doesn't know me or why I thought it'd be a good idea to bring up the time he got punched in the face. Could be both.

"You walk a lot."

I nearly jumped at the sudden offer of conversation.

"I what?"

Bash stayed on the road but I could tell he wasn't listening to the music anymore. "You were walking in that heat wave. And you were walking to the Sticks. You walk a lot."

"Oh. Yeah. Don't got a car."

"Your folks let you walk around on that foot?"

Now I wanted the dead air. "Uh...sometimes. You know? Sometimes they'll drive me though. They're just busy. Like, they work *a lot*. My ma's got, like, five jobs this summer and

Pop's in repairs so his van's, like, never home. They're just busy. It's a lot to coordinate."

Bash's finger was tapping on his steering wheel. He looked like he was trying to do some sort of math. "So...they *make* you walk around on that foot."

I could hear my crutches rattling in the bed of his pickup. I didn't know what to say. The real answer was pretty big but I didn't need to be emptying any purses in some track bro's truck. That would be a very embarrassing way to start the night.

"I mean, like, they told my brother Gio to drive me but he was all *I have a job, fuck off* so they told my other brother, Raph, that he had to drive me because Raph *doesn't* have a job right now but then, like a week in, his kinda-girlfriend Nicki—Nicki Touscani, Dani T.'s stepsister—well, Nicki got knocked up again so now Raph's *getting* a job and suddenly a little broken foot didn't look so bad to Ma and Pop. I mean, I get it. It sucks but I get it."

Or maybe the night was always going to be embarrassing. I have a tendency to overshare when I'm nervous. But Bash just nodded along, that finger still tapping away on the steering wheel. I don't think he knew how to act, faced with all that information.

"And...why were you on your roof?"

I felt my shoulders relax. Maybe because he didn't tuck and roll out of his moving car. He seemed genuinely curious.

"You never go up on roofs?"

Bash shook his head. I smiled.

"I do it all the time. I mean, I did. I got a sick roof, man.

Right by my room. I got a lot of family going on so I'd go up there for some quiet."

"Oh. Cool."

"Yeah. It was."

Bash took the final turn out of the Orchard.

"...Where do you go now? For quiet?"

His finger stopped tapping. I just shrugged.

"I found a spot."

I readjusted my Italy shorts as we drove toward the forest.

At the end of the Orchard, there's this dead end. You're supposed to park there, or preferably a ways away and walk there, then get on the nature trail that spits you out at Square Field, this clearing in the Sticks that's the go-to spot for outdoor parties. People in the Orchard are notorious for ratting on anyone they sense are going into the Sticks for some public revelry so I understood when Bash let out a minute-long *"Fuuuuuuuck"* pulling up to the dead end. At least twenty cars were clustered up at the trail's mouth. Some blocked others in, some parked in the grass, almost all had Moorestown High School parking stickers.

I hopped out and helped Bash with his beer cases. He shook his head.

"Goddamn it, Matty. No way this doesn't get busted."

He seemed weirdly pressed about it too. Like he really needed the night to go well. Half to lighten the mood, half 'cause I was thirsty, I took out two Modelos from a case and gave one to him. "Might as well start now, then."

He looked at me funny, almost like he was trying to remember who I was all of a sudden. But then he chuckled and opened his beer. They were a bit warm from the car but it didn't stop Bash. I always thought of the track bros as light-weights, but the guy could drink. He downed his before I was halfway done, started in on another, and pointed at my shorts.

"So. Where'd you get those?"

"Atlantic City."

The man had the gall to blow a raspberry. "AC's busted. Wildwood's superior."

I just stared right back at him. He cocked his head to the side. "You disagree?"

Cocky cocking prick. I shrugged. "I've learned not to take Jersey beach spot preferences personally. I've gotten into too many fights on the topic in my short life and have developed a thicker skin."

"Good. You'd need it."

"Excuse me?"

"Thick skin. You'd need it to survive an Atlantic City beach."

My nose twitched. Bash smirked. It was bait. I knew it was bait. I took a long sip of beer, just to show him how chill and unbaitable I was, then launched into my defense.

"Wildwood's boardwalk is trash, for starters, and while *maybe* you can argue that its beach access has an edge solely on physical location, it's almost all metered parking, an obvious scam, and any passable restaurant is, like, ten miles away from the water. The sand is oily as hell, the roads haven't been paved since fucking Watergate, and there's absolutely no nightlife to speak of. ESPECIALLY compared to Atlantic City, casino capital of the East. So, yeah. Have fun spending an hour on a mildly nicer beach then spending all night in your Holiday fucking Inn."

Bash just stared at me. I can get a little heated defending things I actually like and I thought I might've freaked him out. His face was kinda frozen like he was taking it all in. Then there was this crack in his eyebrows and he burst out laughing. Like *a lot*. And it wasn't that booming laugh I'd hear from the back of the away bus when Bash the Flash was holding court. It was actually kind of weird. Like a coyote. The kind of animal sound you'd hear in the woods that'd make you think twice about letting your pet walk around. I got the feeling that it was his actual laugh. Pretty soon I was cracking up too.

Somewhere in the laughing, I put my crutches in his truck bed. What could one night on my boot hurt? In the bed, I noticed a bunch of first-draft poster boards of the Beer Olympics tournament bracket. I saw a Sharpie and had an idea.

"Yoooo, what team are you on?"

"What?"

Bash finished his second beer and chucked it into the bed. I popped the marker cap and tapped the big bold **ITALY** on my tank top.

"For Olympics. What team are you?"

"Oh. Mexico."

"You Mexican?"

"Half."

"Nice. Is this plain white shirt particularly precious to you?"

He laughed again and spread out his shirt. "Go for it."

I was **MEX** deep when he started getting fidgety. I kinda fucked up the X but compensated. Without really thinking, I put my hand on the small of his back to steady him. It worked but Jesus he was warm. Not sweaty, per se, but it felt like he'd been sitting in the sun all day. He steadied though. As soon as I put my hand on him. Kinda like when you're brushing a dog. They just freeze. **ICO**. It was Sharpie on a V-neck and I was sure his little buddy Matty would give him shit but at least he'd be regulation.

We probably hung out at the dead end longer than we should've 'cause by the time we were walking through the Sticks it was dark. Bash was super slow, testing every step, but I knew that trail down pat. We were carrying a case each and I was already feeling my three beers which didn't give me too much confidence in my pong potential. Bash must've been feeling his too because he repeatedly remarked how quickly it got dark.

"Damn. Summer must really be over."

I've learned that if a person with any level of intoxication repeats themselves once, it's probably because they're tipsy. If they repeated themselves any more than that, they're really trying to say something else. So, I took him up on it.

"I love summer. Usually. But with my cast and shit, this one was kind of a bust. Past few summers have actually been busts."

It was dark but I could see that he was nodding. He took his time to respond. "Maybe it was just part of growing up, you know? Moving on from summer."

I couldn't see his face and I think he preferred it that way. It was sad, what he said. At least how he said it. Like he really wasn't ready to let go of summer that easy.

I shrugged. "Maybe we just gotta learn to love fall. Leaves and pumpkins and shit."

He laughed. I think he appreciated that. "Yeah. Fall's okay. I like fall."

"Me too."

The trail spit us out into Square Field. Square is sort of like if some rich maniac decided to build a secret soccer field in the middle of a forest but gave up after clearing trees. The ground was probably once fertile but it's been poisoned by years of Moorestown high schoolers' cigarette butts and vodka vomit. The Beer Olympics was already in full effect, smack-dab in the middle of the field. Tiki Torches encircled three pong games running on folding tables. There was an area for kegs and drinks, a group of smokers sitting around a bonfire, and two different speakers blaring competing house music. I'm only ever out in Square to get some alone time so the bacchanalia was surreal. What was originally just a track thing, maybe ten to twenty guys, then a track-and-field thing, at most forty, had erupted. I saw lacrosse girls, choir girls, some kids from the private school, the debate club for fuck's sake. Had to be at least a hundred people.

*"OH, WHAT THE FUCK?! VILLEDA?!"*

Matty appeared in a puff of smoke. He was wearing this tacky poncho and a drawn-on mustache which seemed in poor taste. Then again, I was dressed like an offensive cartoon of an Italian so I guess we all make choices.

Matty scoffed at Bash's newly minted shirt. "Where the fuck— What the fuck are you wearing?! You said you had a sombrero!"

I watched Bash cover for himself, that booming laugh creeping its way back out. I could barely make out his face but the change was clear. It actually made me uncomfortable. Then Matty's drunk ass set his sights on me.

"And *you*. Doug's been carrying Team Italy's ass all night! Table three."

This fucking guy. He pointed me to the pong tables and dragged Bash away. Before he was too far gone, Bash turned back and saluted me.

*"Viva Italia!"*

I saluted him back. It surprised me that he knew that. All in all, Bash Villeda was more surprising than I'd given him credit for. Interesting guy. I was impressed I had the balls to knock on his window. Any other day, I wouldn't do something like that. Maybe I was just feeling ballsy tonight. I certainly wore the shorts for it.

I heard this voice in my head tell me that I should probably go home. I had fun, had some beers, had an acceptable amount of socialization. It was darker now but I knew the woods well and could be home in no time. I could watch a movie with GJ. Snag a nice plate of Ma's leftover ziti before it gets inhaled. Get all warm in my cozy bed. Be comfortable. And alone.

I finished my beer and told the voice to shut up.

# bash

*beer*

I hate the taste of beer.

There. I said it.

I've given it every chance, I've tried all the kinds I could, and it's just not for me. That being said, I am nothing if not competitive. And I am nothing if not a motherfucking beast with a Ping-Pong ball. So, if the only challenge to beer pong is the *beer* half, the Olympics should've been a breeze, right?

*Right?*

I think Matty blacked out somewhere in our third match. It was against the USSR and it should've been a cakewalk. We were four cups up. I had the advantage of my late arrival sobriety and was taking my sweet time catching up to my stumbling opponents. I'd just sunk my second cup in a row, fully heating up, when Matty had to fucking ruin it.

There are three Deadly Fouls in the Olympiad rule book. All easy to follow. All written by Matty himself.

## 1. NO STANDING ON MY DAD'S TABLES!
## 2. NO PEEING ON MY DAD'S TABLES!
## 3. NO PUKING ON MY DAD'S TABLES!

Breaking any of these rules is cause for immediate elimination. Knowing these rules, having WRITTEN these rules, Matty still ended up puking all over our cups while scream-singing along to "Mr. Brightside." Our sober ref, lacrosse captain Ronny DiSario, caught the foul right away, blew her whistle, and that was that.

I would've rubbed Matty's nose in the mess like an untrained dog but he immediately passed out in a lawn chair. I shook hands with the USSR and retreated to the kegs to cool off. It was bullshit. He made me search two separate liquor stores for the right beer, rides me for being late, then can't even deliver us a W? Or, at the very least, not get in my way? Bullshit.

I found myself entertaining the losers' circle, all similarly bitter drunks, and I did what I always tend to do in those situations. I got rowdy. *Flashy.* I pounded two more Modelos and challenged Greg Hudgins to a good old-fashioned game of Whiskey Slap. It's essentially Chicken with whiskey. You take a shot and let the other guy slap you in the face. You keep going back and forth (shot, slap, shot, slap) till someone quits. That simple.

We took our commemorative first shots and I felt a little bad for Greggy. I'd just lost an Olympics I should've swept and while I'm not a sore loser, there were certain scales that needed balancing. I agreed to get slapped first because I'm a gentleman. Also, I know how to game the game. No one ever goes hard on the first one. Your opponent's first slap tests the waters. Your first raises the stakes. Enough to ask: *"There's more of this, bitch. Worth it?"*

Now his second slap's gonna sting a bit 'cause he's feeling braver but that's when you take him by surprise by going all out on your second. Half the time, your opponent quits right there. Figures revenge isn't worth getting slapped like that again. And I knew Greg. He couldn't last through winter training, no way could he survive my infamous second slap.

The game started so I took a breath, took the shot, and took Greg's first slap. Oh, Greg. He barely made contact, mainly hit my chin, and instantly knew he'd fucked up.

He took his shot and I made a real show of winding up. I blew on my palm for luck and let him have it. It was only my first slap so I gave maybe 40 percent of my true slapping power but that was that. TKO. Greg stumbled back like I'd tased his ass, and tripped over an empty Bud Light case. He rolled around like a turtle on its back, holding his cheek and groaning. Everyone was laughing but I wasn't into it. It's supposed to be a game. Fun. And I put a guy on his back from one hit. Maybe I was drunker than I thought. I couldn't bear to watch Greg try to pull himself up so I scanned the party. Matty definitely fucked up on the invites. There were about four times the people I'd expected, about a quarter of them I'd never met. My field advice had backfired. That's when I caught Sandro Miceli watching me from the pong tables.

His partner wasn't a drunk asshole so Team Italy got to the quarterfinals. And still, he was watching me. Bad pong etiquette. Always keep an eye on the table or your opponent could bounce a ball in. But Sandro didn't seem to notice. We just watched each other from across the party. He cocked his head and nodded to Greg, who'd gone full beached whale on the ground. I heard his voice in my head.

*"Why'd you do that?"*

I looked away and searched for anything that wasn't whiskey or beer.

The drink table'd been sufficiently raided so I estimated that the party was in its final act. Ronny had already given up refereeing the games. She'd also hoarded a bunch of mixers from the table to survive her night of teetotaling and snuck me a few cans of Diet Rite. I used to know Ronny pretty well. She's one of those rich girls that like to dress punk to distract you from her wealth. Like Avril Lavigne with a trust fund. She used to be real close with Lucy before Luce got too "art school" for the lacrosse girls. Apparently preferring art club to JV LAX is a mortal sin to some people in our school but Ronny was never a dick about it. I wondered if she knew Lucy dumped me. If she did, she didn't seem to care tonight. With a clearer head, I would've picked up on her obvious come-ons sooner.

"So. Sebastian the Flashtian. What's college looking like for you?"

I sipped my vodka and Diet Rite. "Rutgers. Pretty set on Camden."

"Ew. Why would you stay in Jersey?"

"Jersey's chill. *South* Jersey's chill."

Ronny scoffed. "Sebby. Bash the Flash can do better than Rutgers Track. With those legs?"

She gave my bare calves a once-over. I did some quick mental math on who Lucy would strangle first if she caught Ronny ogling me like that, then shrugged it off.

"I like Rutgers. Solid training program. Good scholarships. Plus, my mom—"

Some drunks booing over at the pong tables cut me off. Another party foul. Ronny groaned, ready to jump back into action.

"Shit in my fist. I don't know why I agreed to this jock crap, I'm not even playing lacrosse anymore. Matty Silva owes me a Friday night."

"I mean…this is kind of fun. Right?"

"Oh, sure. I'm *drowning* in fun right now."

We both laughed. And if the ogling didn't tip me off, her next move confirmed it. Ronny did this thing girls love to do to me where they find any excuse to touch my chest. Ronny's in was admiring my shirt's recent Sharpie addition.

"Well, well. You have *beautiful* handwriting, Mr. Villeda."

I smirked at the sarcasm. Sandro did a real number on it. Ronny was drawing her finger along the *C*, right around my nipple, when someone screamed at the tables. Canada's lone member had puked all over Team Iceland and half of the Newly Seceded Country of Texas. Ronny rolled her eyes and blew her whistle.

"I need to handle this. Enjoy the Diet Rite."

"Thanks. Enjoy the puke."

She smiled and brushed a bit of grass off my shoulder. Her finger lingered. "Come find me later?"

I raised a brow. Message received. She gave my legs one last look and, like the Wildwood lifeguard I only then remembered she was, Ronny sprinted off. I was about to crack into my new six-pack of generic diet soda when I noticed my right nipple was super hard. Huh. Do I have a nipple thing? Something to look into.

I ended up by the bonfire, trying to decide if I was buzzed or drunk, when the Italian Yeti himself plopped down in the folding chair next to me.

"Howdy, camper."

Sandro was fucking soaked. I burst out laughing which only furthered my inebriation suspicions. My laugh does this thing where it sorta pops out. Like a machine gun. *HAH. HAH.HAH.HAH.* Matty likes to give me shit for it but he was passed out under a table in a poncho full of vomit so fuck him.

"What happened to you?"

"We tried contesting our loss to Finland and Anthony Lewis threw a beer at me. Well, he tripped. I think. I hope."

Sandro thought it was an accident, but I knew Ant Lewis. He's a country-club asshole and a mean drunk. Plus, he shared in Matty's pointless beef with the field guys ever since the discus coach told him he should "stick to running." To be fair, the silver-spoon douchebag almost decapitated an innocent bystander with his little discus trick but that's track guys for you. Always making the wrong points.

Sandro produced two beers. "Do you have your keys?"

"Oh. You leaving already?"

"What? For shotgunning."

"Oooooooooooooh." God, I could hear the buzz in my voice.

I gave him a spare key, we stabbed our cans, and we shotgunned. Sandro killed his easy, but I biffed mine and spit most of it up. Got a bit on his shirt. Probably for the best, I was done with beer for the night. We laughed and I felt his further drenched tank.

"You're gonna catch a cold, dude."

He smiled and shrugged. I heard Ronny's whistle and took my hand off his chest. Wiped my face and looked around.

"Hey, I think Ronny DiSario's trying to fuck me."

"Aw, that's nice of her. Aren't you still with Lucy Jordan?"

"No. She, uh… She dumped me."

It just kinda fell out of me. I couldn't remember if they knew each other. Lucy and Sandro. Probably not. And I realized he was the first person I'd told. I never wanted Matty's opinion on the matter and my stepdad and I aren't exactly on gossiping terms right now. But there I was, telling some field guy I think I had home ec with once. This dude I don't even know. Weird.

"Oh. I'm sorry, man."

"Nah. I deserved it."

I opened him a warm cola and we looked out at the party. The Olympics were over. People were getting high and pairing up. Everyone was dancing and booting and rallying. It was a sight. One I'd seen a lot of. One I couldn't wait to get away from.

And as if he was reading my mind, Sandro chuckled. "So. You gonna miss all this?"

"Nooooope. Next twelve months can't go fast enough."

"Yeah. Such a waste."

I've had hundreds of "fuck high school" convos before but no one'd ever called it a waste. I thought that was very interesting.

Sandro shrugged. "I just...like, I don't know what I *thought* it'd be but... It was supposed to be *more* than this, right? This part of our lives? More than drinking beer in a field. Watching people you don't know have more fun than you. More than this." He shook his head. "Sometimes I feel like I did this part wrong."

And all I could do was nod. I wish I'd said something. I wish I'd told him that I felt the same. That I'd felt the same for a very long time. But I saw the flashlights. The music cut and I heard what people were yelling.

**"COOOOOOOPPPPPPSSSSSS!!!!!"**

Before our cans hit the ground, we were in the Sticks. Sandro seemed to know where he was going so I just followed his lead. The woods were black and I could barely make out his white tank. I heard the drunk screams and laughter of other escapees echo in the distance. Sandro stumbled over his boot and I held him up. His shirt was plastered to his chest like papier-mâché and we both reeked of beer. After a few more stumbles, we found ourselves in a clearing. The trees were thinner and it wasn't so dark. The moon lit Sandro up and he lowered himself into this steep ditch. It looked man-made and forgotten. Like someone ran out of money digging up a pool and the forest reclaimed it.

"What is this place?"

"I come out here to think. Safer than a roof. Come on!"

"Promise you won't murder me?"

"Fine."

I lowered myself down. We rested on the incline and caught our breath. I was actually winded. Me, the runner. I could feel my heartbeat in my skin.

"Thirsty?" Sandro cracked open the beer he'd pocketed and it exploded on him. Dude took a full shot of foam, right to the dome. "FUCK!"

We tried to keep our laughter in but it wasn't working. Sandro's face was dripping.

"Jesus *Christ*. It got up my nose."

"Shit, dude. I think you made it mad."

"Shit. Sorry, beer."

After we got our yuks out and our breath back, we were quiet for a while. Just staring at the stars, passing what was left of that beer back and forth, the sounds of the party long gone. The warm night breeze ran across my face and I had a thought. I gave him the can and rubbed the stubble on my scalp.

"Hey."

"Wassup?"

"You like my head?"

"Huh?"

"Hair. My hair."

"Oh. I dunno. It looks good. You usually have it longer, yeah?"

I nodded. In the silence, I couldn't stop thinking about that thing Sandro said before the cops showed. About doing this part wrong. And what Lucy said. And what I asked myself on that Zelley Park slide that night in July. What did I want?

What did *Bash* want? And I think that's it. I want to do this part right. Whatever it is, this part of my life, if it's still possible, I want to do this part right. But how?

I was staring up at the stars and suddenly felt so sad. Well, not sad. Cansado. Tired. Weary. Miserable. I guess it was only a matter of time before it caught up to me.

"Do you know what you want?" I asked, passing Sandro the beer.

He looked confused. "What do you mean?"

"In life."

"Oh. Like…big picture stuff."

"Yeah. You know?"

"I guess. Yeah. Yeah, I do."

"What do you want?"

He looked at me like no one'd ever asked him that before. I had people asking me all the time. Lucy. Del. My barber. Difference is, Sandro had his answer locked and loaded.

"Okay. So, I wanna open a restaurant. But for sandwiches. Not like a deli, though, an actual sit-down place. I can't really cook but I can do sandwiches and I've always wanted to run a restaurant. Like a local spot. So, yeah. A sandwich restaurant."

I chuckled.

When I asked him, I think I was expecting something vague. *To be happy. To be successful. To get superpowers.* Here I was, not even sure what I wanted in vague terms while Sandro had his whole damn life planned out. And he lit up when he described the kinds of sandwiches he'd serve and the seating area arrangement. The apartment he'd own right above the shop. A space to himself.

It sounded great. It sounded kind of beautiful. To know.

"That's cool. I'm jealous."

"It's whatever. How 'bout you? Big picture?"

I just shook my head and felt my stubble again. I wanted my fucking hair back. That's the thing with me. The annoying, awful thing. I knew I wanted long hair and I still let Matty get to me. What if I finally found something I knew I wanted? Would I find a way to mess that up too?

Sandro was looking at me. Waiting. So, I told him what I knew.

"I wanna run."

"Bash the Flash."

"Nah. Just me. Just running. At Rutgers."

"Why Rutgers?"

"My mom worked over there. She wanted me to go. Said it's 'where kids with a future go.'"

I felt my prayer bracelet. Bead by bead. I'd never actually said those words. Not to Del. Not even Lucy. But I did. I wanted it. And it scared me to want something so badly. To only want that one thing.

"That should be enough. Right?" Something was happening with my voice and I needed to stop talking.

Sandro must've noticed. "Hey. You okay?"

I let out a long breath. I wasn't. I hadn't been okay in so long and I think he saw it. I hated that. "Um…"

I wanted to go home. My breathing was getting heavy and I could feel myself closing up. My words weren't coming and I needed to get out of there.

Sandro turned on his side and looked at me. "You remember fifth grade?"

"Like…in general?"

"We were in the same class. Mr. Collins."

"Oh. We were?"

"We ran in different circles. But your mom was our room mom at one point."

"Yeah. Yeah, she was. She loved doing that shit."

"She always brought in muffins. For kids that forgot to eat breakfast or whatever."

I nodded. They weren't great muffins but I'd helped her make each one. Sandro wasn't smiling anymore.

"My family was going through some real shit that year. Bad shit. 'Sleeping in our car' kind of shit. Your mom always made sure I got a second muffin. I don't know how she knew but…it was the only thing I ate some mornings."

"Oh. Wow."

Sandro raised the beer and toasted the sky.

"To Mrs. Branch. Best room mom a hungry little shit coulda asked for."

He drank and I smiled. Because I didn't know about all that. I didn't know this guy. How didn't I know him?

My breathing steadied. "Thanks, man."

"'Course."

He smiled back at me and we didn't say anything for a little. We just lay on the grass and listened to the quiet. And I couldn't hear my breath. I wasn't focusing on my heartbeat or where I should have my hands. We were just listening to the silence.

Then I got curious.

"What would you call it? The sandwich restaurant?"

"It's stupid."

"Good."

He took a second and looked away.

"Bumpin' Grinders."

I burst out laughing and noticed him wilt a bit. Like I was laughing at him. I patted his shoulder and assured him that calling a Jersey sandwich shop *Bumpin' Grinders* is fucking amazing.

"Really?"

"Fucking *really*."

Sandro smiled over at me. "We should go get some. Sandwiches."

"Really?"

"Fuck yeah, dude. Wawa's open 24/7, I'm good to drive."

"You're not touching my truck, Team Italy."

"Come on. I switched to soda a while ago."

"Yeah? Me too."

"They only ever have beer at these things. I hate beer."

"Yeah. Me too."

Sandro laughed and nodded at the beer in my hand. "What about him? And the shotgunner?"

I laughed.

"Oh, you mean the beer *you* gave me?"

Sandro smiled and shrugged.

"Fair. Fair point."

I shook my head and flicked the tab off the can.

"Let's wait. Till we're sure. Just chill a little longer."

"Hey, take as long as you need, man. You *are* a track guy, after all."

I made a face. "What does *that* mean?"

"Track guys are lightweights. No meat on your bones. That's just science."

I cracked up and pushed him. "*Field* guys are lightweights!"

"*What?!* Says who?!"

"Says everyone!"

"Fuck you! I could drink your ass under the Garden State! Fuck *everyone!*"

I busted up laughing and nodded. I toasted the sky. *"Fuck! Everyone!"*

Sandro joined in my toast and I had to give him the beer because I couldn't stop laughing. I had my machine-gun cackle going but I didn't care. We just laughed. Alone. In a ditch. In the woods. In the middle of the night. Everything was so fucking funny all of the sudden. We settled down and caught our breath and laughed through our words.

I rubbed my stomach. "Jesus. Fucking hell. I'm hungry."

"I'm telling you. Wawa. 24/7."

"I do love sandwiches."

"They're the perfect food. That's just science."

"At the end of the day, that's what I want. A good sandwich. Isn't that enough?"

Sandro laughed. "That sure sounds like something a drunk person would say."

I laughed and shook my head. "I'm not. I feel good."

Sandro looked at me. I looked at him. And we smiled.

"I feel really good."

And I heard the can hit the ground before I understood that Sandro was kissing me. All I could taste was beer.

# sandro

*AUGUST 26*

### *JESUS FUCKING CHRIST FUCK*

Why did I do that?

Fuck.

Fuck fuck fucking fuck.

Why did I do that? What the fuck is wrong with me?

College. That was the deal. Get into Northwestern, get an apartment, and get out of Moorestown. Then. *Then.* Fucking THEN, SANDRO.

I'm such a fucking idiot. I'm such a goddamn stupid fucking stupid animal.

FUCK.

He didn't say anything. Not a word. Not in the ditch, not

on the walk, not on the drive. He just stared at the trail. And the road. I could hear my crutches rattling in his truck bed and I had to just focus on that. Focus on that and not say or do anything else.

I couldn't look at him. It was pointless. There was nothing to see on his face. No anger. No disgust. No thought. Nothing. He parked at the top of my driveway and I couldn't get out. I couldn't go home. Not without knowing. I needed to know what he was keeping off his face.

"I'm sorry."

But he wouldn't look at me. I got out and he left. Left me with all my questions. Who's he gonna tell? What's he gonna do? Why did he kiss me back? Why would he kiss my neck? Why did he stop?

I didn't sleep. Maybe I did, I can't tell. It was five in the morning when I got in and if I ever fell asleep, the van woke me back up. The attic's walls are thin and I can always hear my dad and Gio leave for work in the morning. Miceli Repairs. Relief sighed out of me. They wouldn't see. They wouldn't smell it on me. 'Cause they'd know. I know they would. They'd read it on my face. In my mind.

*Dirty.*

*Stupid.*

*Faggot.*

I snuck down to the shower and got to work. Face, feet, hands, nails, face, hands, arms, ears, pits, chest, back, hair. I scrubbed everything twice. Used up all the hot water but powered through. Three different bodywashes. Ma's nice soap. Anything to get the stink off me. I closed my eyes to rinse the shampoo out of my hair and I saw Bash's face. When he pulled away from my kiss. Shock. Like I'd punched him awake. And I felt his hand on my neck. When he dragged me back to him. His lips on my neck. The moan I didn't mean to make.

I threw up on the shower floor and started my washing from the top.

I brushed my teeth. Gargled. Flossed. Gargled again. Brushed one more time. The mirror was all foggy. I tried wiping it but it just got streaky. I took stock of myself. Scrubbed all raw and red. Eyes bloodshot. Hungover. Teeth looked good though. I read somewhere you can fool yourself into feeling happy if you try hard enough. So, I tried smiling at my reflection. My mouth hurt and I could only get up to this sort of grin.

*Weak.*

I thought it might be good to get some food in me. The ziti would for sure be gone but I emptied my stomach in the shower and one more time in the sink so anything would work. Ma was studying for her licensing exam at the stove, beating the shit out of scrambled eggs with one hand and holding my screaming niece in the other. I asked her if she needed help and hoped she'd let me take over the eggs. I wasn't so lucky and spent the next ten minutes trying to keep Lexi from screaming in my ear. She's never not screaming and, hangover or not, it makes me want to puke. The other niblings were watching cartoons at the kitchen table. Neither responded to my "good morning." Ma was running through a list of things she needed to get done today and asked me to chime in if I heard something I could do instead.

"I've got packages coming 'round noon, you can sign for'm,

just use my signature. Should be two boxes, the big one's wine so be careful. My exam's at two then I have to get over to Haddonfield to get Tina's cake. Her scout troop is celebrating all the summer birthdays at once and guess who got volunteered to host? Anyway, then I got to grab some ledgers from the office before they close and you know how Linda likes to close early without telling anyone."

That's the thing with Ma. She'll go twelve days without a word to me then a flood'll break out. Like I'm her assistant and she just got back from a long lunch. The mention of books reminded me of all the summer reading I'd been putting off. I was taking Ms. Morgan's AP lit because I hate myself and we were supposed to come in day one having already read three of her twelve books. I'm not really a reader. I'm more of a math guy but I figured if I could knock out a Lit credit in some no-stakes high school class, I can focus on math in college. I had a lot of plans for college.

"I need to go to the library so I could swing by the office. If Raph can drive."

"Don't be ridiculous. Just walk, it's so close."

Should've expected that. I reminded her what Dr. Kizer said about walking on my foot and she looked at me like I'd cut off her hand. *Obviously*, she knows what the doctor said. *Obviously*, I shouldn't run a marathon on my foot. And, *obviously*, I shouldn't have fallen off the goddamn roof in the first place. *Obviously*.

I apologized for some reason and told her I'd have a friend drive me.

I got dressed then undressed. Considered just crawling back into bed. Trying to sleep through the hangover. Through the day. Maybe if I made it to tomorrow, everything would be okay. Maybe Bash would forget by then. Or maybe I'd die in my sleep. A lot of pros to going back to bed. But I knew I wouldn't sleep. My brain was working overtime and I could feel the heat working up my spine. I still hadn't eaten because I could feel myself getting angry in the kitchen. Angry at Ma. Angry at my foot. Angry at myself. I needed to leave. Leave the house. But I couldn't escape to the roof and I knew what was coming. I was gonna overheat and freak out. Someone would hear and it would all be over.

When I get upset, I can't control myself. I don't keep myself in check. Like if Ma caught me crying and shit, there's a good chance I'd tell her why. I'd tell her how I finally kissed a boy. How I ruined everything. My judgment would get clouded and I'd think she'd be able to help.

With sober eyes, I know what would actually happen. She wouldn't hear me. She'd tell me it was just a stupid mistake. That I was confused. Didn't know what I was saying. She'd tell me I was breaking her heart and we'd never speak of it again. She wouldn't give me the time.

So, I needed to leave. I needed to get to my ditch. I wish I had other options. I really didn't want to go back there. But home felt even worse so I grabbed my crutches and got on my way.

Square Field was also hungover. I'd never related to a dead patch of grass before, but this week was full of firsts. I hobbled across the mess, dodging the crushed cans and broken bottles. All the cigarette butts and beer barf were baking in the hot sun. If I had anything left to puke, the smell of the Olympic aftermath would've got me there.

I was surprised how easy it was to get to the ditch in the dark. It was a bit of a slog today. I think I was worried what I'd find. Halfway down the trail, I had the thought that Bash might be waiting for me there. A trap. He'd have Matty with him and they'd get me back for last night. Make sure I don't do it to anyone else.

But he wasn't. The ditch was just how I left it. The beer we shared was still sitting there. I kicked it across the ditch. Like it was the beer's fault. Well, it sort of was. Not that one in particular but *beer* overall. I never would have done what I did sober. And I did have a lot to drink.

I rested on the incline and looked up at the trees. The sky. Listened to the birds. One called. Another answered. I just looked up and breathed. Let myself calm down. Let the anger run back down my spine.

But I wasn't that drunk. Last night. I'd switched to soda, I wasn't that drunk. I could still run through the woods. I could still find the ditch. We weren't that drunk. I'd made sure of it. I just needed to. Bash looked so beautiful in the moon and I could feel it. That it was worth it. The way he looked. The way he looked at me. Like it might be okay. Like he might need someone too.

I was wrong. I scared him. I ruined it all.

The anger shot through my spine and I boiled over. My breathing got all fast and catchy and sobs hurt my throat on their way out. It was too much. Everything. All the time. I turned over, on my stomach, and pressed my face into the grass. I screamed. I punched. I let everything run out of me. Into the ground. My pain shook the earth and I wished it would open up and take me.

# bash

*aug. 26*

*sorry*

I don't know what to say. I love orange juice. I just do. Pulp, no pulp, Vitamin D enriched, twist of mango, I don't care just give it to me. And if I drink it out of the carton sometimes, so be it. I'm not hurting anyone. Del doesn't even drink juice, so I don't know why he gets on my ass about it.

There we were in the kitchen, me with my carton, him with his coffee, just staring at each other. Groggy. Waiting for someone to speak. Del squinted at my cheek.

"How's the jaw?"

I blinked a few times, trying to wake up. "Been better. But better."

"Mm. Teeth still giving you trouble?"

I shook my head and took a swig. He eyed the juice.

"We have glasses."

I nodded. He took a sip of his coffee.

"You look like shit."

What a thing to say.

I can never tell what Del is trying to get out of me. Conversation? A laugh? An argument? An apology? Sure, I looked like shit. I felt like shit too but that's not the point. What did he hope to gain from saying something like that? I thought the best way to beat his game was not to play. So, I just nodded again. He got back to his coffee, fully aware of what my nods meant.

"So. What'd you get up to last night?"

"Nothing."

"Nothing?"

"...Nothing."

I shrugged and chugged. Del stopped trying.

I killed the rest of my carton and fell onto the living room couch. I was uncomfortably rested. I mean, I was definitely hungover, but I'd slept like a rock. Which surprised me. I'd become incredibly sober by the time I'd left the party and when I got home I thought I'd have trouble turning my brain off but nah. Lights out.

I turned over on the couch and watched the ceiling. I could hear Del puttering around in his room. He had nothing to do up there but I guess it beat being around his dick stepson. When Del decides he can't deal with me, that's it for the day. Suddenly, we're just roommates. In one corner, a forty-something white guy who can build chairs out of tree stumps and recommend a good car tire. In the other, a random brown kid with bad eyebrows and shit posture. Not a thing in common except an address, a penchant for coffee, and my dead mom. Pair up of the century here.

I crushed the empty OJ carton in my hands and wondered what Del would say if I did tell him what I *got up to* last night. Bet that would stop the questions. But then I thought about last night and could feel the juice in my stomach start to boil.

Hot orange juice. Barf.

*"Sorry…"*

I didn't want to think about the ditch. I wanted to shut off.

Del was asleep by the time I got dressed which was good. If he saw me running that early, it would've confirmed something for him. He's always trying to translate my actions. Find the meaning behind the meaningless. But I didn't feel like being translated today.

I started with a few warm-up laps at the school track. It was an odd temperature outside. The sun was out but it was still chilly and I had to adjust my breathing. I read that taking deep breaths in the cold is bad for stamina. Hurts your lungs in the long run. Read that in a running magazine Del signed me up for last Christmas. 'Cause he just knows me so well. Boy, oh, boy, do I love reading about the little bones in the human foot. I wait with bated breath for the postman to bring me this month's edition of *Running Has Taken Over Your Personality Illustrated.*

I moved from my warm-up into some faster intervals. The thing about running is it either helps me think with a new clarity or it completely blocks everything out. I'm usually fine with either but I was really banking on a total eclipse of the brain today.

Not so lucky.

My hangover fog lifted and I thought about the ditch.

*"Sorry…"*

It felt good.

It felt really, really good. I'll admit it.

But that's the thing. I have to admit it. It's something to admit. That's why I pulled away. I mean, I pulled away for a laundry list of reasons. He came in hard. Really hard. Like he was challenging me. Half the reason I reacted that way was in defense. But then he looked so scared. Like I'd just confirmed a million conversations he'd had with himself. The guy had a very readable face and it was reading as terrified.

*"Sorry…"*

He looked it too. Sorry. And he started to get up. And I imagined him standing and leaving and walking home alone on that broken, hairy foot and it was all so sad. So sorry.

For a moment, I was certain. I didn't want him to leave.

I grabbed the back of his neck and pulled him close to me. Closer than I thought I would. Could. And the feeling. He was soft. He was soft in spite of himself. He was this giant, hairy thing. This bear of a guy, all legs and shoulders. His hand was rough on my cheek and the stubble on his neck scratched my lips but he was still so soft. I didn't think it would be like that. Not that I let myself think of stuff like that a lot. I didn't think about it. Them. Other guys. I didn't like to think like that. I don't.

I sped up. I got faster. Hugged my turns tighter.

I didn't want to think about Sandro Miceli. 'Cause what's the point? I'm gonna start kissing guys now? Is that what my senior year's gonna be? Is that what I learned this summer? No.

I sped up and my breathing got heavier.

I'm not. I don't.

I heard Matty's laugh and I picked up my speed. I was breathing so fast and the cold hurt. I fixed my face and broke into a full sprint. Zooming. Burning. Blind. I saw Matty carving **FAG** into Jackson Pasternak's locker. I felt him carve **FAG** into my forehead.

I could barely bring myself to stop in time to puke. All over the track. So orange.

*"Sorry..."*

There's nothing wrong with it but I'm not that guy. I have the receipts. If I were like that, if I were that way, then I had a lot of girls to explain myself to. I've had girlfriends since the second fucking grade. I've felt things for girls that almost killed me I felt them so hard. That was real, I wasn't just faking that shit. So, unless you can wake up one day and just stop liking girls, then no. I'm not.

And I felt like I should tell Sandro that. It felt like something he should know. No hard feelings, guy. I don't care that you are, if you are, but I'm not built that way. My bad.

I couldn't stop staring at my puke. Such a waste of orange juice. My jaw hurt like a motherfucker. Usually, I can walk off a punch but my Cinnaminson fight was taking its time to become old news and throwing up sent the throbbing into overtime. I looked around to make sure no one saw me. Nope. I was alone. No one on the track. No one in the stands. No one to give me shit. No one to ask if I was okay. No one.

I wanted to tell Sandro he shouldn't be sorry. That I wasn't sorry. That it was okay. It was kind of nice.

So, I did.

It's no wonder Sandro's foot didn't heal right, because the Miceli's live in the middle of nowhere. They've got one of the only houses on the Moorestown farmlands and, even with all my shortcuts, it still took me forty-five minutes to get out there. But it's a beautiful area. All fields. Jersey gets a bad rap but that's all North Jersey's doing. South Jersey's the real Garden State. Moorestown's farmland is all corn and tomato fields. But what makes it special, to me at least, is how close it is to the highway. The fields bleed into the Sticks and right on the other side is I-95. You can be surrounded by all this nature and still hear the echoes of speeding cars. It sounds like the ocean. I passed my mom's favorite field on the run over. It's this stripped field I go to when I want to feel close to her. She loved the echoes. The ocean.

Her field is about five minutes from the Miceli's farmhouse. I was worried I'd show up all panting and disoriented but the Miceli driveway was long enough for an adequate cool-down stroll. I knocked on the door then realized how wild I looked. My shirt was drenched in sweat and there were gross orange specks around my collar. I was also suddenly aware that I forgot to put on deodorant. Not my best self. I'm sure I looked like a maniac to the child who opened the door. He was super small, only looking smaller in what was clearly a grown man's *Dragon Ball Z* shirt.

"Sup, lil' man. Your brother home?"

The kid just stared at me. Not threatened. Not scared. Not even confused. Just mildly bored. "I don't have a brother."

"Sandro?"

"He's my uncle. And he's not here."

"Okay… Know where he went?"

The kid shook his head. He was not trying to help me.

"I'm Bash. I go to school with Sandro."

The child considered me for a moment. Well, not me. My shirt.

"I'm GJ. You got barf on you."

And he closed the door. Welp. I tried. I was thinking about the quickest route home when I heard Sandro's voice again.

*"I'm sorry."*

The second sorry. Right on that driveway, by that rusted, red mailbox. After he got out of Birdie. After I said nothing the entire drive. The entire walk through the Sticks. After I kissed him back then made him feel sorry for it. I had an idea where I could find him. Somewhere important to him. That he brought me to. That I ruined. I looked down the long driveway and got my breath back.

My feet were killing me and I had to take my shirt off. I was not ready for all the hungover running but any long-distance training is a win in my book. Square Field looked like it hit rock bottom. I made a deal with God that if I didn't die from the day's cardio, I would come back with some trash bags and thick rubber gloves to clean it up.

I was on my way to the ditch, wondering if I could find it without Sandro's lead, when I caught him. He was on the trail and dirty. Sweaty too. Like he'd just wrestled a deer in the woods. He was definitely hungover. Not that I was one to talk.

"YO!"

He froze at the sound of my voice. When he saw me, he hugged his crutches. Like I was planning on taking them. That sucked. I felt like an intruder.

When I finally caught up to him, I had all the things I wanted to say in my head but I couldn't catch my breath. Christ, I was beat.

"*Damn.* Sorry. One sec."

I doubled over and took a second while Sandro considered his escape route. I don't know what he had to worry about. He could tear me in half, even if I hadn't just run a half-marathon. Dude was big. I've seen him fuck up a shot put with a strength he could easily use to launch my skull into orbit. If I made this guy angry, I had a lot more to worry about than him trying to kiss me.

So, I eased in. "Went to your house. Your nephew seems like a real dick."

I guess I meant it as a joke but, fuck, did Sandro's face get hard. "Why?"

"Probably how he was raised?"

"Why were you at my house?"

It came out cold. He did not want me there. At his house or in his face.

Okay. No jokes. Just say what you went there to say.

But I couldn't. We just stood there. My breath started to steady and I noticed he couldn't stop shifting his weight.

"...Did you walk here?"

He didn't answer. So, yes.

"I think it's fucked that your parents make you walk everywhere on that foot."

I had no business saying that.

"They don't make me."

"But they know you won't say shit, right?"

I didn't plan on saying all that. He just stared at me. Like he was waiting for me to excuse him. Why couldn't I just say what I came here to say? That he didn't do anything wrong. That was all. Just those five words then he could go. And I could go. And it could be over.

Just five words: *You didn't do anything wrong.*

Sandro looked at his feet. His hands. The sky. Anywhere but me. I didn't realize I'd spoken the words aloud. They just fell out. Like last night. Then I couldn't keep them in. "Yeah. I just wanted to tell you that. And that I'm sorry. That you're sorry. You shouldn't have said that. I shouldn't have... I'm just not..." I shook my head. "I'm not."

I couldn't say the word. It sounded like an insult. Another language. A word I knew but never said out loud. And I felt like an asshole just thinking it.

Sandro wouldn't look at me, his eyes glued to the sky. The sun. Like he was checking if it was still there. "Okay." And maybe he was talking to the sun when he said it. "...I am."

Sandro kept his eyes on the sky and I knew that I'd just heard something special. That it was the first time he'd told somebody. Because he nodded a little, after. Nodded to the sun. Like he wanted to make sure they were on the same page. Like he wanted to make sure he was sure. He was though. He was sure.

I nodded too.

"Oh... Okay."

That's all I could say. I think he expected as much, because he turned his gaze to the ground and went on his way. Got on his crutches and continued down the trail. And I thought I should let him go. I said what I wanted to say and he must have too. I could go.

So why was I following him?

"Where are you going?"

"I gotta get my Lit books."

I laughed. Only one Lit teacher required you to get books before school starts. I knew 'cause I was three books deep into her reading list. "Ms. Morgan's Lit? Same."

He laughed back. First time he cracked a smile all day. But it wasn't the same smile from last night. It was more of an *Of course* laugh. I didn't like that.

"Awesome. I hope we get paired up for projects and shit. Become best bros. *Sandro and the Flash*. Blowin' off class, sleeping in the library, fighting in the locker room. Fuck, man, it's gonna be fuckin' sick, bro."

"Sandro." He stopped where he stood and finally made real eye contact with me. I could feel his anger. All that frustration in his voice.

"I don't know you, dude. I don't. We go to the same parties, we've been in some classes, but we don't know each other like that. To me, you're just that loud track asshole who talks shit and fights at meets. So don't come to my house and don't talk about my fucking family. You don't know shit about me."

I could see the red pour into his cheeks. I'd never seen that happen to anyone before. He started off again and I should've let him go. The guy could get angry. I didn't know that. And I didn't know where I got the balls to say it.

"I know something, yeah?"

That stopped him cold. He turned and looked at me like I was the biggest piece of shit on earth.

"*Fuck you.*"

But I didn't mean it like that. I meant it as a connection. That I knew. That it was okay that I knew. That's how he saw me though. The kind of guy who would fuck with him. Who would hold something like this over someone. I hated that he saw me like that. Like Matty.

"I'm the only one, right? That knows?"

But, to Sandro, I was someone to hate. The guy had a very readable face and, right then, right there, that was all I could read. *Hate.*

He threw his crutches to the ground and came at me. Ready to knock me under the ground. There was so much anger on his face. Well. Not anger. Not exactly. He looked tired. Weary. Miserable. I could hear it in his voice. "I swear to God, you try fucking with me, I'll—"

So, I did what made sense to me. I took his face and kissed him.

*Whiplash.*

Our teeth hit and I could feel the shock in his face. The muscles relaxed for just a second then he shoved me. Hard. I almost fell over. He took some steps back and glared at me. Like I'd tricked him. And it was my turn to say it. "I'm sorry."

I think it was the first time Sandro really heard me all day.

"...That's not okay."

"I know."

"You don't get to— You are or you're not."

"It isn't that—"

"Are you?"

I wasn't. I really wasn't. I just didn't know what I was doing. I shrugged like an idiot. A tired, confused idiot. That annoyed him. Or maybe it just confused him.

He took a breather. "So... I mean, what the fuck, Bash?"

I shook my head. Because I didn't know what my fucking problem was. I didn't know what was wrong with me. It made no sense to kiss him right there. It made no sense to come find him like this. To say all this shit. None of it made sense to me. It just felt like the right thing to do. Because of last night. Not just the kiss. Everything. What was so different about that night?

"I don't—I've always had this... I don't know. I don't get it. Just... I liked last night. I liked talking to you. I could just talk to you."

There was just something different about the guy. He was funny and he didn't need to be mean to do it. When he asked me about myself, it didn't feel like a test I'd fail. I didn't have to try to impress him or act like someone else. On that trail, I realized how pathetic I was. How much of my pain was my fault. I was terrified of what people might think of me, what I might say, so I stopped speaking. Let Matty speak for me. Let someone else take over. *Bash the Flash.* What a fucking joke.

I could feel that heat behind my eyes. I felt stupid.

"I'm not myself with people anymore. And I know I'm not and it fucking sucks and I hear it and I want to tell myself to shut the fuck up and stop but last night...yeah. I liked talking to you. I just want to keep talking to you, man."

I watched him soften. He started looking like the guy from last night again. "Then why'd you kiss me?"

"I don't—"

"You wanna keep talking? Talk to me."

I let myself breathe.

*Okay.*

"…Because you were angry. And you looked scared and it was my fault."

Sandro waited for me. Like he knew there was more. I guess I knew it too. I took one more moment because there was no unsaying it.

"'Cause you looked a lot like me. And… I don't know. I just… I wanted to help. I just… I wanted to."

He nodded. Right answer, I guess. "There. You wanted to."

"Yeah. I wanted to."

We just watched each other. Letting it sit. Sandro wiped his mouth. "You taste like barf. And oranges."

I laughed. "I threw up. On the track."

"Oh. Same. Not on the track, but same."

"Nice. I didn't taste it."

"Mouthwash."

"Tight."

We laughed. Like it was all okay. Like last night wasn't the end of the world. Like we weren't terrified of what that meant.

I dabbed some sweat off my shoulders and put my gross shirt back on. "Okay. Sorry, but I gotta eat something. I am literally empty right now."

"Star athlete. Left it all on the field."

That made me chuckle. I pointed down the trail. Back to civilization. "Seriously though. Wanna grab food?"

"Oh. Food with me?"

"Sure."

Sandro rocked on his crutches, considering the offer. "I don't know. I should probably get to the library. Gotta get my books before noon or I'm fucked."

"There's a Burger Town by the library, yeah?"

"Yeah."

"My truck's on the way. Lemme drive you. Two birds."

Sandro almost looked surprised. "Yeah? You don't mind?"

"No sweat, man. It's hot out here. I can drive you."

And the way Sandro smiled. I think that's how I knew it was true. That I wanted it. That I wasn't sorry. That I'd drive that kid anywhere he asked me to.

Because what a fucking smile.

# fall

*And the sun took a step back, the leaves lulled themselves to sleep, and autumn was awakened.*

—Raquel Franco

# sandro

*IT'S LIT*

The grass mixed in with the hair on my chest and I could feel
a bug get confused. The ant thought I was dirt and I didn't
correct her. I just read my book.

"*My life was not my own and I came to know that it would
never become mine in my lifetime. There was an ocean inside of me,
a storm I was not ready to understand. That I might never understand. Standing in the waves of what my life would become, I faced
the epi-tomb of a life unlived. Where ships and—*'"

"Wait." Bash perked up. "*Epi-tomb?*"

"'I faced the epi-tomb of a life—'"

"No, I heard you. Spell the word?"

"E-p-i-t-o—"

Bash sat up on his elbows and smiled.

*"Epitome."*

"Oh. *Ooooooooooh."*

I reread the sentence and he was right. He burst out laughing. That machine-gun cackle.

*"Epi-tomb?!"*

Our laughter was the only noise in the Sticks that afternoon. We calmed down but kept laughing through our words.

"You can read it if you're so smart."

"Nah. I like listening to you."

"Yeah?"

"Keep going. *Epi-tomb."*

I chuckled and found my spot. "This book sucks ass. Anywho. '*...I faced the epitome of a life unlived. Where ships and lost things understood their purpose. And I wondered what the ocean had in store for me.'"*

I peeked over at Bash and thought he might've fallen asleep. I couldn't tell what that looked like on him. But I wanted to. I wanted to be able to read his face.

That image, his face, eyes closed and smiling, stuck with me for the rest of the night. It was actually really distracting and ruined my efforts to read through the syllabi for my new fall classes. I was about halfway through the welcome packet for my new Intro to Guitar elective but my thoughts wouldn't focus. Eventually, I gave up on being a good student and spent the night trying to make sense of the new kernels popping in my brain microwave. Get them out of the heat and into a bowl. Does this metaphor make sense? Is it a metaphor? I don't know. I never said I was good at English.

Here, I'll prove it.

## LITERATURE IS DEAD:
*A Persuasive Essay by (and only for) Sandro Miceli*

Do I suddenly like reading or do I just like hanging out with a hot guy? In this essay, I will take on both sides of the argument and attempt to convince myself of one. I'll address the former first.

I've never enjoyed reading. I don't want to sound like one of those "damn whippersnappers with their Nintendo skateboards" but I just don't love the process. I can never get comfortable.

But lately, I've been doing it for fun. Before I go to bed, after the gym, I just want to read. And it's not for the merit of the book, that's for fucking sure. *Daniel: Last Forever* was just the first book I pulled off the AP lit list. It's about this whiny asshole named Daniel who hates his nice parents, hates his cool friends, and basically hates everyone but himself. He doesn't get his way on his birthday, so he runs away from home on his boat (WHICH HIS PARENTS BOUGHT HIM). Then he gets caught up in a storm (WHICH HE BLAMES ON HIS PARENTS) and winds up lost at sea. I just finished chapter five, a riveting explanation of why seawater isn't potable, and I couldn't dislike a main character more. He doesn't do anything to help himself. He's more preoccupied that no one seems to be looking for his bitchy ass.

Bash says that's the point. He thinks the ocean is a *metaphor for isolation*. At the time, I nearly pulled a muscle rolling my eyes. With further consideration, it's actually super obvious that's what author F.R. Montgomery (ugh) was going for. I've started writing Bash's observations in my copy of the book. They always sound correct. But Bash wears glasses when he reads so maybe he just *looks* like he knows what he's talking about.

Bash's looks bring me to my counterpoint. Looking at him as clinically as possible, Sebastian Villeda is an optically sound human being. His face is symmetrical. He has a defined jawline and aesthetically pleasing imperfections. His eyebrows are unique and he has fully grown into his features. The man is in top-tier athletic shape. Scientifically speaking, he's an admirable specimen. Speaking as a scientist.

Speaking as Alessandro Vincent Miceli, I want to fuck the soul out of him. I'll own that. Dude's hot as balls, what do you expect? He's got abs like bricks and one of those Vs around his hips that points to his dick. His ass looks great in every kind of apparel and he's got this unnaturally clear complexion that looks like the sun.

So, while I don't necessarily have a type, per se, I can see the appeal of Bash Villeda. How couldn't I? He's beautiful.

And of course, this debate may seem obvious. Of course, I've considered that the only reason I like reading now is because he wants to read with me. That reading this awful garbage book means spending more time with this ridiculously good-looking guy. But that isn't it. Because it's not an option. Bash Villeda is not something to consider. It's a nonstarter. I've spent seventeen years getting comfortable with the big G-word and Bash couldn't even bring himself to say it that day in the Sticks. We're just at different points with it all.

Personally? I've sort of always known. I, at least, always knew that I was different. At first, I thought what made me different from other kids was my total lack of interest in other kids. I didn't notice it for a while. I thought my job as a kid was to have fun and not die. But a day seemed to come when everyone started crushing on everyone, stressing over Valentines and dances and who sat with who on the bus. And I was left sitting alone on the playground. I didn't care about girls like the other boys did. But I didn't care about boys either. I just wanted to keep having fun.

I think it was around middle school that I started to feel it, once we started using a locker room for gym class. I've always been hairy—Ma used to have to wax my lip every other Sunday so I wouldn't look like a ten-year-old used car salesman—but it wasn't until that gym class that I realized other guys had hair too. Other guys were big too.

Other guys. That's when I started seeing other guys.

At first, I filed the thoughts away as insecurity. As jealousy. Those other guys knew how to dress. How to walk. Those guys knew how to be guys. In seventh grade, I thought I wanted to look like the eighth graders. But then I got to eighth grade and just wanted to look like the ninth graders. That's when I knew. I didn't want Scotty Travello's body. I wanted his *body*.

Then one night, freshman year, I had the stomach flu and my family went out to dinner without me. I had to babysit GJ and Tina but they were still at that "zonked out by eight" age so I was essentially alone—a rarity in that house. I'd just finished puking up some soup Ma left for me and I looked in the mirror. I don't know why it came out right then. Maybe because I was alone. I had residual barf in my mouth and I could feel my stomach setting up for an encore but I looked at my reflection and said to him:

"You're gay, Sandro."

And my reflection looked back at me like:

*"Fuck. You sure?"*

And I nodded.

"I'm sure, bud."

And I knew I might not get the opportunity to talk to myself like that again for a while so I said it over and over. I was gay. I wanted men. I wanted to know what it was to love a man and for him to love me. It settled my stomach. Like Alka-Seltzer, little bubbles popping inside me. It felt so good.

But I didn't say those words again for a long time. Took me about three years. And all Bash could say was:

*"Oh. Okay."*

It's not that I needed him to say anything more. Not really. It's just that Bash is the only person I've told. This is a big fucking deal for me. I've spent the last thirty-three odd months dead set on never telling a soul till I got out of here. Started over somewhere new. And *there* I would be gay. I would be proud and loud and tell strangers on the bus if I felt like it.

So, for me to tell Bash? Change my life like that? To have someone know? I think that's the extent of what I can handle. Anything more is too risky.

Because what he said on the trail was spot-on. For some reason, I can talk to him. The night of the Olympics and every day since. We just talk well. About the books, about Moorestown, sports, movies, whatever. We'll just post up at the ditch after school and talk till dark. Sometimes read. Sometimes rant. Sometimes we rant about reading.

It's sort of how I assume I'd talk to the last person on earth.

Or if I were stranded on a desert island with someone. As if they were both my best and only option.

But that's why I don't think about Bash that way. I can't. Because we talk about everything *but* the kiss. And if Bash wanted to talk about that stuff, if he wanted to say more than *"Okay"* I think he would. We talk that well. So, there must be nothing to talk about.

In conclusion, I think both options are flawed. *Do I suddenly like reading or do I just like hanging out with a hot guy?* I still don't like reading. Yes, it's nice to spend time in the ditch and not be screaming my brains out into the ground. But it's not because of Daniel. Daniel can get eaten by sharks. But it's not because of Bash either. It's not that he's attractive, it's really not like that. Because I've spent my life just wanting someone. Letting that want be enough. I'm used to that. But I'm not used to having a friend like this. I'm not used to having a friend. And I don't want to mess it up. I don't want to risk that.

Anywho, in conclusion, neither. Or both. I don't know. I don't think I get how persuasive essays work.

# bash

*rules*

I was sitting in Matty's living room, doing the usual nothing I do in Matty's living room. Matty was high and howling at *Just the Tip 3: Suns Out, Guns Out* but I wasn't paying attention. It's one of those "dudes will be dudes" *American Pie* knockoffs and Matty's fave. I've lost count of how many times we've watched it. I looked up from my phone at one point and the main bro-dude had his dick in a slushie.

"*Bro! What happened!?*"

"*I got hot sauce in my dick!*"

"*In your dick?*"

"*In my dick, bro!*"

Matty hit his bowl and choked on smoke, finding this dick-sauce business just as hilarious the hundredth time around. I went back to my phone.

*"How'd you get hot sauce in your dick?"*

*"I fucked a burrito!"*

*"You fucked a burrito?!"*

*"I fucked a burrito!!"*

Matty chuckled, passing me the bowl.

"That's so fucked, dude."

I shook my head. He nodded and hit it again.

"Who you texting?"

I was sending Dro a pic of this dog I saw earlier. He had a fur mohawk, it was fucking sick.

"Villeda."

"Mm."

"Who you texting?"

"...Luce."

I don't like lying. My mom didn't raise me to lie. But I knew Matty wouldn't ask a follow-up if I said I was texting Lucy so no one was getting hurt, right? It was a lie but a small lie. Lately, I've been letting myself off on the small ones. A new rule.

Matty was repacking the bowl so I took the opportunity to go sit in the bathroom for a while. Sandro was at the Johnson's Pumpkin Patch with his nieces and nephew and sending me updates. He texted me a picture of him in a tender embrace with a scarecrow. I laughed without laughing and deleted the pic. I didn't keep pictures of him on my phone. Another rule. They were getting on the hayride so Sandro signed off and I put my phone away. I sat on the toilet for a bit longer, tracing my finger over the weird sandy wallpaper the Silvas had through their apartment, and ran through all the new rules I'd been making with myself lately.

The following is my very own *New Rules Playlist*.

## 1. *"FREE YOUR MIND"* by EN VOGUE

All we ever did at Matty's apartment was watch movies. If we weren't at a party, track, or the diner, you could usually find us sitting on his couch, silently watching *Superbad* or *Scary Movie 3* for the thousandth time. During last Sunday's couch session, *2 Fast 2 Furious* was on and I decided I would try picturing Tyrese Gibson the next time I jerked off.

Stay with me.

If you'd asked me last year who my favorite actor was, I'd probably say Tyrese Gibson. I just always liked seeing him in shit. I actively sought out his movies outside of the Fast franchise. Lately, I've been wondering why because I could not tell you one Tyrese Gibson movie that's actually good. I like *Baby Boy* all right but more for Taraji. It had to be something else.

After that day on the trail, saying all I said to Sandro, I'd started opening my mind up to the things I tried not to think about before. So, after grabbing some late-night burgers with Dro at B-Town, I came home and showered. And by *showered*, I mean I stood in the shower and went to town on myself. Thought of my normal stuff. Penélope Cruz in *Vicky Cristina*. Penélope Cruz in *Blow*. Penélope Cruz in that perfume commercial. Then Tyrese. We were speeding down

95, bags of cash in the back seat, cops on our tail, when he put his hand on my thigh. And...yeah. That was all it took. Interesting.

### 2. *"THE BAD TOUCH"* by BLOODHOUND GANG

I was helping Lucy and her mom clear some dead wood from their yard when Ms. Jordan asked if things were ever awkward between us, going from childhood friends to boyfriend/girlfriend and back again. Me and Luce looked at each other. I think we were both wondering the same thing.

*"Is it awkward for you?"*

It wasn't for me, we basically just took kissing back off the table. I could see that it wasn't awkward for Lucy either. I knew her looks and that was her "you couldn't bother me if you tried" face. We were fine. Even though we weren't talking like we could, we had history. All these roots. The safety net of a lifetime of memories. That's why it wasn't weird to hug her. Or why I didn't feel guilty if our knees touched a little too long. Not like with Sandro.

On the walk back from a particularly boring alien invasion movie, Sandro and I were talking about how neither of us really fuck with overly touchy people. The bad CGI of the face-sucking space creatures reminded Dro of his aunts and uncles down at the shore and their aggressive brands of affection. Apparently, the guy grew up under a family tree full of vise-grip huggers and wet-cheek kissers, none of whom had any respect for Little Sandro's personal space. The guy comes from an intensely physical family and he really hates being touched when he's not ready for it. Which is funny, given how he kissed me. Which is less funny, given how I kissed him. But in the name of respecting this pet peeve, I made a rule very early on that I would do my best to not touch Sandro. Like, at all. I mean, I wasn't gonna bolt if he patted me on the back but I didn't think I'd be a very nice person if I did something like kiss him like that again. That wasn't okay. It's not like I didn't like it. Well, the one on the trail kind of hurt, but the first one. The soft one where he touched my cheek. Where he made that noise when I kissed his neck. That was nice. But I had some shit to figure out. I had my own rules about when and where and how I'm ready to be touched. And it wasn't fair of me to get involved with Sandro like that if I couldn't come correct. Like, what if we started touching and I had a panic attack or something? It could happen, I don't know. How could I? I knew literally zero gay people. Well, zero plus Dro now. But I had no roadmap for this guys-touching-guys shit. They didn't exactly cover the topic on *Full House*. All I know for sure is I will not be another face-sucking alien disrespecting Sandro's boundaries.

So yeah. No touching. Not until I can be sure.

**3.** *"DON'T STOP BELIEVIN'"* by THE CAST OF *GLEE*

I watched the pilot of the show *Glee* online because it seemed like the kind of thing that gay people would watch. I was curious. Because studies show that, between my age, gender, and income level, I am literally the person most movies and shows are made for. But there had to be other things, right? There were no gay characters in my movies, not really, so they had to be somewhere. I guess I wanted to see what the world had to offer gay people. I liked the pilot fine but didn't want to watch past it. The songs were good and it made me listen to a lot of Journey that week but I don't know if the show was meant for me.

I just wasn't a musicals guy. My mom was obsessed with them but something about just bursting into song embarrassed the hell out of me. So, no. *Glee* is not for me. Which was a slight bummer. I thought maybe I'd see something to latch onto. Something that'd make some sense of all these new threads in my head. I made a note to myself, a rule, that I didn't have to like something now just because it was a *gay thing*. "Freeing my mind" didn't mean I had to become someone I wasn't. I still thought musicals were corny as hell. Sorry, *Glee*.

**4.** *"DON'T SWEAT THE TECHNIQUE"* by ERIC B. & RAKIM

Things have been simple so far. It's how I always thought making friends should be. We hang out. Have a good time. Explore the woods. Try to out-eat each other at B-Town. See movies and sneak into second showings. We don't even gotta talk. Sometimes he just comes to the diner and does his trig homework while I bus. It's been simple. So simple, so fast, that I wanted to make sure we were on the same page with each other. Especially with what we were telling people.

It didn't seem like a big deal, us hanging out, but when we started back at school, people really liked to ask me about it.

*"Since when did you start hanging with Miceli?"*

It's not like Dro's disliked. Track-and-field pettiness aside, everyone actually really likes the guy, not that he believes me.

But I understood it. To the outside world, we were a bit of a random pairing. It was like if you saw a goat playing with a horse. Not the wildest sight but certainly worth some follow-up questions.

So to the outside world, Sandro was my workout partner. That was the rule. The simple, easy lie. I'd been helping him with foot-healthy cardio and he was helping me with weights. That's how most people saw us anyway so why not lean in? We agreed it would make the most sense to them. Those *other people.*

*"Sandro and Bash? That goat and horse? Why would they hang out? They're probably jerking each other off, right? Oh? Workout partners, you say? Aaaaah, they couldn't be gay because sports. Nevermind!"*

As far as Moorestown was concerned, Sandro and I were simply spotting each other.

But when it's just the two of us, Dro's a reliably chill time. But not "let's sit on a shitty couch I found in the Sticks and watch Comedy Central reruns at my place" kind of chill. I feel legit relaxed when I get home from the ditch. And, with all the reading we do together, I was absolutely crushing AP lit. The guy's a good sounding board for essays and I was two books ahead of the class.

All signs told me that this was a good move. Me and him being friends. Sandro was, as my mom would say, a good influence on a growing boy. And I guess I was rubbing off on him too. He said he hasn't "overheated" since that day on the

trail. I had my suspicions, but Sandro told me he struggles
with his anger. Not just anger, emotions in general. Apparently right before I found him on the trail, he'd had a break-
down in the ditch. Cried into the ground. Screamed. I felt
bad for him. To have all those feelings, to feel that much, and
have to keep them together. Especially from that family of his.
I haven't met them yet and I'm not trying to. The way they
treat him? Never thought I'd feel lucky not to know my dad.

Point is: so far, so good. We're good in the ditch. We're
good in Birdie. I even felt okay having him come over a few
times, when I knew Del would be at work. It wasn't that I
didn't want them to meet, it'll have to happen eventually,
but it's just gonna open the door to questions I won't want to
answer. Because Del asking about Dro will make this simple
thing more complicated than it has to be at this point and I
just wanted to keep it simple.

## 5. _"CRYING"_ by ROY ORBISON

A low note to end on but I thought it was important. I
don't know what I'm doing. I never thought this was an option for me, you know? It wasn't just that I didn't let myself
think it. It truly never occurred to me that I might be able
to have something like this with someone like him. Because
he's nice. A lot of people in my life aren't nice. And I don't
think I've been all that nice. Not for a while. He's a good
guy and it kind of terrifies me. I feel so stupid around him
sometimes. Maybe 'cause I haven't been talking so well for a
while but it's like I forgot how. I'm always speaking too fast

or too slow and my tongue gets whiplash. I end up babbling like an asshole. And in my head, it's worse. I say one thing off the cuff and my brain reels.

*Am I flirting with him? Was he flirting? Is this what flirting looks like between guys? Am I being fair? Am I wasting his time? What about rules? What if I make him angry again? What if I ruin this? Ruin what? What is this?*

But then he speaks and the noise stops. I listen. I listen to him the best I can because I owe him that. It's a give-and-take. He deserves an ear just as much as I do. 'Cause I get the feeling people don't listen to him like they should. And I get the feeling that really hurts him. Fucking kills him. And that's what's been driving me up the wall. Why should I get that feeling? What am I drawing from? This guy was ostensibly a stranger to me in July so why do I feel like I know him? Know what hurts him? It's this intense familiarity. It makes me nervous.

This whole situation with Sandro has me so on edge that I'm running laps just to get to sleep. I need to tire myself out or I'll spend all night thinking. About the book. The ditch. How he snores when he naps on his back but almost purrs when he sleeps on his chest. I think about everything. It's exhausting. In the five weeks since we started talking, I've cut my long-distance time a few seconds every check-in. Coach Bianco's thrilled.

I think what scares me here is me. Sandro's been great so far. I'm the problem. I'm doing things that don't make sense to me. Like we got our senior portraits done. I hate mine, my eyebrows look extra bushy, but Sandro's is something else. Obviously, he hates it, because who likes their own yearbook picture, but I asked him for a copy. I got a wallet-sized and put it right in, you guessed it, my wallet.

Now, why would I do that? I could've put it in my locker, my backpack, any number of my pockets, but no. And it's not like I'm pulling it out and making goo-goo eyes at it in between classes but what if someone saw it? What if Matty took my wallet as a joke or something and saw it? How do I explain that away?

The wallet thing kept me up that night. I'd gotten home from a run around ten and sat on my porch. It was just for a breather but then I got to thinking about Matty. The look he'd get on his face if he saw that picture in my wallet. And I thought about how my only option would be to sell Dro out. Say I found it in the locker room or something. Say we should give him shit for it. Rag on how he smiled with every part of his face. Call all the life in his eyes *"faggy."* Just so Matty wouldn't turn on me. Just to keep a part of myself I didn't even like safe.

Then Del was there. Just getting home. Asking if I was okay. I must've lost track of time because it was 1 a.m. He said I looked like I was ready to kill someone.

"…I'm sorry."

He tried asking more but I felt this nauseous need to get away from him. I rushed to my room because I wasn't breathing. I just kept making these gasping noises. My eyes and my nose stung like I'd dived face-first into the ocean and I realized I was crying. I thought I knew what crying was for me but I'm learning a lot about myself lately.

So, what's the rule here? Maybe it's more of a reminder. Sandro is affecting me. It's sudden and I can't predict it. It can be as scary and nerve-wracking as it is easy and simple. And thrilling. And terrifying.

So, I guess the rule, the one I need to follow, would be: *If he's affecting you, let him.*

I might not know what I want but I know it involves Sandro Miceli. As a friend, as a workout partner, as a goat-and-horse traveling band, I don't know. But I'm glad we're starting with friends. Because I could use a friend like Dro.

# sandro

*SEPTEMBER 30*

*HIS SHINY TEETH AND ME*

The thing about me and guitar is that I'm bad at it. Well, I'm good at the playing part but ask me a single question about chords or technique and I'll self-combust. The only reason I even started playing was to prove a point. My first guitar got dumped at my feet around age twelve after my brothers both tried and failed to learn. Ever the student, I taught myself how to play within the year. Never took a single lesson. Couldn't have afforded them if I wanted to. All this to say, tween Sandro was very vocal around the farmhouse that he did what his big brothers couldn't.

He didn't give up. He picked up the guitar. Then he fell off the roof with it.

It was a weird summer being stuck at home with no roof and no guitar. That's why when I saw the available electives for my first marking period back to school, I leaped at the chance to take Intro to Guitar. I knew it would be a lot of what I already knew and I was bound to be the only senior in a class full of little baby freshmen but still. I thought learning actual technique would be nice and the class description promised to put a guitar in your hand day one. And so far, between Ms. Morgan's Lit making me read every book in existence and AP calc and AP stat pan-searing my ass, Intro to Guitar with Mr. D has become a welcome oasis in an otherwise packed schedule.

I had no choice but to take Guitar during my last period of the day. The more logical seniors opted for senior privilege and get to go home early after eleventh period but those are kids who have homes they enjoy returning to.

The first half of class, Mr. D has us all play through that day's assignment as a group again and again. I find the monotony of a dozen teenagers playing one chord incredibly soothing, especially once we're all in unison. It's like math, a little bit. When all the numbers and letters line up like they're supposed to and the results are clean and clear. But, just like math, if there's one little error, even if it's the smallest mistake in your calculations, everything else gets thrown off.

Like, we were doing this exercise where we all strummed an A minor 7 for two measures then switched to a C major for two and back and forth to help us get comfortable with transitioning. People would trip up every so often but they're pretty basic chords so it was easy to get the group back into that unison. Except for Phil Reyno.

*"Fuck my face."*

Phil sits at the table right behind mine and he just wasn't getting it. And that's okay, it's an intro class, we're all here to learn. But what bothered me about Phil, what made me want to ask Mr. D for a seat switch, was all the muttering. If you fuck up, just take a second, feel where the group's at, and jump back in. But every time Phil fucked up, he'd groan, cuss, and stop playing altogether.

*"Fucking bullshit."*

Phil Reyno is a famously angry guy. It's what he's primarily known for in my senior class. Well, no. He's primarily known for being outed by his boyfriend in front of the entire school. Well, actually, he's primarily known around town for the way that he dresses. Okay, to put it into a list, Phil Reyno is primarily known for:

1. Dressing like a pop punk singer from the '90s
2. Getting outed at a dance sophomore year
3. Being an angry little shit

Can't say I don't blame the guy for hating the world. If I got outed like he did, so loudly and publicly, I'd be sticking safety pins in my earlobes too.

*"Gonna break this guitar over my fucking... Fuck."*

Maybe I had a chip on my shoulder, knowing how to play already, or maybe I felt some sort of secret queer solidarity with the guy but, in the spirit of helping, I turned around.

"You good?"

Phil stopped playing altogether. So did his tablemate. Punk besties Phil Reyno and Ronny DiSario stared at me like I'd just asked them how my asshole looked up close. Ronny's lip curled in disgust.

"Um...turn the fuck around?"

Phil joined in. "Focus on yourself, Easter Island Head."

Wow. I rolled my eyes and turned back around. You try to help a guy. I filed the interaction away as proof that just because reaching out to a certain conflicted track bro recently yielded positive results, it didn't mean I should be reaching out to every struggling stranger I came across.

For the second half of the class, Mr. D let us free play. As long as we were making music, the time was ours to use. I was sitting at a back table alone, going to town on some Red Hot Chili Peppers, when the punk posse approached me. Phil Reyno and Ronny DiSario eyed my guitar playing with interest so I slowed to a stop. Maybe I was sitting in their spot?

Ronny shook her head, snapping into a Twizzler. "No, no. Keep going."

I took my feet off the table and sat up straight. "Can I help you?"

Ronny gave the remaining half of her Twizzler to Phil. He talked with his mouth full. "Why are you in Intro?"

"I'm allowed."

"Yeah, but you already know how to play."

I didn't understand why they were talking to me. Sure, we're the only seniors in a class full of fifteen-year-olds but just ten minutes ago, they were looking at me like I'd just slapped their mothers.

"Call it an easy A, then."

I felt my phone buzz. Bash texted.

B: Need ur help


Phil sat on my table. "You're a sports guy, right? Big ol' sports man?"

"What?"

"Sports. Jockery. That's your thing, no? How you usually fill your days?"

"I don't... What are you asking?"

Ronny cut to the chase. "Look, you're good at guitar. We are not. I'm more of a keyboard girl and Philly's basically useless off the drums."

"Okay?"

"Okay, and I want to record a demo for my NYU application so we're desperate for a passable bass player. And you aren't exactly busy this fall, are you?"

She kicked my boot under the table. My brain was having trouble catching up to the conversation. My phone was still open in my hand. I texted.


S: meet u at birdie


There were only a few minutes left in the period so I grabbed my backpack and stood.

"I don't play bass. Excuse me."

I headed for the back door. The punk parade was quick on my heels.

"But you play guitar. Well. Bass is just guitar with less strings, anyone can figure it out."

"C'mon, Miceli, it'd be fun. Jamming. Talking shit. Spending some time with people above a 2 IQ."

I stopped in the doorway and looked back. "Thanks, I appreciate the offer but you guys are dicks and I have enough of those. I'm sure there's a freshman you can trick into thinking your whole punk thing's still cool."

Phil and Ronny gasped, all mock-offended. They said it at the same time.

"*Bitch?*"

I shrugged off Fall Out Boy and left class early. Call it "senior privilege."

Bash was relaxing in the back of Birdie when I got out into the parking lot. He opted out of last period because he respects his own time but always sticks around to drive me home. I'd call that courteous but I know he really does it to get some extra time on the school track.

I threw my backpack in the bed and nodded at his very wet hair. "Wassup, sweaty?"

"I just showered."

"Because you were sweaty."

"This is true."

Bash put his sunglasses on and looked up at me. "Hey, so, I got a favor to ask."

"You've earned exactly one. *Shoot.*"

"It's kind of...a lot."

"I'm intrigued. *Shoot.*"

I crawled into the truck and sat on the side. I always made sure to sit a good bit away from him when we were in public. Not like we're sitting on each other's laps when we're alone in the ditch but I knew how Bash felt about eyes. On himself and on me.

Bash sighed. "I was gonna have Lucy help but... I don't

know. It could get complicated. Involving her. But now there's you and... I don't know. You might be more...whatever. Ideal."

"Bash, you're gonna have to *shoot* eventually here."

He sighed again and pointed to his jaw. The bruise was gone but it was where I saw him get clocked that day behind the diner. "I need a tooth out. Teeth. Wisdom teeth."

"Oh. Shit."

"I've been putting it off for a minute but that punch kinda forced my hand. I had it my way, they'd just stay in my mouth but..." He shrugged. "I'm hurting. They need to go."

He turned away. There was something I wasn't getting. "Okay. And...what's my part here?"

"I need someone to drive me home. After. Pick me up and... I'm gonna need some help afterward."

"Sure. That's fine. Your stepdad busy or what?"

Bash sighed up at the sky. Shit. What wasn't I getting? "Del's gonna be home. That's the other part of it. The favor." Bash turned around to face me, looking like he was gearing up. "Look. You ever see one of those videos? The wisdom teeth ones? Kids get all zooted, tell their moms and dads they're the devil or whatever?"

"Sure. They're funny."

"Sure."

Bash rubbed his jaw.

"I don't want to be around him, Sandro. When I'm not acting...you know, after? When I'm high? He'll already be pissed at me that I didn't take care of this a year ago when the dentist told me to."

"Oh. *Ooooooh.*"

"Like, what if I say something? What if I say something I shouldn't? What if I say something mean? Or, like, wrong? Something about him? Or my mom? Or…"

He trailed off but I heard the rest of the sentence in my head. *What if I talk about you?* Bash looked so fucking nervous right there in his truck bed. This worry had been plaguing him for weeks. Months, really. A whole year with this festering shame burning a hole in his jaw.

I nodded. "I get it. I get it, Bash, it's cool. I can help. I'll get you home." I sat up straight. "I am at your service."

He breathed a sigh of relief. "Okay. Thank you, Dro."

"Happy to, bud. It'll be fun, chauffeuring you for a change."

"Yeah. Yeah, it's the least you could do."

"Fuck offfff. You love it."

"I bear it."

"Sweaty."

We laughed and hopped out of the bed.

I once lost a front tooth to an elbow from a brother over a Super Bowl bet but that's what baby teeth are for. Otherwise, I haven't spent much time at the dentist's office. The one I drove Bash to felt more like a lawyer's office though. No fun posters. No fish tank. No stack of moldy *Highlights* magazines. Not the ideal waiting room so I opted to zone out. Around minute thirty of idly daydreaming about my future life as a successful restauranteur and active homosexual, I got a text from my brother Raph.

R: whats the wife password?
R: *Wifi

I sighed.

"Gotta be fucking kidding me."

Another buzz. My oldest brother, Gio, was joining in the fray.

G: What's the wifi passwrod?

I groaned and searched through my Notes for the overly complicated password, wishing my brothers would write something down for once in their goddamn lives. But my phone wouldn't stop buzzing.

R: where the fuck did u go?

G: Wait are you not home??

R: ur supposed to b watching the kids fucko

G: You said youd watch GJ what the fuck??

R: wait r u in ur room?

G: Oh found the wifi password

R: r u asleep? Im coming up

G: This is the wrong password nvm

R: put clothes on

G: Raph just fell down the stairs.

I put my phone on silent and let my brothers sort themselves out. I'd already confirmed with Ma that she'd be home early today so the kids and the Wi-Fi would survive without Uncle Sandy for one night. I had other responsibilities.

It felt good that Bash would trust me like this. I mean, I was his only option but it's nice to know he'd pick me over plan B: hiring a stranger off the street.

*"Villeda?"*

I guess it was time. I stood and walked up to the receptionist. "Hey, hey. I'm here for Bash Villeda. Uh, *Sebastian*. Sebastian Villeda?"

"You're his escort?"

"Yes'm."

"You have your own vehicle?"

"I have his?"

"Super. They make me ask that. This way."

She led me back a few rooms. I heard his voice before I even reached the last one.

*"Because you KNOW I'M RIGHT!"*

Then laughter. I popped my head in and saw Bash covering his face, machine-gun cackling his ass off and nearly falling out of his chair. The dentist was sorting a folder together, happy to play along with what was probably his thousandth high client this week.

"You're very right, Mr. Villeda. Horses are very friendly."

Bash propped himself up, ready to make his case. "No. No, I said *they're our best friends*. That's different."

Oh, wow. I put a hand to my mouth and just watched him go.

"We've been friends for so long, Dr. Hirsch. Horses have helped us since before we even started recording our history. And we've helped them." He got so serious then. Like Matt Damon at the end of *Saving Private Ryan*. *"We've helped them too."*

Then Bash saw me and his whole demeanor changed. All smiles. "AY! MICELI! Como stai?!"

"Italian. Wow. Bene, amico."

He gave me the sloppiest dap up I've ever received and made himself chuckle. Dr. Hirsch handed me Bash's folder and a little baggy of post-op supplies.

"Kid took it like a champ. You're a friend? He's a championship athlete, you know."

"Ah, yes, so he *often* tells me."

"Probably my most impressive client. Not a lot of kids like him in this town."

Hm. Weird thing to say, Doc. I helped Bash up and out of the chair. Dr. Hirsch guided us out the door.

"All the instructions are in that bag, he should heal fine, just keep an eye on his drooling. Soft foods, ice packs—"

"I know the drill. My brothers all got theirs out, I'm well trained in the ol' saltwater gargle."

"Perfect. Just get him sleeping. No straws."

Bash put his hand around my throat. *"I want my fuggin' straws, you son of a bitch."*

He busted out laughing and hugged me. I couldn't help but smile because Bash the Flash, the "too cool for school" track god of Moorestown High, was giggling in my ear and drooling on my shoulder. Like a fucking toddler. He started squeezing me too tight so I removed his bear hug and held his hand all the way to the elevator.

"Okay, buddy, let's get you home. Say 'Thank you, Dr. Hirsch.'"

Bash pointed at his dentist as the elevator doors closed. "I know you killed my wife!"

I pulled the wild man's finger away from getting clipped by the doors and steadied him.

He wiped his hand across my face and snorted. "Got a real face on you, Miceli. Real big face."

I'd never seen a higher person. I mean, when Gio and Raph got their wisdom teeth out, I remember them being loopy but more in an "Oh, my God, is this forever" kind of way. Bash was off his ass. He definitely made the right decision calling in a ringer here. Who knows what he would've said to Lucy? God knows what he'd say to his stepdad.

"Yo, big man." Bash put his hand in my hair and rubbed my head. "I need to poop."

"Oh, fuck. Shit."

Bash cracked up and stumbled into the elevator wall. "I'm joooooooking. Your face. Imagine."

"You're a dick."

"Yuuuup. A big floppy one."

"Wow. You're not gonna remember a second of this, huh?"

"Yeah, here's hoping. Big man."

The doors beeped and opened. After a few cautious steps forward, Bash put a hand on my shoulder to steady himself. "I'm fine. Just making sure you don't fall down."

"Thank you, Bash. Very courteous."

"Hey, I'm a courteous guy."

The trip back to the duplex was quick. I managed to drive Birdie and keep Bash from hollering at too many strangers out the window without totaling her. I'd never driven a pickup before but found it was essentially the same as any other car. I did need to shove the seat way back to accommodate my legs which made Bash furious.

"You break my Birdie, I break your face."

"I'll return your seat good as new. Not my fault you're short."

"Every tree is short to a sequoia."

"That's beautiful. Write that down."

I parked on the street and undid his seat belt for him. There were no cars in the Jordans' side of the duplex's driveway which was good. It assuaged my looming worry that we'd run into Lucy Jordan on the way in, rendering this entire plot useless.

I hopped out, ran around the truck, and opened the passenger door to help Bash but he wouldn't move. His eyes were also on the Jordan driveway. I guess he noticed it too.

"Lucy's not home."

"Yeah. That's ideal."

"She's my day one, you know that? I don't got memories before Luce."

"You told me. It's real sweet."

"I really... I really fucked things up with her."

He shook his head. His mood was dropping quickly.

"Bash."

"I'm such a fucking asshole, Sandro."

"Hey. Come on. Let's get you upstairs."

"Why do you even hang out with me?" I moved to help him but he slapped my hand away. "No. Really. Why do you like me? I'm a fucking dick, man."

"Bash, let's talk in your room, huh?"

"You should've found a reason by now. I suck."

Bash rested his head back on his seat and sank a little. I moved my hand back but he didn't slap me this time. "Come on, bud."

He grabbed my arm and let me help him out of the car. I got his key off his chain and did my best to open the door quietly. The first floor looked empty. Hopefully, Del was in his room or stepped out. Either way, the coast was clear and I didn't plan on lingering.

"We're good. Let's go." I guided Bash to the steps but he didn't want to move. Like a dog pulling on a leash. I kept my voice down. "We gotta go."

Bash leaned on the wall and closed his eyes. "Head rush. Fuck."

I heard a creak in the house. Someone was home. Which side of the duplex, I didn't know. But I didn't want to find out. Bash nodded and tried a step. His center of gravity instantly rocked back and he nearly fell on his ass.

"Shit!"

"Shhh!"

He was being too loud. I called an audible and moved in front of him. "Come on. I'm picking you up."

"You can't pick me up, you're not that—"

"And lift—"

With a quick inhale, I pulled Bash's arms over my shoulders and put him on my back.

*"Oh, fuck."*

Bash quickly picked up his legs and tightened them on my hips. He linked his arms and buried a laugh. "Oh, my God."

"You're lighter than you look. Shh."

With my Bash the Flash backpack tightened, I lumbered up the steps as quietly as one could manage. He couldn't stop laughing in my ear. He got squirmy around step eight and I had to jostle him up to keep him from dropping. He cackled into my back.

"Who's driving this bus?"

"I will drop you."

We crested the mountain and headed down to his room. There were only three doors. One was a bathroom, one was shut, and one was open. From the hall, the open door looked like a teen boy's room so I figured the shut door was Del's. Bash had mentioned Del had an affinity for midday naps and I thanked God for our luck.

Once we were in Bash's, I locked the door and dumped his ass on his bed. He sprawled out like a tabby in the sun.

"Yesssss. I can die peacefully."

"I'm putting all your important shit on your desk."

"Careful. I got a system."

I took two steps and tripped on his "system." Sebastian Villeda might have the messiest room I've seen in person. And growing up with my brothers, it's stiff competition. It's like he had an allergy to putting his clothes away.

"Jesus, dude. Is there a carpet under all this?"

"I have…a system."

I put the post-op baggy on his desk next to this Spanish word-a-day calendar. Bash was digging his face into his pillow and I could tell sleep was coming. Good. All the internet research I did during my waiting room stint said rest was best.

"Sandro, can you get me some water?"

Actually, it said fluids were best and rest was a close second. Bash was stretching his mouth as wide as it would go. "I feel like sandpaper."

"I gotchu. Stay awake for, like, two seconds."

"Then we gotta talk." I stopped in his doorway. Bash was looking at me from his bed, suddenly serious. "We need to talk about it, Sandro."

"Talk...about what?"

I felt nervous all of a sudden. What did Bash need to talk about? Who knew what he'd let himself say right then?

He pointed at my face. "*Daniel. Last Forever.* We need to discuss the boy on the boat."

I rolled my eyes and left him to stretch. I headed downstairs and guessed my way around the layout of the kitchen. I'd only been over a few times and I'd seen the kitchen exactly once so it took a minute to track down a water glass. I got some ice, figured tap would be fine, and turned the sink on.

"The tap is crap."

The glass just about shattered in my grip. I hit the faucet off and turned to find Bash's stepfather staring at me from the doorway. He looked like he'd either just been ousted from a nap or was five seconds from taking one. Groggy. But, moreover, confused.

He gestured at the fridge. "We got filtered in there."

"Oh. Thank you."

"You're welcome. What are you doing in my home?"

As if to answer the question, a big THUNK shook above

us. Bash was up and at it. I pointed at the noise. "I'm, uh... in English with Bash. We take English together, we were just reading."

"Reading? That's what you've been getting up to today? Reading?"

"We got paired to read a book. For English. So, that's what we've been...doing."

I didn't know why I was lying or why it was such a bad lie. I was usually better at lying to parents.

Del scratched his beard. "Y'know, Dr. Hirsch's office called earlier. Said the operation went well. Said Seb might be a little whacky tonight, might need an eye on him."

My face dropped. I wanted to jump out of the kitchen window. "Oh."

"Yeah."

"I'm sorry. I don't... I don't really know what I'm supposed to say here, sir."

Del shook his head and walked over to the fridge. He pulled out a pitcher of filtered water. "Dr. Hirsch also said a very polite boy picked Seb up. Made sure he didn't embarrass himself too much. Drove him home and everything."

He held out a hand. I smiled and gave him the glass. "Just doing Bash a solid. He'd do the same for me."

"Would he now? Interesting."

Del filled up the glass and gave it back to me. It felt like the natural end of our talking. I could feel him giving me an out. But there was an offer there too. What he wanted me to take him up on. Bash always said Del wasn't a talker. But maybe Bash just didn't know how Del talked.

"What do you mean? Interesting?"

Del raised a brow. I think he was surprised I was taking him up on something. I have to imagine it's something Bash never does. He put the pitcher away.

"Just that you're the first friend that kid's had over since the eighth grade."

I made a face. "That can't be true."

"It is. It is very true."

"C'mon. What about Lucy?"

"Well, Ms. Jordan's family. This is just as much her home as ours."

"What about Matty?"

Del leaned against the stove and shrugged. "Who?"

It took me a moment to realize that Del wasn't kidding. When Bash told me he'd been distant with his stepfather lately, I thought I'd understood. I get being distant with your family, I have the scars to prove it. But ask anyone about Sebastian Villeda, nine times out of ten Matty Silva will be the second face they think of. The guys are a package deal in Moorestown. How could this man not know about his stepson's dickhead shadow? I get being busy or distant or whatever but how detached can you be from a kid's life?

I got it in my head then that this man was just one more adult too busy to care.

"He's some kid. Track kid. No one important." I toasted the glass of water. "Better get this to Bash. The internet said fluids were key. Nice to meet you, sir."

Del nodded and watched me go. "You didn't."

I stopped in the door. Del smiled a little. "Huh?"

"You didn't meet me."

I must've looked confused. Del pointed a finger at himself. "Del. Del Branch. I'm Sebastian's stepdad."

"Oh. I know."

My stupid brain snapped to and I realized I'd never told the dude my fucking name. "Oh! My name is Alessandro Miceli. I mean...just Sandro. I don't know why I said the full...thing."

Del nodded and went back to the fridge. He pulled a beer out and smiled my way. "Well. *Just Sandro*. It's nice to meet you too. Thank you for taking care of Seb. Making sure he's okay."

"Sure. Anytime."

This time I took the out. I nodded and was about one step from the doorway when Del called after me. "Is he?" I turned back around. Del opened his beer and sipped it. "Is Seb...do you think he's okay?"

"For sure. The dentist said—"

"Not his teeth. *Him*."

Del's eyes drifted up. The thumps and thunks from on high had stopped. It had been silent for a while.

"Is my kid okay, Sandro?"

I swallowed. Del didn't look so groggy anymore and I saw it then. The care. I saw care on a father's face. Something simple and innate and obvious. Something I had no clue what to do with. Because what did I know about a father's care? I didn't know about that. But I did understand that whatever distance there was between Del Branch and Sebastian Villeda, it might not be Del's fault.

"You don't gotta tell me anything out of school. I get that Seb wouldn't like that. But...if he's in trouble—"

"He's not." I reentered the kitchen. "Really. He's not in trouble, Mr. Branch. He's just...working through something."

That seemed like something Bash would be okay with me saying. Because it was true. He was working through something. I didn't need to say what. Or with who.

But Del seemed relieved. Just a little. He nodded. "And you're helping him? He's letting you help him?"

I just nodded back. Del smiled. Just a little. "Well. That makes me happy." I smiled back. He looked at my glass of water. "Go. I'll make him something to eat. Thanks for talking to me, Mr. Miceli."

"Thank you, sir. Soft foods."

Del chuckled and started on dinner. I headed back upstairs. Bash was asleep and hugging a pillow when I came back in. His shoes had been chucked to opposite sides of the room and I have to assume that was the thunking. He stirred when I closed his door and sat up a little when I put the water on his nightstand.

"You still here?"

"You still high?"

"Mm-hm. I don't like it anymore."

He took the glass and swallowed the whole thing in two big gulps. It was jarring. "Jesus, dude."

Bash wiped his mouth on his pillow and squirmed away, making room for me on his bed. He pointed at the edge of the mattress so I sat.

"How you feeling, bud?"

"I can't get to sleep. I just...wanna sleep."

"Want me to turn a show on? A movie?"

"Can you read to me?"

"Read?"

Bash tried to rub a headache out of his temples. "I just wanna listen to something, dude. Can you?"

"I don't have a book. But Del's making you dinner. Maybe we find something after?"

"You talked to Del?"

His eyes opened. I nodded.

"I told you not to talk to him."

"Uh, no, you told me not to let *you* talk to him. We barely spoke, Bash. But he wanted to. He's actually pretty chatty if you give him—"

"It's fine. Whatever." Bash closed his eyes then turned away from me. Made a big point of showing me his back.

"Bash."

"You don't gotta stay, Dro. You can go."

"C'mon."

"I appreciate the favor, Sandro, I do. But I just wanna sleep now. Okay?"

"...Fine."

I didn't stand up. I just stared at his back. Watched his breathing. Because it didn't feel right to leave yet. Bash asked me to look after him and I wasn't done doing that yet.

*"Anywho."* I dimmed his lights and plugged in his phone. "I think Phil Reyno and Ron DiSario asked me to be in a band with them today."

Bash didn't budge. I pulled his desk chair close to his bed and sat. Gave him his space. Got comfortable.

"They're in my music class. I think they took it to hunt for guitarists. That must be the reason 'cause they can't play for dick. We were doing these chord progressions in the first half of class and I just heard them behind me plucking away, all off time. They were kind of hopeless, honestly."

I just kept talking. Talking and talking and talking. I talked about A minor 7. The C major chord. I talked about the day I got my guitar and the night I lost it, just waiting for him to tell me to go. But he didn't. Bash let me talk like I knew he would. Because I know how noisy guys like us can get when it's just us and our heads and I knew he didn't want to be alone with that noise that night.

I was starting to understand that Bash didn't want to be alone. No matter what he did to keep himself that way, Sebastian Villeda was tired of being so far from the world. Exhausted. And he had no idea how to tell the world he missed it. He'd lost his tools. He'd forgotten how to fall back to earth.

"You know, I usually avoid guys like Phil but Ronny can be funny. They want me to play bass which, I mean, I've never even picked up one before. They don't even want me, really, they just want my hands. I'd just be a walking instrument to them. I don't know. It's interesting though. Would definitely be a way to fill out my fall. And I do like music."

Bash kept his eyes closed but eventually he turned back around. Listened to me talk. I knew he understood what I was doing for him and he drifted off to sleep while I told him about my day.

"Maybe I'll do it. Maybe I'll join a band. Maybe that's what fall's supposed to bring."

Bash's face went from tight to still in the matter of minutes. The stress faded from those big, bushy brows and his jaw stopped looking like it might shatter. His breathing got easy. His cheeks got soft. His eyelids fluttered and I had to smile.

Because not a lot of people must know what I know now. I must be one of the lucky few. It's got to be a short list of people who know how beautiful that boy looks when he sleeps.

I thanked him for trusting me enough to see it.

# bash

*eyes*

The Micelis have this driveway that rivals the New York Marathon. They live on the edge of town and the only street that leads there devolves into gravel about a quarter mile away from the place. You're driving along the road then BAM, once you pass their mailbox it's this long stretch of rocks with a big ol' farmhouse looming on the horizon. Very pastoral. Very tiring to walk down.

Yet every morning, rain or shine, Sandro insists I park by their red, rusty mailbox. At first, I thought it was for my sake. Maybe he thought I wouldn't want to be seen escorting him to and from school every day. Maybe he thought I'd find that too risky. But lately, I've started to suspect that it's more for him. That the risk he's worried about isn't "Me re: the World." He's more afraid of "Me re: the Micelis."

My suspicions started last Tuesday, after school, when I offered to drive him all the way to his door. I'd never questioned the perimeter he was keeping between me and his homestead before but it was raining and crutches plus umbrellas don't exactly mix. I asked him why he wouldn't just let me take him all the way to his front door and he got all flustered. Sorta cagey. But before I could press him about his sudden shift in mood, he uttered what I'm now realizing is Sandro Miceli's trademark catchphrase.

"Anywho."

The second there's a lull in the convo, whenever things get a little too close to home, the moment Sandro considers talking about some of his own shit, I see this switch flip in his head. Some ad-blocker in his mathematical robo-brain that seems to scream:

*ERROR! ERROR!*
*BASH IS THE ONE WITH BAGGAGE HERE!*
*REROUTING! REROUTING!*

And he'll give a little sigh and a shrug and move the conversation onto something less personally invasive. Weight lifting. Hoagies. My relationship with God.

"Anywho."

Just covering up all his worry with a smile. I mean, hey, it's a great smile. A great cover.

Today was a foggy kind of morning. Everything was moving slower and my windows were misting up after a minute of idling by that rusty mailbox. I spotted Sandro halfway up the driveway so I turned the radio down and unlocked the passenger door. Dro tossed his crutches into Birdie's bed and climbed into shotgun, looking like he'd just rolled right out of bed and into my truck.

"Morning."

"Morning. You sleep well?"

"You know I didn't, dick."

I laughed. Sandro smiled and buckled up. Last night, the Miceli family had some big funeral or wedding thing in Philly, leaving Dro on babysitting detail for his nieces and GJ. It wasn't the first time he'd been assigned the role of de facto parent/warden for his niblings, but apparently his baby niece Lexi was crying her eyes out from sundown to sunup and, by midnight, Dro was ready to leave the children in the woods. I was up half the night distracting him with phone calls but the sound of Lexi's wailing on his end kept my efforts nice and short.

"Want the second half of my coffee?" I offered up what remained of my large Wawa to-go cup. Sandro's eyes lit up.

"Did you go to—"

I nodded at the glove box. He opened it up and just about cried. Every so often, if I'm out of bed early enough and feel up for the extra stop, I'll swing by the Wawa on Main before heading to Dro's. This morning, I'd grabbed him a bacon-egg-and-cheese along with my coffee. He once told me he could probably survive solely off bacon-egg-and-cheeses for the rest of his life, which is funny because he's always skipping breakfast.

Sandro was three bites in before taking a breath. "You're a fucking prince, Bash Villeda."

"Thought you might sleep through brekky. Extra salt, pepper, ketchup."

"A fucking prince."

I smiled and looked up the driveway. Someone was standing outside the house. Sipping his own coffee. Watching us. Even with the world's longest driveway between us, I could feel the man's eyes.

"Hey. Who's that?"

Mouth full, Sandro looked where I was looking. His chewing stopped. With one hard swallow, he nodded at the steering wheel. "My pop. C'mon, we should go."

"Why's he watching us?"

"Come on, dude, seriously."

I raised my brows and shifted into Drive. The gravel crunched under us and we pulled away from the foggy farmhouse on the edge of town. As we drove away, I kept a watch on my rearview. Mr. Miceli's eyes stayed on us until the very end.

"Your dad looks tall."

Sandro's eyes were still on his window. He was taking his time on the final bites of his breakfast sandwich. "I got his height. And his feet."

"Huh?"

"We both got flat feet. None of my brothers got them, just me."

"Aww. Lucky."

"Yeah, I'm truly blessed."

Sandro polished off the last of his roll and shrugged. "Anywho. You finish chapter twelve?"

I had to keep myself from snorting. King of segues, San-dro Miceli. He fished his copy of *Daniel: Last Forever* out of his backpack and found his spot in the book.

"I think Ms. Morgan's gonna quiz us today."

There was no use trying to ask about Dro's family. I never pushed past an *anywho*. Because we're getting really good at this whole conversation thing. The way me and Sandro talk, that shit's simple and easy. I've never had that with another guy before. We get what the other wants to talk about and we respect what the other doesn't. I don't push Sandro on the way his brothers bully him. He doesn't push me on my silent shit with Del. I don't ask him about the scar on his eyebrow. He doesn't ask me about the kiss in the woods. Who knows? Maybe one day we'll get there but for now I'll settle for simple. Because nothing else in my life stays simple for long. If Sandro needs to *anywho* his way out of sticky conversations, that's fine by me. Because we can always find better things to talk about.

After eleventh period, I dropped my books off at my locker and headed to the senior locker room for a run. It wasn't a cross-country day but some of the older guys and I were planning on getting some laps in during senior privilege. To be honest, though, I hate running in a group. Having to keep pace with people. Slow down for them. Running is a solitary activity, that's what's so great about it. You can be the best all on your own. If it weren't for what that Rutgers coach told me last spring, I would've just spent my fall run-ning on my time but if *Cross-country Captain* looks good to the eyes of Rutgers admissions, you can bet I'll be the fastest lemming in the herd.

Matty was midchange when I got to my locker.

"Yo, bitch tits. Tryna light up?"

"It's a Thursday."

"You used to be fun."

"Mm." .

Matty has gotten into a big "running while high" kick since school started up again. I never took him up on his offers though. I made a hard rule with myself that, whatever bullshit Matty roped me into, I would never do it on Moorestown High property. Maybe it's my mom's influence. She always made sure I got the lines clear in my head. School is for school. It's where you go to work, it's a job. A lot of kids don't get to go to school, much less one as nice as Moorestown, so keep your head down, keep your nose clean, and keep it off school grounds. I was also keenly aware that if I got caught doing half the sketchy shit my friends get away with, I'd be punished twice as hard. Because Bash the Flash has a lot of eyes on him. That's his point. His purpose. But in a town like Moorestown, a name like Villeda catches eyes too. All it takes is one wrong eye. My mom made sure I got that line clear.

I took off my prayer bracelet and zipped it up in my backpack. I always worried I'd lose it on the track. I yawned into my hand for the thousandth time that day, really regretting staying up so late with Sandro on the phone.

I guess I'd been quiet too long because Matty snapped in my face. "Yo. Stares. What, you smoke without me?"

"Nah, man. Just thinking."

"'Bout?"

"Thursday."

"What?"

"Thursday. I'm thinking it's Thursday."

I shook off another yawn. Matty rolled his eyes and laced up his shoes on the bench. "You've been moody as fuck lately, dude. What gives?"

I rolled on some deodorant and shrugged. I could've said more. Could've made a joke. Kept this dead end of a conversation going. Because that's what Bash the Flash does. Stokes the flame. Talks his shit. Backs his boy Matty up. But I was tired. And I felt eyes on me. Anthony Lewis and the rest of the cross-country guys were filing into the locker room and I needed to keep it chill. Matty didn't press me. He had entertaining to do, after all. He left me to change and bopped over to Ant Lewis and the gang to compare running shoes and dick sizes.

Our group finally finished dressing and headed out to the track. It was always empty during the last period of the day on Tuesdays and Thursdays because there were no gym classes. The rest of the guys stretched out in the lanes but Matty told me to wait back around the captain's entrance gate. I swallowed my sigh. I just wanted to start running but ignoring Matty would've only caused a bigger conversation.

"Sup, man?"

Matty looked at the herd of guys talking shit and messing around on the track. "Ant asked about the shit with Cinnaminson. Heard there was a fight."

"Was that supposed to be a secret?"

Matty scoffed. "No, asshole. But I told him we stomped those fuckers. Hear me?"

I got it. The record shows that we won the fight that day. Even the Cinnaminson crew would cop to that. But we didn't exactly come out clean. My sore gums and round of antibiotics would prove that and Matty got it even worse. Those guys busted his nose and kicked the shit out of his ribs before I even joined the fight. But I guess that's not the story Matty told Anthony Lewis. Because, to guys like Ant, it's not good enough to win a fight. You need to make it look easy. Tough guys like that don't want wins, they want war stories. Domination. If Matty and the Flash were gonna be *Matty and the Flash*, they needed to be untouchable.

"So, if he asks—"

"Sure. We stomped those fuckers."

"That's right. 'Cause we're not the guys who get punched."

"Sure."

"And if those Cinnaminson fucks say otherwise—"

"We'll stomp them again. Sure."

Matty smiled. He patted my shoulder and we joined the herd. We ran as a group, a cluster moving as one. Seven people keeping each other's pace, matching each other's speed, and hugging each other's turns. I ran at the head of the group, slower than I would on my own, and my team followed my every move. It got to the point where I could swear our breathing aligned. The sounds of our shoes hitting the ground seemed to sync up and in just two laps, we'd become one runner. One cluster. One person.

Around lap eight, I lost track of who was saying what. I tried my best to ignore them but they just wouldn't stop.

"You hear Bruvik got his dick puked on?"

"Fucking foul. Who?"

"Syd DeStefano. At Ronny's house, last weekend."

"Syd *the Stuffin' Ho*."

"You're fucking corny."

"Was she drunk?"

"Bitch is always blackout, she just can't give head. Gags and pukes and shit."

"Not what I heard."

"Yeah, I heard Syd does anal."

*"The Stuffin' Ho."*

"Nah, girls don't take it up the ass."

"Well, Syd does."

"Yeah. 'Cause her dad left."

"Dude, shut up."

"What, he did. She told me at CCD."

"That she takes it up the ass?"

"That her dad left, dumbass."

"Daddy issues."

"Gag reflex issues."

"It's Bruvik's fucking fault. What do you expect?"

"Slut."

"Dude."

"Sorry. Devil's advocate, you fuck with a girl like that, expect to get your dick puked on. Sorry."

"Like you get girls."

"Eat shit. Pepperoni nips."

"Lard ass."

"You got a confusing dick."

"Your balls look like an old woman's neck."

"Your facial hair doesn't connect."

"Your pubes look like a ten-year-old boy's."

"How you know what a ten-year-old's pubes look like, faggot?"

"'Cause I was one, cocksucker, were you?"

How boring. All of it. How stupid and small and boring this

all was. These jokes. These people. This existence. Running in the same circles, with the same guys, with the same conversations. This track. This closed loop of a life. The same beginnings, the same endings, over and over again. I was so tired.

When I slowed down, no one seemed to notice. When I ended up at the back of the pack, the conversation never stuttered. And when I stood completely still, the group kept on without me. I'd been spending so much time trying to match their pace, trying to stay in step, because I thought the cluster would crumble without me. Their captain. I'd been holding myself back, running how I thought they would run, because I thought that's what was expected of me. I made myself slow for them. For years. I made myself so much worse for these fucking people and they won't even miss me when I'm gone.

And I was gone.

I cut through the side of the track and took the shortcut to the locker room. It was empty when I got in and I checked my phone before changing. I had two missed calls from Sandro. Weird. He texted too.

S: so sorry. Can u grab my booik out of Birdie? I left it there this morning.
S: supes cool if not, im just bored in Guitar

I smiled and figured I might as well. My free period had suddenly opened up.

B: Be right there.

I decided I'd shower and change after getting the book to Dro. I headed out the side entrance to the parking lot and found Sandro's copy of *Daniel: Last Forever* under Birdie's passenger seat. I used the faculty entrance since it's closer to the music hall. Students aren't allowed to use that entrance but there isn't a teacher in Moorestown High School who doesn't love my ass. Lucy's deemed me a Teacher's Pet but I can't help it if I'm "an enthusiastic learner" and "a delight to have in class." Luce can call me a brownnoser all she wants, I'm allowed in the teachers' lounge and she isn't. Sorry I'm a delight.

When I turned down into the music hall, I could hear the orchestra messing around with some warm-up tunes. I thought I heard the one about the bumblebee but didn't stick around to confirm. At the end of the hall, the big double doors were propped open and I heard guitar. Not a class's worth though. Just one. Some pretty strumming. And some decidedly unpretty yelling.

"THIS IS NICE! THIS IS GOOD MUSIC!"

I popped my head into an empty practice room and saw Sandro playing an acoustic guitar, screaming down at Phil Reyno at his drum set. And Phil was screaming right back.

"THE SMITHS ARE '80s SHIT! WE ONLY PLAY '90s SHIT!"

"IT'S THE SAME SHIT! THEY'RE ALL THROW-BACKS!"

"IT'S A DECADE OF DIFFERENCE, YOU BIG FUCK!"

Ronny DiSario was sitting at a keyboard, sipping a Slurpee and checking Twitter. She noticed my presence and played a loud, dissonant chord. The boys shut up and Ronny smiled at me. "Bash the Flash? As I live and breathe."

Phil scoffed at me. "Oh, now this. Hey, this is our practice room, *bro*, we reserved it. Find a locker room to hotbox."

Sandro looked embarrassed. I shrugged off Phil Reyno's glare and held up Dro's book. "It was under the seat. Sorry to interrupt."

Sandro put his guitar down and walked my way. "He's cool, guys, I invited him."

Phil stood behind Ronny, arms all crossed. "Oh! Well, if *Sandro* says he's cool..."

Ronny gave Phil a pat on the butt and cooed, "Come on, Philly. Bash the Flash is just passing through, huh? I'm sure he's got better things to do with an afternoon. Babies to kiss. Ribbons to cut."

"Yeah, Flashy, don't you have a trophy case to jack off to?"

Sandro closed his eyes, instantly regretting putting me in these particular crosshairs. I don't know what I'd done to incur the wrath of Hot Topic's own Phil Reyno and Ronny DiSario but if I've learned anything from my time with Sandro, it's that I don't have a great sense of how I've been coming off these past few years. Especially to people who could not give an iota of a rat's ass about track, field, or Bash the goddamn Flash. These two, with their black nails and pink gauges and *fuck you* glares, saw me as part of the herd. Another track jerk with his head up his ass and his mind on his dick. Who called a girl a slut because her dad left her. Who called each other faggots for any reason they felt like. They saw me as Bash the Flash. Moorestown's Golden Boy. And why wouldn't they? I was still wearing his clothes.

I put the book on a chair and gave the room a nod. "The music sounded good. Sorry."

And I left.

"*Bash.*" Sandro followed me out. I was halfway up the hall when he put a hand on my shoulder. I ducked it.

"It's fine, man. I get it."

"Bash, c'mon. They're just dicks."

"It's nothing I haven't heard before."

Sandro sighed. "You're not upset?"

I just shrugged. "Not worth getting upset over. Are you upset?"

"What? Oh, the screaming? No. That's just...how they talk. It's a whole thing."

"Sounded lively."

"It was. It's been..." Dro smiled. "It's been really fun, actually. Like...we argue a lot and it's a lot of yelling sometimes but, I don't know. It's like the *right* kind of yelling, y'know? It's actually about something I can get passionate about, not some fucking football game or who the best Flyers coach is."

"That's good, man. That's really good. I'm glad you're making friends."

"I don't know if I'd say *friends* but..." He considered it. "Yeah. We could be friends. I could make friends."

I watched Sandro smile. And I wanted to tell him about my friends. My run. What those boys said and how it made me feel. What Matty said and how it made me mad. And tired. And bored. I wanted to tell Sandro how much better my afternoon would've been if I just could've spent it with him. Talking in our ditch. Driving in my truck. Moving at our pace. I wanted to tell him how much better I felt just standing in that hallway with him. With two punks staring holes in the back of my head and my running clothes starting to stink. I wanted to tell Sandro that I knew why he didn't want to talk about his family but I wished he would. I wanted to thank him for taking care of me after my surgery and I wanted to tell him how much better my year has been now that he's in it.

The bell rang. Free period was over. The day was done. My classmates flooded into the hallway and I had a choice. I could go with the flood or I could find a life raft. A buoy. Something to anchor me from floating away. But I felt eyes on me. Ronny DiSario. Phil Reyno. Anthony Lewis. Matty Silva. Lucy Jordan. Sandro Miceli. I felt all of their eyes on me and I didn't know who to be right then. Which Bash. What to say. So, I let the eyes make my choice for me. I took a step back from Sandro's smile and just shrugged.

"…Anywho."

The eyes had it.

# sandro

OCTOBER 15

### SOLVING FOR WHY:
### THE POINT OF YOU AND ME

So, we were in the weight room and I was about to shove my size thirteens up his smug ass.

Wait.

This is a disingenuous place to start.

Let's roll back to tenth period.

So, we were skipping study hall in the senior parking lot, Birdie's seats in full recline, and we were breaking down Bash's different *Bashes*. It was sort of like Pokémon cards, the way we were tossing his different moods around. We'd discussed *the Flash*, his cocky streak around his trackolytes, we'd covered *the Ex*, his mellower side around Lucy Jordan, but there was one Bash in particular that I'd been dying to unpack.

"How 'bout *the Stepson*?"

"What do you mean?"

"How you act around Del."

His smile slowed down. "How do I act around Del?"

"I mean…"

While annoying and way too aggro for my liking, at least Bash can have some fun with the Flash. At least he's talking. Engaging. But he gets so weird around Del. I've met his step-dad a few times now and he's a really nice guy. A little mopey and always tired but he's made me feel very welcome in their home. I even helped him fix up Birdie when a cracked cool-ant tank turned her into a ticking time bomb. We made a whole day of it. Grilled on the lawn, played music, he even "forgot" to put away a case of beer. And it's not like Bash was brooding in the corner but I don't think they said more than three words to each other all afternoon. They would talk to me or through me. I can't imagine what they're like when I'm not there.

Personally, I think *the Stepson* is the worst version of Bash. It's the only one I don't feel him putting on. It just comes naturally.

"Come on, man. You're not exactly your *best* around Del."

Bash fiddled with his prayer bracelet and shrugged. "I don't know what you're talking about."

"Really? It's kind of obvious, dude."

"You don't know what you're talking about. *Dude*."

Okay, bitch.

I'm glad his eyes were glued to the roof because I made quite the face. I seriously thought he might kick me out of the truck for a second. I considered backtracking or explaining myself but decided better of it. Best to just abandon ship. Keep things easy-breezy.

"Anywho. Wanna work out?"

Bash considered it then smiled. Exercise always refocused him. It's one of his few character flaws. We'd been working out together pretty regularly since the top of the school year and found it to be an excellent smoke screen for our sudden friendship. Sports people don't question the pair-up because they wouldn't dare question their king. Nonsports people don't question the pair-up because they wouldn't dare ask about the boring world of sports. Suffice it to say, *Sandro & Bash: Workout Buds* is a far easier pill for people to swallow than *Sandro & Bash: Kissed Twice in the Woods and Now Awkwardly Half Flirt at Each Other over Sandwiches.*

I was sitting on the locker room bench, undoing my laces, and Bash was changing out of his school clothes. We were about ten minutes into my latest hypothetical when Bash nodded, decision finally made. "I think I'd rather...yeah, I'd rather eat my arms."

"That's ridiculous, Bash."

"It's less to eat. I'd be over with it sooner."

"That's not the point, man."

"Yeah, it is. *Would you rather eat your arms or your legs?* My arms, asked and answered."

I laughed. "It's not about the action, dude. It's about the aftermath."

"The aftermath?! This is a bad hypothetical, Dro. One of your worst."

"It's not about the eating, it's—"

Bash slid his jeans down and they took a bit of boxer with them. I caught about an inch of curliness peeking over his waistband before shooting my eyes to the tile.

I swallowed. "It's, uh…it's about the result. Dealing with it. The after."

I kept my head down because I thought I'd gotten flush. Bash chuckled. "So, would I rather live without arms or legs? Yeah?"

I looked back up. He was just in boxers then. I nodded, doing my best to keep a casual face. Not look anywhere I shouldn't. Not think about this guy I'm simply friends with or his astonishingly thick set of pubes.

"Yeah. Which would you rather?"

Bash looked up at the ceiling and scratched his stomach hair, really considering my question. I realized I was getting hard and decided I'd change in the bathroom stall. But before I could hide myself and before Bash could answer, Anthony Lewis strolled into the locker room.

"Dios míos, it's Sebastian el Flash!"

My nose twitched. This fucking guy. The last time I saw Ant Lewis, he was chucking a full Solo cup at my chest for contesting his win at the Beer Olympics. He told me he'd tripped which might have been the first time the snooty douche ever spoke to me with eye contact. Anthony is one of the biggest believers in this bullshit track vs field rivalry. He once tried to get a petition going that the track team shouldn't have to share a bus with us Fieldies because we were "two different breeds." Personally, I think Anthony's an insecure closet racist who's just mad his daddy couldn't buy him a captain's spot.

I looked up at Bash but he wasn't where I left him. I'd been so preoccupied on not watching him change clothes, I didn't catch him change people. Bash the Flash's booming laugh echoed around the locker room and the two track bros high-fived. Suddenly, my workout buddy looked a lot less cute in his Joe Boxers.

"Sup, Ant? How's your girl?"

"Good question. Which one?"

"All right, you fucking dog."

It's truly unsettling to watch Bash turn it on for people. All the new words he uses. The intricate handshakes everyone seems to know. This Anthony run-in wasn't as bad as I've seen it, not "Heckling Long Jumpers at an Away Meet" level, but it was still weird. Didn't help that Ant never so much as looked at me the entire exchange. Neither did Bash.

After, when Ant was gone and we were alone again, we finished dressing and stretched out on the benches. But the whole time, I could tell Bash was thinking about it. That I saw him change like that.

He laughed a little. "I hate that fucking guy. LAX bro asshole."

I grunted. I didn't feel like commenting on a conversation I wasn't invited into. I think Bash got that. His eyes were trained to the floor. He felt bad. He wasn't hiding it. He took another second then looked at me, still a little sheepish.

"I mean… I guess I'd rather live without my legs. I like my hands and the leg prosthetics look easier to manage."

I looked back at him. Bash wanted to move on. Ignore
that he just ignored me. Get back to our rhythm. Our pace.
Whatever this thing we're doing is.

So, I nodded. "Oh. Right. Yeah, and you could get those
blade legs."

"Exactly. Like a superhero. Also, I put a lot of work into my
legs and... I don't know. I think they'd probably taste better."

"Logical. How would you cook them?"

"Just a bit of Lawry's. Finish on the grill."

"Nice. It's simple but it's good."

Bash smiled but I knew he wasn't letting himself off the
hook for Ant that easy. It's not a simple thing to shake for
him. This need to put on and impress. And while I might
find it annoying and super unflattering, I really do get it. It's
no different than how I am in my house. Sandro *Miceli* and
Sandro *Sandro* are two different dudes. It's just how I survive
my family. Bash is just surviving. Only he has more dudes to
worry about. Some garbage fucking dudes.

So, after hours the school gym is open to all students but
the weight room is only available to captains of pre- or in-
season sports. As luck would have it, that was us. As luck
wouldn't have it, that was also Matty Silva. As soon as we entered the room, Bash's spine went all limp like a pool noodle.
His eyelids drooped and his head bobbled around on a spring.
I sighed. Twice in under an hour. A new record, perhaps. At
least he was consistent. Bash nodded a "Sup" at Matty, busy
with leg presses. Matty nodded his "Sup" back to Bash and
only Bash. Before the BFFs could "sup" themselves to death,
I dragged my workout buddy away to the free weights.

According to my schedule it was a chest and back day, so

I picked out a comfortable pair of dumbbells for Bash and grabbed my usual forty-fives. We faced the mirror and I guided him through our first few curl sets.

I always prefer working in the weight room. It's established field territory if you bought into that sort of thing but, pointless rivalries aside, I just feel comfortable there. I can be impressive there. Bash can kick my ass all he wants with cardio but on strength days, Sandro knows best. Because while I don't consider myself a "Big Sports Boy," I do know what I'm doing with weights. My brothers made sure of that.

After our first few sets of curls and raises, we moved onto the bench for some standard presses. Bash thumbed through the weight rack. "What weight should I do?"

I cracked open my workout log. Bash wasn't trying to gain muscle mass with these workouts, just to keep fit for his long-distance regimen. The plan was to start him steady and move him up to some bulkier workouts once sprinting season kicked back up. But for now, we were starting light to keep him from hurting himself.

"Last week, I had you at one-eighty. How'd that feel?"

"Good. Real good. Sometimes I get this crick in my neck when I bench but last time—"

*"One-eighty?"*

I'd never heard a scoff echo before. I watched Matty approach from the mirror. "You've been clearing two-flat easy since sophomore year, Bashy. You slouching?"

I went to give Bash an eye-roll, but Bash had left the building again. The Flash shrugged. "Just taking it easy. It's Friday, y'know? Fuck it."

"That the big guy's idea? Taking it easy?"

He was talking around me, not to me. Was I just invisible to track assholes today? The smart play was letting Matty tire himself out. But I wasn't being smart today. I was being a jock.

"You wanna talk shit, you can look at me when you do it."

Matty laughed and did what I asked. He looked me up and down. My workout clothes suddenly felt particularly tight under all that condescension.

"No one's talking shit. We're just fucking around, paisan."

I could force myself to work out or I could force myself to talk to Matty. I couldn't do both and I wanted to do neither. But I smiled. "Bash is looking to retain muscle mass without losing tone. Dropping to a lower weight will keep him from bulking out or hurting himself."

"Yeah? And you'd know all about bulking out, huh?"

"I know the basics of physiology, yeah. You just need Google. And common sense."

Matty gave Bash a little look and a sneer. "You catch that one, B-Boy?"

Bash was fiddling with a ten-pound plate. He just shrugged. I'd missed something.

Matty laughed. "Yeti's so focused on sounding smart, he didn't even hear it."

"Hear what?"

Matty put his hands up, all *Beats me*. "What'd he miss, Bashy? What went over the field captain's ol' watermelon?"

We both looked at Bash. He was counting ceiling panels at that point. When the silence became too much to out-chill, he met Matty's impatient stare and sighed. "He mentioned bulking. And you made a joke about...bulk."

Matty cackled and slapped my stomach. Bash clocked the

vein pulse in my neck. He knows all about my thing with being touched. *Especially* by fuckers who I never gave an invite. I felt my belly shake against my workout tank and quickly played out a scenario in which I punched Matty's nose-bone into his brain. I'd definitely get suspended but with the right character references, I might be able to walk that back to a week or two of detention. I'd get so much homework done.

Matty kept up his cackle all through my hypothetical. "I'm just fucking with you, bubba! Those thunder thighs bring home medals!"

I was about to shove my size thirteens up his smug ass. I could've too. I had nearly two feet and at least seventy-five pounds on the runt. Matty patted my back a few times before Bash cut in.

"Chill, Matty." Bash had let his face go full Flash at that point. "You don't gotta touch him, man."

"C'mon. We're just fucking around! Captains!"

"You don't always gotta be touching dudes. Fucking weird, man."

Matty made a face. And if I weren't trying to keep my cool, I would've joined him. Things needed to de-escalate, the unwanted contact was definitely getting to me, but that was not the road I would've taken. It wasn't a look I liked on Bash. Any Bash.

"What's wrong with him touching dudes?"

Matty and the Flash both looked at me. Then each other. Then the three of us just sort of stood there in this weird, homophobic standoff. I didn't mean to ask the question. In my right mind, I would never have shown my hand that much but I was angry. I'd been getting angry since I heard that first scoff. Since Anthony Lewis didn't bother acknowledging me. Since Bash didn't bother acknowledging me either. God's honest, I think I'd been getting angry all day.

Bash backed down. He knew there was no good answer to my question. Not in the weight room. Matty, in true Silva form, didn't know so well.

"What, you like me touching you, Miceli?"

He cackled again and jiggled my stomach again and before I knew it, Matty was in the fucking air.

On a good day, I can bench one-ninety. On a game day, I can bench over two-flat. But with proper motivation, dangling Matty Silva in the air was like carrying groceries. I felt like Rafiki holding Simba up for all of Pride Rock to see. I couldn't hear what Matty was yelling. I couldn't hear what Bash was yelling. I just shook Matty Silva up in the air. Because I could. Because that little fuck needed to know that I could. All I could hear was my own voice. My own screaming voice.

**"WHAT?! YOU LIKE ME TOUCHING YOU, MOTHERFUCKER?!"**

Something had taken over me, this anger that creeps up my spine, and for a minute I couldn't see faces. I could make out the shapes of some rubbernecking field guys but I couldn't see their faces. I think some of them had their phones out. That calmed me down a little. Not the roaring team support. The eyes. The realization of what I was doing. The hand slapping my back.

**"SANDRO!"**

I started hearing words again. Seeing faces again. Bash's face. Angry. Confused. Scared. Suddenly, I wanted to run away.

I put Matty back on his feet and waited for the hit. I deserved one, right across my jaw. But Matty had no comeback. No scoff or sneer. I never even saw his face, he just went straight for the door and left. Bash took in the room of eyes, silent.

"Ba—"

His glare cut me off. His throat shook. Like all the things he wanted to scream at me were fighting to get out first. Instead, he just followed Matty out. Yelling his name. Asking for his friend to wait up.

I didn't know what to do. But I knew I wasn't supposed to follow him. So, I worked out a little longer.

After I'd showered and changed, I saw that Birdie was still where we left her. Bash hadn't left. But he hadn't returned any of my texts so I resorted to walking the halls. I needed to apologize. Not to Matty. Matty could go fuck himself. I wanted to apologize for embarrassing Bash like that. Because these last few weeks, we've never hit a road bump like this. We've gotten annoyed with each other but never mad. Of course our first snag would be my fault. It was just a matter of time really. Bash just has this weird thing with attention. It's like he wants everyone in a room to acknowledge his presence then completely ignore him. He hates having eyes on him but doesn't know how else to judge himself. And that weight room had a lot of eyes.

When I got to Bash's locker, I found someone. Not the person I was looking for, but certainly someone. Someone very cool. I've never really known what *cool* is, but there's no denying that Lucy Jordan is fucking cool. The braids, the fashion, the withering stares. Seeing her leaned up against Bash's locker was like stumbling onto a runway. Because not only did I feel inadequate just looking at her, but I got the feeling that I was in her way.

She clocked my staring and stared right back. "Are you being helped?"

"...What?"

"Can I fucking help you?"

I held my gym bag closer to my stomach. "Sorry. No. Sorry. Um..." I pointed at the locker she was leaning on. "You seen Bash?"

Lucy sighed and returned to picking at her purple fingernails. "All track-and-field inquiries should be taken up with Coach Bianco."

"I'm not—"

"Look, I don't have the time or the patience to deal with jock shit today. Okay, Hoosiers? I'm not his damn secretary."

She eyed the bathroom door across from us. *Men's.* She was waiting for him. I nodded. "He's in there?"

I didn't wait for her response, I just went for the door. Lucy snapped to attention and slipped in front of me. "Hold the fuck up, Italian Shrek. He doesn't want to talk to anyone right now."

"I know. It's my fault. I want to apologize."

"And just who the fuck are you?"

I backed up. That sort of stung. "We had a whole year of gym together. Eighth grade? C'mon, Lucy, I was like a yard taller than everyone."

Lucy nodded, a little surprised. "I remember. I just didn't think you did. People don't usually remember me like that."

"I mean...same."

We held for a moment as Mr. Bart, the thousand-year-old custodian, pushed his cart through the hall. Once we were clear, Lucy smiled a little. "I don't know what you did but it probably doesn't matter. Trust me. I don't know half the shit I did to get him all Moody Booty."

*"Moody Booty?"*

Lucy took a moment to put her explanation together. "Seb... *Bash* gets into funks. Sometimes it's like he becomes someone else. And when people do...whatever it is that you did...he can get mighty funky. When he gets burnt or burnt-out..."

"Moody Booty."

She shot me a finger gun. I looked at the men's room door. "So, what do I do?"

"Are you his friend?" I nodded. Lucy shrugged. "He hasn't talked about you."

"We're workout partners."

"Oh. Thrilling."

"But we're...we're friends first. Bash is my friend."

Lucy gave me a look. Probing. Like she might ask to feel my face if I maintained the eye contact. "If you're friends, he'll come back. If he still wants you around, you just need to wait."

"Big ifs."

"Or you can do what I do and ambush him. But that's just me. And next time, if you're very lucky, maybe he'll call *you* to stand guard outside a bathroom." I laughed at that. Lucy checked her watch. "You should go. He never sulks in bath-room stalls for over twenty minutes."

"He's consistent like that."

Lucy chuckled. I gave her a little salute and got out of there. I could feel her watching me the entire way.

That night, I was in bed reading when I thought about Bash's different Bashes again. I guess I like the Ex the most. It was something I caught glimpses of at practice last spring. Everyone would rag on him, call him *whipped*, but when-ever Lucy Jordan was around, Bash chilled a bit. He was still flashy and loud about it, but you could tell he was filtering it through Lucy. That was promising. I thought it might be good to get to know Lucy somewhere down the line. If there still was a line.

Through my floorboards, I could hear the faint grumblings of my parents. Dad was heading into town to pick up dinner from the bistro on Main, which meant Ma was having hot flashes. I heard Lucy's advice float past my ears.

*"Ambush him."*

Before I could let myself think about it too much, I was throwing on socks. I slapped on deodorant, jumped down my house's three flights, and caught my dad in the foyer. All my downward momentum nearly ended in me cannonballing him out the door but I found my footing, caught my breath, and asked to tag along as casually as possible.

Gio Sr. eyed me with an inconvenience he usually saved for shit on his shoe. "It's a school night."

"It's school-related."

"It's after eight."

"It's important... *Pops*."

He grunted. *Casual* wasn't working. Why would it? We were never casual with each other. I changed tactics and straightened up my spine. "I have band practice. My friend needs my help."

I knew how to speed this process along but, first, I took a moment to weigh my integrity. It would be a lie, yes, but with time I think I could forgive a necessary lie. I couldn't forgive sitting on my ass and doing nothing. So, I gave myself a pass and smiled a little.

"She really needs me."

The little flicker in my dad's eyes. *She.* That little shred of pride, hiding out behind his pupils. I wanted to spit in his face. But this was simpler than calling a cab.

You know, running it back, the last time I went for a drive with my father was probably the morning he brought me home from the hospital. I missed that. Newborns aren't expected to make conversation.

After eleven minutes of driving in silence, Pop tried to do the heavy lifting for me. "Y'know, when you said you were in a *band*, I thought...you know." I didn't. But I nodded anyway. He smiled. "But now I get it. What's her name?"

I was digging a hole into my knee, counting the seconds before I could responsibly get out of Pop's van. "Ronny. Ronny DiSario."

Stupid. Stupid, stupid, stupid lie. Pop perked up. "*DiSario?* Like, the rich *DiSarios*? Paul and Janey, over in the Orchard?"

STUPID. STUPID. STUPID. It felt like I was digging straight through my kneecap. "Oh. I forgot you...forgot you knew them. Shit."

"Your mother knows every Italian in a five-mile radius,

Alessandro. She put the DiSarios in that McMansion they got over there, they're loaded out the ass. You're fucking a DiSario?"

I sank in my seat and wondered if it would be painful to choke on my own tongue. "It's not...like that. We're just friends."

"*Friends.* That's my boy."

I wanted to slap that smile off his fucking face. I wanted to punch him in his giggling throat. I needed to get out of this van.

I basically jumped out of the moving vehicle and said I'd walk the rest. Pop didn't question me as we'd met our quota for talking this month.

When I got to the duplex, I banked on the fact that Del would be working nights all month and rang the doorbell. I banked wrong.

Del rubbed his eyes.

"Evening, Mr. Branch. Sorry to bother you."

"Mr. Miceli. It's late."

From the looks of it, I'd woken Del. Though, rested or not, Del had a sleepy way about him. Bash has it too sometimes. You couldn't find two men who looked less alike but they still shared that. A walking exhaustion. It's in their eyes.

"It's a school night, Sandro."

"I know. I'm sorry. I just... Bash around? I sort of... I gotta talk to him."

Del eyed me, only then starting to wake. I braced myself to feel bad, but his look wasn't pointed. It was curious. Not cutting or suspicious or inconvenienced. Nothing like my dad. Del didn't look down on me. "Are you all right, Sandro?"

It was odd, having an adult ask me that and it not feeling like an accusation. After a moment, I shook my head. "I made Bash mad. And I don't like that. I wanted to apologize."

"Apologize?"

"He has enough shit. I don't want to be another problem for him. I wanna be better than that."

Del didn't invite me in but he didn't close the door either and when he went upstairs, I stayed on the porch. After a light knock, a heavier knock, and a few quiet words, Bash came down the stairs. He had a big hoodie on and his hands were stuck deep in the pockets. When he saw me, he stopped on the steps and looked upstairs. Del wasn't following. We were alone.

I waved. He took a moment to consider something then nodded at the door.

"Outside."

Bash locked up behind him and we walked onto the lawn. His hands stayed in his hoodie pockets and he shrugged up at the moon. "Sup?"

I almost smiled. The "Sup," the shrugs, the hoodie. It was exactly what Lucy was talking about. *Moody Booty.* How Bash can get when he gets burnt or burnt-out.

I nodded to the sidewalk. "Wanna go for a walk?"

"I'm cool."

"Oh, trust me. I know."

Bash's top lip curled in that "the fuck you say?" sneer I'd seen him give rival track captains. But I saw through it. You don't grow up in my house with my dad, with my brothers, without a keen nose for macho bullshit. Once he knew I wouldn't blink, his lip settled.

"It's late, Sandro. Say whatever you came to say and go."

"What do you want me to say?"

"Del said you wanted to apologize."

I nodded. He still had a voice on, his hands were still in his pockets, but I could hear Bash in there. He wanted me to apologize so the blame could be simple and this snag could be settled. And I could do that. I could bite the bullet and let this be as easy as *Oops, I got mad. Oops, I shook your friend like a Shake 'n Bake.*

But there was more to it than that. He knew that. Whatever it is we're doing, it does not feel simple. So, why settle for that? Why settle for simple?

"I do. I want to apologize to you."

"Fine."

"But I wanna say something first."

Bash stood up a little straighter. Looked me in the eye a little more. He was listening. He was actually listening. So, I fought past this old instinct to back down. To keep things light. This thing in my brain that told me to cover up my hurt and hope the bad feeling passes. If I wanted Bash to open up, I needed to meet him halfway.

I met his eyes. "I've got a thing with being ignored. When people treat me like I'm not right in front of them. That's something about me. Something I want you to know. And I hate when people talk about me, not *to* me. Discuss me like I'm not right in front of them. It's something my family does every day and…that's what Matty and you were doing. You and Ant Lewis. You all just—"

"That's not—"

"I need you to let me talk."

Bash's hands were by his side. Out of the hoodie. He nodded. "Okay."

I took a breath and continued. "I think you are really... I think you're great. I think you're really great, Bash, I'm not gonna hide that. It's been easy. And, yeah, today wasn't my best and I'm going to apologize for getting mad, I really am, but... I need you to apologize with me, dude." I took a step closer. "Because whatever we're doing, whatever this is... I need to know you're in it with me. Even when it isn't easy. Or simple. I need to know that you're not just fucking around with me and by November you'll—"

"Sandro."

"You'll just go back to making fun of guys like me with guys like them."

"Sandro. Stop." Bash took a step back. He looked almost sick. He nodded at Birdie on the street. "Let's go for a drive. Okay?" He looked back at the duplex. I don't know which side he looked more afraid of. "Can we go for a drive, Dro? Please?"

I nodded. It didn't sound like an ask. More of a plea. So, we went for a drive. It seemed aimless at first, like he just wanted to catch his breath and get away from the house, but eventually we made our way to the farmlands. He parked along this dead cornfield, this cropped lot on the edge of the Sticks, and I knew something was really weighing on him. Like he knew what he needed to say, what he was ready to talk about, but didn't know how. So, we just sat there for a while. Like tenth period, all over again. Only this time, I wasn't saying anything. Like that might help him get it out.

"...This was my mom's favorite spot."

"Oh."

"She used to take me here a lot. To talk. Or not. She loved it here."

I looked around the field. It looked like someone had salted the earth. Not an inch of green to be found for miles. Just dead cornstalks and barren rows of dirt. "It's...cute."

"It's not supposed to be pretty."

He pointed around the field. All that quiet, dead corn. A scarecrow's graveyard. "They let this field die. End of every season, farmers set aside a certain section of their crop just to let it die. It's more helpful that way. Fuel. Glue. Cow food. Works better than the pretty stuff. You just gotta let it die first."

"Wow."

"Yeah."

"...There's probably a metaphor in there, huh?"

Bash shrugged. "Probably. I've been trying to figure one out for years. Lemme know if one pops up." He stared at the dead corn for a little while longer. Chewing on his thumbnail. "I'm sorry about that. On the lawn. I got in my head. I thought someone might be listening to us and... I just had to get out of there."

"Someone like Lucy?"

He sniffed and shook his head. "...Del." He wouldn't take his eyes off the field in front of him. "I know we're not okay, okay? I know I should be better with him but I just...it's not my fault."

"I didn't say it was."

"But you think it. You think it's my fault, Sandro."

"Hey."

He rolled his eyes. "You got family shit too. Since you wanna talk about it all the sudden. I could say shit about your family too, Dro, I could blame you too."

"I'm not… Bash, I'm not blaming you. Stop." I turned in my seat to face him. "But would it be the worst thing? Talking to him? Del knowing what you're going through?"

"Not all that. You were saying a lot, Sandro. That was a lot."

"I was trying to be real with you. That's the point, isn't it?"

"The point?"

"The point. The point of you and me. Saying a lot. Opening up. Talking."

After a bit, Bash nodded at his steering wheel. "And that's… that's something you want? You want to hear that sort of stuff? The heavy stuff? Stuff that's not…easy?"

"Yeah, Bash. I do."

He stared at the windshield for a long while. Our breath was fogging up the glass. He swallowed. "Because…like, I have something. If you want to hear it."

"I do."

"Okay. Yeah. Okay." Bash nodded and took a steadying breath. "I might stop. I don't know."

"Okay."

He was gripping the steering wheel hard enough to break it. He cleared his throat. "Um. So, when Del knocked on my door, I was sleeping at my desk. I'd been filling out some Rutgers app stuff and I guess I nodded off. And I was having this really…it was a really shitty dream and I thought I might've been… I don't know. Screaming. Whatever. I thought Del had heard me."

"What was the dream about?"

Bash exhaled, real slow. "I, uh… Sometimes…" He swallowed and tapped his temple. "Sometimes there's this, like, replay thing my head does. Like my brain's too tired to make something new up so I just sit in memories instead. And sometimes it's great. And quiet. And easy. But this time…"

I could see his jaw moving under the skin. Grinding away.

"When my mom… Fuck. Toward the end, I was hanging out at the hospital a lot. I'd just read a bunch. Sometimes to her. I think I got through twenty books altogether. And there was this one night, a school night, she had this real bad seizure. Not one of the usual ones. And the nurses threw me… the nurses made me leave the room."

He was pushing himself to get it out. To not get upset. It's a thing his big eyebrows do. They tense up. Almost vibrate. Like he's focusing so hard, they might crack off.

"That never happened before. I didn't know where to go so I went to the cafeteria and I, uh… I broke down. I got a cup of coffee and I couldn't stop… I was just standing still in the middle of the cafeteria and I couldn't stop crying? And everyone was looking at me like I was this fucking…"

He shook the thought away.

"Next thing I knew I was burning off laps in a parking lot next door. Jumping around cars. Trying not to get hit. Burning. Just fucking…just *screaming*."

His voice cracked a little. It was taking a lot out of him, telling me this. His jaw had locked up and I was worried his teeth were gonna grind to dust. All because I wanted him to open up more. He was hurting and it was my fault and I didn't want him to hurt anymore so I touched him. Just on the wrist. How I touch GJ when he's having a night terror. Just enough to remind some part of him that I was there.

"I was really fucking scared, Sandro."

And he let me. He let me touch him. And he eased up on his brows. His jaw. He stopped clenching Birdie's wheel so tight and I thought, for a second, that Bash might take my hand. And I had this sleepy memory of sitting in the back seat of Pop's van, coming home from a day at the Atlantic City beach. Gio was driving and his high school girlfriend Eunice was in shotgun and they were holding hands. I was maybe ten and I thought: *One day. That's gonna be me. I'm gonna know what it feels like to hold someone's hand. Feel how warm it is. Feel someone's pulse on mine.*

But Bash didn't take my hand. Instead, we took a breath.

"I'm sorry."

"I'm sorry."

I don't know who said it first.

After I apologized for Matty, after we got to joking about it, even after Bash drove me home and we said our good-nights, I sat in my bed that night and thought of the different Bashes. And I wondered which Bash was there with me in his truck. In his mom's field. Who was that kid? Was that the real Bash or was it someone new? Someone he's becoming?

I don't know. But I'm learning more about Bash every day. He likes early 2000s horror movies, strawberry shakes, rain over snow, dogs over cats, and Carole King (a surprise). But as for his larger traits, which Bash is the *real* Bash, I'm still in the data-collection phase. Sure, as a devoted student of math, I have my theories. It's just a matter of breaking down his issues and solving for $Y$. Collating the different Bashes and finding a common denominator.

The Ex lets me know that he has intervals. He can adjust. That if he trusts someone, he doesn't need to be as Flashy. The Flash lets me know that he has a need to be the best and that need makes him miserable. Moody Booty tells me he knows when too much is too much. When the volume gets too loud, Moody Booty knows how to shut it all down. How to save face. How to stay cool.

With the congruent factors between these three integers being his overall need to please, the obvious conclusion would be that Bash bases his self-worth off how others see him. But these integers aren't the complete set. There's also the worst dude, *the Stepson*. That variable is throwing off my theories. Because if Bash needs to be liked, then why wouldn't he put it on for his stepdad? If his mom's death left this gaping wound in his side, why can't he open up about it with the person who'd understand most?

Inconclusive. More data required.

# bash

*branch*

Dro was falling asleep at his desk in Ms. Morgan's classroom. He was going on nod #8 in the vicious cycle of nod/drift/ snap back to it and I suspected that one was going to take him. He'd been up all night helping GJ make a last-minute family tree for school and I knew he was working with three hours of shut-eye, tops. I would've nudged him or thrown a shoe at his head but we sit on opposite sides of the room.

"Mr. Miceli?"

From the reflection in the window, I watched Sandro straighten, all faux-casual, and smile up at our AP English teacher.

"Yes, ma'am?"

Ms. Morgan only looked slightly amused. "Mr. Reyno just popcorned you to read?"

From the other corner of the room, Phil Reyno tried to contain his chuckle and flipped Sandro the subtlest of birds. I scoffed. Cheap shot. Sandro cleared his throat and nodded, committing to the reality that he wasn't just caught napping. "Sorry. I was just...absorbing."

He picked up his copy of *Daniel: Last Forever* and flipped around the pages. I sighed. The guy was completely lost. He caught me watching him in the window reflection and made a face. Just as subtly, I motioned to him like a third base coach.

**1**

**1**

**9**

Ms. Morgan was losing patience. "Mr. Miceli, we are on page—"

"Page 119, I know. I'm there. Just giving everyone...a moment."

Sandro turned to the right page and stared at the book. Shit. How could I tell him what line Phil left off on?

*"Miceli, Jesus Chriiiiiiiiiiiist."* I saw Ant Lewis's blond brohawk whip around from the front row. "AP still stands for *advanced* placement, right, Ms. M?"

Sandro went completely still. I now know that's his way of keeping himself from getting red. He'd much rather look like an unplugged robot collecting dust in some storeroom than give an overstuffed prick like Anthony Lewis the satisfaction of seeing him embarrassed. And he was embarrassed.

Ms. Morgan gave Ant a look. "Well, Mr. Lewis, if you'd like to run the show, why don't we hear how you'd read it?"

Ant stifled his groan and got to it. Sandro gave Ms. Morgan a quick appreciative smile then buried his face in his book. I watched Dro in the window for another few popcorn rounds. Waiting for him to look at me. Waiting to give him a smile.

But he stayed in his book. Sandro is one of the smartest guys I've ever met but will fold the second someone makes him feel stupid. He's literally taken every single math class this school offers, aced them all, but I guess a GPA isn't strong enough armor when you're surrounded by people who call you the *Italian Yeti*. When you're raised in a house that treats you like an unpaid intern. Sometimes your bad won't let you hear your good.

When class let out, I headed for the door immediately. Sandro found us a nice post-English rendezvous spot beneath a stairwell that's great for uninterrupted check-ins between classes.

But before I could get gone, Ant slipped right in front of me. "Yo, yo, amigo. You're applying to Villanova, right?"

I froze up. My brain had already started transitioning from *Diligent English Student* Bash to *When I'm With Sandro* Bash and I couldn't remember who I was around preppy assholes like Ant Lewis.

"Uh...maybe? Why?" Sandro was standing by the door, unsure if it'd be okay to wait for me.

Ant looked around and got in close. He smelt like the kind of cologne you don't refer to by name but by price. "My dad's tight with the alumni board and set up a lunch for me and the Nova coach last week. And he said he remembered you."

I was confused. Did I remember a Villanova scout? I knew I put up some pretty solid sprints last spring and I remembered a lot of people wanting to talk to me afterward. But I only remembered the Rutgers scout. He was the only one that mattered to me.

"That's…dope."

"He said he doesn't remember anyone. Seriously, bro, the man couldn't stop talking about Bash the fucking Flash."

"Great. That's…why are you telling me this, Ant?"

I felt my phone buzz. I could see Sandro texting me from the hallway. I had to go. I needed to check in with him after all that bullshit with the reading. But Ant just laughed.

"I'm telling you 'cause that'd be sick, my guy! You and me, tearing it up in Nova next year? I'm sure you could get in easy."

"I mean, I'm kind of set with my college choice—"

"You wouldn't even need that affirmative action bull, dude, you're a fucking beast."

I felt my phone buzz again. Or maybe I didn't. Maybe the buzzing was me. Maybe I'd been buzzing our whole talk. This whole class. You know, I think I'd started buzzing the second that silver-spooned, boat-shoed, yacht-clubbed dick decided to embarrass my friend.

I cocked my head a little. Completely unbothered. "Why would Nova track want a guy who couldn't make captain his senior year?"

Ant's mouth closed. "…What?"

I didn't blink. I didn't shrug. I didn't let that racist fuck off the hook. "Your dad bought you a playdate with the head of a D1 track program, and he couldn't stop talking about *me*? Wow, Ant. Sounds like you got your money's worth."

Ant looked around the empty room, assuming someone

would be there to back him up. But we were alone in there. Just Ant Lewis and a teammate who'd heard enough of his shit.

"That's...a really messed-up thing to say to me, Villeda."

"Yeah, well, I'm a messed-up guy. See you at practice, *amigo.*"

I brushed by him and headed out to meet Sandro. He looked concerned. "What was that?"

I shrugged and walked clean past our stairwell. "You know. Just bros being bros."

I held open one of the double doors leading out to the parking lot. "Skip Guitar today. Let's get food."

"Really?"

"Really. You're a senior. Call it a privilege."

Sandro raised a brow and looked around for teachers, scandalized by the potential rule breaking. "I mean...what about your run? The cross-country guys? It's Thursday."

I shrugged. "I don't wanna run. I just wanna talk to you."

Sandro smiled.

With an open afternoon of endless possibilities, Sandro and I found ourselves back at our usual favorite spot doing our usual favorite shit. Chilling in the ditch, eating some Wawa, and reading *Daniel: Last Forever*. Well, *trying* to read. We'd been distracted by our new game and it was my turn.

"...My eyebrows. They're too bushy."

"They give you character. The hair on my shoulders."

"It's cool. Real macho-like."

Sandro smiled at his shoulders through the neck of his sweatshirt. "Yeah?"

"Like a bear or some shit."

"Nice."

I sipped my Wawa coffee, happy for the warmth, and tried to think of something else I didn't like about myself. "Hmmm... My laugh."

"I'll always be able to find you in a crowd."

"I don't laugh like that in crowds."

"You should. It's a good laugh."

"Maybe people should just be funnier, then."

"Maybe."

Sandro stared up at the trees. The squirrels watched us, curious why these two humans were intruding in their space so deep into October. "...My smile."

"You don't like your smile?"

"It's goofy."

"Says who?"

"My brothers. Teachers. That yearbook photographer. This priest, one time."

He wasn't looking at me then, but I wished he would. Or maybe I didn't. I still wasn't sure if I wanted Sandro looking at me. "...I don't think it's goofy."

"Yeah. Me neither."

He yawned and his eyebrows started to get heavy. What he barely survived in Ms. Morgan's class was coming back with a vengeance. Before I could even say goodbye, he was out.

I cracked my book back open and found my spot. I'd been taking my time with *Daniel*, trying to go at Dro's speed, but I've always had a bad time pacing myself. Sandro's snoring scored the painfully anticlimactic last pages of *Daniel: Last*

*Forever* and I closed the book for good. There's nothing more
disappointing than reaching the end of an unsatisfying book.
You always hope it can pull itself together and make all the
time you spent reading worth it but then you turn that last
page and wonder why you bothered.

"Meh."

I didn't want to wake Sandro up so I settled for watching
him sleep. You know, like a creep. I thought about napping
too but I can't do it like him. In nature. In class. In public. If
I don't feel safe when I'm trying to sleep, that's all I'll think
about.

I watched Sandro's chest rise and fall and rise and I thought
about putting my head there. Maybe his chest was comfortable. I thought I might be able to sleep there and I wondered
why I might think something like that.

I let Sandro hold my hand a couple nights ago and I'm regretting it. I mean, he held my wrist and it was more a sign
of support than interest but still. Maybe I'm making a bigger deal out of it than it is. He was essentially just taking my
pulse, and it probably didn't mean much to him. But still. I
keep thinking about it. How he was so quick to reach out
after I said all that about my mom. Even though I was mad
at him for the shit with Matty, he knew what was more important. It's like he could tell how badly I was hurting. It
made me wonder if I'd know when he was hurting. If I'd
take his pulse.

Sandro had some dirt on his cheek and I thought it would
be pretty harmless to flick it off. I ran through my list to see
what number "Touching Sandro's Cheek" would be.

*times i touched dro:*

**1.** When he drew the **MEXICO** on my shirt. (Hand on Back)

**2.** Feeling his beer-soaked tank at the Olympics. (Hand on Chest)

**3.** Holding him up running through the Sticks. (Arm over Shoulder)

**4.** When he thought I was making fun of Bumpin' Grinders. (Pat on Shoulder)

**5.** The Kiss. (Lips on Lips, Lips on Neck, Hands on Hips)

**6.** The Kiss: Part 2. (Lips on Lips, Teeth on Teeth, Hands pushing Chest)

**7.** Slap-fight over radio outside B-Town. (Hands on Various)

**8.** Living room couch during *The Ring Two*. (Knee on Knee)

**9.** Carrying my high ass up the stairs. (Chest on Back)

**10.** High-five after he fixed Birdie's coolant tank. (Palm on Palm)

**11.** Hitting him when he picked up Matty. (Palm on Back)

**12.** When he calmed me down. (Hand on Wrist)

Number 13. Unlucky. But interesting. With Sandro's thing about touching, I guess I thought it would be less. Look at me, respecting personal spaces. I flicked the dirt off his cheek and he smiled, eyes still closed. "Can I help you?"

"I finished."

"On my face?"

That cracked both of us up. He sat up and thumbed through his book. "Please tell me Daniel gets swallowed by a whale at the end."

"That sailor lady finds him and he returns to school."

"That's *all*?"

"Completely unchanged."

Sandro Frisbee-flung his book across the ditch. It hit a tree. "Fuck you, Daniel."

"Oh, and you know that light in the sky? In chapter three?"

"The mirage?"

"Not a mirage. Lighthouse."

"Oh, my God. So—"

"He could've been saved right away if he wasn't stubborn trash? Yup."

Sandro groaned and turned on his belly. He took my readers and tried them on, letting out this big yawn. "How long was I asleep?"

"Not long. I can't do that. Fall asleep in public. Well, in places that aren't my bed."

"I do it anywhere. Here, school, bleachers. It's how I fell off my roof actually."

"Fuck, Dro. You were sleeping on your roof?"

"I didn't mean to. There was all this screaming in my house one night and it was lasting longer than usual so I went up there with my old guitar and...yeah. Woke up on the ground with a broken foot. I felt so...so stupid."

"God. You and that word. You're not stupid."

Sandro took off my glasses. "I don't know."

"You're in AP trigonometry, Dro. I can barely spell *trigonometry*."

"It's not a school thing. I just feel stupid sometimes. A lot of times. Like any time I mess up or forget something, my family'll be like *What a Sandro thing to do.* Get the wrong milk? *Classic Sandro.* Spill paint in the garage? *That's Sandro.* Break my foot?"

"Talking about you like you're not there."

"Yeah. It's just a lot. Everything. All the time."

"That sucks. I'm sorry."

I don't know how someone so decent came from such a miserable group of people. Sandro's not like me. He's not so confused about the things that hurt him. He knows every wound on his body. But just because you know what's hurting you doesn't make it hurt any less. I wished I could do more for him than *sucks* and *sorry*.

He shrugged and gave me back my glasses. "Anywho. Them's the breaks. Here's hoping I'm not too stupid for Northwestern."

"That's your top choice?"

"Yuppo. Just gotta get in, get out, and restart. Get a nickname, maybe some tattoos. An apartment all to myself."

"Right above Bumpin' Grinders?"

"Hell yeah."

He smiled and we just stared at the sky. It was silent. The

birds, the wind, everything decided to take a moment. Silence.

This connection I feel to Sandro is something else. I thought it was just the communication thing but I feel just as heard in silence. I think he feels it too. So maybe I am doing more. More than *sucks* and *sorry*. Because our lives are loud. I thought I needed the noise. Because silence never felt right before Sandro.

I got a text.

M: gotta pick costumes dude

Matty. God. I took a moment to scroll up our texts together. I'd gone a few days not texting him back and he still hadn't noticed. My last genuine response was last weekend. Matty hit me up all hyped 'cause his older brother got us a hookup for fake IDs. All we had to do was fill out some forms and send in a picture and we'd have the IDs by January. We'd been talking about doing it for years, but it took me forever to agree to a time. Because other than work and the occasional run, I haven't been hanging out with Matty much lately. I just don't know what to say to him anymore. I don't know who to be around him now. Some part of me is growing, I can feel it, and that part doesn't speak Matty's language. Hanging out with him, sitting on his couch, listening to his bullshit, it feels like one of those bad dreams where I'm in a play and I can't remember any of my lines. I've been getting stage fright around my best friend and I want more than that. After the weight room, after how we treated Sandro, I wanted more.

That's why last weekend, when I finally agreed to a time for our fake ID photoshoot, I invited my good ol' workout bud.

It had been mostly funny but somewhat jarring to see Dro sitting on my milk crates behind the diner that day. Using my dumpster to fill out his ID form. He had officially, irrevocably invaded my bubble, the only place that felt truly mine, and I didn't care.

"How about *Gino Natoli*? I wanna stay Italian but maybe more subtle than Alessandro Miceli."

"*Dominic* Natoli. I feel like Gino's half a step away from Luigi Pizza-Pie."

"Fair. I got a cousin Dominic, down by the shore."

"Wow. What a *New Jersey* sentence."

"Garden State, baby. How 'bout you, whatchu feeling?"

I wrote out my freshly chosen name, all pretty in pen. "I'm thinking *Daniel. Daniel Branch.*"

"*Daniel* like the book?"

"And *Branch* like my mom."

"Hm. Doesn't feel very Latino."

"I guess I don't feel very Latino."

Sandro gave me a nod so I committed. At the end of the day, it didn't really matter much. These were for the sole use of purchasing booze, *maybe* getting into concerts. But I liked the idea of *Daniel*. And I really liked the idea of *Branch*.

I never felt like a Villeda. How could I? My dad gave me his name, some eyebrows, then bounced. I barely remember the guy. But it was my legal name and by the time I even considered dropping it, my mom was *Mrs. Branch*. I liked *Daniel* too. The character in the book is a jerk but I sort of identified with him. He's a lonely guy. Pissed. More angry that no one notices he's missing than he is about being lost. All these misplaced emotions when really he's just mad at himself. All he needed to do was trust the lighthouse. No one should want to be alone.

Matty wasn't happy that I brought along the guy who made him look like a Tickle Me Elmo in front of the field team. Sandro did the honorable thing and apologized but even after they shook hands, I knew the memory was still eating Matty up. He stomped out of the diner with his mom's camera and a rejected Beer Olympics poster board.

"Let's make this quick. Miceli first."

The picture needed a white backdrop, so I held up the blank side of the poster board and Sandro stood against it. He smiled. It wasn't anything out of the ordinary. Just his normal, earnest smile.

But Matty grumbled. "No dumb faces. They gotta look legit."

"This is just how I smile."

"Well, fix it."

Sandro's smile dropped. Faded away into something passive and stung.

*What a fucking asshole.*

I don't think there's a worse thing you can tell someone—that their smile is "dumb." Or their laugh is "weird." 'Cause smiles are smiles. Laughs are laughs. We don't plan them. They happen when we're too surprised or happy to care about what we look like. And to make someone question that? I think that's a really cruel thing to do.

I was up next and didn't try smiling. I just wanted to get Dro away from my dick coworker. Back to the ditch. Get him

smiling again. But I had the rest of my shift and Sandro had
to pick up GJ at karate. We still had lives outside of our talks
and I'd have to wait. Hope something else got him smiling.

Dro finished up and started off on his crutches.

"Text you later, Bash. Thanks a bunch, *Matt.*"

I stifled a laugh. Matty despises "Matt." Says "Matt" is a
boring-ass white guy who drinks LaCroix and Frisbee golfs.
I couldn't remember if I'd told Dro that but it was the perfect dig for the situation. We watched Dro go and, once he
had some distance, Matty huffed. "Some guys can't take the
fucking hint, eh?"

"Whatchu mean?"

He ignored my question. "Hey, you get a costume for
Spooktacular yet? I'm thinking we do this Greek gods thing.
Really show off the abs."

*Spooktacular.* His Halloween party. I tried bringing him
back to what he meant about "the fucking hint" but he had
moved on. "I heard Ronny DiSario's doing some haunted
house shit at her place and, honestly, it feels like an attack.
Our party's *gotta* kick ass. I got kegs, got us E, we're going
hard. I'm only inviting track guys and soccer girls. *Maybe*
basketball girls."

"Oh. No field guys?"

I knew what Matty was doing. Matty knew what he was
doing. He had this look I recognized but couldn't place right
away. "Bashy. You got your friends, then you got your *teammates.* That's what went wrong with the Olympics. Too many
guys we didn't know. Not *really.*"

It took a twitch of his brow for me to place his look. It was
the same one I saw in my rearview that night. When I drove

Dro home from the Olympics and did everything I could to keep the emotion off my face. Matty was thinking loud about something and trying not to show it. I wanted to figure it out but Avi barked at us to get back to work.

We didn't talk about it again and I spent the rest of the week avoiding him. But even in the ditch, with Sandro snoring beside me, Matty's texts could still find me.

M: gotta pick costumes dude

My fingers moved to respond but none of the letters looked right. I didn't know what to say. Stage fright. The wrong kind of silence.

I've known for a long time that I didn't love hanging out with Matty anymore, but it's new that I can't stand being around him at all. He's this cackling reminder that I've spent the last four years being a dick to people. Being a loud, showy asshole so people wouldn't notice what I was really feeling. How much I was feeling.

I heard Sandro clear his throat then he sat up with me. "Sup?"

I guess nap time was over. I showed him my phone. "Matty's big Halloween party's this weekend."

"Mm. *Mateo Silva Presents: Spooktacular?*"

"*Mateo Silva Presents: Spooktacular 3: Son of Spooktacular.*"

"Ah. My secretary musta lost my invite."

"I was thinking about skipping it."

Sandro rubbed the crap out of his eyes and stretched out like a cat. "Really? Bash the Flash skipping a classic Matty S. throwdown?"

"Yeah. Thought we could hang out."

"We're hanging out right now."

"But we could be hanging out in costumes. With a full liquor cabinet. In my empty house. Real spooky shit."

"I do like spooky. But no Ouija boards. I got a functions exam coming up and really can't afford gettin' possessed right now."

"Deal."

I extended a hand. He looked at it and made a face. Like he was acknowledging my unspoken rule. This rule about touching that I thought I made for his sake but was maybe always more for me. I guess Sandro knew. But he shook my hand anyway.

**14.** When we shook on it. (Palm on Palm)

We shook for a good long while. Maybe too long. It was funny. Because we were getting so close. I felt close to this person. Yet I was still kicking up all this sand about touching him. Something as simple as a handshake. Or his hand on my wrist. He laughed and pulled his hand away and I felt like Daniel again. Lost at sea. Ignoring the lighthouse. Too stubborn to accept a helping hand.

And I decided it was time to come in from the sea.

# sandro

*OCTOBER 31*

## *THEY DID THE MASH*

Ronny, Phil, and me were sitting in a circle on the floor of the practice room. Mr. D had started letting us three use the free play half of class to jam down the hall and today's session had quickly devolved into a very important conversation.

"*Exit 40.*"

"*McFist.*"

"*Bathtub Screaming.*"

"*Panic, Panic.*"

"*Kiss By a Fist.*"

"*Jersey Devils.*"

"*There Might Be Fists.*"

"Why all the fists?"

"Oh, that's a good one."

"That wasn't a suggestion, Philip, that was a question."

"I dunno. Fists are punk."

*"Fist Patrol."*

"I just don't like the fist thing."

"Yeah, I don't know if I want a band named *Fist*."

*"A Band Named Fist."*

"Oh, actually, y'know, that's nice."

*"Bloody Knuckles."*

"No, we're getting further from it."

Ronny was braiding Phil's hair. She looked over at my foot. "Hey. Can I sign your boot?"

"What? No."

"Someone else did."

I turned my brace over and looked at the tiny Wite-Out handwriting along the side. "He had specific permission."

Ronny made a face. "Oho. Was this the Running Man's handiwork?"

I shrugged. Phil perked up. "Oh, right. I always forget you hang out with Bash the Trash. Such a random pairing. Like if Michael Jordan was buddies with Clifford the Big Red Dog."

Ronny yanked on Phil's braid. "Hey, that reminds me. I'm having this Halloween thing tonight. My parents are gone all week, we're gonna tear the place to the ground."

I picked up the bass Ronny loaned me to help with her demo and checked the tuning. "Neato. That's fun."

"It *is* fun, thank you. And costumes are very mandatory. I'm going as a sexy lamp. Phil's going as Seasonal Depression."

After some dead air, Phil and Ronny fixed their blackeyelined gazes on me. I was supposed to respond. I never knew when I was supposed to join in with them. With their constant shit-talk and terrible attitudes, the line between *bandmate* and *friend* was frustratingly vague and I never knew which side they wanted me on.

"Oh. I don't... I haven't picked a costume this year. Don't think I'm dressing up."

Ronny tsked. "Well, you have to, Sandro. Costumes are mandatory. And don't show up in some football jersey saying you're David Akers or some jock cop-out. Don't let my cool vibe fool you, little boy. I expect investment."

I wasn't getting something. Why would Ronny be expecting me at all? "Wait, did you want to play music? Like, a set?"

"God, no. We can't even land on a name, we're not even close to playing for people."

"Okay. Then, why would I need a costume?"

Ronny squinted at me, matching my confusion. "Sandro, Jesus Christ, I'm inviting you to my party. As a guest. Guests wear costumes."

Phil swooned. "Noooo. Sandro, do you not get invited to parties? Tragique."

I let my embarrassment roll off my back and focused on my bass plucking. It's not my fault I didn't expect someone like Ronny DiSario to want me over at her home. Harshing her party vibe. Tainting all her cool. "I actually get invited to everything. I just never go."

Ronny laughed and stood up. "Yeah, Phil. Ask around. Our bassist here isn't like us. Everyone in school can get on board with Mr. Miceli. He's universally approved."

Phil smiled at me, disdain on his lips. "Aww. Like tap water."

I rolled my eyes. "Sorry I'm likable."

"Thank God, someone *finally* apologizes for it."

I guess I laughed at that. Ronny sat at her keyboard and started playing "Chopsticks." "So, you coming? Will you bless our jaded asses with your likable presence?"

To be honest, I thought Ronny didn't like me. I assumed Phil hated me. That was just the pair's general demeanor. They're always screaming about something or someone and they couldn't give less of a rip about my "jock shit." I thought this arrangement, any time we were spending together, was all contingent on me playing a passable bass guitar. Because I was used to getting invited to parties I had no business attending. Only I wasn't used to people caring if I showed.

"I just…didn't think y'all would wanna hang out after practice."

Ronny and Phil shared an overly sympathetic look.

"Aww. He's so sweet."

"A proper good lad."

"If we're gonna be a band, Sandro, we should probably start to enjoy each other, no? Why wouldn't we want to hang out with you?"

I shrugged. "'Cause. You two are dicks."

Phil and Ronny burst out laughing. Phil flipped me off and moved to his drum set. "We're all dicks, Miceli. I see you. You're just better at hiding it. Got that Good Boy face."

"Hey, I am a good boy, you fuck."

"Then come to the goddamn party!"

Ronny smiled and picked up her tempo. I sighed. "It sounds really fun, Ron. Really. I appreciate the invite."

"Boo. This sounds like a no."

Phil groaned and picked up his drumsticks. "Told you. You're probably going to Matty Silva's thing, right? Sounds like a *rad* occasion, Bro-Bot, good choice. I'm sure it'll be a hella hetero time."

Phil joined in with Ronny's "Chopsticks," drumming along to the rhythm. Now, I was expressly not invited to Matty Silva's Spooktacular (something about a weight room if I recall?) and Ronny's invite did have potential. Ever since Beer Olympics went so tits up, she's been slowly chipping away at Matty's party supremacy with a series of counterprogramming and I really respected her hustle. But I had plans for my night. Very set, very important plans. Plans I guess I needed to lie about.

"I was gonna stay in. Babysit my little nieces."

Ronny gave me a genuinely sympathetic look. "You could always bring them. Do they party?"

I laughed and joined in with their impromptu "Chopsticks" jam. Bass was a lot easier than I thought it would be. Once you have your guitar basics down, it's really just a matter of reverse engineering your brain into the bass mindset. A supporting instrument. A part of the band.

Ronny was looking at my boot again, at the words Bash painted on me a few days ago in the back of Birdie. A phrase I groaned after a particularly heated session of venting about my family and my mother and my life.

"How about that? For the band name?"

Phil looked at my boot and read. "'Everything All the Time.'"

We mulled it over as a group. Phil and Ronny nodded.

"Evocative. Very moody."

"Very pop punk."

"And we didn't even need a fist."

Ronny smiled. "*Everything. All the Time.* That'll look good on a demo. I like it."

I smiled at my boot. Bash's neat, white handwriting. "I like it too."

We all repeated our new band name out loud and in our heads a little while longer, never letting our pointless jam session go quiet.

It was actually killing me that I couldn't tell Panic! or The Disco about my real plans for the holiday or my costume for the night. Because little did my bandmates know, I fucking LOVE Halloween. I just do. I love everything about it. The bats, the black cats. That decoration where it looks like a witch crashed her broom into your garage. I love the chocolate (Rolos at the top, Kit Kats at the bottom), the candy (Skittles at the top, Sour Skittles at the bottom). It's just a magical time of year.

Any other Halloween, I would've been over the moon to get an invite to a surefire rager like Ronny's party. Her place is huge, her parents are never home, and the nights always end with some big scandal that rocks the school come Monday. But tonight I had better, spookier plans.

Bash's house. Bash's *empty* house. Bash's *empty* house with *alcohol* and *costumes*.

Our costume idea started as a joke but, as it often does

with Bash, became a competition. Who could do the other better? I'd dress like him and he'd dress like me. Since we weren't planning on seeing anyone, we figured we might as well go all out.

I knew I wanted to do his running getup. It's his signature look. Like if they were making Sandro and Bash action figures, the Bash dude would have a white V-neck, shorts over compression pants, and a kung-fu grip.

I hit up Target after school and found most of Bash's ensemble in the workout section. The compression pants were a challenge to find in a size that wouldn't cut off circulation. I finally tracked down an XXL in clearance that technically fit around my waist but I was bulging out pretty hard and they made my legs appear even ganglier. Overall, I looked pretty hilarious in them. They probably would've won me the contest flat out. But I didn't want to look hilarious. Bash invited me to his house. It would just be us. And I knew all about his unspoken rules and limits. He wasn't just respecting my space; I knew that he was holding back. But ever since that night in Birdie when he let me touch him, something felt different. We'd moved past something. I didn't want to look hilarious. I wanted to look good for him.

I opted to go bare legged for the costume. But I wasn't trying to lose this competition so when I got home, I had GJ spray me with the hose. On the mist setting, to make me look all sweaty. I was going for Bash: *Hangover Edition*. To really clinch the gold, I sprinkled some drops of SunnyD around my collar to simulate barf.

GJ asked where I was going and I told him the truth. He knew about Bash. Well, he knew Uncle Dro had a new friend and he asked if he could come with. I hate saying no to GJ. He's my little guy. The only thing I like about my house other than my roof. But I had big plans for the night and they hope-fully wouldn't be kid friendly. So, I told him it was Adults Only and he told me to go fuck myself.

I biked over to Bash's, avoiding all the mini ghosts and gob-lins on the sidewalk, and knocked on the duplex door. Bash answered, landline in one hand, bowl of candy in the other. He was mid-convo but burst out laughing. He dropped the receiver on the porch and I had to take the bowl from him. That's when I got a full look.

My God.

I have no fucking clue how he tracked them down but Bash found the EXACT shorts I wore to Beer Olympics. My Italian flag boys with the criminally short inseam. They're not some-thing you could pick up at any old Target and I truly believed that he'd drive all the way to AC just to win our competition. He had a homemade **ITALY** tank on and he'd drawn fake curlicue hairs all over his chest in marker.

Fuck.

*FUCK.*

I was half mad that I was bound to lose the competition, half wildly turned on by how much chest he was showing. Legs too. Those shorts really are too short.

He picked up the receiver and wrapped up his convo. "Yeah, he's spot-on. Really. I mean I think I'm still gonna win but I'll send you a pic. Sure thing. No, it rained yester-day so I put the toolbox in your room."

Based on how he was talking, I never would've guessed it

was Del on the other end. I don't think I've ever seen Bash look so casual talking to him.

"Yeah, I handed it in Friday. I think so. Ms. Morgan likes me. How's Maine? Nice."

Then he turned away from me. Went into the kitchen nook. I wish I'd gotten there five minutes later so he could've finished the call in peace. 'Cause it was really nice seeing him talk like that.

I could still hear him from the kitchen. He sounded smaller. Like a kid. "I'm sorry. That I didn't come. I... Yeah. I know. Okay."

There was a short silence. I thought he might've hung up on Del but then I heard a quieter voice. "...Love you too."

I felt intrusive. But it was interesting. Interesting, interesting, interesting. The Stepson loves the Stepdad. And he's telling him now. Very interesting.

Since that night in his truck, Bash has been trying to tell me more. Bigger stuff. Heavier stuff. Lately he's been letting me in on his unique situation with Del. Del married his mom when Bash was ten. Things were fine then. Got on well. He wasn't calling the guy *Dad* or anything, but they could talk. Then, five years later, his mom died. It was sudden and neither of them handled it well. It's gotta be weird. This guy you only know so well becoming your only family? But apparently, it was never a question that Del would raise Bash. It's what his mom wanted. He told me all this in the ditch. We'd just finished a particularly frustrating chapter of *Daniel: Dickhead at Sea* and it got us talking about family.

"The last real talk we had was about family. What we owe

to family. She told me to keep him close. We'd need each other. I hate that I can't just do that for her."

"What's stopping you?"

"I don't know. I want to. I do. But something just stops me. When he's around, I just feel bad. Like I'm not grateful. Wanted."

I watched him test his own water. See how much he could say about himself before he closed up again.

And, from what I heard on this phone call, he was only getting better. I munched on a Milky Way, annoyed that it wasn't a Snickers, and added it all to my data.

Bash hung up the phone and leaned into the living room. "Yo. Bash the Flash."

I laughed and gave him my best bro nod. "Sup, brah."

We couldn't keep a straight face for long and pretty soon we were cracking up loud enough to completely miss the trick-or-treaters ringing the doorbell.

After a few rounds of giving out candy, Bash declared that he wanted to start drinking so we put some of the candy on the front porch and brought the rest up with us to his room.

Now.

I've been spending the past two months both overanalyzing and trying to ignore signs. What does it mean that Bash wanted a copy of my yearbook photo? Why did he invite me to get fake IDs with him? To say nothing of the Wisdom Tooth Saga. Well, when we got to Bash's bedroom, there was no need for analysis. Because that room was fucking spotless. The bed was made. Laundry done. I could see vacuum marks in the carpet. The only other time I'd been in there, it looked like an unwashed gym bag had given birth. Boxers, jeans, socks, shirts, I could barely see the floor. But that All Hollows' Eve? There was a concerted effort to make that bedroom presentable to visitors.

*Visitor.*

Bash was looking through his closet so I sat on his bed. This wasn't a move, my foot just hurt. It also wasn't a move for me to sprawl out as immediately as I did. His bed was comfy as shit. Memory foam, down comforter, the man slept well. Though I'd been sleeping in an attic for the past two years so maybe I was just starved for comfort.

Before I got too comfortable, I sat up. "Del coming back tonight?"

"Nah. His uncle died so he's up in Maine for the weekend."

"Well, damn, Bash. And you stayed?"

"I don't really know his family. And we're...you know. It would've been weirder to go, honestly."

"You sounded good. On the phone. You were talking well."

"Really? Huh. Cool."

He sorta smiled to himself and reached up for a high shelf. He moved some towels around, trying to unearth something. His Team Italy tank was a little short on him and when he reached up, I could see his stomach. That V around his hips. All hairy and shit. Ugh.

"You've got a hairy stomach."

"I know. It's a bitch sometimes with running."

"It's good. Nice. *Off the record.*"

He gave me a look and went back to his search. He pulled out a bottle of Jack and a half-drunk two liter of Coke. "This is from the Fourth so it might be flat. Unless you wanna take it straight."

I was fine either way. I'd never drunk much liquor, but I really wanted to start. He poured the rest of the Jack into the Coke bottle, nearly filling it back up, and shook the mix together. He hopped over me and we sat across from each other on his bedspread. He nodded at my V-neck. "...Lemme see yours."

"You tryna get my shirt off?"

"Nah. Just lift your arms. That's the sweet spot."

I laughed and did it. My stomach's thicker than his, in hair and fat, but he didn't seem to mind. We laughed.

"I always clock it. The fuzz."

"Same."

He unscrewed the Jack & Coke cap slowly, expecting an explosion. Nothing. "Wow. Super flat. This actually might be older than the Fourth."

We both took some pulls and shook off the bite. It was mostly Jack, but the flat Coke was hard to swallow. Like lukewarm syrup. I winced and tried to stay on topic. "Bolu Olowe's got a great one. Super dark happy trail."

"Oh, I'm aware. We had gym last year. Looked like he was wearing a fur tie in the locker room."

"Matty's got an oddly pronounced one too."

"Yeah. He's weirdly proud of it."

I took another pull and decided to just ask it. "He hates me, right?"

"He's never said that. But yeah. He hates you."

"Weird. I assume a bunch of people don't like me, but I've never actually gotten a confirmation."

"Don't let it knock you. Matty's not worth the time."

"Why do you hang out with him, then?"

Bash took a drink. I think he hated it but was definitely determined to get it down. "I don't know for sure. After my mom… Matty was there. Around. He didn't expect much out of me. I think I needed that. Low expectations. Simple shit. *Bash the Flash.* Hard to let that go."

"Haven't seen the Flash in a minute."

"Dude's benched. Don't need him. Half my conversations with Matty consist of me shitting on someone so he won't shit on me. You don't make me nervous. Not like that."

He passed me the bottle and I could tell he was getting himself ready for more. Like that night in Birdie. I could feel him getting ready for wherever this road seemed to be going. The signs were there. But I decided not to rush anything. To let whatever would happen happen.

But something was eating at me. Something that'd been stuck in my craw for months. And I figured, if Bash was in an open mood, I might as well probe. "Was Matty the one who keyed **FAG** into Jackson Pasternak's locker?"

Bash winced. "They never caught the guy. But, *off the record*, yes."

"That was fucked."

"Yeah."

"Weird word."

"Fag?"

"Yeah. Always feels weird out loud."

Bash smirked and opened his mouth wide. Really enunciated. "Faaaaaaaag. Yeah."

"Fags. Faggot. Faggots."

"Faggy. *Faggier*."

"Faggiest?"

Bash threw up his hand like he was hailing a cab. "Ayo, FAG!"

"What it do, my faggot?"

We started cracking up at that. Not for long though. Something kind of fell over us and we got quiet. When you say a word enough it gets funny. Starts to lose all meaning. But that one always kept its meaning for me. Even when it was a joke, I was always so scared of that word. When I might see it, where I might see it, who might be saying it. And I wondered what it meant to Bash. "Anyone ever call you one?"

"Nah. Not, like...for real."

"Same. Not for real."

That was technically true.

My dad called all three of us fags at various points throughout our lives, but it was never an actual accusation. I know this because, whenever it'd happen, I would spend the next four days dissecting every element and circumstance of how and why he'd use that particular word in that particular scenario. If only for peace of mind. And it was usually 'cause we were goofing off. Nothing gay about goofing off.

"You ever call anyone one?"

Bash had to think about it. I guess that's good. I was ready to accept he had. Not that I'd ever heard him, it's just the kind of thing I expected from *Matty and the Flash*.

"Like bad drivers. Or friends. Just kidding around. Mostly." Mostly. Couldn't fault him for that. I was right there with him. The shame of mostly. Not all the time but not never. Stuck somewhere in mostly. "You?"

"…I called Joey Tan a fag in sixth grade because he had one of those folders with the cartoon bunny on it."

"Oh, yeah. Those. Weren't they more for girls though?"

"I mean, yeah, that's why I called him it. I was just joking around but he must've thrown the thing out. I don't think I ever saw him with it again."

Bash isn't the type to make me feel bad about sharing something shameful, but I instantly regretted telling him that. That memory made me feel like shit to this day.

"What's up?"

I guess I was too quiet. I shook my head. "I just think about that a lot. Like, a *lot* a lot."

"You were a kid."

I shrugged. "I knew better."

I still remember how fake the word sounded coming out of me. How put on. And then I remember who my brothers are. How my family is. Who I become when I'm not careful. "It just makes me feel bad."

Bash nodded. "…Good."

I socked him with a pillow. He laughed. "It's better than the alternative, right? Most guys just drop it without thinking. At least it means something to you. You're allowed to change."

Bash handed me the bottle and lay down on the bed. I took a sip and tried not to stare at his sliver of stomach showing.

He wiped his mouth. "I got called into the principal's office 'cause Pete Frey told the teachers I called him a faggot. It was fourth or fifth grade, I think."

"Oh, damn. I forgot about him. Freckles? Asshole?"

"Yeah, that was Pete. They were like 'Peter says you called

him a mean word.' But then they said 'Faggot' and I was like 'Who?' It's how I learned the word."

I lay down next to him. We stared at the ceiling. "They believe you?"

"Nah. I had no clue though. They said it was something you only call people you hate. And I felt bad. I didn't hate Pete. He was my friend."

*"People you hate."*

"Yuuuuuup."

Bash took a long pull. A lot to unpack there. Before I could try, Bash let out an incredible belch. Lasted six whole seconds with key changes and everything. He wrapped up and graciously bowed.

"Wow. That's considered an art form in the Miceli house."

"Your mom let's that shit slide?"

"Nah. Ma woulda smacked the shit outta you for that. But my brothers would love it."

"Damn. She smack y'all a lot?"

"Like she has the time."

"Just wondering. They sound like smacky people."

"They?"

"Your fam. I mean, just off what you've told me, the violence barometer in the Miceli household sounds a little broken."

I shrugged. He wasn't wrong, I just didn't want to get into it. We were supposed to be having fun. "Look…if you're asking if my parents hit me, no. I mean, they've *hit* me but like head slaps and shit. It's not like I'm getting punched in the face or nothing. We're just a physical family. It's normal. Like my dad once threw this jewelry box at my head."

"What the fuck? Sandro."

I didn't mean for it to sound that harsh. Because the story's not, like, this "I survived" trauma. I shook my head. "It's not a big deal. We were clearing out the garage and I saw this box marked Halloween and I wanted to see if we still had my Goku costume. But when I was reaching for it, I knocked this bigger box over and all this paint spilled on the cement floor. Dad happened to be holding a jewelry box my ma never used and, bing bang bong, now I got *this*."

I pointed to this little white mark that runs through my left eyebrow. It's small and you wouldn't even notice it unless you were really looking but, yeah, I guess I'd been maimed.

Bash squinted. "Oh, shit. Hold up, lemme see."

He got really close to me. Closest he'd been in months. In two months, five days to be exact.

"Damn. Almost got your eye. It's kinda cool though. Some people do that intentionally. Shave a gap."

"Welp. Lucky me."

He stared at me. The guy was always staring. And I thought he might touch me then. Finally touch me. I thought he might finally be ready.

But it was me who turned away this time. I didn't give him the invite. I didn't like him looking at me like that.

Because Bash was looking at me carefully. With care. And that made me uncomfortable. Why would that make me uncomfortable? Someone caring about me? And for a second, I remembered sitting in the van as a kid. It was night and I was cold. I'd just thrown up and Ma was crying. She wouldn't look at me. But I didn't want to think about that. I wanted someone to care.

I did my best to meet his eyes. "...Do you think we're gonna be fucked-up?"

"I think we're already fucked-up."

"Seriously."

"What do you mean *fucked-up*? Like are we gonna become serial killers?"

"No. Like...how we came up. The way we are. It can't be ideal, right?"

Bash rubbed his stomach. "Do you think you're fucked-up?"

"Kinda. I get too angry. And I cry a lot."

"I mean, same. But that's normal. Right?"

"I don't know. Maybe it's just normal for us."

"It's not like we're all that different from other people though. It's really just..."

"Just the big things."

We were silent for a little. The ceiling fan clicked above us. Around and around.

*Click, click, click.*

"Things could be better."

"A lot could be better."

*Click, click, click.*

"Maybe if my mom were here."

"If my ma talked to me."

"And if I knew my dad."

"If I liked my dad. And if I weren't..."

Bash took a long breath.

"If we weren't."

*Click, click, click.*

He smiled, kinda sad, and laughed. "But people out there got it a lot worse than us."

We stared at the fan and wondered if that should make us feel any better.

*Click. Click. Click.*

*Click. Click. Click.*

*Click. Click.*

"I don't think you're fucked–up, Sandro."

I turned to him and he was close again. Looking at me again. Less careful. More curious. Then he touched me. He put his fingers on my jaw like it was no big deal and moved my face toward the light.

"What are you doing?"

"You said you had brown eyes."

"I wasn't lying, I swear."

"Nah. They're like…golden? Didn't know that was an option."

"I paid extra at the hospital."

He kept moving my face around at different angles, trying to catch the light. I felt like Silly Putty and I didn't know what to do. Then he stopped. Held my face in place. Catching the light.

"There. Yeah. *Golden.* You just gotta know how to look at them."

"Yeah. It's… Yeah."

Bash was looking at my eyes but not making eye contact. He was just taking them in. Then I felt his thumb rubbing against the stubble on my cheek. It was faint, barely moving, but he was feeling my face. Then eye contact.

"What's that look, B?"

"I'm just… I'm touching you."

"Really? I don't know if you are."

He swallowed and his touch got heavier. More intentional. The tips of his fingers along the rough of my cheek.

"Is… This is okay?"

I nodded against his touch. His fingertips landed in my hair and his palm rested against my jaw. Like his hand found a comfortable place to sleep. And Bash smiled. His hand on my jaw, his eyes on my eyes. He just smiled.

"This is okay?"

And I had to roll my eyes. Because, really?

"Bash."

"What?"

"I just…"

He chuckled. *"What?"*

I smiled back up at him. "…Do it or don't."

He got it. He understood. We were on the same page there. Whatever rule, for whoever's sake, that was gone. Or altered. I didn't know for sure and, honestly, I didn't care.

Bash nodded and he kissed me. It was light. More like he was resting his lips on mine. I think he was nervous. I felt a shake in his shoulders come and go. I thought it'd help to lighten the mood. Ease in. So, when he finally took his lips off mine, I cracked up and howled. *"FAAAAAAAAAAAG."*

We laughed and he hit my chest. "Shut the fuck up."

Then the real kiss. The deep one. The kind of kiss that started all this. Passionate. I could feel his warmth, his skin, finally on me. His care. His hand was in my hand and he was touching me.

*Bash was touching me.*

I pulled his body onto mine and heard the candy bowl fall to the floor.

# bash

*tails*

So.

So so so so so.

Soooooooooooooooooooooooooo.

So, I had sex with a dude.

I don't wanna get into too much detail, but I will say this:

**1.** Sandro is proportionate. Apparently everywhere.

**2.** Sandro is loud. Apparently everywhere.

**3.** Senior year, on the whole, is not what I expected.

Okay, whatever, I guess I do want to get into detail.

*Viewer discretion advised.*

From the top, let me say this. Sandro smells amazing. Which was surprising because males, in my history of locker rooms and middle school, smell like ass. But not him. When I got close to Sandro, he smelled like skin. Like sweat, but good sweat. The guy smelled like the ocean. Salt in the air. All I could think about at first was how good Sandro smelled. Well, when I wasn't otherwise preoccupied.

We made out for a while and it was A+. It's all I was planning on doing that night, really. Just some good ol'-fashioned necking and maybe some bumping and grinding if we were feeling it. But as soon as he pulled me onto him… I don't know, man. You forget how big a guy is until he picks you up. I liked it. Him picking me up. Moving me like that.

And God bless Sandro. It was his first time on the field, but he played like a pro. Dove right into my crotch, headfirst, no parachute. He was worried at first because I wasn't making noise. A complaint I've received in the past. Apparently, my lack of moaning and groaning when receiving a blowjob is "confusing" and "unmotivating." It's not like I wasn't enjoying myself, and Sandro was doing some gold-star work. I'm just an internal person. Knowing what I know now, I feel like an asshole for never giving girls audio clues before. Because if Sandro wasn't the loudest, most sensitive motherfucker in South Jersey, I would've been similarly lost down there.

Three takeaways from my time in the Miceli trenches. First, don't touch Sandro's balls. Just don't. He doesn't like it and thinks they're "too sensitive," which, I mean, sort of the whole point but whatever. Second, I could tell I was doing a good job when Sandro was making noise. I could tell I was doing my best work when he stopped making noise altogether. Once I got a handle on things and got into a good rhythm, his voice just cut out and his back arched. It was hot as fuck. Last takeaway: I want to get really good at giving head. I think, with some practice, I could crush it next time.

I don't know when we got naked but at some point I noticed all our clothes in a heap, along with Dro's boot. I couldn't remember taking them off but there they were. The shorts I drove to AC for. The boxers I bought for cross-country season. The socks with the holes in the heel. I became so suddenly aware of how naked we both were. It was all a big, surreal blur. Because I've been naked with loads of guys before, but I'd never seen them at those angles. In those positions. In such proximity. All these new ways to see a person. But I couldn't get a clean look. In the blink of an eye, everything was moving so fast and the images wouldn't stay still. All these new parts. All these things I never let myself think about. The image of Sandro there in my room and my bed and my arms overwhelmed me and I needed to find control. That's why the waltz started.

We did this little dance, Sandro and I, of who was kissing who. He'd be on top of me, pressing my hand against the bed then **STEP 1, 2**, I'd turn him over and get on top. I'd be feeling his chest, his hips, his shoulders then, before I knew it, **STEP 3, 4**, I'd be on my back again. It was this unspoken argument. This need to find control. And somewhere in the squeezing and pressing and the lips peppering my chest, I realized the argument was my own. An argument I felt a need to win. And maybe it's the competitor in me but at some point the argument just got too loud. Too heated. Two voices shouting their loudest.

One Bash cheering: *You're gonna fuck him!*

The other screaming: *YOU'RE GONNA FUCK HIM?!*

Sandro's sweat was mixing with my own and I didn't know if I could handle all that heat. I could feel the guy poking at my hip and I realized that I'd never been *poked* before. The sensation was entirely new to me. The only other time I'd even made contact with another man's junk was the time Doug Parson teabagged me at a group sleepover and that ended with me breaking a broom across his back. And Del would kill me if I broke our broom, it's a great broom. And maybe it was the thought of my stepdad or sleepovers or Doug Parson's nuts on my forehead, but the poking was becoming too much. The heat. The theme from *Space Jam* started up on the randomized Jock Jams playlist I had going on my speaker and I needed to stop.

*"Time-out."*

I pulled back. Sandro's fingers paused their exploration of my balls. "Oh. Not good?"

"Just...gimme a second." I rolled away from him and looked anywhere else. The *Space Jam* theme played on, for no one.

"Hey. You okay?"

I stared at our pile of clothes on my bedroom carpet. Both our outfits, mixed up together. I thought that would be the hard part but I didn't even notice them go. This is the part I thought was going to be easy, but there I was in my head. I was drunk on this feeling two seconds ago and then *poof.* The feeling ran out of me and left me sitting on the edge of my bed, fully nude, making a big show of fiddling with my speaker. "I'm fine. Just...yeah. Just fixing this."

"The speaker?"

"The...song."

While I mindlessly scrolled for something less *pep rally,* Dro was silent. Catching his breath. I guess I was too. I heard him pull one of my pillows closer to him and knew he was covering himself up. Sandro has a thing with his stomach. I think it's tied to his thing about people touching him. Anytime he sits, nine times out of ten, if there's a pillow handy he'll sort of cuddle with it. He says he just likes having something to do with his hands but I know it's because of his stomach. What he'd call a gut. That's Dro though. Something I've learned about the guy these last few months. The guy loves to cover up. The pillow. A smile. *Anywho.*

"Bash?" His hand was on my back then. Like he might be able to feel whatever it was that stopped our rhythm. "I do something wrong?"

I looked back at him before the question could linger. "No, Sandro. No." I didn't want him thinking like that. Because it wasn't his hang-up. It rarely is. "I just needed...a breather."

"A time-out?"

"Yeah. I just needed to stop."

His hand stayed on my back. Feeling my breath. "...You wanna stop?"

I shook my head. And I told myself to start kissing him again. I told myself to stop overthinking things, to stop arguing with myself.

*You wanted this.*

*C'mon, you want this.*

*Right?*

*What do you fucking want, man?*

"Dro?"

"Yeah?"

"Can…" After a quiet moment, I pointed across my bedroom. Right over to my desk. "Can you go over there?"

"Huh?"

I looked back at Sandro and smiled a little. "It's okay. Just for a second. I don't wanna stop, just… I don't know. Humor me."

He gave me a sort of look. Like he wanted to question me but didn't know where to start. But he rolled off my bed and hopped up, a little stumbly without his boot on. He stood a few feet away from me, in all his nude glory. Well. Almost nude.

I held a hand out. "Pillow?"

Sandro sighed and tossed his cuddling pillow at my face. I put it back on my headboard and looked at him. He kept a hand on his junk. Not enough to fully cover up, he didn't want to show his nerves that obviously, but I could tell he felt a little insecure.

"What, uh…is this? Cavity search?"

I didn't want him feeling insecure so I got up too. Right across from him. I put the length of my bedroom carpet between us and just took him in. He got a little giggly.

"What's that look?"

"Whatchu mean?"

"What are you looking at?"

"You." I smiled. "Can I just…look at you a little, Dro?"

"What?"

I motioned at his body. All of it. Hairy head to hairy toes. "I wanna look at you. All of you."

"Oh." He thought about it for half a second. Then he grabbed at his crotch a little. "You know, I usually charge by the minute."

He tried a smile. I didn't smile back. "I'm not joking around, man."

I took a moment to get my words together. Because I wanted to do this. Whatever we were about to do, I wanted it. And I know he did too. But the second I kissed him, the moment he pulled my body onto his, the night had become a blur. I didn't want a blur. I wanted to take my time. I wanted to see the man I was about to be with.

"I never look. Ever. All my life. And whenever I wanted to, I felt... I felt so shit about it. I never let myself look." I shrugged. "I just wanna look at you, Sandro. And I want you to look at me."

Sandro smiled. He moved his hands to his sides, off his stomach and himself, and brought his shoulders back. "Okay."

"Okay?"

"Yeah, okay. Look at me."

He nodded. So, I looked.

Sandro's feet are huge. Thirteens in the gym, fourteens for comfort. They've got hair on the knuckles and very little nail. He's got this shiny purplish scar on his right shin that always peeks out when he wears tube socks. Says he got it walking into a table back in July. And his arms. Dude's got these super long arms that a swimmer or pterodactyl would pay good money for. Reach all the way down past his hips with these big-ass hands to match.

"Can you grip a basketball?"

"I can."

"Damn. Lucky."

"I know, so lucky, it's so useful."

"Shut up. It's cool."

His chest is a scouring pad of dark black hair. It's thick. Like armor almost. I'd only been under Sandro for a few minutes but I could still feel the friction of that patch rubbing against me even then. You can hardly see the skin underneath at points. Just hair. And his chain. And his nipples.

"What are you looking at?"

"Your chain."

"What about it?"

"I mean…your nipples."

"Oh. What about'm?"

"Nothing. You just…have nipples."

"WHAT?!"

I cracked up. He did too. After we settled, I pointed at them. Two pink reminders that there was a person under all that hair. "They're nice. Very pronounced."

"Gotta be. They grew up in a rough neighborhood."

"Low-key jealous of the hair. I can't grow shit."

"I dunno. You're growing something."

He smiled down and I realized I was about three more seconds of nipple talk away from half-mast. He laughed. "Is that a birthmark down there? I couldn't tell for sure under the covers."

The question held me in place for a moment. Because I realized then that no man alive had ever seen my birthmark. My mother had, of course, and Lucy caught a peek or two over the years but not Del. That's for damn certain. And my father never bathed me. And even with a lifetime of locker rooms, the mark's unique placement is sort of hidden. I looked down at myself and held up my penis. Under the tip of my dick, right where the head meets the shaft, there's this almost triangle-shaped dot. Like the Great Pyramid. It's actually kind of cool looking. I might even say I'm a little proud of it if I ever told a soul it existed.

"Yup. Had it as long as I can remember. My lil' Bermuda Triangle."

"It's cool, man. Like an arrow."

"Yeah. Lucy once told me I came with a built-in compass." I wagged it at him. "You've now entered into rare company, Miceli. You're the first dude to see it. Ever."

"Bullshit. No one?"

"Nope. Not a one."

"Wow. Exclusive."

I felt my eyes wandering and switched topics from my dick to his. "So. Why aren't you circumcised?"

Sandro's answer shot out immediately. "Why the fuck are you?"

It was like I'd triggered some automated response installed in the guy many years and gym locker rooms ago. Shit. I shook my head. "I don't mean... No, it's cool. I like it."

"Oh."

"When I got your boxers off, I just... I didn't expect it."

Sandro nodded and looked down at his situation for a moment. "Oh. Well...yeah. Here's my dick. *Tada.*" He did this little jazz hand thing that made me smile.

"It's cool. Uncut. You don't see that every day."

Sandro shrugged, ready to move off it. "I don't know, man, it's just how we are. My family. My brothers and me."

"Oh. Is that an Italian thing?"

"I think it might just be a Miceli thing. You'd have to ask my nonno."

"For sure. Yeah, I plan to."

He laughed at that but I could see Sandro's hands twitching on his side. He wanted to cover up. Or at the very least get the spotlight off his hog.

Dro made a little motion with his finger. "Give us a twirl. Lemme see your butt."

"My butt?"

"C'mon. I wanna look at you too."

I sighed and turned around. I felt a bit silly at first because I guess I'd never showcased my ass before. The concept of mooning someone never strongly appealed to me. I thought about shaking it a little, getting a jiggle going, but settled on just a little sway. Back and forth. Nice and easy.

"How'm I looking?" I let the question hang for a little, keeping my sway going, but Sandro wasn't saying anything back. I couldn't see his face and, for a second, I got worried. Did I have a bad ass? "Dro?"

Then he laughed. "I mean…" He really, really laughed. "I mean, *come ON*."

"Yeah? Good?"

"Amazing, dude. Just how I pictured."

The laughter was contagious and pretty soon I was right there with him. "Shut the fuck up. You picture my ass a lot?"

"Blame those Adidas sweatpants. They frame it well. It's very…perky."

"*Perky.*"

"Pronounced."

*"Pronounced?"*

Sandro groaned. "You got a big, round ass, Bash, what do you want me to say? I wanna play bongos on those cheeks till the sun comes up. Sue me."

If I was a blushing guy, I think that would've got me there. I turned back around and waved off the sentiment. "Blame your squat routine. How 'bout you?"

"What about me?"

"Come on. Don't think I haven't noticed you in basketball shorts, Dro. You fill out."

"No, no. You have a *big* ass. I have a *fat* ass. There's a difference."

I made the same little finger twirl back at him. "I'll be the judge. *Bongos.*"

Sandro stared up at my ceiling for a second then let out a long sigh. He turned around, resting his fists on my desk. There wasn't much hair on his back save for a patch above his ass. But his cheeks were basically hairless. I was honestly surprised. Because how could someone so big and hairy have such a cute butt? No other way to put it. Sandro Miceli had a cute little butt.

"It's a good butt, dude."

He was shifting his weight around. Really leaning on the desk. His foot was gonna start hurting him soon, I could tell. But it was more than that. He was starting to get uncomfortable with my little experiment. With my time-out. My eyes on him. Me.

"...It's sexy."

"What?" Dro turned back around. I could tell he was genuinely surprised to hear that. The guy's "don't fuck with me" face is one of his easiest to read.

"Your ass is sexy. So's your chest. Your feet."

"*Sexy?*"

"Sexy."

As if on instinct, his hand found its way back to his stomach. Covering. I got serious. "Your stomach. Your fingers. You're sexy."

Sandro snorted. "C'mon."

"That so unbelievable?"

"I mean…there's no accounting for taste."

"No one ever call you sexy before?"

He made a face. "Bash. Who in my life would *ever* say that to me?"

Fair. Dro wasn't like me. He didn't have people he could experiment with. He didn't have hookups or play school girlfriends. He didn't have vacation flings or summer crushes. However new all this felt to me, Sandro must've been feeling it ten times harder. We were both in uncharted territory, in different and similar ways, and I decided right then that if I was gonna be this guy's first, I was gonna earn it.

I stood up a little straighter. "When I saw you in those little Italy shorts…the ones you wore to Beer Olympics?" My fingers grazed the hairs on my stomach. "I wanted to touch them. I wanted to feel what they felt like. Those legs. On mine."

Sandro's face got more serious. I nodded. Then I nodded at his dick. "And if I saw that earlier… I mean, if I caught that in the locker room, man, I don't know what I would've done. That might've been it for me. I don't think I could've handled it."

Sandro laughed. "Like...in a good way?"

"In the best way. It's fucking...that's sexy, Dro. You're so sexy to me, Sandro." I smiled. Because it was true. But it's like I was realizing it just as I was saying it. "And I think the way you clear your throat is hot. All deep and shit. And your sweat smells like...you smell so good, dude. Like the beach. And that time you broke that big stick over your knee? I fucking... I thought about that. *A lot.*" I laughed with him. "I know! I don't know! I just thought it was hot and I think you're hot and your hands... I just want them."

"My hands?"

"I just want you."

Sandro wiped some sweat from his forehead and smiled. "I want you too, Bash."

I smiled back. But my eyes stayed on his dick. He was holding it and, even soft, that basketball-grip hand couldn't hold it all. I felt my knees get a little shaky. The whistles were blowing, halftime was over, and I wanted to touch him.

Sandro chuckled. "Oh, what's up, birthmark?"

There was no use hiding it. I was almost painfully hard watching him. And I felt the heat again. But this time was different. Quieter. There wasn't an argument worth having anymore. Sandro looked me up and down, his grip starting to move. "How do you like it?"

"How?"

"Yeah. What do you want, B?"

I was working on myself then too. Showing Sandro what I'd like. What I was ready for him to do to me. My free hand moved to my chest. "This." I felt my nipple. Something I'd been working on lately. Something I wanted Sandro to know about me. My body. "When you touch me...touch me here, okay?"

"Either?"

"Both. One at a time."

"Okay."

His hand never stopped moving. He never took his eyes off me. "You are..." But he smiled. "You're so beautiful, Bash. I've been dying to say that, man. For *months*. You are so beautiful. How'd you fucking do that?"

I felt this warmth rush down my chest. Like a swallow of hot mint tea. I let it spread through me, watching Sandro watch me. Seeing how he took me in. And the way he looked at me. The way he fucking looked at me, man. However that boy must see me, to put that kind of smile on a person's face, that's how I knew. I knew I'd be okay. Whatever was about to happen, I knew Sandro would keep me safe. Because I knew what I wanted. And I knew what he wanted too. He couldn't cover up if he tried. He couldn't cover anything anymore. Neither could I.

I was ready.

I walked across the carpet to Sandro and I kissed him. I felt his hands on my ass and that poke in my hip. He pulled me close to him and squeezed. That basketball grip.

"So fucking beautiful."

"*Sandro.*"

"So...so fucking..." His hands rubbed my bare ass and I could feel a chuckle. "How the hell is your ass hairier than mine?"

I cracked up laughing and buried my face in his chest. His hands kept squeezing me, feeling every part I wanted felt, and I shook when his whisper scratched against my ear. "You wanna?"

I nodded. It was an easy question to answer. "I wanna. I really wanna."

Sandro started kissing on my neck. I held on to his ass and kissed along his shoulders. He moved to my lips and his hands found their way back to my ass. Pretty soon, we were making out in the middle of my bedroom, squeezing the hell out of each other's asses. It was hot. Then it was funny. Not *ha ha* funny, more *huh* funny. And there was something about the slowing in our panting that told me we both thought the exact same thing at the exact same time.

Sandro's lips left mine. His hands stayed put. "To clarify…"

I didn't let go of his ass either. "I want to have sex with you, Sandro."

"Dope. Okay, dope."

"Is that… That's what you wanted to clarify?"

"Yeah. I mean, no, but yeah. Ultimately, yes."

"…What?" I pulled back, hands still firmly planted. His hands wouldn't budge either.

"I, uh… I don't know how to ask this."

And with that boy's fingernails in my butt-meat, it dawned on me. "Ah."

"Yeah. Ah."

Neither of us blinked. We hardly even moved. Naked on my carpet, asses stuck midclutch, a stalemate. No more waltzing. No more **STEP 1, 2**. We'd been waiting to dance for fucking months now. It was time. It was happening. But the question still remained.

Who would lead?

"...I think there's a quarter on my dresser."

Look.

I didn't plan on getting fucked in the ass this Halloween. I just didn't. But tails is tails. Them's the rules, quarters don't lie. And between you, me, and the watercooler, it's actually really amazing once you get past the whole "getting fucked in the ass" factor. I mean, yeah, it hurt like a motherfucker at first. But only at first. Then it turned into something. The hurt didn't go away, it just changed. Became part of it. Became *fantastic*.

Jokes aside, I loved it. The whole night. I really loved it. I loved the talk, I loved the costume thing, I loved the crappy Jack & Coke. How he touched me. Sandro held me like I could break. No one has ever treated me like that. He was so careful with every move, even the rough ones, and I needed that. I needed the care and he made sure I was okay. I've never been so scared and so safe.

He wanted to shower after, so I was alone for a minute. I just sat there in this bed I've had since I was a little boy, and I was so happy. I was so happy with me. That just doesn't happen. Ever. I was proud of myself. Impressed that I let myself do that. That I found something I wanted and let myself go for it. I was eating a Mounds bar, looking at all the smeared curlicue marker on my chest, when I started smiling. I couldn't stop. I must've looked unhinged. I felt high. I looked at the picture of my mom and me sitting on the nightstand. I'm small but my hair is huge and we're sitting in the back of Birdie.

In our field. My head in her lap. The sun on my face. I can still feel her running her hands through my curls. I was so little then. And look at me now. This laugh burst out of me and I rubbed my face. Jesus. What a night.

Sandro came in dancing, wearing just his boxers. "Sick shower, brah. All kinds of nozzles and shit. I'm impressed."

"Yeah, we ball out."

He smiled and sat on the side of the bed. He looked at me. Really took me in. He still had that care in his voice. "You good?"

"Oh, I'm chillin'."

"It was okay? I don't have anything to compare it to. So."

"I mean, I don't either."

"You and Lucy never..."

"Yeah, but that was different. In...at least three ways."

He nodded and took a bite of my Mounds. He nearly spat it out. "Coconut sucks ass."

"I knew this wouldn't work out."

We laughed and he lay back on me, resting his head on my chest like a pillow. I rubbed my hand through his hair. Felt his ears, his jaw, his scalp. All of him.

"...It was really great, Sandro."

"Yeah?"

"Yeah."

"We're not gonna freak or anything?"

"We don't gotta."

"Or think about what it all means?"

"Not tonight."

"Super."

He ran his thumb up my arm. Took my wrist, like he did

that night in the truck. He rubbed my prayer bracelet and I felt like sharing more. Like there wasn't anything worth keeping anymore. I wanted him to know everything about me.

"My mom gave it to me freshman year. When things were getting bad. I put a new bead on it once a year. On her birthday."

"I like that."

"I don't know if it's an actual tradition, but it feels right. Keeps me close to her. I don't really pray or anything but… I don't know. It's comforting."

He fiddled with his chain. Held the little golden cross between his big fingers. "I pray. Sometimes. Not always to God or nothing but, yeah. It's nice to think that someone's thinking 'bout me."

"Exactly."

Sandro killed the bottle of Jack & Coke. I could feel a burp rise through his chest and get swallowed. It was unreal, being that close to someone. I rubbed my face in his hair and smelled my own shampoo. "You know, one of these days, that quarter's gonna flip heads."

"It is a statistical probability, yes."

"Odds are in my favor. You ready for that?"

Sandro shrugged. "Maybe. Still trying to decide if I wanna fuck you again."

"Asshole."

"Hey, you are what you eat."

"Jesus CHRIST."

Sandro cracked up. I pushed his goofy ass away from me but he pulled me back onto him. He kissed me soft.

"You're so good, Bash. You're so… God. Thank you."

"Thank you?"

"Thanks for finding me."

Sandro rubbed his face into my chest. I scratched my nails along his hair. "Thanks for finding *me*."

He kissed my nipple and giggled at all the Sharpie smudges on my chest. "You wanna shower? You've got marker hair all over you."

"Honestly? I don't know if I trust my legs right now."

Sandro busted out cackling. I got in there too with my machine-gun laughs. I guess we were both still a little buzzed. From the Jack. From the sex. Still riding the buzz from that night in the ditch two months ago.

In some ways, we finished what we started that night. That night asked: *Should we? Can we?*

This one answered: *Why would we ever stop?*

# sandro

*NOVEMBER 24*

*AIN'T NO LIE, BABY, BI BI BI*

At first, it was like sucking off a statue. No change on his face, none of the moans or groans I expected from a lifetime of porn. I believed I was the world's worst fellator. I've seen the guy sneeze with more excitement than when I got him to bust that first time. But I got him there, darn it, and that's a win in my book. Things have steadily improved since then, but I still wonder what the snag was. Maybe he was nervous. Maybe he felt like he'd be betraying some part of himself by enjoying a blowjob from a guy. Or maybe he just needed to trust me. I guess I earned his trust 'cause now Bash won't shut the fuck up during our festivities. The body is a mystery.

It's too cold for the ditch now but so far we've hit Birdie's driver seat, passenger seat, back seat, his living room couch, his shower, his bedroom floor, his bedroom wall, and this one time we started in the kitchen but ended in his room. A grand total of thirteen. Oh, duh, and his bed. Fourteen. Not that I'm counting. Okay, I'm counting. Sex is a good time. Not what I thought it'd be. Better. And it's not like it's all we can think about now, but there's a definite vibe looming over our hangouts lately. Like we'll be watching a movie on the couch and he'll look at me, midscene, and his big Bash eyebrows will be all:

"Okay, *Scream 2*'s great and junk but how 'bout you take me upstairs and throw it down real quick?"

But after our post-Thanksgiving sleepover turned into an all-night event (three times before sunup, thank you very much), a very tired Bash declared that lubrication needed to be invited to the party. Ever the gentleman, I offered to be our designated **Lube Coordinator™** and pay to support our active lifestyle. It was literally the least I could do as, so far, I've been kind of a pain wimp when it comes time to flip-flop. The one time we tried it the other way, I nearly broke his shower door and my foot all over again. I'm just not there yet but Bash has been patient with me. Plus, not for nothing, the guy just enjoys getting fucked. Who'd a thunk?

I biked over to the Cinnaminson CVS to buy our lube because I'd eat my own head in embarrassment if someone from Moorestown caught me with it. Once inside, I tiptoed right for the Family Planning aisle and selected some bottles of the brand with the simplest packaging. A lot of the pricier ones had these sexy logos and suggestive names. Really trying to

jazz up the cool factor for the luber on the go. I didn't need
bells and whistles. This was gel that was gonna be shoved up
someone's ass. Be humble.

I was worried the cashier would think less of me if I showed
up with a bunch of lube like some dry-skinned sex deviant
so I grabbed Doritos and a Hallmark card. I guess I preferred
them to think I was a dry-skinned sex deviant who also loved
Cool Ranch and Bat Mitzvahs.

I was aimlessly looking at different kinds of batteries when
Lucy Jordan and I locked eyes from across the store. She was
with another girl I couldn't see. I instinctively slipped the
three bottles of lube into my butt pockets. What the fuck was
she doing there? She definitely saw me because she made one
of those lazy little waves that say: *"I am acknowledging that,
yes, we know each other and, don't worry, I don't need to talk to
you either."*

That was comforting because me, Lucy, plus some bottles
of K-Y would make for some terrible, unexplainable small
talk. She'd at least have to wonder who all this lube was for.
Bash told me Lucy is incredibly perceptive and he would a
hundred percent throttle me if I set off any of her alarms.

But then I saw who Lucy was with. I hid behind a display
of off-brand Hot Wheels and whispered up to God. *"What
the FUCK, man?"*

For some inexplicable reason, Lucy was yucking it up with
Ronny DiSario. How the fuck did they even know each
other, let alone enough to be hanging out? It was one thing if
Lucy caught me lube-handed, but Ronny knew me. Ronny's
taken a decided interest in my whole deal. And she knew I'd
been hanging out with Bash. Ronny knew just enough of her

favorite bassist's shit to help Lucy fill in some deeply closeted holes about my life. Bash's life. And it would only be a matter of time before Lucy connected some dots, blew up my spot, and took the best/only sex I've ever had back off the table.

*Damn it, Ronny.* This is why I don't make friends.

The girls walked over to the drinks so I crept up the opposite side of the store. I just needed to get out unseen, get back to Bash's, and never talk to Ronny DiSario ever again. Well. Maybe not that. Never talk to Ronny DiSario *about Bash* ever again. Better.

But it wasn't like I jabbered about him 24/7. If anything, she brought him up more than I did. Which reminded me, didn't Ronny try to fuck Bash at the Beer Olympics? Fresh off his breakup with Lucy? And now they hang out at Cinnaminson CVSs together?

Weird. Maybe I didn't understand girls.

I saw them heading into the Frozen Food section so I slowly backed into Mouthwash and Eye Care. I ducked low and scurried up the aisle, almost tripping over a basket someone had abandoned in front of the Crest Whitestrips. I saw a straight shot to the exit. But then I heard Lucy's voice.

"I think I could do twenty."

I almost dropped to the ground. They were one aisle over in Allergy and Children's Health. Just a pack of Pampers separated me and certain death. Then I heard Ronny.

"No. You're underestimating how hard it would be to actually fight a third grader."

"I don't think I am. I think I have a realistic understanding of myself."

"Third graders are bigger than you think, Lu. You'd be tired after ten."

"And I'd tough it out till twenty. I know my body."

"I want pho."

"Yesssss."

They were walking up the aisle, toward the exit. I could wait them out. See if they left first then make my escape. But what if they catch me in the parking lot? See me on their way out? Too many variables.

A woman was staring at me over a bottle of cinnamon mouthwash. I waved her off. She didn't need to get mixed up in all this.

"Do we think Matty Silva would be interesting in bed?"

"Ronny, bleh."

"Merely positing a question."

"Also, I assume Mr. Silva doesn't go down on girls."

"Oho. Based on experience?"

"*No.* Simply vibes."

"Does Bash?"

I perked up. They'd stopped walking and so had I. My exit window was open but I found myself curious to hear what Lucy had to say.

"Seb and I... I mean, the guy knows what he's doing. He just..."

I leaned in. It was none of my business. But I leaned in.

Lucy sighed. "He could never stop thinking."

"Like, about someone else? Fucker."

"No. Like, about everything. He was always in his head. Like he thought he'd get caught doing something he shouldn't. He never got lost in it, you know?"

"Damn. Good thing he blew me off at Olympics."

"Very good thing. It would've been real inconvenient to have to murder you."

"I was bored. And sober. And I probably wouldn't have done it anyhow."

"You just wanted to know you could."

"You get me. If we order pho now, it'll be at mine in twenty."

"Do they do those little pork meatball things? I'm craving."

"That they do. Oh, shit, I need mouthwash."

Fuck. On impulse, I chucked my bag of family-sized Doritos over the aisle wall. It crashed to the tiles and made the girls yipe.

"What the hell?"

Before I could question the logistics of my diversion, I ditched the Hallmark card and rushed out the front, unseen. My heart was racing by the time I reached my bike but I hopped on and sped away before any Moorestown girl or Cinnaminson cop could stop me. I was a good three blocks clear of the CVS parking lot when I realized that I'd not only stolen three bottles of lube but had also sat on two. My ass was sopping. Super.

I biked straight to Bash's and caught him up while my boxers and jeans bounced around in his washing machine. He thought the run-in was hilarious, namely that my first act as **Lube Coordinator™** was to shoplift and cream my jeans. I guess it was a little funny. The washer had thirty minutes to go so we passed the time breaking in the surviving bottle on top of his dryer.

Once the load was finished, we knocked out an encore in

his room. After, I was sprawled out on his wonderfully comfy bed, something I'd come to love, while he worked at his desk. Bare ass on his chair. Thing about Bash, if he gets naked, he stays naked. He says he likes to "let his skin breathe." I'm not complaining, it's a nice sight, I just hope he washes his desk chair from time to time.

He was eating an old Wawa hoagie and reading a Princeton Review workbook. It was full of Post-its and liner notes. Del's been getting on him about college apps lately. Says that, however much he wants to go to Rutgers, it'd be foolish to *only* apply to Rutgers.

I didn't wanna say it, because he really does wanna go for his mom and all, but I think he can do better. He's a smart enough guy but those legs of his open a lot of doors. I told him I agreed with Del, that backups are wise, so he's been window-shopping around. Maybe it's just to get us off his back but I'm happy he's trying.

I was staring at the picture he keeps of his mom on his nightstand, with him so small and cute and loved, when I had a random thought. "It must've been nice to have Lucy."

"Huh?"

He took his earbuds out. I hadn't noticed them. "Lucy. It must've been nice to date someone you're so close with."

"Yeah. It was. Most of the time."

"But, like, confusing too, right?"

"Whatchu mean?"

"I don't know. Something I was thinking about on my bike ride over."

"Me and Lucy?"

"You and me. I'm wondering who has it harder."

He swiveled around and took his readers off. "In what sense?"

"Well, I like you. I like people like you. But you like people like me AND other people. Like Lucy. Both are confusing and shit, but, yeah. I wonder. Which is harder?"

"You mean, is it harder to be gay or..."

"Bi. Bisexual."

He grunted. Bash is weird with terms. I don't think I heard him actually say the word *gay* till about three weeks after I came out to him.

"That's liking both?"

"According to the internet. And porn. And Phil Reyno, yeah."

*"Bisexual."* The word hit my ear weird coming out of his mouth. Like Bash was worried he'd mispronounce it. "I don't know. Sounds made up."

"I'm sure it wouldn't if you let yourself say it enough."

"Fair." He stood up and did this stretching routine he does that's his own personal blend of yoga and nervous pacing. "Bisexual. *Bi.* I am a bisexual. I am bisexual. I have bisexuality."

"Look at him go! Though I don't think it's something you *have*."

"I caught bisexuality. I'm riddled with it." He took a bite of his hoagie and spoke with his mouth full. "But to answer your question, I sorta wish I was more like you. Maybe I wouldn't worry as much."

"I worry. I worry a lot. It's, like, one of my main things."

"Sure, but only about the one thing. I have both balls in the air, y'know? Not to mention..." He leaned back in his chair and fiddled with a pencil. "Like, I feel like if I ever were to tell someone… Like, if I told Lucy about everything. You and me. My whole deal. I feel like she'd think I was lying."

"About being bi?"

"No, like everything she and I had was a front."

"I don't think Lucy's like that."

"Not Luce in particular, just in general. I don't know if people would believe me. That I like…both."

"It's not a hard concept."

"Try telling me that in July. I didn't think it was a real option and I was living it. So, yeah. It's hard. *Harder.*"

I sat up in bed. I suddenly felt very naked and pulled his comforter around me. "Fair. But you had someone. You had options. I could never…"

"What?"

"Like, if you wanted, there's a world where you never have to tell anyone. You know? Like, you could find some great girl and fall crazy in love and all that and…yeah. That'd be it. I don't have that. *Harder.*"

"I mean… I'd still tell people."

"Would you?"

Honest question. If Bash was completely happy and satisfied and in love with the perfect woman, would this side of himself even exist? Would he let it? I really didn't know.

I don't think he knew either. He really mulled it over. "I would. I think I would. I think I'd need to. Or I'd be lying. I think it'd feel wrong."

"I get that. That's why I haven't… Like, I never wanted to fake it. I could've, I've had offers. But faking it felt mean. To the girl."

"Offers? From who?"

"Syd DeStefano."

"Fuck you. That's a lie."

"Seriously. Seventh grade. We were in the same Latin class and hit it off."

"Sydney flirts with everyone, Dro. She's a little hard-core for a guy like—"

"She invited me to Passy's."

"Oh. *Fuck*. No bullshit?"

"No bullshit."

In Moorestown Middle, you didn't invite someone to Passy's Pizzeria unless you were looking to fall in love or get fingered in the alleyway. Often both. But I turned her down. At that point, I didn't have the words for what was going on in my head, but I knew that they didn't involve Sydney DeStefano or Passy's Pizzeria.

"Wait. So, you've never had any kind of girlfriend?"

"Nope. Not even a date. That surprises you?"

"I mean, I assumed but I didn't…wow. So, I really was your first *anything*?"

"Yup, yup, yup."

"Huh." He took a contemplative bite from his hoagie. Gears were turning in his head. His mouth was full of ham and bread when he said it. "You wanna go on a date?"

"What?"

He finally swallowed. "Wanna go on a date?"

"No, I somehow made that out. What do you mean *date*?"

"Like a date. Like go out. To dinner or something."

I tried to respond with words but they came out as laughing. I could feel all the red on my face which just doubled down on my embarrassment. I wish I had some damn clothes on right then.

"I'm serious, Dro! Come on. I wanna take you out. Really do it up."

A big laugh burst out and I hid under the comforter. I heard him walk over and felt him start punching on my chest through the blankets.

*"Okay?!!"*

"Okay!"

"Okay. Good. Okay."

I could hear him sit back in his chair. Heard him chuckle to himself and take another bite of sandwich. But I couldn't get out from under the comforter. I didn't want him to see how much I was blushing.

A date. A *date*? With Bash? Holy shit.

Holy. Shit.

# bash

*sayno*

I woke up looking for the man in my doorway. He wasn't
there. Fuck. I hate dreaming. Dro was snoring on my chest.
I shook his face.

"Dro. *Hey.*"

His noises cut off and he blinked himself awake. "Mm?"

"I just had a dream."

He was barely up. "While you were sleeping? Dude, no
way."

"It was about my dad."

That got his attention. He sniffed and got the crap out of
his eyes. "Weird."

"Yeah."

"Talk to me."

The dream already felt so far away. What happened? What about the doorway? The more I tried to remember it, the farther it felt.

"Bash?"

"...I don't remember."

"Jesus."

"Something about angels. With tattoos."

He peeled my arm off him and pushed me over. "Turn around. You've lost big-spoon privileges."

"Works for me. I go both ways, bitch."

"Ugh."

He put his big arm around me and I repositioned my hips to find his. His meaty forearm was like memory foam. I pushed my head into it and got comfy.

He grumbled. "I'm getting you a dream journal for Christmas."

"I'm getting you a CPAP machine."

"Fuck off, I barely snore."

"I think I'd know."

He kissed the back of my neck. "...Is it bad?"

"Nah. I kinda like it. It's like whale sounds. My white boy's white noise."

I felt his chuckle shake through his chest into mine. "Good night."

"Night, Dro."

I waited eight seconds and the snoring picked up behind me. It was more like purring this go-around. I smiled and followed the noise to sleep.

Sandro made me promise that I'd stop running multiple

times a day. Well, to quote him, even a single daily workout was "near masochistic" but I got his point. Running two or three times a day wasn't exactly healthy if I was only running to stop thinking. But I've liked my thoughts lately. It was an easy promise to keep.

The next morning, after my single run of the day, I happened to catch Lucy leaving her place with her canvas grocery bag.

"Bash Ketchum."

"Luce Cannon. Careful, I smell like ass."

"Charming."

She untangled her headphones and gave my sweaty self a once-over. I think she was loading up on all the things she'd been meaning to tell me. We hadn't really caught up in a minute. It wasn't on purpose, we just kept missing each other.

"Where you been? You were missed at Spooktacular. I was a hamster."

"Nice. It sounded sick. I was in Maine. Del had this family thing."

"Travel. Fun."

"Yeah. Lobsters."

"Matty was pissed. Says you keep bailing on him."

I didn't want to tell Lucy about my turn on Matty. How I haven't said a word to him since I bailed on Spooktacular outside of "Table Eleven needs straws." I just nodded. "Matty's Matty."

She crunched up her nose at that. Lucy Jordan is allergic to vague sentiment. "Yes. Matty is Matty. A spectacular observation."

"I'm nothing if not observant."

"And so humble."

She unscrunched and smiled. "Feels like I haven't seen you around much. How are you?"

"Good. Fine. Cross-country kind of sucked but winter track starts next week."

"Oh. Joy."

"Been reading a bunch too. Eleven books since August."

Lucy laughed. "Ms. Morgan's Lit? You read the one about that douche on the boat?"

"Hey. Don't come for my boy, Daniel. Aced that report. Well, *A*-. I rambled."

"You? Talkative?" We laughed. And I realized I was talking. I'd been talking for minutes without thinking about what I needed to say next. "Hey, did Sandro ever find you?"

I spoke too soon. My body went still. "Huh?"

"Sandro Miceli. *Mitchelli?* However you say it. He was looking for you, little while back. Said he needed to apologize for something. Said you were friends."

"Oh. Yeah."

"Y'know, I'd completely forgotten about it but I saw him at CVS the other week and… I don't know. I didn't know you knew him like that."

If people ask me about Sandro, I tell them about our workout schedule and our training regimen and how our coaches wanted the squad captains to yadayadayada. I have all these deflections for people. But Lucy knows me, and I know when she's digging. My tongue started feeling heavy in my mouth and I couldn't stand still.

"He's been helping me with math so I'm driving him

around. He broke his foot. Plus, we're both captains. So, you know. It's not weird."

Unconvincing.

"I didn't say it was weird. It's just... That's very nice of you. Helping him like that. I always liked Sandro. He's...polite."

"Sure. He's chill."

"Sure. *Chill.* You know he's in a band with Ronny? Ronny DiSario?"

Good, a diversion. "Yeah, wait, since when did you start hanging with Ron again?"

"She got a lot more sociable once she quit lacrosse. And I guess I missed talking to people who wanted to talk to me. Who told you we were hanging out again?"

My spine froze. Lucy Jordan, Kid Detective. I did my best to shrug casually. "...You did."

Lucy stared through me. It was an easily disprovable lie but I wasn't thinking at full capacity. Lucy only had to say Dro's name and I'd fallen back into my hole. This place I put my-self where I could barely put words together.

Lucy nodded. "Hm. Maybe I did."

"Yeah. You did."

She had more to say. I think she was assessing whether it would be worth getting into it at this moment. I was assess-ing whether it would be worth pushing her into the grass and bolting down the street. We must've stood there silently assessing for a whole minute before Luce shook her grocery bag. Like a parachute out of this stalemate of a conversation. "Welp! Mama needs romaine."

"Tight. Susan loves lettuce."

*Oh, my God, shut the fuck up.*

Lucy made a face and nodded. She started off but stopped. Looked back at me. "I got back from Spooktacular kinda early. Around sunup. Coulda sworn I saw Sandro Miceli leaving here. Dressed kinda like you."

My stomach fell out of my ass and broke through the sidewalk. Hit the earth's core and ran right through to Australia. I just shook my head. "...I was in Maine."

She seemed to accept that. Or maybe she was just over holding a conversation for both parties. She put her headphones in and was gone. I started breathing again and ran inside. Dro had left at four in the damn morning. We couldn't have been more careful. And I did us no favors, stumbling over my words like that with Lucy. Like there was something to cover up. And I was talking so well before that.

I ran through every incriminating beat of my conversation with Lucy that night after dinner. I was at the kitchen counter, trying to focus on my college app notes, when I got distracted by a scribble hidden in the margins.

*Tell D 2 slap?*

I guess I'd written it that night in my room. When I was researching colleges after LubeGate. I chuckled to myself.

"What's so funny?"

I forgot Del was in the room. He was researching financial aid packages on our laptop. What *was* so funny? It wasn't so much that I'd left a reminder to ask Sandro to try giving me a little slap next go-around. I think it was the fact that I wrote the note at all, where anyone could find it.

"Nothing. Just something stupid."

I erased the scribble. We were about an hour deep into Del's postdinner campaign to get me to expand my college choices and, while I was a little over it, I was impressed at how easy the conversation was flowing. It's not usually like that.

Del turned the laptop to me. "How 'bout Drexel?"

"Too expensive."

"Villanova? That scout last May loved you."

"I don't have the grades."

"Sure you do. And it's a great school. Great track program."

I know Nova's got a great track program. That's why it's on my fake "backup" list. All the schools I'd go to if Rutgers was wiped off the map. But I knew what I wanted.

"You need other choices, Seb. Deadlines are coming up quick."

"And my Rutgers app is good and submitted."

Del stood up. Leaned on the counter. We were talking better, sure, but I still felt that pang of guilt when he looked at me sometimes. He just makes me feel watched. "Take Mom out of it for a sec."

"Why?"

"She wanted you to go to *college*. And I think Rutgers is great. I hope you get it, I do. But with your times and some effort? You have options."

I didn't think we were ready for this kind of conversation. But I took a page from my time with Sandro and tested my own water.

*Start with a fact. Something you know for sure.*

"...I wanna go for her."

My voice did something around Del. It got quieter. Like a

kid apologizing for losing his bike. Like I thought he'd chew me out if I didn't come in soft.

He nodded. "I know. But she wouldn't want you just going for her. It should be your decision, Seb. What *you* want."

Del calls me Seb and it always hits my ear wrong. Lucy does it too sometimes. I'm not *Seb*. I haven't been *Seb* since I was a kid. But Del saw me as this kid that I wasn't anymore. Maybe that's why we couldn't talk. Maybe that was my problem.

So, I sat straight and looked at him. Stopped sounding like a kid. "Del... This is all I've wanted. For a long time. I get having the backups and we should do them but I just... I know. I know it's what I want. I want to go to Rutgers. And I just gotta follow that."

I could tell he heard me. Was really listening to me. I think it surprised him, that I was actually speaking to him like that.

"You remember the race car bed? The red one you *had* to have?" I smiled. The race car bed was bitchin'. I used to rush to the mailbox every weekend just to grab the new Toys R Us catalog. Clip out another picture of the bed for my wish list. "You never asked for anything. Every Christmas your mom just had to guess then, BAM, you saw that bed. It was all you talked about for months."

"Then I got it and was pissed it couldn't drive."

"Which we told you a thousand times."

We laughed. 'Cause I was such a brat about it. I refused to sleep in the thing unless Del slapped an engine and some real tires on it. A couple weeks later, they replaced it with the bed I have now. It was the first Christmas Del was a part of our family. I hadn't thought about that in years. I could feel where he was going with it.

"You don't want a lot, Seb. So, when you find something you do, you get tunnel vision. It's the sprinter in you. You stop thinking about the long run." I looked at my feet. I forgot what people like Del can do. Like Lucy. They can see all the places that you're weak. "It's about finding the right way to want something."

I could feel myself retreating. I think Del could feel it too. He backed away and poured himself some coffee. Poured me one too. Cream for him, black for me. My eyes were still on my feet.

"Where's Sandro applying?"

"Northwestern. Rutgers as a safety. But he'll get it. He's smart." My voice had gone back to quiet. Del did nothing wrong but I still felt like I'd been screamed at.

"...He's a good kid." Del slid me my coffee. "You both are."

He put his hand on my shoulder. I smiled a bit. Del thought I was good. Good like Sandro. He didn't know. He wouldn't think I was good if he knew all the things I'd done. The kids I've hurt. All the terrible versions of myself I became after Mom left us. But I smiled. 'Cause it was a nice thought. Being like Sandro.

Del and I hadn't talked like that in years. That's how it used to be with Del. He might never be my dad, but I used to be able to check in with him like that. Get real advice. And he's right, I should be looking into other schools. I do get a little too focused when I find something I want. I guess the lesson there was that talking didn't have to be easy. Sometimes it was work. But it was better than the alternative.

Between Lucy and Del, the week was feeling like a pop quiz on my conversational skills. A little midterm review to see if I'd learned anything from my time with a certain Italian man. Though if those chats were quizzes, this morning's phone call must've been the final. The real test. But I guess if I didn't pick up, I never would've put a voice to all the stories.

It had been a chill morning. I was sitting on the couch, icing my ankle after my one run of the day. I started feeling this weird click during my last mile and I thought I'd better be safe than sorry. Then I got a text from Dro.

S: sayno

Then my phone rang. I put my icepack down and answered. Dro was somewhere loud and midconversation with someone.

"—*twenty different kinds of red sauce, I don't know!*"

"What?"

"*Yeah, it's him.* Bash? My mother would like to—"

I heard the phone change hands and Sandro take the Lord's name in vain. The new voice was a lot like Dro's. Raspy and a little tired. But a lot more direct.

"—*take the Lord's name in public, my God.* Sebastian?"

"...Speaking?"

"Sebastian, this is Claudia. Claudia Miceli. Dro's ma?"

I'd just read the word *shanghaied* in a book and had to look it up in the dictionary to make sure it wasn't racist. It's funny how you learn a new word one day then it seems to pop up in your life.

On this call, I felt *shanghaied*.

"Oh. Hello, Mrs. Miceli. What can—"

"Listen, so Dro's dad and the boys are all gonna be home Friday and I want you to join us for dinner, okay? We're doing chicken but I can do a salad too if you're not big on chicken. You like chicken, Sebastian? *Tina. Tina. Tee, I am so clearly on the telephone. What did—*"

"Hello?"

"—*bother your brother.* Yes? Perfect. It's Dro's favorite. Right? *Dro? It's his favorite.*"

"Uh, wha—"

"Okay, superb. I am just so excited to meet you, we all are. When this one told me he'd been letting someone drive him to school every day for months without ever letting me feed him, I nearly broke a plate over— *Well, because it's rude, Sandro. It's rude! I didn't raise you to—*"

"Hello?"

"Okay, sweetheart, it's so nice finally talking with you. Dinner's at seven."

And she hung up. Jesus. My phone screen returned to my texts.

S: sayno

Oh. *Say no.* I was supposed to say no.

I guess there was still room for improvement on the speaking front but two out of three successful conversations this week wasn't bad. Sixty-six percent. Which, hey, not an F. I was busy patting myself on the back when I felt a pang again. This throbbing itch somewhere in me. But it wasn't my ankle. Another text popped up.

S: were fucked dude...

It was my stomach. Folding in on itself.
I was having dinner with the Micelis.

# sandro

### *BASH THE FLASH*

Bash has never stepped foot inside my home. This was on purpose. The last time I had a friend over was Drew Udell in the sixth grade. We weren't really *friends*, but he was fun and we teamed up for a history project. Within an hour of Drew's stepmom dropping him off, GJ threw up on our book bags, my shirtless dad came through screaming at his phone, and Raph pushed me into a wall for playing his *GTA* save file. Drew's stepmom was back before I had time to defrost the pizza bagels I'd bought for the event.

The problem with tidying up my house is everyone reads into it. *"Who you trying to impress?"* I didn't want to show my hand with all my cleaning and primping. I didn't want them

to smell that desperation on me. How badly I wanted the
dinner to go well. Because we've shared a lot, me and Bash.
But we weren't prepared for something like this.

It was almost seven and I was searching everywhere to find
Lexi's Binky. She was screaming like I'd just poured salt in
her eyes and no one had any clue where she'd left it. I was
running around when I got a text from Ronny.

R: Recording sesh tonight?
R: Just learned the keys to Black Parade :O

So tempting but so not the time, Ron.

S: familyt dinner. Supes busy

I scanned the upstairs for Binky because Tina recently developed a habit of stealing random objects and letting them
marinate in the bathtub. I hollered down the hall for assis-
tance but Gio was at work and Raph was too busy "sending
emails" in his room to help. I found the pacifier in the half-
full tub along with my shot put and the spare van keys when
I got another text.

R: demo deadlines coming up
R: ur gonna have to hang with us one of these day dro
R: we don't bite

Wow, Veronica, not now. I grabbed some towels and
cleaned the bathwater off Tina's contraband with one hand,
texting with the other.

S: sorry just very stressed rn. Ill call you later

R: wtf don't call me, never call me, just text

I rolled my eyes and gave myself a once-over in the mirror. I was plucking the odd nose hairs when I felt another text buzz on my thigh. Jesus, Ronny, take the hint.

B: Here?

Fuck. Bash. I ran face-first into the closed bathroom door then rushed to the stairs. Bash was just standing in the open doorway, looking in from the porch. I jumped down the stairs, almost falling, and dragged him in.

"Sorry. The door was wide-open."

"Of course it fucking was."

"Is someone fighting?"

There was indistinct yelling coming from somewhere in the kitchen area. Definitely Ma but the male voice could've been Gio, Dad, or Raph. "Probably."

"I brought this."

Bash offered me one of those Yankee Candles I always stop to sniff at Target. All the smells of *White Winter Wonderland* in one glass jar. "...Why?"

"You said your ma like candles. My mom said you always bring—"

"Leave it outside." I took it out of his hands and placed it on the porch. He looked confused. "It's too much, man."

"Uh, it's a *candle*."

"It's too considerate. They'll think something's up."

"Oh. Okay."

"It's sweet but... I just wanna be safe."

Bash nodded and I finally took a moment to look at him in the nice navy polo he bought for this. God, he looked good. It wasn't fair. Bash was wasted on my family. He could tell I was ogling him and smiled. I wanted to tell him how sorry I was that this night was about to happen when, from the depths of hell, Ma screamed.

*"Is he here?! SANDRO!?"*

I cocked my head skyward and screamed back. "YEAH!"

*"WELL?! How long's he been here?! Bring him IN!!"*

Bash chuckled. I'm glad he found it funny then. He wouldn't soon. I could already feel my heart rate rising. Something that hadn't happened since October. The weight room. I had to stay calm tonight or this house was gonna burn down.

I tried breathing and Bash rested a hand on my shoulder. "Hey. It'll be fun. Or, at least, *fine.* We'll—"

I moved away from his touch. There were just too many ways my family could fuck this up for me. I didn't need to hand them their shot. He nodded. He got it.

"Okay. We just gotta get through one—"

My mom screamed my name again from the kitchen and I gave up.

The meal was chicken parm, a staple in the Miceli home that Ma could and has made in her sleep. To her credit, my mother knows how to make something as basic as discounted deli chicken and bread crumbs into something impressive. She's always been good with presentation stuff like that.

It wasn't that a dinner at the Miceli table was a surefire recipe for disaster. If that were the case, I would've told Ma that Bash had moved to Paris or got drafted or something simple. Anything to keep him from facing this particular firing squad. But the Miceli dinner table could be a fun night of all right pasta and good conversation if nothing went wrong. If we could keep things civil and light. If we could be a respectable Italian family, like my cousins down the shore or any other branch of our family tree. If we could just be easy for one fucking night, Bash would be okay. We could be okay.

I made sure to sit across from Bash so I could keep an eye on him. Gauge how he looked through the ordeal. Ma hadn't even sat down yet and Gio and Raph were already halfway through shoving their plates down their gullets. Ma slapped the table and they stopped. I watched them settle and wondered which Miceli might ruin this night.

Luckily, GJ and Tina ate earlier so they were locked away in the TV room and out of the running. My dad was slammed with work and holed up in his office which most nights I would find rude but felt like a gift from above tonight. If, by the grace of God, he could stay in there the whole time, I'd really only have to worry about my brothers. Ma can be careless and sometimes hurtful, but a guest is a guest.

Ma started pouring everyone wine. "Red okay, Sebastian?"

Bash had remained perfectly still in his seat thus far, only speaking when spoken to. Smart strategy. He gave me a look and I nodded, ever so slightly.

"Yes. Thank you, Mrs. Miceli."

"Please, call me Claudia, sweetheart." She all but emptied the bottle into his glass. Bash drank enough to keep it from spilling over and smiled his polite approval. Ma sat down and served herself salad. "And I am so, so sorry about my husband. We usually eat as a family but he told us to start with-out him. Just wrapping up a call in his study."

Gio swallowed a burp. "*Our* study."

Everyone but Bash stifled a groan. Gio's got this stick up his ass about Pop's repairs business being "their business" now that he's got his roofing license. Ma pointed Gio to *their* study. "Then go check on him."

Gio grumbled and got up. Bash took another sip of wine and smiled at Ma. "Thank you for having me. The chicken's really good."

"Glad we could finally get you here! It's the least we could do with all the gas you're wasting coming out to the edge of town."

*Wasting.*

Raph sucked up a noodle and pointed Bash's way. "The Cinnaminson Trials are coming up soon, yeah? Winter Trials? How's Coach feeling?"

Bash looked confused. I never should've told Raph about the running.

"Raph used to be long-distance captain."

"No shit."

Bash caught himself and apologized to Ma for swearing.

"Why? People curse."

"Yeah, I was captain junior and senior year."

I mumbled to no one that Raph's senior year was a decade ago. But if the men in my family like to dwell on anything more than my shortcomings, it's their glory days.

"I still keep up with Bianco. Heard all about you."

"Oh. All good things, I hope."

"Yeah. You've made a real name for yourself, *Bash the Flash*."

I'd doubled down on my suspicions that Raph would be the one to ruin dinner when my dad and Gio stormed in, vying for the belt. As is custom, Pop was winning whatever they were arguing about.

"It doesn't matter who he knows, we can't work with that Greek piece of shit." Ma and I took a long sip of wine as Pop zeroed in on the new face at his table. "Who the fuck are you?"

Bash had been doing really well up to that point. He'd complimented the chicken, drank a little but not too much wine, knew all the words to our grace. He even stood up to shake my dad's hand, one of those pointlessly classy acts that go a long way with guys like Gio Sr.

Then he opened his mouth.

"Hey. Hi. My name's—I'm Bash. My name is Bash. Sebastian. Villeda. I know your son. *Him*."

Bash pointed at me and I could read the *What the fuck am I doing?* in his eyes. He was nervous. He's shit with words when he's nervous. That was not good. Everyone sat down and Bash drank a bit more wine.

Ma refilled his only half-drunk glass. "This is the boy who's been driving your injured son around every day."

"Which, again, is really no—"

"Why y'gotta say it like that? You could drive him around."

"You could too."

"So could Raph."

"So could Gio!"

"Fuck you, I work."

"We all work, Gio! Watch your mouth."

I couldn't tell who was saying what because I was very focused on cutting my pasta into tinier and tinier pieces. Anything to not be at that table. My dad cleared his throat loudly. Gross throat-clearing is essentially my dad's catch-phrase. It's a disgusting byproduct of years of smoking cigars that he uses to control conversations. "Where you going to college, Sebastian?"

Odd question.

"Uh, Rutgers. Hopefully."

Raph smiled, practically drooling over what he could add to this conversation. "On a sprinting scholarship, I bet. This kid's crazy fast. Pop was a sprinter too. At Moorestown."

Bash smiled. "Yeah? Sandro never mentioned."

Thanks for the shout-out, pal. I never mentioned this to Bash because why would I? I do field because they did track. I play guitar because they played football. I don't talk about their pasts because it's all they ever do. So, I just shrugged.

My dad snorted. "Dro's just pissed he can't run for shit. What's your four hundred?"

"Just broke fifty."

"Fuck off."

Bash nodded, seeming grateful that his speed was making up for his weird introduction. "Forty-nine, six. For real."

My dad slapped the table. Hard. It shook the wineglasses. "Forty-nine!? Damn!"

Ma winced at Pop's language. "What, is that good?"

My brothers nodded along, impressed because Dad was impressed.

"*Good?* Bianco's gotta be wiping your ass for you."

"Yeah, yeah. He's a fan."

I watched Bash laugh and take a drink. Something was off. Raph patted him on the back, very chummy. Like a brother. My dad spoke with a mouth full of chicken. "Keep that pace and you got your pick of schools. Why slum it at Rutgers?"

Ma motioned for him to close his mouth and chew. "Sebastian, Rutgers is a great school. And it's so close, you could practically commute."

I felt an invisible kick in the shin. This again. *"Ma."*

"What?"

My dad leaned in closer to Bash. "Sandro's ma here wants him to go to Rutgers so he'll stay close."

"It would just be so helpful."

I couldn't keep having this conversation. "I'm going to Northwestern."

Raph chuckled. "Like you're getting into Northwestern."

"Fuck you, fat ass."

Ma slapped the table and we quieted down. Raph kicked me like a fucking asshole but I swallowed the hit. I'd made a career out of swallowing dinner table kicks from my brothers.

Gio reached for the wine bottle and cleared his throat, I assume trying to copy my dad. "You date Lucy Jordan, yeah? Her brother and me go back."

"Oh, shit. Yeah, Perry's awesome. Taught me how to dunk."

"Guess who taught him?" Gio tipped his glass and patted himself on the back. Bash laughed.

I hated this. This obvious bonding my brothers were trying to do. I considered just getting drunk. Ma smiled at Bash, happy to find a segue out of our usual sports talk. "Cutie, you have a girlfriend? How long have you two been together?"

"Oh. We, uh, no, we actually broke up. But I've known her my whole life. Neighbors."

"Aww, that's too bad. Nothing like a high school romance."

My dad laughed. "Speaking of romances, give us the dirt on lover boy over here." Bash went still. My dad punched me in the arm which, of everything that annoyed me about him, was probably the one thing I truly despised. "Sneaking out every other night to see his little gal pal. You know Veronica? The DiSarios are good people."

"Oh. Uh…yeah. I know Ron."

Pop smiled over his wine. "Look, we all did it at your age. Snuck out. Kept secrets. Every man should have a secret fling or two. Get it out of his system before settling down."

Ma toasted her husband. "Very romantic, G."

My parents both took sips and Pop's hand clamped onto the back of my neck. Another laugh I didn't like. Another touch I didn't ask for. "How 'bout it then, Flash? Sandro got a secret friend he's too afraid to bring home?"

I bit my cheek. I tasted blood. Bash looked for my cue but it was a lose-lose. He could blow up my lie and make me look like an ass or continue my lie and make me look like a coward. There were no good answers at this table.

So, Bash shook his head. "Nope. Definitely, no. No secrets."

He just shouldn't have answered. Or I should've prepped him more. You never answer bait like that. That's how they get you.

Raph chuckled. *"Definitely."*

"No, I mean—"

"Dro can't keep a secret worth dick."

My brothers laughed at Bash. I watched him struggle to find the right words. Land whatever case he felt a need to make for me. He was trying to speak through his nerves. To get back control.

"I just meant that some guys don't do that. Girlfriends. Some guys are...you know. Late bloomers."

The table burst out laughing. Everyone but Bash and I found that hilarious. Pop patted Bash on the back, just eating up this fresh voice at his dinner table. Raph touched my cheek and I swatted his hand away.

"*Late bloomer.* Kid's had a mustache since he was eight."

Ma reached over and put her hand on my face. "My hairy baby. I remember, every other Sunday, I had to trap him in the bathroom and wax that dirt off his mouth."

Everyone laughed again. Wave after wave of well-meaning, shit-eating laughs. Bash smiled, happy the focus moved off our secrets. "Aaaah. So, he was born hairy?"

"Please. The doctors thought I'd given birth to a monkey."

Ma tickled my lip and I pulled away. She made the ticking sound she makes when I'm *not being a good sport.* "Aww. Don't get angry, baby, we're just having fun. He get this pissy with you, Sebastian?"

Raph all but raised his glass in a toast to Bash. "Please. *Bash the Flash* don't take that shit. I heard you once knocked a kid out cold for stepping in your lane. In the middle of a race."

Pop smiled in appreciation of the stranger he already preferred to his actual son. "Amazing."

Bash finished his glass and laughed. Not his machine gun. His booming laugh. His flashy one. "Nah, hey, come on now.

It was *after* the race. And this dude was full-on LIVING in my lane. I had to fucking leapfrog over him just to pass."

My family laughed with Bash the Flash. My dad had to catch his breath, he was laughing so hard. The Flash could really work a room. I just watched him go as all the voices blurred together.

"That's a fucking sprinter for you. Knocked him out cold?"

"One hit, floored his ass."

"You box?"

"When I need to, y'know?"

"Atta-fucking-boy."

"We bought a group pass to this boxing gym in Lenola."

"You could take Dro's spot. He never comes with us."

This is what they do. They take everything good in my life and make it theirs. I don't get to be Sandro. At this table, we're just The Micelis. And I'm the worst one.

I tried speaking. "I have a broken foot."

Bash refilled his wine. Didn't even look at me when he said it. "You could box on that foot." *Look at me, Bash.* "I once medaled in relay with a broken arm."

Raph and Gio made impressed grunts.

"Bash the fucking Flash."

*Bash the fucking Flash.*

"That's not the same thing."

Pop and Gio turned on me. Offended I'd come for their new best friend.

"It's impressive, Sandro."

"More than you could do."

My jaw clenched. "I'm *hurt.*"

They laughed.

"Whose fault is that?"

"Yeah, the two of us are on roofs every day and we've never fallen off."

Bash chuckled. "Well, y'all are prolly not sleeping on them."

He took a long drink.

*No.*

Everyone turned to him. Ma put her glass down. "...What?"

Then the eyes were on me. I could feel them turn. But I didn't look at them. I just stared at Bash and wondered if he understood what he'd said.

"Sandro, you were sleeping on the roof when you fell?"

Bash the fucking Flash. My dad cleared his throat just to scoff. "You fucking *idiot*."

Bash got it then. "Wait."

But it was too late. Their voices piled onto me.

*"Are you fucking kidding me?"*

*"Why were you sleeping on the goddamn roof, Sandro?!"*

*"Fucking idiot."*

*"I had to take off work for you."*

*"Just a fucking idiot."*

*"The doctor's bills alone—"*

*"And you got the fucking balls to complain—"*

*"And we're supposed to be chauffeuring your ass—"*

*"Dumb fuck."*

*"Dumb fucking—"*

*"Fucking dumb—"*

*"Always so goddamn—"*

It rose and rose, and I could feel that scratching in my heart. I couldn't see. My face was on fire and I could feel tears burning up my throat. Then Pop slammed his fork against his plate, silencing the voices. I saw Bash jump before I glued my eyes to my lap.

I needed to leave. Or something was going to happen. My ears were scalding. Popping. Then my dad's voice. The disappointed anger. "I took you to the ER in the middle of the goddamn night because you fell asleep?! On the fucking—" His hand slapped the table. Glasses rang. "**LOOK** AT ME when I am **TALKING** TO YOU."

I did. I looked him in the eyes. And I knew he could see it in me. That I was about to cry. Break. Crumble under all the emotions he didn't like me having. He was fuming. I could see the red pouring into his face. I'd never seen that happen before. "...Un-*fucking*-believable."

He tossed his napkin down and stomped out. Gio followed. I was back to my lap. It was almost over. I could hear Ma apologize to Bash. Say it's not usually like this. That my family isn't always like this. Then she was gone too. Then silence.

"Sandro."

Did he want me to look at him? Is that what *Bash the Flash* wanted?

I didn't think it would be him. I knew it would end like this but I never would've guessed that he'd be the reason. I should've. The signs were there. All the data. I should've known. How disappointing. How fucking disappointing.

The last thing I heard before the front door slammed behind me was Raph. "Classic Sandro."

My crutches never worked on all the loose gravel in my driveway so I threw them down and walked. I was breathing fast. So fucking fast it hurt. The air was cold but if I could just get to the Sticks. I didn't even need the Sticks, if I could just get away. I just needed to go. I needed to be alone. I could hear him running down the driveway.

"Sandro! DRO!"

He was fast but his footsteps were unsteady in the gravel. They stopped behind me and he put his hand on my wrist. The balls to think I wanted his hands on me.

*"Don't touch me."*

I ripped my arm away from him and walked faster. I passed our mailbox and slipped on some gravel. I could barely see in the dark. I could barely see at all. But Bash wouldn't stop.

"Sandro, you need to talk to—"

He grabbed me by the shoulder. His grip was tight and desperate and wouldn't let go. He wouldn't let me go.

"Dro, you need to calm—"

"DON'T FUCKING TOUCH ME."

I pushed Bash off of me. Not hard but not soft either. Then it was just sounds. Gravel slipping under a dress shoe. A gasp. The crack of metal on bone. A cry. His back knocking against the ground. His head knocking against the stones. Panting. Breathing.

It was hard to see in the dark. But what I understood was Bash had tripped. A push, then a trip, then my mailbox. And when my eyes adjusted to the night, I could see that Bash's eyebrow had split open. Clipped on some part of that old, rusted thing. His blood looked black in the dark and it ran down his cheek. Into his mouth. Onto his new navy polo.

"Sandro."

He just looked up at me. The moon on his face. His beautiful face. He didn't even try to stop the bleeding. Like it hadn't sunk in yet. What just happened. What I just did.

"Sandro."

I covered my mouth. What did I do? What the fuck did I do?

"Sandro?"

I was backing away. I couldn't see where I was going but I couldn't stop. He should have left me alone. Everyone. I needed to be left alone.

"Sandro...wait."

I shook my head. *"I'm so sorry. I'm so sorry."*

I turned away and I left Bash alone.

# winter

*In the depths of winter, I finally learned that within me there lay an invincible summer.*

—*Albert Camus*

# bash

*help*

I once told Sandro that I'd never been called a faggot before.
  That wasn't true.
  I grew up with that word. Because of who I am, the guys
I hung out with, I've been called a fag more times than I've
been called Sebastian. It's just one of those words you put up
with. On the away bus. In the locker room. In class. In fun.
Liking dudes was a joke. I wasn't lying when I said it was
mostly joking around. It was. Mostly.
  When I was little, I went trick-or-treating with these older
kids on my block. It was getting dark and they wanted to
sneak off to the Sticks and drink these beers they stole. We
were near the duplex and I *knew* if I went off with these boys,

Mom would find me out. Things always got back to her. Or she'd ask, "How was trick-or-treating, Seb?" and I wouldn't be able to lie to her.

I said I didn't want to go. I just wanted to keep trick-or-treating. So, Tank Lombardo called me a faggot and shoved me into a telephone pole. It was one of those old wooden ones and a splinter tore into my cheek. Ripped the Ash Ketchum costume Mom made me. Some other big kid gave Tank shit for it, but the night was done for me. Halloween was over and I needed to go home.

When I got back, Del caught me before Mom could see what happened. I couldn't tell him, but I think he knew. He bandaged me up and we didn't say a word. And when I started crying, he hugged me and let me cry. I was ten. It was the first time I let him see me cry.

It was a lot like Halloween that night. After that dinner. I was running home in the dark. Bleeding. Hoping no one would see me. Del told me he'd be at the Zelley site till late so, if I ran fast enough, I could've hidden the polo, showered up, and stopped the bleeding. If I was fast enough, I could've gotten into bed before he had time to see me.

People kept honking at me on the street. Maybe they thought I was dying. My face was caked in blood and dirt and my new shirt was ruined. I just had to run faster. At some point, I threw off the polo and sprinted home in my undershirt.

The door was locked so I sat on the porch and tried to think of my next move. The spare key was in Birdie with Del. Lucy had one but I couldn't let her see me like this. I could go to Matty's. Tell him I got jumped. Maybe by those

Cinnaminson kids. Maybe he'd forgive me for thinking I was too good for him. But Matty's was so far and I was so tired.

I watched my breath in the cold air. Still breathing. Guess I wasn't dead.

"Seb?"

But I wasn't fast enough.

Del was at the curb, pulling paint cans off Birdie. Maybe if I'd driven, none of it would've happened. Del wouldn't have dropped me off early. I would've had the drive to myself, time to get my head right. If I drove, I could've reminded myself what I was risking. If I drove, Del wouldn't have caught me there.

"What are you doing back? I woulda come and got ya."

Then he saw my face. Del dropped his paint cans and ran up through the yard. He knelt by me and took my busted face, moving it into the moonlight. I could feel the split skin move open. My face felt loose. Like it could've fallen off right on the porch.

"Who?"

Of course Del thought someone had punched me. I couldn't have just run into a stop sign or fallen down some stairs. Smashed my face into a mailbox all on my own. That's not me. *Bash the Flash* fights. He can't help it.

I moved Del's hands away and tried my best *Flashy* laugh. Aloof. Above it all. Like this sorta thing happened every week. "Chill, man. It's cool. I just—"

*"Sebastian."*

He wasn't letting me lie. If he just let me do what I do and lie to him, it would've been easier. Getting punched would have been easier. I got into some shit with some dude over some bull. None of it mattered. It didn't have to matter.

"Del, it's fine. This asshole was mouthing off and I had to—"

"Where's Sandro?"

*Where's Sandro?*

Like we're some inseparable pair? Like I knew where he was at all times? Like I could feel it like a punch in my stomach that he was somewhere in the Sticks, angry and terrified and alone? My jaw was grinding and I could taste the blood drying on my teeth. I tried to look away. To lie.

"He fuckin—"

The words tripped in my throat.

Why couldn't I just lie? Say Sandro pissed me off, so I bounced? Say I got into it with some private school punk? Talk shit like I have been the last four years? I've spent all this time trying to let Bash the Flash die, then when I actually want him, when I'm not at the fucking Miceli dinner table, I can't do it?

"Sandro—"

I couldn't. I couldn't do it anymore. This stuttering sob cut me off. It sounded like a laugh. My laugh. A machine gun. Quick and pained and never-ending. It all melted away and I broke down into Del.

And he held me. Like I was that sad little kid on Halloween. I dug my face into his shoulder and tried to stop. But I couldn't help myself.

I just couldn't help myself.

# sandro

### *A CRYING SHAME*

When I was little, we lost our house. It was a nice place. Right off Main Street, behind our old church. My room was by the front door and we had a piano no one played. I don't remember much from that house. But I know things were quieter. My brothers were still trying to do something with their lives and my parents didn't have so much to survive. My life was allowed to be simple and the sounds inside me still made sense. Then Pop's partner fucked him over and the repairs business went under. That was the end of everything. All the quiet. We had no place to go. Ma's family wasn't an option and my dad didn't have much family left. So, we split up.

Raph hadn't alienated his football friends yet and had a network of couches to surf. Gio's girlfriend Eunice had one of those carriage houses in her backyard and kept him hidden the whole time. G had it easiest. Probably too easy 'cause GJ was born within a year. Dad found work with a college buddy in AC. Three short-term construction gigs that would get us above water. Ma and me were supposed to hole up in a motel until he got back but the money just wasn't there. So, we slept in the van.

I spent the first week trying to convince her that it was fun. That I didn't mind. It was a warm September and I'd always liked camping. It could be fun if we made it fun. We'd been through so much together already, this was another problem to get through. Claudia and her baby. Her sweet boy. Her favorite helper.

I spent the second week with a stomach bug. It wasn't so fun anymore. I got them a lot as a kid and they took so much out of me. Out of Ma too. She would have to hold my hand from start to finish. I'd get so scared. I was always convinced that something was wrong, this time was different, I was dying. And that time around, when I threw up all over the steering wheel, Ma just broke. It was too much.

She'd been so steady up till then. Her home was gone, her family was divided, and she'd spent the past two weeks sleeping in a van, showering at the gym, and working retail all day. It took her remaining child painting half her new home in vomit to finally crack. She screamed at me. At God. At Pop for choosing a shady partner. At McDonald's for giving me the ammo. At her parents for not helping us. At herself, for breaking.

But she stopped when I started to cry. Her tears shut off and she reset. Took my face and looked me in the eyes.

*"No more."*

I'll never forget her expression. So much need staring back at me. Like all would be right in our world if I could just stay strong. Stay smiling. Stay helpful. That's when I decided the best thing I could do for my family was hide. Wait until Ma slept to throw up. Never let them see me cry. If I was going to have all these emotions, this orchestra inside of me, they had to be mine. That's how I could help.

It wasn't so hot outside Dr. Kizer's strip mall when I went for my follow-up. New Jersey didn't get a white Christmas but the clouds made up for it by icing over everything. Tip to taint.

I was back on that exam table, freezing my toes off, while Ma talked to Dr. Kizer about my foot meds. I was barely listening.

"He can run out his prescription on these yella fellas, but let's wean off any pain relievers once he's feeling comfortable."

"And he's done, yeah? After this?"

"He's a strong boy. Healed well, considering all the walking."

"Oh, we won't be making that mistake again."

I couldn't stop looking at my foot. Finally free. No more cast, no more boot, no more crutches. No more questions, no more pity, no more shame. *No more.*

I thought about all the things that were over in my life. No more Sticks. After that dinner, I spent the night in the ditch. Had a runny nose the rest of the week. I don't think I can go back there anymore. No more sex. That sucks. I think I was getting good at it. No more discovery. All this data wasted. No more sharing. Even with all these things I still needed to say. No more Wawa. No more driving. No more talking. No more Bash.

And I thought about how small my world was. It had to be pretty small if one night can knock it all over. But that's what happened. The world had knocked over. Because of me. What I did.

I hated Bash for ten minutes. I hated him from the moment he laughed his *Bash the Flash* laugh to the moment my hand touched his chest. I told him not to touch me. I told him a thousand times, a thousand different ways, I don't like being touched like that. When I'm like that. But then his head hit my mailbox and everything stopped. All that heat, all that anger boiling inside of me, evaporated. The hate I felt for Bash, for my family, steamed out of my pores and into the air and I could see again. I could see the boy I'd hurt. Bleeding on the ground. His face. What I'd done.

Then all that hate and all that anger found me again. It collected in the air and sank back into my skin and it told me I was disgusting. An animal. A dangerous, nauseating beast that didn't deserve people. Didn't deserve Bash. Didn't deserve to learn or grow or escape. I was always going to be a Miceli. A loud, mean bully who leaves people hurt. Leaves them in the dirt. I wanted to learn what to do with all this noise that lived inside of me but maybe that's all it ever was. Anger and hate. Ways to hurt.

I didn't mean to hurt him. I never wanted to leave him. But he was better off without me. It had to be the safer road. Because maybe Bash was right. Maybe my barometer's broken. Maybe someone broke it. Maybe when you're a kid and you make a mistake and your dad splits your eyebrow with a fucking jewelry box, maybe that splits something inside too. Maybe that scar changes you. Changes how you take your hits. How you hit back. And now we match, me and Bash. Now we both have reminders. Right above our eyes, a reminder that someone hurt us. Someone important hurt us then left us. Someone who was supposed to love us. 'Cause that's the thing. That's what knocked over my world. I think I was supposed to love Bash. I really think that's where this road was taking me, but I couldn't even do that right. And now I won't get the chance.

That thought made me want to cry. And how pathetic would I look if I started crying in Dr. Kizer's office? That thought made me angry. Because they wouldn't try to help. Dr. Kizer would make some joke about school or hormones. Ma would ask if I was sick or hungry. But never if I was okay. Never ask if I was hurting.

That's what these past few weeks have been. Thoughts of crying. Thoughts of anger. But when I'm at dinner and my family is fighting and I see all the reasons to get angry, nothing. When I'm alone in my bed, in my attic, hearing the sound of a head hitting a mailbox, tears don't come. There's nothing. All my noise is gone.

"No more."

I said it to no one.

# bash

*smile*

I was on the away bus, keeping my eyes to myself and trying my best to disappear into my hoodie, when I wondered if I was born an asshole or if the universe was determined to make me one. I've just been in a dick mood lately. These past few weeks felt like I'd been in a really nice coma, having some real nice coma dreams, then suddenly my insurance got rejected and now I'm back on the streets, dealing with all these fuckers wondering where I've been. Only I can't tell them I've been in a coma. I can't tell them what was so good about my life.

The other day, Del asked me where I disappear to every

night. I can't tell him that I need to burn off a few miles on the track to get to sleep. Avi asked where my "nice attitude" went. I can't tell him that my nice attitude left me bleeding out in his fucking driveway. I can't tell them that. I can't tell anyone much of anything since that dinner.

I've just been simmering in this frustration the past few weeks. The holidays were a bust and I couldn't even enjoy the gift my mom left for me. On Christmas morning, Del brought me a random selection off her gift pile and it was the first bright spot in my crappy winter. I was almost excited for a moment. The present was in an envelope and we both assumed it'd be a letter. She'd written me a bunch of letters and I'm sure Del thought some life advice might do me well about then. I still reread the one I got for my sixteenth birthday weekly. She talks about how I would cry all night as a kid and the only thing that'd calm me down was a drive in our truck. A talk in our field.

But the Christmas envelope just had a small card. Three letters, her handwriting.

## DAR

Not a word, right? I scoured the internet for what it could mean. *Daughters of the American Revolution?* What a caveman would say if he got confused? I was certain Mom was just fucking with me. The card was an elaborate prank from the beyond. It wouldn't be out of character for her.

To throw more frustration in the works, the envelope was full of seeds. SEEDS. What the hell, right? Do I eat them? Do I plant them? What kind are they? Maybe I'm weird or whatever but I can't just identify seeds off sight, I'm not Johnny fucking Appleseed.

If the seeds were supposed to help me solve *DAR*, or vice versa, they didn't. The riddle eluded me all winter break. It continues to elude me. Normally, Mom's little puzzles make the present feel bigger. A scavenger hunt through our memories together. But the mystery of the seeds just added to this low boil in my stomach that's been cooking me from the inside since that night in that long gravel driveway. Of course, she couldn't have just sent me a nice fucking note. That'd be too easy. Not enough hoops to jump through. Not for Bash the Flash. That guy loves a hurdle.

I haven't lost it yet. I'm barely keeping it together, but no one's pushed me over. I did come close. With Raph Miceli of all people. He was one of the romantics slumming it at the diner yesterday. To be clear, Raph brought his seven-months-pregnant girlfriend to a Valentine's lunch at a diner by the highway. I'd not seen hide nor hair of the Micelis since the dinner and Raph was near the bottom of my People I Want Interrupting Me at Work list. He'd really pissed me off that night. Buttering me up like we were best buds, like I didn't just see him shit on Sandro. He's the exact type of Jersey-specific asshole that can get me nervous. Got me nervous. Got me *Flashy*.

Raph took one look at the scar on my eyebrow and told me I was lucky. I didn't understand him at first, but I guess Sandro told the family that I got in a wreck. That was why I hadn't been coming around. Why Raph's had to drive him to school. It was a good lie. Sandro was good at lying to his family. Probably better when he didn't have some asshole telling his secrets at their dinner table. I thought of Dro sitting in shotgun every morning with Raph. Not talking, not laughing at the bad jokes, not singing along to the morning radio. He wouldn't put his big leg up on Raph's dashboard. Raph wouldn't bring him a bacon-egg-and-cheese to scarf down before homeroom.

I don't know if I gave Raph an excuse for leaving midconversation but next thing I knew I was standing by the dumpster. Head against the brick. Eyes closed so tight they could break. Feeling each bead on my prayer bracelet until I could breathe again. I left my shift an hour early and went right to sleep. Fuck Valentine's Day.

My mood followed me everywhere I went. At the diner. At the duplex. At school. But it finally caught up to me today. On a run. Not just any run. The Cinnaminson Winter Trials. What a shitshow. When a sprinter underdelivers, they throw up their hoodie and sulk on the bus ride home. When *Bash the Flash* underdelivers, he sits in the front seat and tries to ignore everyone staring at him. Even the bus driver wanted to know what the hell was wrong with me. I couldn't even beat my own teammates. I couldn't even beat Matty. Bad. I was just fucking bad. And everyone knew it. Especially Matty.

Mateo Silva doesn't leave bed without a pocket full of salt to rub in people's wounds. He's a master gloater. It's an undeniable factor in what kept me constantly gunning for success. So, when he followed me off the away bus, all the way across the school parking lot, I knew to prepare for the worst.

"YO!"

He ran up holding two Chinese take-out containers. He shook them at me like he really wanted me to ask about them.

I assumed they were props in an elaborate pun-based diss he'd developed, just waiting for me to fuck up so he could unveil it. *General Slow's Chicken.* Something annoying like that.

I picked up my pace. "Not now, Matty."

"What? You sucked ass and made us all look worse as a team. No big. Now *take.*" He offered me a container. I eyed them, unsure. "They're not rigged."

At least he knew his rep. I took the container and opened it. Under some fortune cookies, two shiny IDs. The fakes we'd ordered in October. One for me, one for Dro. Sandro's face knocked me off balance. That look, when Matty made fun of his smile, captured and laminated. *Dominic Natoli* was an organ donor from Michigan. Six foot three, brown eyes, and miserable.

*"You're welcome."*

"Oh. Thanks."

"No problem, pal. Your boy's came out great. Looks real cute."

I stared at Matty and wondered why he'd say something like that. It's possible he knew. Found out somehow. Saw us kiss through my kitchen window or something. But I don't think he did. I think Matty was just being a piece of shit for no other reason than his being a piece of shit.

He pointed at the scar on my eyebrow. "Ooof. Fighting without me, B-Boy?"

I'd been in enough scrapes with Matty by my side to know what it took to lay him out. I could probably knock him out cold in two hits. One if I really clocked his jaw just right.

"That shit's nasty, man. Can't imagine what you did to deserve it. Fieldie not got your back?"

If I surprised him, he'd hit the cement a few seconds before his teeth would. He's quick but has no stamina. But people might see.

"Don't talk about Sandro, man."

And the fucker laughed. That laugh that was burned into my memory. My shame. "I got no problem with the Italian Yeti, dude. I'm just worried for him. See, he doesn't know 'bout you. How sooner or later, you're gonna get tired. He doesn't know how easy it is for Bash Villeda to forget about his best fucking friend."

I didn't care. People would want to see. There's a yearbook full of students and teachers who would've loved to kick Matty's ass if I hadn't always been nearby. I was edging closer to him. Just enough to let him know I'd do it. If he kept talking, he'd see what I could do.

And he met me halfway. Got right in my face. Still calm. Still rubbing that salt. "What? You mad? You mad, *Flash*? What'd I do?"

I knew Coach would bench me for the season, but I could use the rest. Just one goddamn moment of peace. I felt the mailbox crack against my skull and I grabbed Matty by the collar. The scar on my eyebrow twitched and I jerked him close.

My words spit out of me. *"I should fucking..."*

And then something happened. Matty's face changed. It went soft. His eyes were almost always moving but not then. There was no sneer in his expression. No laugh on his mouth. I didn't know that face.

"What'd I do? What did I do to you?" His jaw locked and he spoke through his teeth. *Just tell me what I did.*

It felt like this was the first time Matty ever really spoke to me. Actually said something to me. Even when my mom died, he never really talked to me. Just asked if I was "cool." But he was real with me here. For the first time in our knowing each other, Matty didn't want to talk with his fists. I let go of his shirt.

I knew what he meant. He wanted to know how it was so easy for me to cut him out of my life. After all these years, how could I just drop him? Even though Lucy could see all my weaknesses and Del could make me feel so guilty, I only cut Matty out. How did I do that? Why was it so easy?

"I don't…"

A passing car honked at us. Emma Sutter and the rest of the Senior Girls Relay squad. They waved our way and we covered. We nodded back, cool and unbothered. Untouchable. *Matty and the Flash.*

Alone, we just watched each other. I could feel every year of our friendship between us. How small and far away they all seemed right then. Every late-night run, every double shift, all the parties, all the fights, all the movies.

*Matty and the Flash.* We were supposed to be untouchable.

"I'm not like you, Matty."

"Bash."

"I don't *want* to be like you."

Matty shook his head. "Bull. Bull-fucking-shit, dude. We're… Come on. We're…"

He couldn't find the word. Because he didn't know. He didn't know what we were anymore either. I think Matty finally understood me then. Because when he nodded and backed away, he almost looked real for a second.

But when Del closed Birdie's door and asked if we were good, he turned it right back on. Smiles and waves.

"Just talking to my teammate, Mr. Branch. Captain stuff. Right, Villeda?"

But I couldn't look at him. I couldn't pretend anymore. I couldn't be like him.

Matty said something in Spanish I couldn't make out but I could hear him walk away. When I finally looked, his hoodie was up. I couldn't get that out of my head. The whole drive home, I just saw Matty walking alone with his hoodie hiding his face. This kid who, to the world, was so much like me. Who didn't know me.

"You get me anything?" Del pointed at the take-out container. I forgot I had it. Or that he was in the car. "Who was that?"

I swallowed. "Matty. Matty Silva."

"Oh. I don't know him. What were you two talking about?"

"Running."

"Fascinating. What about running?"

Maybe it's because we'd had a couple of good talks but it was like Del had forgotten the telltale signs that I wasn't in a talking mood. "Running. We talked about running and track and running track. What difference does it make?"

"Okay."

I thought after that night, when Del found me bloody and crying, things would go back to normal. He didn't ask me about what happened and I didn't tell him. He just let me cry and that was that. I thought we would go back to not talking. But nope. That night opened some door in Del.

"What's in the takeout?"

A door my mom would want me to walk through.

"...Fake IDs."

Del laughed. "Ballsy." He reached into the container and pulled one out. Sandro's. "They're getting better. Huh..."

"What?"

"He looks sad."

"We couldn't smile. To look real."

"That's a myth, y'know. You can smile if you want to. You just have to smile small."

I knew what I wanted to say. The first thing that came to mind. A piece of information that was useless to me now.

*Sandro can't smile small.*

I took the ID back and inspected it. But Del was watching me. Why was he watching me? I froze. 'Cause I'd said it out loud. Something I really loved about someone I really liked.

I couldn't look at Del. I didn't want to read whatever might be on his face. Feel whatever it was that I felt around him. That kept me from loving him like I should. But I felt his hand on my head. Running through my curls. And I let him. And my body breathed. I breathed for the first time in weeks.

I felt okay with Del touching my hair. Touching me like she used to.

I felt okay.

# sandro

*MARCH 10*

## *EVERYTHING ALL THE TIME*

According to my latest poll, there are nine Micelis under my roof. In my life, we have lost one house, flipped another, and settled in the half-completed, mice-riddled farmhouse I call home today. That's nine Micelis under one poorly constructed roof. We have bought, sold, lost, crashed, restored, and lived in too many cars for me to keep track of and have had five separate but equally loud relatives come to live with us for no shorter than eight months at any given time. Everyone in my family is an uproariously fair-weathered Eagles fan and has, at one point or another, made a poor but deafening attempt to learn an instrument. All this to say, when I say I have a lot of family going on, I mean:

## I HAVE A LOT OF FAMILY GOING ON.

I did my best to explain this to Ms. Morgan after class when she asked why I'd fallen behind on my reading. The chaos of my house wasn't exactly "reader-friendly," a fact she didn't seem to understand. She was one of the rare teachers in Moorestown who hadn't endured my brothers, which was initially a real asset to me. Most teachers assume I'm going to be a disruptive asshole once they see the Miceli name on their attendance sheets but Morgan's always given me the benefit of the doubt.

"You just need to carve out space, Alessandro. Find some quiet in all the chaos."

I wanted to tell her I had found quiet spaces. A roof. A ditch. But then I'd have to tell her why I couldn't go back to them.

"Well. That's some very *English teacher* advice, Ms. Morgan."

"That's *AP English teacher* to you, Mr. Miceli." She smiled up at me from her desk. "Personally, I like to read on the toilet. Is that less floral?"

I almost smiled back. Ms. Morgan had a habit for breaking through my bad moods. I left her classroom promising to try "carving out space" but it was more for her peace of mind than my own. I did need to get some reading done though. I was falling way behind and it wasn't exactly easy to engage in class. I'd spend all period trying not to look at the windows. Keeping my eyes off reflections. Terrified I might see it. The look on his face. The scar on his eyebrow. Him.

I decided I would try something positive and give the ditch another chance. It would be freezing but my options were limited and I couldn't avoid it forever. Because the reading thing was becoming a legitimate problem and maybe a quiet (if chilly) afternoon in the Sticks might pull me out of my slump.

I was halfway through the senior parking lot, queuing up my walking playlist, when I heard a car honk. I sighed. Always something. A very nice, very vintage lavender convertible pulled up next to me and kept my three-miles-per-hour walking speed.

"Howdy, stranger."

I didn't stop walking and hoped enough silence would make Ronny give up and drive off.

Phil zipped up his big puffer jacket. "Y'know, for a guy everyone likes, you're really hard to track down. No one seems to know where you've been lately. Don't you have friends?"

I gave them a quick up and down. It was deep into winter and two seconds outside was already giving me the sniffles. Yet there was my band, driving around with the top down in Ronny's fancy Mustang. All bundled up like they were heading to Santa's Village.

"...Why is the top down?"

Ronny wiped her nose, her car slowly rolling along. "It's been broken since junior year and I'll ask the questions. Why are you avoiding us?"

I kept my eyes forward and my mouth shut. The truth was, I'd been avoiding everyone. But the bigger truth was, if I let myself talk to them, who knows what I'd say? Who knows what I'd do? Look what happened to the last friend I made. Everyone was better off without me.

Phil whistled at me. "YO! STRAIGHT BOY! YOUR BANDMATES ARE TALKING TO YOU!"

The Mustang sped up, blocking my way out of the parking lot. I stopped. Ronny and Phil stood up in their seats and looked down on me. Waiting for an answer. But I wouldn't budge. I had nothing for them.

Phil took his sunglasses off. "What, did the Eagles lose? You burn a lasagna? Seriously, Miceli, what's your fucking problem?"

Ronny shook her head. "Had to finish my demo without you. Thanks for that. Almost missed my late deadline because you fucking flaked. If you don't want to be in our band anymore, fine. We'll find someone else. But don't waste my time, Sandro. I thought you were a nicer guy than—"

"You don't know me."

I closed my eyes. I tried to keep it back. Stay calm. But they needed to get away from me. They needed to get the fuck away.

Phil raised a brow. "We don't? I thought everyone in school knew the Italian Yeti?"

But it wouldn't stay inside. The best I could do was say it calmly. I walked around the Mustang, not looking at them. "You're not nice people. You're loud and rude and you don't treat people kindly. I don't want to be around that anymore."

"Sandro. Don't be a dick."

"I have no investment in you as people and I have no interest in you as friends. Goodbye. Good luck on NYU."

"Miceli, what the fuck?"

I passed them and headed for the street. I heard Phil scoff. I heard Ronny spit her gum at me. But I didn't look back.

Phil yelled after me. "Y'know, I guess people DON'T

know you! 'Cause everyone thinks you're a REAL GOOD
GUY!"

The Mustang kicked back up and spit gravel out behind
it. They peeled out of the parking lot and sped around me.
Their voices whipped by.

"I WANT MY FUCKING BASS BACK!"

"YOU'VE GOT A WEIRD ASS!"

Then the Mustang was gone. There went my band. For
the best.

*Anywho.*

I put my headphones in and turned for the sidewalk. That's
when I saw her. Lucy Jordan was watching me from the back
of her mom's Volvo. She had an art easel in her hand and a
question on her face. Was it a question for me? For her good
friend Ronny? I didn't stop to ask. People needed to stop
fucking looking at me.

It was nice walking through the Sticks without a cast or
boot or crutches. Just me and the trees. There was no more
snow on the ground and the path to the ditch seemed shorter.
Before, it felt like a journey. The trek getting there was half
the reason to go to the ditch. But I guess when you're just
walking to walk, not talking or messing around, it's not as
special.

The ditch looked the same, untouched since the last time I
was there. After. When I woke up at dawn with leaves in my
hair and dirt on my face. It looked just as sad. As ordinary.
But I got in anyway. Plopped down and got to business. The
ditch was just a ditch and I was there to read.

So, I read.

It surprised me that Bash wore glasses when he read. The

first time he busted them out I thought he was joking. Like they were costume glasses he brought for a gag I wasn't in on. It was the first big change I saw on him. Physically, I mean. It was like seeing your teacher at Walmart. Not necessarily a shock, but a surreal hint that the black-and-white image you'd built up in your head of a person might have more color than you expected.

*Stop.*

I didn't come to the ditch to think about Bash. I was carving out space. I was reading. And if I started thinking about Bash, I'd start thinking about the dinner. How well Bash the Flash fit in at the Miceli house. It didn't help that I couldn't get into my new AP lit book. It's not even the book's fault this time. *His Garden* is straight-up soap opera–level of batshit but it still wouldn't grab me. I'd just finished the first chapter where this rich old German dick tells his estranged triplet daughters that their late mother strangled her brother/lover to death while pregnant with them and I simply could not give a shit. Like, that's some grade A Jerry Springer drama but I just couldn't focus.

I saw Bash running last week. I was helping Ma set up an open house in the Orchard. I was driving one of her gaudy *CALL CLAUDIA!* signs into the front lawn when I spotted him. Across the street, a few houses down. He was in full sweats. New running shoes. Headphones in. That was new. He hated running to music. I didn't even stop to think if he'd seen me. I was just stuck on that.

What made him start running to music?

*Stop it.*

Bash isn't my problem. I'm not solving for *WHY* anymore. There's no point trying to figure him out. He's got too many variables. Too much risk. This was supposed to be a year of slipping by, not making waves, and tiptoeing to graduation. That was the deal.

The best thing I ever did for my family was sit back. Lie low. Keep my hands to myself. That's what I needed to be doing. Just getting through and getting out. Then, when I'm in my big-boy apartment and have my two dogs and my college friends, *then* I can look into the variables. Because it doesn't matter if he made you happy. It doesn't matter that he made every day feel like your best day. None of it matters because he made you stupid. He made you doubt the things you hate about yourself. He made you stop keeping yourself in check. That's why it happened. Bash made you think you weren't an angry, emotional animal so you stopped keeping that shit at bay. You let your guard down and look what happened. You hurt him.

You *left* him.

*Don't.*

That's what happens. That's how Micelis show they care.

You love Ma but she screamed at you when you cried. You love Gio but he pushed you down those stairs. You love Raph but he knocked your front tooth out. You love Pop but he hit you with a goddamn jewelry box.

*Please stop.*

You love Bash's eyebrows but you split one open. You love to talk to him but you never asked if he was okay. You love that boy but you left him bleeding in the fucking dirt.

**"STOP!"**

Everything came back to me then. All the anger, all the tears, they all found me again. Everything I tried to put into the ground burned out of me and the scream torched the sky. And I thought all the noise in me had died.

"Sandro?"

*Oh, God, no.*

My eyes opened and there she was.

"It's okay."

I stood up, real quick. Like I wanted to scare her. Like I was the kind of guy who'd scare a girl in the woods. But I was still crying. I just couldn't turn off the crying.

"Please leave."

"Hey. It's okay."

No one was supposed to be there. I wanted to bury myself. I only have the ditch left. Just let me have my fucking ditch.

She came closer and I stood taller. Threw my arms up. Like an animal. A Miceli.

**"LEAVE ME ALONE! EVERYONE! WHY WON'T YOU JUST—JUST—"**

I heard my screams echo in the woods. And I bit my lip. Cut everything off. Because Lucy didn't flinch. She just stared at me. A calm worry on her face. Like she understood something about all that noise. Like she might be the only person on earth who could.

So, I turned away. Let myself cry. No use trying to stop something I do so well.

*"I'm sorry."*

And when she came close and held my hand, I let her. She

asked me what was wrong. I couldn't remember the last time someone asked me that.

Her voice was as soft as her hand.

I get why Bash loves her.

# bash

*mar. 15*

*luce*

It's been a funny couple days. An interesting few days to be sure.

It started with Del. I'd just gotten back from a run and he was drinking coffee in the kitchen, prepping for a night at the lot. It was this new fancy espresso stuff he's been about recently. Not my speed. Nevertheless, I joined him for a cup.

Del hasn't said it, and I'm certainly not going to, but after that talk in the car, about the IDs and Sandro, things have been different. Like the wall is finally down. We're not discussing the secrets of the universe, but I told him about the Beer Olympics. About the weirdness with Matty and why Lucy dumped me. The bigger, heavier things like my problems with talking. Even smaller, pointless shit like how I find peaches deeply unsettling. Like biting into a hairy arm. Disgusting. We even workshopped possible answers to my mom's unsolved mystery. The gift of seeds. *DAR*. Del knows my mom's antics maybe even better than me and he's at a loss too. But he says that's good. That she'd want me to really think it over. He told me the answer would come to me when I stopped trying so hard to solve it. It was good advice.

When I noticed him looking at me over his cup of fancy coffee, I didn't feel so guilty anymore. Just curious. "You watch me a lot."

"Do I?"

"Yeah. Why do you do that?"

"You just have an interesting face."

"Interesting?"

"Impenetrable. Hard to read. Does that bother you?"

"It used to. A lot."

"Why?"

"Not sure."

"Huh. Well, I'm sorry. But not anymore?" I shook my head and unlaced my shoes. Del laughed. "You ran this morning."

"I know, I was a big part of that decision."

"You've been running a lot lately."

"Yeah, it's kind of my thing."

"Seb. You were still faster than half the guys out there."

I guess my face wasn't *that* impenetrable. Del could see how the embarrassment from the Cinnaminson Winter Trials was still eating at me.

"I wasn't faster than Cinnaminson's guys. I looked like a punk."

"You've been bringing Bianco medals for years now. You earned a bye."

"They don't want *byes* at Rutgers." I was stretching my hammy against the wall and I felt Del staring again. Maybe I wasn't so over it.

"Oh. So, you think this'll keep you from getting in?" Impenetrable, my ass. But I just shrugged. Del shrugged right back. "Maybe it will. They probably heard all about it and threw out your file."

I didn't mean to but I flinched. I actually flinched. "...Why the hell would you say that?"

I didn't feel so talkative anymore so I kind of stormed off. He was probably joking, but that was an obnoxious sort of joke. He knows what Rutgers means to me. I don't like jokes like that. He should know that.

I got to my room and slammed the door. Probably a bit much but I wanted him to know that I was pissed.

I regretted it right away. 'Cause there it was.

There, on my bed. All neat and situated, propped up on my pillow. The envelope. The *big* envelope. I picked it up. Felt the weight in my hands. I traced my finger along the scarlet *R* stamped on the seal.

I got it. I fucking got it.

I almost fell down the stairs on my way back to the kitchen. Del had two glasses of whiskey at the ready. I could hear some spill on the tile floor when I bear-hugged him, but I didn't care.

'Cause I got into Rutgers.

People started getting their letters last week. Ronny DiSario

got into NYU. Ant Lewis got a full ride to Auburn. I heard
Matty got into Vanderbilt, which makes no sense but good
for him, I guess.

We cooked a big dinner that night to celebrate. Jambalaya.
My mom's go-to comfort food. We even got kind of drunk.
Something I never would've thought was possible with Del.
It was fun. It was really, really fun.

Later, still a little buzzed, I found my way onto some message boards and saw Northwestern's letters hadn't gone out
yet. Before going to bed, I rubbed my beads and said some
prayers. Added that letter to my prayer list. It was a short list,
nothing too official. But he was all over it.

The next morning, I found out Lucy got into UCLA. The
art program. Her first choice. She told me the news after
jumping me.

I was running some laps at the track, nothing too stressful,
and I was feeling pretty good. I didn't even feel the need to
listen to music. I liked my thoughts that day. Rutgers. Mom.
Running. A future.

I didn't see her coming.

I was rounding a bend when she came at me. Stomped clear
across the track and shoved me into the grass. I fell right on
my ass. Rolled a bit with it. I'm lucky I wasn't sprinting because Lucy could derail a train if she was mad enough.

And she was mad enough.

"What is your FUCKING problem?!"

"Lucy, what the—"

"What the hell happened?"

It was still pretty early and I was three kinds of unprepared for all she was throwing at me. I managed to get up and assume a steady, hard-to-knock-over stance. "The hell are you—"

"What happened with Sandro?"

My brain deflated and I felt my face go pale. "What do you mean?"

"I found his giant ass crying in the Sticks."

I had to look away, so I tried my feet. Like maybe I was inspecting my laces or something. "What does that have to do with—"

"Stop. Stop it."

Lucy shook her head.

"I barely saw you all summer, Seb. Fine. You're you, you like your space, I gave you it. I broke up with you, but I gave you it. You start hanging out with some guy we barely know and, surprise, I start seeing you again. Not as often but at least you were looking like you again. I didn't press. I was just happy to see you smiling again."

She got closer.

"Then Del tells me you're out running for hours every night. No one on the team sees you anymore. Matty won't even say your fucking name. I watched Sandro Miceli cry in the woods for almost an hour and he wouldn't tell me why."

Her voice was so serious then. Not angry, not upset. Just worried. Lucy was scared. "You tell me. I'm tired of this, Seb, just tell me what's fucking happening with you. If you aren't okay…"

I wanted to look at her. She knows what it means when I can't look at her. "Sebastian. Look at me."

I've always been shit at saying no to Luce. But I didn't want her seeing me like that. I wanted to go home. She touched my cheek and I could feel a tear between our skin. Tears. I don't know when they started.

"...I don't know what to do, Luce."

Lucy and I were really bored the afternoon we decided to start dating. We'd just played tennis at Zelley Park, something we only did when we were a very specific kind of very bored, and ended up at the school track. We must've sat on those bleachers for hours just talking about nothing. Eventually, like it always did, that nothing turned to something. Then everything. And we came to the decision that finding someone you can talk to like that, anywhere on that range of nothing to everything, must be love. Maybe even better than love. Rarer.

We were back on those bleachers when I told her about me.

"I don't know when I knew. I mean... I'm still not exactly sure *what* I know but... I know. I thought it might pass or whatever but..." We sat close. Like the stadium was full and cold and we were the only things keeping each other warm. "I don't think it will."

She nodded, taking all of it in, but I really needed her to say something. I needed to fill the silence. "When'd you find out?"

"Halloween? Maybe a little after. Del said you didn't go to Maine and... I think I'd already known."

"What do you... How do you feel about it?"

"I mean... I've known you my whole life. And I've known all the *yous*. Seb. Bash. *Bash the Flash*. That one summer you tried going by Bastian." Ugh. Not my best summer. The only movie I wanted to watch was *The NeverEnding Story III* and I didn't know any better. I groaned. Lucy smiled. "Now... I just know you better. And you know you better. That's good."

"You're not mad?"

"What? Why would... No. This doesn't change anything for me." She took my hand. Looked me in the eye. Really made sure I understood. "You're still who you've always been to me, Seb."

Her voice and her hands. They were the first things I thought of when I thought about Luce. I loved her for their softness. "And, shit, if you had trouble making your mind up *before...*"

And I loved her for that. For knowing me. As hard as it was for me sometimes. Lucy knew me enough to give me shit. To care about my weaknesses. That's why I could never lose her. Never cut her out. Even if I wanted to fall off the face of the earth, Lucy would know where I jumped. She would know how to find me.

That's the difference.

"I keep thinking about Matty."

"Whoa."

"No. Not like... Something Matty said. After Sandro, I just stopped talking to him. Like I didn't need him anymore. And, yeah, Matty's a dick but...it's not a good way to treat people." I gripped her hand. Looked her in the eye. It was my turn to be understood. "You know me, Lucy. I haven't let a lot of people know me like you do. But you know me. Del knows me. All these parts of me, even the weak ones. And that...it scares me." I wiped my eye. I didn't want to cry for this. "Because you love me. You and Del love me. And when you look at me sometimes, I just feel so guilty."

There was no use fighting the tears. They were polite enough to not mess with my speaking, so I let them run. I needed to hear myself say it. "Because of how I am. How I've been. How disappointed she'd be in me. If she could look at me, she'd be so ashamed."

"Seb…"

"I just disappoint people. I let them get close then I punish them for it. Like Del. Like…like Sandro. And I did the same thing to you and… I'm sorry. About everything. About not trying with you or fighting for you or… I'm sorry."

Lucy watched me with those eyes. So much like my mom's. Not green. Not like an island. Not how they looked at me. How they saw me.

"Seb… Are you fucking crazy?" Despite myself, I smiled a bit. Lucy laughed. "You're right. I like to look at you. Always have, even when we were little. Wanna know why?"

I did. She wiped my cheek.

"Because you see everything. You might not talk well, but you see so much, Seb. You see me. You see Del. Sandro. We just want to know what you're looking at." She rubbed my head. My curls. She liked my hair long. "She loved you. She loved every part of you. We all love you. Every part."

I leaned into her touch and she spoke softer. "'Cause we see you too, dumbass."

I smiled. I smiled and I hugged her.

But it wasn't over. The smile faded. "I don't know how to fix this, Luce."

I said it into her hair. I could feel her nod. "Well, what do you…" She trailed off and gave me a look.

"…What?"

"I can't keep asking you what you want, Seb. Don't make me that person for you."

I nodded. Stood. Paced. "We only have a few more months. I don't want to waste them. I don't want him hating me."

"Then tell him that."

"He doesn't wanna see me. If he wanted to see me…"

I thought about Sandro leaving me on the ground that night. How mad I made him. How guilty. How horribly I fucked things up for him and how easily it came to me.

"He doesn't want to talk to me anymore. He wants space."

Lucy groaned. "Boys and space. Y'all think it's this big gift. You know what happens after you leave everyone alone?" Lucy stood up too and shook the pins out of her legs. "He didn't want to talk to me either. But he asked about you. Asked if you got into Rutgers. *'Cause it's important to him.*"

Lucy did a surprisingly good impression of Sandro. It made me happy. Not the impression but the idea of Sandro asking about me. Wondering about my future. Still thinking about me.

I smiled. Lucy cocked her head. "Huh. Your smile's different."

No. It wasn't. It was just real. It felt real. I couldn't smile small when I thought about Sandro. I hugged Lucy tight and wondered how many times I've hugged her. Smelled paint in her hair. Felt her hug me back. "I really didn't deserve you, Luce."

She pulled back and made her "no one deserves me" look. "Yeah. You really didn't."

She rested her head on my chest and laughed when she said it. "But you might deserve Sandro's goofy ass."

I smiled big and kissed her forehead. Hell fucking yeah, I might.

# sandro

*MARCH 18*

### *A PEARL, STRUCK BY LIGHTNING*

I didn't know where we were driving. I don't think he did either. We'd done the errands, we'd done the burgers, there was nothing left for Gio Sr. and his boy Sandro to do on this earth. We never spend more than an hour alone together and for good reason. We have nothing to talk about. Nothing in common except a wife/mother who insisted that I *stop moping around the house* and we *have a boys' day together.*

We were driving along the edges of the Sticks and I thought he might take me to the woods and put one in my skull *Sopranos*-style. What took you so long, Pop? It had been a long day and none of his forced efforts to strike up a conversation were working. To be fair, my dad's idea of conversation is telling me a never-ending allegory about cacti in the desert to teach me fiscal responsibility or something.

"Y'know, clients, the good clients, they figure, 'Hey, we've got a crew that works for us, that works for us cheap, that won't fuck us over at the end of the day.' So they keep us on. It's about reliability. Consistency, Sandro. That's why we get the work these out-of-staters try scooping up. We show up, we do good work. Every day. Consistency. It's about finding out what kind of man you are and bringing that man to the table. Being that man every day."

Some invisible hand tugged on my collar, trying to get me to point out his inconsistency. Get angry about his hypocrisy. Make him look at the scar on my eyebrow. Instead, I watched the Sticks. Wondered what I might see if I stared hard enough.

"I just want you to be a good man, Sandro. I understand what you're going through. Your brothers all went through the same thing. We were all seventeen. We were all stupid. We all…"

*We all liked boys.* He wouldn't understand. *We all kissed boys.* He would kill me. *We all hurt boys.* I'd disgust him. If he knew me, if he cared to know me, I would disgust him. So, maybe it's better this way.

"Is it that girl? The DiSario girl? Is that why you're…" I kept my eyes on the woods and crawled back into myself. "I just want you to be a good man, Sandro. Just…grow up."

We turned the corner for home pretty soon after that and I went back to bed. I could hear Ma grill my dad beneath my floorboards about our big day. I smothered myself with a pillow so I wouldn't hear what Dad had to say about me. Hear

Ma not defend me. Hear them come to terms with the fact that they were dealt three defective, unhelpful, angry boys.

When I grow up, I'm going to make sure my kids have soundproof walls. Soundproof floors. Roofs with railings. And when I get angry or sad, I'll tell them why I'm crying. I won't hide myself from them. I'll tell them I love them and I'll make sure they know everything about me. If I can't give them silence, at least I can give them peace.

I think I'm gonna be a good dad. Maybe everyone thinks that though. Lately, I've got it in my head that some parents can be amazing at parts of parenting. But only those parts, you know? Like, Ma is wonderful with kids. She puts Lexi and Tina first, no matter what. She lets GJ do his own thing, but she'll still move heaven and earth for him when he needs her. That's how she was with me once. When my problems were as easy as crusts on PB&Js and stomach bugs. Before all the noise. Maybe some parents aren't ready for all that noise. Maybe she just didn't know what to do with it.

I'd been sitting on my Rutgers letter for that very reason. I knew how she'd react. And it's not like there aren't plenty of great apartments at Rutgers. I'm sure there are loads of sweet, funny, fosterable dogs and I'm sure I could make some real friends. But it's not my future. Rutgers would mean commuting from home. Errands and odd jobs on the weekends and living with one foot in my past. I saw it happen to Gio and he couldn't even last a year. It's not what I want. Hence my stalling.

I was burning through *His Garden* in the van, out of sight and in full stall mode. In the lucky few times it wasn't in use, I found the van to be a suitable place to read. I'd just finished my favorite chapter so far (Anna, the only nice daughter, finds out she's pregnant with her own set of triplets and rips her billionaire father a new one at the family psychiatrist's funeral) when I decided to take a break for a bit. Digest the literary drama. I didn't have it in me to go to the Sticks so I settled for walking up and down my driveway. It's long enough to merit exit ramps and always makes for prime pacing material.

About halfway up my driveway, I thought about my band. *Everything All the Time.* It was a good name. And it lasted maybe a month. Shame. I felt some lingering guilt about how I talked to Ronny and Phil that day in the parking lot. I just didn't know how to be a good communicator lately, much less a good friend, and it's not like they bring out the positive in a situation. We just weren't a fit. Guess I'm too emotional for the emo crowd. I know they were just checking in on me but they should've just let me be. Honestly, I'm surprised I didn't blow up on them harder.

And I'm actually shocked I didn't pop off on my dad during our "boys' day." Because it was coming. I could feel it. The noise. Since that day in the Sticks, that day Lucy let me cry, I felt awake again. I was all sobbed out. My noise was back and I felt like I was going to fucking explode.

I decided to stop at the mailbox. See if my second-grade pen pal ever got back to me, or perhaps I received a love letter from one of my many suitors fighting overseas. Despite feeling guilty any time I got within fifty feet of it, I'd been super on top of the mailbox since the Rutgers letter came. I'm lucky GJ found it before Ma because I really didn't want to have that conversation. I wasn't in the right headspace for the big college fight.

But fate doesn't give a shit about your headspace.

The envelope fell out of the mailbox, straight to the ground. Hit the dirt with a comically loud THUNK. Like a drunk passing out in the snow.

### NORTHWESTERN

*"Oh, fuck."*

I knew I wouldn't have the balls to show Ma the Rutgers letter, right headspace or not, if I didn't come with ammunition. And even then, it was going to be a battle. I had to come correct. So, before the war, I just let myself walk up and down the driveway. Rocks in my bare feet. Reading the only letter I cared about again and again.

Again and again and again and again.

*Dear Sandro.*
*Congratulations.*
*Considerable academic achievements.*
*Impressive character.*
*Dear Sandro.*
*Congratulations.*
*Dear Sandro.*
*Congratulations.*
*Congratulations.*

I couldn't tell you the last time I felt tears coming and cheered them on.

*The years you spend here will be among the most memorable of your life.*

I did it. I made it.

I fucking did it. Northwestern.

*Congratulations.*

I read my letter again at the kitchen table. Held on to that feeling. Let that hope harden my resolve. Ma was making meatballs with the kids at the counter, rereading the Rutgers letter. Her letter. She hadn't put it down since I gave it to her.

"*Model student.* That's so nice of them to say. I mean, I'm sure it's in all the letters but it's still a very nice thought. I think we can give you the van once your dad pays off the new one. And if Raph doesn't find a gig by then."

She had one hand on the paper, the other stirring a sauce. Always moving. Pop was having work friends over for dinner so my achievement had come at an inconvenient time. I don't think she actually looked my way after I gave her the news.

"That way you could come back some weekends. But only if we need you. Don't need you flunking out."

GJ combined three meatballs into a Mega-Ball. "Like Gio?"

Ma chuckled. "Just like your father. Smaller balls, they won't cook."

GJ nodded and gave Mega-Ball a face.

Ma went on about the van and the campus but I wasn't listening. I just kept rereading one line of my letter. *One of tens of thousands of applications. Tens of thousands.*

In an AP statistics unit, I read you had a 1:12000 chance of getting struck by lightning. Also, the odds of finding a pearl in an oyster are 1:15000. *Tens of thousands. Tens.* The odds were abysmal. I was one of tens of thousands and they still picked me.

They saw me.

"And, you know, it's actually perfect. Sharri says Joseph—you remember the Russo's?—well, Joey worked as a valet when he was at Rutgers and I'm sure he'd—"

I put my letter down. "I'm going to Northwestern."

She didn't hear me. "What? Don't be ridiculous. Rutgers is great, it's close and you'll never— Sandro. We need you close."

She didn't *hear* me.

"That's not fair."

Ma finally looked at me. "Things aren't always fair, hon. That's something you gotta learn."

But she never heard me.

Raph came in and tasted the sauce with his finger. "Salty. What's not fair?"

Ma moved off of me, discussion over, and pushed Raph away from her stove. "It'll cook down. Sandro wants to go to Northwestern."

"He's not gonna get—"

"I got in." I stood. Tapped the kids on the head. "Guys, go watch TV."

Before Tina could complain, GJ nodded and took the girls away. That stopped Ma. I think she could see it on me. See that something was about to happen.

Raph must've too. "What's your problem?"

Ma didn't look his way but her voice was solid. "Raphael, go to your room."

Raph knew that voice. He grabbed a meatball and vanished. Ma set the burners to simmer and wiped her hands clean. Got ready. I forgot how immediate her attention could be when she gave it, but I had it now.

She nodded. So I looked her in the eye and used her attention.

"I didn't say shit when you put me in the attic. You were busy and GJ and Tina needed my room. I get that. That's fair. You had a lot to take care of, I understood that." My voice wasn't as confident as my posture. I could stand as tall as I wanted to but I couldn't keep my voice from shaking more and more. "...There were bones sticking out of my foot, Ma. Three, right by my toes. I stared at them for half an hour because I couldn't go inside. 'Cause I thought y'all'd make fun of me for falling."

She flinched. Just a little, right in her lip. Because they did. She did.

"I had to beg Tina not to wake you guys 'cause I knew what you'd say. And you *said* it."

"Sandro."

"*No.*" There were tears rolling down my face. Different from the ones in the driveway but not angry. Not sad. Necessary. They needed to get out. She needed to see. "I told you Raph wasn't driving me but you didn't do anything. I could feel the bones breaking again but I didn't want to bother you!"

She put her hand on my arm but I shook it off.

"You were so busy and I only wanted to help you. I didn't want you to worry about me so you just fucking stopped! You don't talk to me, you just fight me or scream at me or make me feel stupid!"

I slammed the Northwestern letter on the counter. I didn't mean to, but I screamed at her. "I'm **NOT!** I'm **NOT** stupid!"

She jumped at that. She was holding herself together but that shook her. I wiped my face. There was no heat on my cheeks. That surprised me. I cleared my eyes and got my voice back.

"I know what's unfair, Ma. You taught me that shit early."

I took my letter and left her with that. I said all I had to say. I went to read my book on my roof and I didn't give a fuck if she heard me.

# bash

*mar. 18*

*dar*

I got into Villanova?

It's not a question but that's how it sounded in my head. Not a fact yet.

The big envelope came this morning with brochures and pictures and stats about the school. It's still close. Ish. And it's got an amazing track program. It's a great school. Truly. But it's not Rutgers.

It's not the big scarlet *R* that's been hanging above my bed for over a year. It's not what I've wanted for so long. So why do I keep reading the brochures? Why did I email the athletics department for more info?

Why the big question mark?

I was reading the brochures in bed when I started feeling my prayer bracelet. Thinking about Mom. Her gift. Those fucking seeds. *DAR.* I was beginning to suspect that the entire point of DAR was that there wasn't a point. An antipoint. Some existential cop-out that seemed very far from my mom's usual MO.

But then, while reading a Villanova pamphlet about student diversity and working on this crick in my foot, I remembered that, hey, I'm diverse. And it clicked.

"...Oh. OH. Oh, FUCK."

I threw the brochures aside and grabbed the new Spanish word-a-day calendar off my nightstand. Mom's calendar got me in the habit so I gave myself one for Christmas. I cheated and looked ahead, day by day, word by word, until I found it.

August 25. **DAR.**

*DAR (basic verb)*
*Give*
*Yield*
*Show*

I had to sit.

When I was really little, my mom would take me walking in the Sticks. It was a morning routine of ours, something we'd do after long winters to make sure the snow was really gone for good. She'd pick up a coffee at her spot and we'd walk the nature trail. I was too young for coffee but sometimes she'd pour a little splash into my cup of hot chocolate and we'd drink our morning drinks. I was so in love with the forest and, each time, I'd find a new favorite tree. But Mom's was always the same.

Toward the end of the trail, there was a clearing. I'm pretty sure it's a picnic area now but, back then, it was just an open clearing with one single tree. One lonely oak. That was her favorite. My mom told me that forests had their own magic but, in her eyes, there was nothing more beautiful than finding a solitary tree. She said it was like the forest letting you in on a secret.

The more walks we went on, the more I understood what she meant. What she felt. That lonely tree didn't have a forest. It had to find its own space to grow. It became its own forest, deserving its own attention. Walking with my mother, I began to see the beauty of being alone.

That's why she left me the seeds. Because she knew how lonely I could make myself. How much I could put between myself and the world. My mother knew how hard it was for me to show myself and she knew how desperately I wanted to be seen. To give. To yield. To show. All that want wrapped into a word. That's all she ever hoped for me. For me to give myself to the world. To find my own place in the forest. She wanted me to see the beauty of being found.

I put the seeds back in the envelope and ran to Sandro's.

When I got to his driveway, I noticed his mailbox was open. I considered drop-kicking the thing then and there but decided my revenge would have to come another day. I ran up his forty-three-mile driveway and knocked on the front door.

I guess I wanted him to answer. Or maybe I didn't. I don't know. Not his dad, for sure. Maybe his ma. But there in that giant *Dragon Ball Z* shirt was GJ.

"Hey. GJ."

He was holding a wad of ground beef. I think it had a face. "Where have you been?"

"Oh. Uh... Around."

"Are you here about Sandro?"

"Yeah. I am."

"What's wrong with him?"

I knew Sandro would be upset but he was always so sure to keep that shit from his family. He must've been real pissed if even they noticed. "Oh... Is he mad?"

GJ shook his head. Even with his giant shirts and big eyes, it was the first time he truly looked like a little kid to me. "He's sad. He won't tell me why."

Damn. That was worse.

I didn't know what to say. GJ nodded like he could smell my hesitance. Without another word, he left, leaving little drops of beef in his wake.

The house was surprisingly quiet. Mr. Miceli's office door was closed and I could hear deep voices coming from the kitchen. It sounded like Raph and Gio. I poked my head into the living room and saw two little girls watching a movie. *Saw IV*, if I'm not mistaken. Seemed liked a problem but I had bigger fish.

"Sebastian?"

I turned to find Mrs. Miceli sitting at the dining room table. Alone. Like she'd been sitting there since our dinner.

It's a funny thing with the Miceli men. GJ looks like Gio who looks like Gio Sr. Same with Raph and Sandro. Big hairy apples under a big hairy tree. It was all I could think when I finally saw them together. But I couldn't find Sandro in Claudia's face. Their connection wasn't so clear.

Not until right then. Alone at that table. I knew that face.

"You okay, Mrs. Miceli?"

"Claudia, sweetheart."

She didn't try smiling at me. She looked like she'd just been gut punched. All winded and dazed. Her hand sat on the table and her fingers were doing this weird dance on the wood. Like she was playing a concerto from memory.

Her fingers stopped. "Are you Sandro's friend?"

I nodded. I didn't understand the question, but I nodded. "Yes, ma'am."

She nodded too. "He doesn't have friends. I don't know why, he's such a nice boy. He's always been nice. Raph and G had friends. Girlfriends, each other..." She shook her head. "But they're not nice. Not like Dro."

I didn't know what to say. So, I went with the truth. "...Sandro deserves better."

She nodded again. And I saw where Sandro got his thinking face from. When he's close to solving some math problem that's taken him all of study hall.

I think she solved it. "He never talks about you." She smiled at me. It was a sad sort of smile. The kind you save for harder days. "I wish he could talk about you, Sebastian."

I wanted to tell her what I wished for Sandro. Everything. But I didn't want to say more than I should again. Words never came well to me at that dining room table.

She must've seen me holding my tongue. A Miceli specialty. She gave me a nod and looked at the ceiling. "He's on the roof."

"Yes, ma'am."

She smiled. Less sad. More tired. "Claudia, sweetheart. Claudia."

And I left her.

I'd never been in Sandro's room. It was never an option for us. I peeked my head inside, in case he was there, but the attic was empty. And small. Fine for an attic but small for a bedroom. To think I was worried what his impression would be of my room.

I took in Sandro's world. The only decorations were the dozens of multicolored tank tops thrown around the room. A dirty shot put in the corner next to some cleats. A chunk of neon green cast proudly displayed on a shelf. I inspected the tiny desk by the window. Knickknacks and souvenirs from trips I'd heard about. An AC beach token. A picture of him as a boy with an older couple on a sailboat. A legal pad covered in possible logos for Bumpin' Grinders. His copy of *Daniel: Last Forever.* That fucking book.

I thumbed through it. The margins were full of notes. I stopped on one.

**B thinks lighthouse is meta4 4 self-sabotage. Steal 4 paper.**

Fucker. I knew he stole that idea. I flipped to another page and found a bookmark. Not a bookmark. A picture.

My senior portrait.

I'm not afraid of heights but you'd be foolish not to get a little cagey on that roof. It's a drop. I don't know how Sandro survived it.

I found him lying on the shingles. His eyes were closed and he had a copy of *His Garden* open on his chest. A ballsy move to be sleeping on the roof again. Very carefully, I made my way up the slant and stood over him. Maybe it was my shadow hitting his face or maybe he could just sense a presence, but his eyes opened. He looked at me. Not that I'd been counting but it had been just shy of one hundred days. By six.

It'd been ninety-four days since Sandro looked at me.

I pointed to the book. "How far are you?"

I only had two books left to read on Ms. Morgan's list and *His Garden* was low on my favorites. I did my best to follow along in class but it was just so ridiculous.

Sandro just looked at me. Gave me nothing.

I shrugged. "I didn't get it. I mean, I got it. I just didn't like it."

Still nothing. He closed the book and started lowering himself down the roof.

*Shit.*

"Sandro, plea—"

I turned a little too quickly and fell on my ass. Hard. I heard a shingle fall somewhere and hit a tree branch. Sandro stopped and whipped around. I steadied myself from slipping further and breathed. We watched each other.

"...You can't stand up here."

"Okay."

"And I wasn't sleeping."

"Okay."

Sandro nodded. He crawled back up to my level and sat. Opened his book like he was planning on reading through whatever I had to say. I'd take it. He thumbed through and found his place. "I don't get it either. This is like the eighth chapter in a row where Anna just screams at her family but no one ever does anything."

"It makes sense at the end."

"What, is she a ghost?"

I gave him a spoiler-free, wishy-washy shrug. Sandro rolled his eyes and Frisbee-tossed the book off the roof. That made me smile. He leaned back and rubbed his face. Probably pissed he'd be searching for his book all afternoon again. He did the same thing once with *Daniel*. Back then, we made a game of it. First to find the book got free Wawa that week. I found it within the first two minutes but he got me to love Wawa, so he won in the long run.

I wanted to help him find this book too. I wanted another bet.

I wanted my friend back.

"I'm sorry, Sandro. I'm so sorry. I should've just kept my fucking mouth shut. Or I shouldn't have... I could've said something. I could've stood up for you. I was just nervous and got in my head and I don't... I'm sorry."

He took his hands off his face but kept his eyes on the sky. I felt like I was right back there on that trail. The morning after our kiss. Just trying to break through to him.

"Talk to me. Please. I need you to talk to me, man."

He nodded. Sat back up and sniffed. "I've, uh..." He took his time with it. All of it. "I've been angry. Really angry. For a long time. At myself and my family. And how they treat me. And...my foot and the hair on my shoulders and...and I'm not good at dealing with it. I keep it all... So, it all... And sometimes I just get so fucking angry that my head feels like it's cracking open. And when you... When we started hanging out, I wasn't so angry."

He was soft and calm and only stopped to wipe his eyes. "I thought you were gonna fix it. And that was stupid and it's not your fault and... It's something I need to fix myself. Moving and restarting and Northwestern won't mean shit if I don't. So, *I'm* sorry. I shouldn't have pushed you. I shouldn't have left you. I'm so...so fucking sorry."

"Sandro, it's okay."

"No. It's not."

"I was an asshole. I told them you—"

"I fell asleep on the roof. It was a stupid thing to do. I deserved it. You didn't." He shook his head. He was trying to stay calm. "I *hurt* you. I pushed you into a mailbox, your face... I hurt you."

"Dro. It was an accident, Sandro. You gotta know that."

"But I left you there. Alone. That wasn't an accident, I did that. That's fucked-up. I'm... I'm fucked-up. I shouldn't be around people. I deserve to be alone."

I shook my head. Awed. And I thought of everything I wanted to say to his mother before. All the things I wished for her son. "You deserve so much better than this, Sandro. You deserve parents who care about you and brothers who care about you and Northwestern and the apartment and Bumpin' Grinders. You deserve the fucking world, man. Look at me."

And he did. I smiled. "I am so lucky I know you. I can be myself with you. I like who that is with you. You're nice and good and you smile like... Fuck, I love your smile." I got closer to him. Took his hand. "And people don't treat you like they should. I haven't treated you like I should. Like you deserve."

Strong like Lucy. Honest like Del.

"And I want you to go to college and I want you to get the chance you deserve. I want these last months with you and I want to drive you when you go. I need you in my life, Sandro. You're my best friend. You're my fucking lighthouse, man."

They were the easiest words that ever came out of me.

Sandro looked at me. Watched me and took me in. I knew what that meant now. He put his hand on my head and pulled me in gentle. Still so soft. He held me like we were still in the ditch. Like if he held me tight enough, we could fall back to summer and try it all again.

I smelled the salt on his skin and smiled. "You got into Northwestern?" Sandro nodded against my head. I sniffed. "I'm so proud of you, Dro."

I felt his teardrop hit my T-shirt.

My face in his shoulder, I mumbled something like *I love you.*

I could feel him smile back.

"Me too, bud."

# spring

*You can cut all the flowers but you cannot keep spring from coming.*

*—Pablo Neruda*

# sandro

*MARCH 30*

*BOTTOMS UP*

All right.

We went camping this weekend because I decided that, if we were going to embark on such a big next step in our relationship, I would need a nice, quiet, secluded area to feel comfortable. But that comfort comes at a cost. A lot can happen in the woods and, believe you me, I thought up just about every way this trip could go wrong.

Here are my main concerns in no particular order.

## SANDRO MICELI'S TOP FIVE REASONS NOT TO LOSE YOUR BUTT VIRGINITY IN THE WOODS

## 1. My Ass is a Minefield

I knew the day would come. I mean, it's homosexuality's big-ticket item, right? You tell someone you're gay and their first, second, or third thought is:

*"Oh, so he's cool getting a dick in the ass?"*

Growing up the way I did, I was inundated with the idea that all gay guys do is gasp over brunch and sit on some cock. Which sounded like a nice Sunday. The concept of butt stuff was never unattractive to me, given the right guy, and I'll admit my fingers have gone spelunking during the occasional long shower. But I know me. I know my body. I have lived with my ass for nearly eighteen years and he is not a friendly neighbor. My ass is the old man from *Up*. Selfish, loud, and comfortable living a solitary life. But much like the old man from *Up*, my ass would need to open up and learn to let that special someone inside.

So, after spending an entire morning washing my war zone obsessively, Bash picked me up and we drove Birdie two or so hours upstate to a camping area Del recommended. It was a really nice spot. It was like the Sticks but more alive somehow.

That's sort of how I'd been feeling about everything lately. Since that day on the roof, everything felt new.

We hiked all afternoon, mainly for the hell of it, and Bash held my hand the entire time. At the top of our trek, we realized we'd never actually held hands before and Bash was very eager to right that wrong. *Making up for lost time.*

Three hours and two sweaty palms later, we found a good stopping point under some trees and set up Del's tent near this amazing lake we'd stumbled onto. I didn't tell Bash all the big plans I had for my ass, but I think he could tell I had something up my sleeve. We were arguing over the best way to start a fire, neither one of us wanting to admit that we didn't know the first thing about it, when he kissed me. He keeps doing that. Just out of nowhere. We'll be talking or sometimes just doing nothing, and I'll see a change in his face. Like he suddenly remembers he's allowed to kiss me. It's nice. And the exact opposite of what I needed right then.

Because even with my morning of cheek-scrubbing, I hadn't accounted for the two-hour drive, three-hour hike, and (God's greatest prank) the sudden recurrence of early spring humidity. All this to say, a refresher in that lake was looking mighty fine right about then. It's not like I'd crapped myself but this was a big step so forgive me if I was feeling a bit anal.★

★(**Feeling a Bit Anal** was the original title of this list)

## 2. Bears

Self-explanatory.

## 3. The Eggplant

We were alone in the woods and, my God, did I want to fuck. We hadn't gone that far since December and I could feel us both wanting it. But I suggested skinny-dipping first because why the hell not? We stripped naked and Bash immediately folded our clothes. He's weird like that. I was watching him fold my boxers into a neat little square when, staring down the barrel of it, I remembered just how big his dick is.

*Goddamn it.*

Allow me one quick sidebar.

I am not a picky eater. Even as a little boy, I was always a big "try anything once" kind of kid. But somewhere between the original *American Idol* getting canceled and the new *American Idol* getting rebooted, my mom went on this big health kick. Suddenly all my favorite meals of hers were getting converted into whatever veggie-forward, carb-free, no-cheese recipe Ma ripped off the internet that week.

So, innocent Lil' Sandro was understandably upset when he bit into WHAT HE WAS TOLD to be his all-time fave, chicken parm, only to find a stringy, wet imposter swimming in his marinara. Eggplant Parmesan. *"Just as good as the original, and only half the calories!"*

**NO.**

**DECEPTION.**

Baby Sandro just about threw that fucking plate across the table. Don't get me wrong, I love vegetables. When they're honest. When they're not gallivanting around, pretending to be something they aren't. Because chicken parm is my ultimate comfort food. And part of that comfort is expectation. In knowing what you're getting into. I know what will make me comfortable. Stay in your lane, aubergine.

Okay. Sidebar complete.

Now, this seems like an incredibly long road to get to my point but, believe me, it is the best way to describe what I was looking at by the lake. A familiar feeling of surprise. Be-

cause in sex ed, they had us put condoms on bananas. I was
ready for a banana. I had mentally prepared myself for the
concept of a banana in my future. I knew what I'd be getting
into. But Bash had an eggplant. Bigger, thicker, and harder
to handle than what I expected on my plate.

### 4. Jason Voorhees

All I'm saying is those movies have to get their ideas from
somewhere.
You don't know.

### 5. I AM NOT A REAL ATHLETE

The thing you never consider when you visualize the loss
of your virginity is the positioning. The body rolls and leg
cramps. The *hold on*'s and the *oh, sorry*'s. But, aside from some
pain in the beginning, the sailing was pretty smooth on Halloween. We were lucky. But I have literally studied the odds
of lightning striking twice.

After our swim, we were naked in the tent and drying off
under a quilt. The lake was pretty cold so our bodies were tense
and, how you say, *shrunken*. Bash was talking about going ex-
ploring in the morning but all I could think about was my legs.
In our short career as bed partners, Bash has experimented with
a great many positions. He's a real completionist so, those first
couple of goes, he never stayed in the same position twice. A
true D1 athlete. But I'm not like Bash. I've been stuck in a cast
for most of the year and can't be folded into a pretzel so easily.

Being frozen in a tent only hampered my mobility further. If you haven't gathered, I am not a small person. My legs alone are taller than most elementary schoolers. For both of our safety, it was best that my tree trunks stay out of the air and, if necessary, be strapped to the ground. This limited me to basically one position. As the old masters once wrote:

*Face down, ass up.*

Not exactly the most dignified of positions but decidedly more than the "baby on a diaper-changing table" position the internet recommended for first-time drivers.

At the end of the day, I just didn't want to look stupid. I really didn't want to look stupid for Bash. I just got him back. Things have been going so fucking well and I didn't want my giant legs or hairy gut or uncooperative ass to get in the way of what was supposed to be a really special night.

That's just five of the hundreds of reasons that ran through my head that night. That's my problem. It's kind of both our problems. We spend all this time living in our heads, watching and observing and thinking of all the reasons something could go wrong. But when we were lying there in the tent, trying to get warm, I couldn't think of that list. I left all my reasons to worry in that lake and I could only think of one thing.

## SANDRO MICELI'S TOP REASON TO TRY SOMETHING NEW

### 1. I Love Bash

Hey, big surprise, I love the guy. I really do. And he said he loved me too. He actually said it first which is wild. So, yeah. I guess we're in love.

*Ta-daaaaaa.*

I cannot begin to express how wild that is. Like he's said it a couple of times now, that he loves me, and every time I just start laughing. Like he just told me he saw a dog mowing the lawn. Like I don't believe it but wouldn't that be awesome? I mean, obviously, I believe him. He's my best friend. He wouldn't lie about something like that. I guess I just don't believe that it happened to me. That I would find someone like him and he'd see whatever he sees in me.

The sun had officially set and Bash was holding me. It wasn't our usual MO but it helped with the cold. He's always so damn warm. Like he just hopped out of the dryer. I could feel all that heat against me and thought, *Eh, fuck it.*

Our Songs to Be Nude To playlist was going on the speaker, "U Got It Bad" had just started, and my hips did this sort of shaking/rubbing thing to the beat. Something Bash has done before to me to let me know what he wants. I thought it was time to return the favor.

"Oh. Really?"

"Sure."

"We're in the woods."

"I am aware."

"Bigfoot could be watching."

*"...Let him."*

Bash laughed and pulled me closer to him. He nuzzled my neck and kissed it like he did that first night in the ditch. And I wasn't so cold anymore.

After a few hours of tests and lube and failures and lube and successes, I snuck off to the lake to clean up. I took a minute in the water to laugh at the surreality of the situation. I was buck-ass naked, washing myself in a lake, having just had earth-shattering sex with a boy who loved me. In North Jersey of all places.

"Jesus."

I kissed my chain and thanked God I decided to go to the Beer Olympics that night.

When I got back, he was asleep. Bash once told me he could never fall asleep anywhere but his bed. Especially in public. It probably meant something that he could sleep so soundly now but I was too tired to decipher it. My body had been pushed to the edge. I was done for the night. So, instead, I got under our blankets and held him. Warmed myself up again. Traced messages into his chest and listened to him breathe.

Bash mumbled something nonsensical about hats. I didn't know he talked in his sleep. I stored that fact away in the newly reopened Bash Villeda Database and made a note to ask him about it later. It felt good to be learning more about Bash again. Even with all this data I've collected so far, I'm still learning more and more every day. Day after day. Days and days and days.

I heard the number in my head.

*One hundred and forty-three.*

I looked at Bash's watch. It was after midnight.

*One hundred and forty-two.*

That number's the real reason I worry. Why I needed the night to go well. Why I laugh when Bash says he loves me. Because our time is running out. Already. Every day, a little less.

It's not fair. To get something so great, so late. I just want more time with him.

I traced *RUTGERS* into his chest and tried to go to sleep.

# bash

*apr. 16*

*family*

We rolled up to the B-Town drive-through and I had to cover Lucy's mouth to hear the speaker box.

*"Welcome to Burger Town, can I take your order?"*

Sandro was in the back seat, yelling. "Bullshit! BULL. SHIT."

I tried to get their attention, but Lucy argued through my fingers. "It is NOT bullshit. Mayonnaise is DISGUSTING and I WILL NOT—"

"But how can you say that if you've literally never—"

The speaker crackled and I rested my head on my seat belt. I was regretting my suggestion to spend a Saturday together, just the three of us. It had been twelve straight hours of arguing. Over what? Couldn't tell you.

Lucy whipped around to face her opponent. "Have you tasted shit?"

*"Okay."*

"Okay, but you know you don't want to eat it?"

"That's not the—"

"THAT IS THE ENTIRE POINT, YOU BIG BITCH. Seb, come get your friend."

"Back me up, B."

The two people I love most in the world were looking at me, waiting to see whose banner I supported. So, I turned to the speaker box.

"Yeah, can I get a Number Three, extra cheese, no onion, and a small Sprite, a Double Chicken with B-Sauce, large curly fries, and a root beer, and I'll get a Number Seven combo with sweet potato fries and a Diet Dr Pepper."

I sunk back into my seat. They were still looking at me. Lucy smiled. "Awwww. He knows our orders."

"I'm a good waiter."

Sandro rubbed my shoulders from the back seat. "…Sweet potato fries are fucking nasty, bubs."

Lucy shot him another dirty look. "You have *terrible* taste."

Sandro just snorted and rubbed my head. "Eh. I'd argue we got the same taste."

Thankfully, that got a laugh out of my ex. I smiled at the worker in the pickup window as Lucy and Sandro fought over napkins. I handed them their food and listened to my best friends go. B-Town got our order wrong and we ate in the parking lot, but it was the best dinner I'd had in a long, long time.

On a less tender note, Sandro just about puked up that burger the next day. Since track season started, it's been my personal mission to get my workout buddy excited about running. It's not that Sandro's a bad runner. It's just that he's not good at it. He runs how I'd imagine an unmotivated T. rex would. Head forward, arms tucked up, and making weird noises throughout. On this particular run, he bailed after one loop around my block. My *warm-up*, mind you. We passed the duplex and he veered straight into my front lawn. Fell face-first into the grass and pretended to die. I jogged circles around his corpse.

"Come on! One more block."

"My foot hurts."

"You have no stamina." He mumbled something presumably dirty into the ground and laughed at his own joke. I stopped. "No wonder you only throw things."

"I also wrestled for a minute." He grabbed my ankle and tripped me with his shoulder. Before I had time to cuss him out, he was sitting on my chest. "Plus, two older brothers."

He slapped my cheeks. I had the instinct to give his giant ass my lunch money then I heard a door close.

"*Kinky.*"

I looked up to find Lucy on her porch. I tapped out and Dro rolled off me. We both jumped up, at attention, like we'd been caught throwing a football in the house. She told us to cool it and I invited her to dinner at ours. Del wanted to congratulate us all for getting into our first-choice colleges and

I'd insisted on a Cajun theme. My mom grew up in Louisiana so I was raised on a steady diet of peppers, okra, and shrimp.

"But y'all can't be bickering the whole time, okay? Del's sensitive."

Lucy rolled her eyes and linked arms with Sandro. "We don't bicker, Sebastian. Bickering implies *both* parties are incorrect."

Sandro agreed, happy to let Lucy save him from finishing his run.

I'll give it to them, they kept it civil for the rest of the evening. Just to be safe, though, Del and I handled most of the cooking. We thought it best to keep Punch and Judy away from knives and fire.

After some superb fried okra, some okay catfish, and a banging gumbo, we took a break to digest. Del and I got to our usual dishwashing routine while Lucy and Dro ate ice cream in the living room. They weren't bickering, but we would pick up the occasional outburst.

*"Get off the floor! What are you doing? Sandro."*

Sandro does this thing when he's full where he lies on the ground like a starfish. Got the idea from Ms. Parente's class terrarium. Apparently, lizards rest on hot stones after big meals. Helps with the digestion.

Del laughed and passed me a plate. "They seem to be hitting it off."

"I know. It's scary."

"Worlds collide."

We paused to hear their argument boiling up.

*"You're wrong. You're very wrong."*

*"No, gelato's just cream. Custard has egg, Froyo has milk, but gelato's ALL cream. That's the dif—"*

*"You are so wrong and I don't know why you won't admit it."*

I laughed and shook my head. I knew it was a mistake leaving them alone with that ice cream. I put the dry plate away and Del handed me another. "They're both wrong and both right at different moments. Funny."

"It's been like this all week. They're both wildly stubborn about food."

I almost dropped the plate when they started yelling.

*"BOY! YOU ARE ITALIAN! YOU SHOULD KNOW ABOUT GELAT—"*

*"I AM ITALIAN SO TRUST ME WHEN I TELL YOU—"*

I had to smile. Because by all accounts, Sandro and Lucy's only real connection is a gym class they shared in eighth grade but, somehow, they act like they've known each other for ages. Like brother and sister. They had a rhythm. Maybe that's just how it is with the right people. All that groundwork just appears.

I'm glad it was easy for Dro. I know how hard it's been for him to make friends. He caught me up on how the whole Ronny/Phil situation blew up in his face. It's tragic really 'cause, even if you strip away the sex and the love I feel for him, Dro's still the best friend I've ever had. And it sucks that the world doesn't see that. Everyone could use a friend like Sandro.

My train of thought slowed my drying and, of course, Del was watching me. "I swear to God if you keep staring at me..."

Del laughed and shook his head. Got back to washing. "They're showing my uncle's cabin up in Maine soon. I thought we could visit before it sells. Go fish or swim or whatever. If you want."

Maine. Del's family. The last leg in this relay we seemed to be running together. We still hadn't talked about how I couldn't bring myself to go to his uncle's funeral. How I'd rather let him go mourn alone than come along as Del's Dead Wife's Kid.

So, I took the baton and set my sights on the finish line. "Will your family be there?"

Del nodded. "Brett should be."

He said the name like he'd mentioned *Brett* a thousand times. It killed me that I didn't know who he was. There was so much about Del I didn't know. This man who raised me when my own dad couldn't bother. Who held me when I cried and never pushed me when I pushed him away. He was my family. It was time to know my family.

"Which one's Brett?"

Del smiled. "Older brother."

"Oh. How many brothers do you have?"

"Just him. He raised me. Him and my uncle."

We got back into our dishwashing routine and the conversation got moving.

Brett worked in New York for years in advertising. Then he up and quit one day and became a writer. Over the past decade, he's published three nonfiction books about illegal hunting practices in the Northeast and he loves to ski. Del thought the world of Brett. Wanted to be just like him grow-

ing up. The way he talked about his older brother made me
pissed I was an only child. The pride in his voice.

"He started renovating the cabin early last year. They've
been living up there since the funeral."

"Who's they?"

"Justin and the kids."

"Who's Justin?"

"Brett's husband."

I stopped drying my plate.

So much I didn't know. So much I could've known. All
this time I wasted, watching. Falling off the face of the earth.
How much easier my life could've been if I just talked. Asked
questions. How much easier my life could be.

As if to guide us along, we heard Sandro's laugh boom in
from the living room. It filled the silence hanging around
us. And I nodded. Just enough to answer what Del already
knew. He nodded back. We did what came naturally to us
and said it all with a look.

"...I'd like to meet them."

"Yeah. I'd like that too, Seb."

I thought about one of the last things my mom said to me.
It was about family. What we owe to those who know us.

Del calls me Seb. So does Lucy. This kid that I wasn't anymore. This kid I could still be. It wasn't too late for Seb.

Del told me he'd finish up and to go see my friends. He
patted me on the shoulder and I thanked him. I think I'm
gonna be thanking Del for the rest of my life.

That night, Sandro slept over. He fell asleep pretty quickly,
happy to be my little spoon, but I stayed up watching him.
Something I've been doing since I got him back. Take in

his face at rest. Try to guess what he's dreaming. I know it's weird, but I missed him. Leave me alone.

I've been thinking a lot about dreams lately. What they mean and why I have them. Why some nights my memories replay. Those nights when the dreams about my mom are calm and normal, it's like my brain is rewarding me. It lets me live in those quiet moments with my mother again. I'm helping her cook. We're driving. She's painting the living room and I'm reading to her. There's always a moment where I realize that I'm dreaming but, when it's quiet, I can stay in the dream a bit longer. We can buy ourselves more time. It's that afterglow that's most interesting to me. The calm moments after I realize I'm dreaming but before I wake up.

Living in a dream.

That's what it feels like, watching Sandro and Del laugh together. Listening to Lucy and Dro argue over something pointless. Having all these people I love together and talking and laughing. All these people who love me.

I felt myself drifting. And for a second, I wondered if I'd locked my bedroom door. Something I'd always double- and triple-check before. Dro had slept over dozens of times but tonight was different. Because he wasn't my workout buddy anymore. At least in the duplex. Sandro wasn't my best bro to Del and Lucy.

I kissed his forehead. He smiled in his sleep.

"I love you, Sandro."

Under my roof, I had a boyfriend.

# sandro

## *SWEET BOY*

Ronny DiSario might have the tallest house I've ever seen. I say tallest over biggest because the base of the house is actually pretty standard. It sits on a large, empty property and just keeps going up, like a fucking hotel planted in the middle of the Orchard and a heavy wind might be able to send it toppling down.

I planted my bike in front of *Chateau DiSario* and walked up the driveway. The garage/recording studio door was wide-open but nobody was inside. Thousand-dollar music equipment filled the space and lined the walls. There was nothing stopping a passerby from robbing the place. Maybe rich people don't think about stuff like that. Maybe they wouldn't even notice.

"Care to steal anything?"

I looked to my left and Ronny was at my side. Sipping a Red Bull. I didn't hear her approach.

"I wouldn't know what to do with it."

"Fence it."

"I wouldn't know how."

"Google it."

She offered me her can. I accepted because I'm a good guest. Also, because I was nervous.

"Phil here?"

"No. Why? You think we spend every waking minute together?"

"I think you try."

Ronny shrugged. "He's with his boyfriend. But he's coming over after if you wanted to scream at us as a pair."

"Ronny—"

"Only, I've got a headache brewing so if you could just wait for my Advil to kick in—"

"Ron."

She picked up a stray lacrosse stick and cradled it about her studio. "You were very clear, Sandro. You're a special little boy and we're awful, terrible influences. Message received. I don't think we need to relitigate."

"I came to apologize. It's really...*really* overdue."

"Super. I don't want it. So, where does that leave us?" Ronny tossed her ball in the air and caught it with finesse. "Seriously. What's the point? Best-case scenario, you apologize, I say 'no sweat,' and we skip into the sunset. Then what?"

"I don't... I don't know."

"Exactly. It's almost May, Sandro. We're just about done here. Whatever you came here for, I *promise* you it's not worth the trouble." Ronny chucked the ball into the lawn. She flung the lacrosse stick out with it and plopped down at Phil's drum set.

I shook my head. "That's... I don't like that."

"That's life, big boy. We're all just trying to get to the end of it."

Ronny DiSario had a habit of speaking like a song lyric. But I'd be lying if I hadn't thought those exact words, not too long ago. Before senior year started, I was determined to army-crawl my way to graduation. Just keep my head down, keep my grades up, and get to the end. Keep this town at arm's distance because what had this town done for me lately?

But if I kept limping down that path, I never would've knocked on that truck window at the stop sign. I never would've fallen in love with this boy who changed me. I'd changed. It wasn't too late for that. It was never too late to try.

"Can I be real with you, Ronny?"

Her sigh echoed in the empty garage. "If you must?"

That made me smile. But it faded quick. "I don't know how to make friends." I leaned on Ronny's mixing table. "People always tell me, *'Oh, you? You're so fun, you're so funny, you must have a lot of friends.'* But every time someone says something like that, there's just this asshole in my head screaming, *Hey, fucker, why'd you never learn how to make friends?! Why can't you...why can't you keep a friend?"*

I took a breath. "High school's almost over and I never made any fucking friends." Ronny put the drumsticks down. I shook my head. "I just... I don't know what someone would get out of me. I don't know what I bring to the table that would make someone say, *'Yeah, him. Yeah, Miceli's worth seeing again.'"*

I thought of Bash on my roof. All those things he told me.

That I was good. That I deserved the world. A boy who saw me. A friend who proved me wrong.

"But I wanna try." I looked at Ronny. "I don't care if it's just a summer. Or if it's just about the music or if we won't be friends for long. But I want to be your fucking friend, Ronny. You and Phil, I want to be your friend. I want to talk about guitar and records and the intricacies of Avril Lavigne's career. I want our shitty sort-of band back. This is worth the trouble to me. Apologizing to you isn't pointless to me, man. You guys are worth the trouble."

Ronny just stared at me. I thought I'd stuck some sort of landing there but her silence was making me question it. But eventually she nodded. "Hell of an apology."

"Yeah. Well. No one in my family ever apologizes for shit so... I'm self-taught."

"It was good. Very thorough." She smiled. "It'll be fun to watch you repeat it for Philly."

I laughed and shrugged. "He can get the abridged version."

Ronny stood up and walked around Phil's drum set. Before I could question it, she shook my hand.

"I knew you were a good guy, Miceli."

"That's the rumor, huh?"

She smiled and punched me. I looked around the expensive studio. The Killers' *Hot Fuss* was playing softly. "Jenny Was a Friend of Mine."

I pointed at the speaker. "You finished your demo?"

"No help from you, but yes. NYU said it was *impressively competent*."

"High praise." I sat on the arm of the ratty old couch Ronny kept in there. Maybe the only thing in that garage that cost under 1K. "Could I listen?"

"To my demo?"

"Yeah. Till Phil gets here."

"I mean, it's only a few songs. Philly's gonna be at his boy's for a while. They...take their time."

I smiled and shrugged. "Then we'll just have to hang out till he gets here."

Ronny rolled her eyes and grabbed the remote. "Fine. But if you think it's bad, I need you to lie to me."

"Oh. You just want me to stroke your ego?"

"Keep up, Miceli. That's what friends are for."

I laughed and joined Ronny on the couch. I passed her the remote and got a little closer. Sort of dropped my voice, like anyone in the Orchard could be eavesdropping.

"Wait. So, Phil has a boyfriend?"

Ronny tapped the remote to her lips.

"Mm. Inner circle shit. Top secret, very lock and key."

"*Come on.* Someone from school? One of the theatre guys?"

"I'm not snitching, you gossipy bitch."

"Ron. Are there other gay kids in Moorestown?"

I had this silly, scandalized smile on my face. Ronny just scoffed at it.

"Miceli. There's a lot more going on in our school than track and field. Where have you been?"

All I could do was laugh. Sort of intrigued. Sort of amazed.

"Out of the loop, I guess."

Ronny snorted and elbowed me. She pressed Play and we rested our heads back on the cushions, staring at the cement ceiling together as my bassline shook through the garage. I sounded good. We all did. We sounded like a band. The piano. My bass. Phil's drums. Ronny's voice. Everything. All the time.

After an afternoon of jamming with my friends, Bash and

I squeezed in an evening workout. I spent an hour practicing my throwing form, now that field season is up and running, while some hot asshole ran laps around me. We tired ourselves out until the sun set then blew each other in Birdie as a reward. Incentives are key in maintaining a worthwhile fitness routine.

Plus, I didn't hate that it gave me an excellent excuse to be somewhere that wasn't my house. Since Bash and I got back together, I'd been going to his, going to field practice, and pretty much just coming home to sleep. It's an unspoken arrangement that works for everyone. Ma hasn't said a word to me since the college letter blowup and the rest are busy enduring Raph's new baby. I don't want to be there and they've made it clear the feeling is mutual. If they weren't going to bother, why should I?

After our evening workout (and some exemplary mouth stuff), I sat on my roof and watched the sun set over Moorestown. My house is far from the neighborhoods but some nights I can see the little lights in the distance. The baseball field, Zelley Park, the cul-de-sacs, and the streetlamps. Whenever I see those lights, it makes me think about living in the city. Somewhere not so small. I think I'd do well there. I'm ready for it. Despite being in the middle of fucking nowhere, this farmhouse has prepared me for city life. The noises, the smells, getting mugged, I'm used to all that shit. My house never sleeps.

It was three in the morning when I heard footsteps on my stairs. Ronny had given me a copy of her demo so I was in my room listening to it for the hundredth time and reading. *Daniel: Last Forever.* I thought it might deserve another shot. The steps creaked and I put the book down, annoyed and bracing myself for the intrusion. Instead, a knock. It might've been the first time someone knocked on my door.

I sat up in bed. "…GJ?"

But it wasn't my nephew. Ma pushed through my door with a laundry crate. She looked busy. Or as busy as someone could look at three in the morning. "Dirty clothes. Doing a load."

Sentences. Incomplete but sentences, nonetheless. I was surprised. Ma never comes up to my room. Too many stairs. But there she was.

"It's three in the morning."

"Yeah. Newborns are a bitch."

She pointed to a stain on her shoulder. Spit-up. Raph's newborn Angelo was a fat little volcano. He'd tagged me earlier that day.

"You gotta wear the bib things."

Ma shook the laundry crate, surely full of soiled shoulder bibs. She almost smiled and looked around my room. It was not clean. I didn't tend to have company to clean for. She put the crate down and sat on the edge of my bed. That was weird, hasn't happened since I was a little kid.

"Cold in here."

"It's an attic."

"Mm."

Ronny's cover of "For You" by the Used played on my speaker. Ronny added it to her demo because I said I'd always loved it. I didn't tell her I only loved it so much because the lyrics sounded like Bash. Her singing was the only sound in the room for what felt like minutes.

"This is pretty. Radio?"

I shook my head. Ma just nodded. I could've told her about the song. The singer. Who was playing guitar in the background. But I felt no responsibility to carry this conversation for her. If she had something to say to me, I didn't need to help her say it. But even with my mother's silence, I heard her voice in my head. Those words that drift back in when things get too silent. I was back in the van. A kid. A crying, sick kid.

*"No more."*

And I could feel that wall building back up in me. I was sick and she yelled at me. I broke my foot and she ignored me. When I needed her, she was too busy for me. Who was she to sit on my bed? Interrupt my reading?

"So. Sebastian's back. That's nice. Been a while since he came around. Were you two fighting?"

Who was she to talk to me about Bash? I let my face go blank. I didn't want to talk to her.

She nodded. "Okay. But things are good now? You boys doing anything fun for your birthday? *Eighteen.* That's a..."

I flipped through my book. It was just a prop, just to show her that I wasn't going to do this with her, but I caught a note. I'd written it in the margin toward the end.

*b a lighthouse*

I'd drawn a crappy little sketch of a lighthouse shining its beacon over the ocean, lighting up lost boats on dangerous waters.

"Sandro, please." Ma's hand was on my knee. I hadn't noticed. "I... I had an awful thought. And I couldn't stand it."

Her voice sounded angry. Not at me though. She took my hand and looked at me. Her thumb rubbed my knuckle. "I know you, baby. I do. I've known you your whole life and... and I know when you're not telling me something. I know we don't... We haven't been so... I know *what* you're not telling me, Dro, and—"

She was starting and stopping, trying to say it right. "And I always wanted to give you your space. And your time. I wanted to let you tell me when you were... But after what you said in the kitchen—"

Her voice caught. She was getting upset, but she still held that anger. "Sandro, do you think I'd make fun of you? If you told me?"

"Ma."

She looked at me like a mother. Like my mother. Like who she is for Tina and GJ and Lexi. Now Angelo. Fierce. Protective.

She pointed downstairs. "You think I'd let any of those fuckers make fun of you? For that? For who you are?"

Ma knew. Ma's known. How long has she known? I couldn't stop my eyes from filling up. I wished I could be angry then, but I was just embarrassed.

*"Yes."*

I didn't mean to say it. I didn't mean to speak. I wanted to put my hand on my mouth but my brain wasn't letting me move.

"Yes. I think you'd let them make fun of me."

Ma started to cry and I couldn't move. I didn't want to make her cry but she needed to know. "How could...how could you think that, Sandro?"

"How could I not?" A tear ran down my cheek. "When it's them and it's me, you choose them. You always choose them."

"They're your family. We're your family, Dro. Your brothers and your father, we all love you so much."

I laughed. "How could I know that, Ma? How could I?"

"Sandro."

"No. *No.*" I fought through the tears choking in my throat. "If I'm not solving a problem for you, you don't see me. The last time I told you *I love you*, you asked me what was wrong. You never say it. You don't show it, no one shows it, I can't—"

My face got all tight and I tried to shake it away. "I can't see it. I can't. I shouldn't have to look so hard to find love in this fucking house." I felt his book in my hand. Our song in my room. "I'm so tired of looking for it, Ma."

She just stared at her lap. For a second, I thought she was about to get up and leave. Find another chore that wouldn't make her talk. The music played over our silence. Ronny's stripped-down rendition of "I Wish I Was the Moon" by Neko Case.

Ma nodded. "That's why Northwestern. That's why you want to go so far." I didn't know what to say. She shook her head. "You know, Rutgers is a fine school."

"Ma."

"It's more than anyone in this family ever got."

"That's not the poin—"

"Sandro." Ma looked at me. Steady. It was her turn. I let her speak. "It's selfish. I know it's selfish of me to want you at Rutgers. To want you close. But…"

She sniffed. "I just thought… I thought we'd have more time, Dro. There's never enough time in this goddamn house and I always thought, you and me, we'd find the time. We'd talk. We'd get it out and we'd talk about…all this. About you. What you go through."

She took a little breath. "Because I see it. I do, baby, I see what it's like for you. I understand it. Because we get through things the same way. We cover up. We power through. We stomach. And when things get hard, we go it alone. All this time, I thought we were in the trenches together, getting through it, getting through the days, but…"

Ma took my hand in both of hers. "But that was wrong. I was wrong, Sandro. You're just a kid. You're still a boy. You're my sweet boy and I… I guess I thought that meant you were easy. I thought our talks could wait. I took your sweetness for granted, that amazing…that *beautiful* patience in you…because I thought we'd have more days. I never made the time and now it's running out. That's why I wanted you at Rutgers. That's why I want you close, Dro, I can't… I can't let you go yet. Not like this. I can't let you go to Chicago hating me."

Her hands were cold on mine. Like smoothed stone. They were always cold. I'd forgotten that.

"I don't hate you."

It came out of me like an instinct. She shook her head and I needed her to believe me. I never hated her. That's not what this was.

"I don't hate you. I don't. I just…"

I let go of her hands and tried to hug her. But it felt wrong. Like I didn't know how. It broke my heart that it didn't come naturally anymore.

"I need you to talk to me, Ma. I shouldn't have to scream for it. I need you in my corner. I need you to tell me you love me and I don't wanna feel selfish for needing that. I need it. I need you to hear me."

She kissed my forehead. Like she used to when I was little and simple and easy. I missed that. I missed that so fucking much.

"I hear you, Dro. I hear you, baby."

She hugged me back and we remembered how to hold each other.

I thought I was helping my mother, keeping myself from her. I thought it was the easy road. A road she made really easy for me to take. But did I hate her? No. I never hated her. I just needed her to hear me. That's all I ever needed.

A new song came on. "Call It Fate, Call It Karma" by the Strokes. I smiled, still hugging her. "This is...this is my band. That's me. On bass."

"Oh. You sound good, kid."

"I practiced all year."

"...Is Sebastian in your band?"

I laughed, my face in her hair. "Bash can't sing for shit. The one thing he's not good at. Sounds like a hungry cat."

We giggled and her head leaned into mine. I felt her hand running through my hair. "...Does he love you?"

I closed my eyes and nodded into her shoulder. "He loves me so much, Ma."

I could hear it in her laugh that she was crying again. Ma held my head close to her and touched my face. "I love you more. My sweet, sweet boy."

We talked that night. We talked till I could see the sky change in my window. Till baby Angelo woke up screaming and Dad and Gio drove off to work.

And my house never felt so quiet.

# bash

*track*

I prayed to God to give me more time and He sent me five days of rain.

Time worked differently under the sheets. People stayed home. The sun never moved. Days slowed down during the storm.

On the first day, we washed our hair in the downpour.

Sandro was afraid at first. He didn't trust the wind. I told him I'd protect him so he grabbed a bottle of shampoo and we ventured into the empty streets, daring for cars to run us down. We were soaked to the bone by the time we reached the storm grate, but we didn't care. We worked the gel into a lather and let the rain do its job. Sandro made a spike out of my hair. It'd gotten its length back. I rubbed the suds out of his eyes. We obeyed the bottle's instructions and repeated the steps.

Sandro only ever sang in the shower. Even with a band, he only sang when he was alone. This beautiful, powerful voice with nowhere to go. But there, in the intersection of Duquesne and Third, he sang for the world.

"Islands in the Stream."

I didn't know the song, but we sang it all day.

On the second day, Sandro showed me how to shot put. After a morning of heavy rain and a *Final Destination* movie marathon, the sky turned misty and we wound up at the track field. I'd seen him coaching his freshmen and wanted him to teach me. There's something about watching Dro in his element that fascinated me. I think it's because he's usually too modest to own up to all the things he's good at. Or maybe too embarrassed. But whenever he's talking about all he knows, he gets into his rhythm. It's this excited, stumbling state, and I can't help but stare. Shot put, trigonometry, the composition of an Italian hoagie, there's this well he dives into.

Like how he went on about Atlantic City that first day, before the Beer Olympics. I barely knew the guy but he still said more to me in a minute than anyone had in months. All this uncensored enthusiasm. It made me want to talk to him. It's the first thing I loved about him. He awes me, Sandro.

I threw my first shot. It made a gross SPLERT on the muddy turf. Specks of mud managed to splash the short distance to my shins.

Dro sighed. "You're gonna hurt yourself."

"Show me again, Captain Miceli."

He rolled his eyes and got behind me. Full captain mode. "Shot rests on the middle finger, right under your jaw. Bent knee." He slapped my thigh, so I bent my knees. Carefully, he extended my free arm and adjusted my legs into position. I let myself be coached. Moved. "Eyes up. Keep your left locked." He got into a power position and acted out the throw. "You power from your legs, but it's all about the punch."

I copied his moves. Watched him work. After a few cycles, I took a deep breath and dismounted. The new shot soared past my sad first attempt.

Sandro hooted. "Yeah, buddy!"

He high-fived me and wiped the mud off my face. He got close and I could smell the waffles we'd made during the very ignorable *Final Destination 4*. It's funny. When he was coaching me, it was all business. He was wet and his sweats clung to his body in a way that really worked for me but, still, nothing. That's kind of how it's always been for me. Lucy recently asked if I ever checked guys out in the shower or ogled any particularly tight spandex on the track but there's always been this clear divide in my head. Sports are sports. I'm there to learn. Compete. Be the best. Nothing sexual about it.

But the second Sandro's coach voice faded, all bets were off. He was an inch from me and grabbed my shoulder. "You're a natural. But stay in your lane, track bro. Don't need you showing me up in front of my freshmen."

The rain picked up and I kissed him. I wanted him to teach me everything he knew.

On the third day, I went for a run.

The morning was mist again and I was the only person reckless enough to be running in it. It was my day off but something guided my feet to a diner I'd seen more than enough of. Some lingering itch.

Maybe I thought I'd catch him on a break. I didn't know if I wanted that but there he was. I ran along the chain-link and saw my coworker sitting by the dumpsters. On the milk crates I'd stopped claiming months ago. I didn't feel a need to hide on my breaks anymore but I guess Matty still did.

I slowed my run and stopped at the fence. I couldn't tell if he saw me or what he was thinking. Matty was sitting in the rain, barely keeping dry, and I wondered why he would do something like that. On a day like that, why would he let himself sit in the cold? Did he like to be alone that badly? I felt the mist soaking into my shirt and remembered what we still had in common.

So, I did something that was starting to make sense to me. Something I didn't understand when the roles were reversed. Something I didn't have the tools to appreciate from the other side of that fence.

I waved.

I know Matty saw me. I know he considered waving back. Taking an olive branch. Taking a chance. He gave it more thought than I did in his shoes and that surprised me. And it surprised me how deeply it stung when he walked back inside.

I waited for the screen door to slap, for him to reconsider. I waited until the rain picked up and I decided I needed to get out of the cold. I had people at home. Del. Sandro. Lucy. My friends. Matty wasn't my friend anymore. Matty wasn't my fault.

On the fourth day, Sandro told me he wanted to go to Rutgers. I thought he was joking. He wasn't.

"For your mom?"

"For us."

"Sandro."

Sandro has never wanted to go to Rutgers. I know this because it's what I wanted for so long. He understood that about me but never agreed with it. He thought I could do better. I know he can do better.

"What about Northwestern?"

He sat up in bed. Held my pillow close to him. "Rutgers has an Applied Mathematics program. Just as well rated as Northwestern's."

"But...you don't want to go to Rutgers."

"I can do everything I wanted to do at North at Rutgers. And it's closer. We'll have Wawa and we can come home whenever we want. See Del and GJ and—"

"Sandro."

He turned to me. Made that eye contact he makes when he's really trying to convince me of something. "And Ma and me are good now. Better. We're actually talking, she's really making an effort with me. And she'd be so... We could be so—"

It wasn't me he was trying to convince. I needed to tell him. "Dro, I'm going to Villanova."

That stopped him. Honestly, it stopped me. I didn't know I'd made the decision until I said it. There'd still been that question mark. But I knew where that road was heading. I knew the second I found those seeds.

He just stared at the pillow. Not upset or mad or nothing. He just stared.

I sat up and took his hands. "It's...it's wild, I know. I just... They have a better track program. And it's still close. Ish. And it's... It would be *my* thing."

He nodded. Still staring.

"Dro, look at me."

He did. And he smiled. Sad. "It was stupid. I shouldn't have... I'm sorry."

"No. I get it. I do. I've thought about it."

"Really?"

"Obviously."

He rubbed my knuckle with his thumb. He was quiet. Like he'd done something wrong. "I just... I always thought Northwestern was a long shot. And I knew it would hurt if I didn't get it. But...at least I'd have you."

"But you got in. You can go, Sandro."

"I know, I get that. I do. It's just... It's like there's this world where we go to college together. We get to do that. This one path we can take and we can keep..."

I took his face in my hand. I could feel his jaw, so tense it might snap. This was killing him. This was weeks of thought, nights of worry, going up in smoke.

"B."

He sniffed. Didn't need to say it. We understood each other.

"Yeah."

"Yeah."

I pulled him onto my bed and we lay back down. He rested his cheek on my chest. I could tell he was still thinking. Kicking himself for even bringing up this ray of hope. I stared at the scarlet *R* still hanging above my bed frame. I remembered when I put it up. I'd just spent the day in Camden, touring the campus. Walking the streets, eating the food, taking it in. Trying to look into my future.

A very different person put that *R* on the wall.

"Rutgers was all I wanted. For so long. It was all I could see. But...sometimes better things come into your life. Things you didn't think you could want." He buried his face into my shoulder. I breathed. Tried to sound strong. "I can't just go for her, Dro. She can't be my reason. And us... What we have? It can't be the only reason either."

He nodded into me. I blinked back a tear and pushed forward. "We'd just be going for someone else again. And, as bad as I might want it—as bad as I might fucking want it—in the long run, Nova's better for me. Northwestern is better for you." I held him. I held him so close to me. Because it really hurt to say. "It's not enough to want something. You gotta find the right way to want it."

He was breathing heavier then. Still nodding. "...That's very mature."

There was a pop in my laugh, and I guess I was crying a little. So much damn crying this year. Sandro wiped my face and felt the scar on my eyebrow. I took his hand. "And Nova's an hour closer to Chicago. I looked it up and, I mean, it's still a drive but I'll come see you. You can show me the sights. Your apartment. It'll be cool."

Now I was trying to convince him. Convince him that something so great wasn't ending so soon. As quick as it had begun.

On the last day of the storm, we woke up in each other's arms.

"Is it morning?"

I couldn't tell. The rain washed out my window. "I think so."

We looked at the window. The neighborhood was a blur. Everything was silent.

"...Dro?"

"Yeah?"

"How many days?"

He didn't have to think about it. He just sniffed. "One hundred. It's one hundred today."

We couldn't stop the numbers. We could only keep track.

My boyfriend and I stared at the ceiling together and listened to the rain click on my roof. It was getting softer. Sandro gripped my hand tight. So tight.

"I wish I knew you sooner, B."

The storm would pass soon. And time would only move quicker.

# sandro

*MAY 21*

*ALL THIS TO SAY*

I wish there was a movie of my life. Something I could turn
on when I wanted to know what was coming. Even if it meant
I'd know the ending, at least I'd know what to do next.

But there aren't movies for boys like me. Growing up, I
could never find myself in the Hollywood endings or music
montages. I wasn't giving speeches at prom or racing to the
airport. I grew up watching movies for other boys. Learning
from the wrong playbook. Stealing notes off someone else's
paper. Maybe that's my problem. Maybe that's why I can't
stop counting down the days.

Because the things I want tear me apart. Bash. Northwest-

ern. I can't have one and the other. Time's running out and
the worst part, the thing that really kills me, is that there's
no choice to be made. I don't need a movie to know what
happens next.

I'm going to Northwestern.

I'm going to get my apartment and my dogs and my new
friends. I'll wear boat shoes and bike to class. I'll get new
nicknames and tattoos and drink too much and he won't be
there. I'm going to have to find a way to be happy without
Bash. The guy who taught me what happy meant. The guy
who got me to stand up for myself. The guy who's always
been too good for this town. The best.

If you ask around school, ask about Bash, people always
say the same thing.

"Villeda? He's the best."

He was so many people to so many people but always
stayed "the best."

But I wonder what people would say if you asked them
why. What makes him *the best*? The gold medals? The college scouts? His body? His jokes? That's all great but only a
few people get to see the real reasons. Because the rumors are
true. Bash is the best. He's the best reading partner. He's the
best dining companion. He's the best pillow on a cold night.

Bash is the best friend I've ever had.

But now he's the world's problem. Give it a year and I'm
sure everyone at Nova will say the same thing about Sebastian
Villeda. And they won't know how lucky they are. Because
they're going to see how great he'll become. How much he'll
keep growing. And I can only hope I do the same.

*Ninety.*

My birthday fell on prom which gave us the perfect excuse to ditch prom. Our first excuse was neither of us knew who was supposed to ask who but that was more of a joke anyway. It's great it worked out this way, though, because I think we both wanted an out.

We ended up at the ditch after practice one day, sharing an Italian hoagie like a joint, when he finally brought it up. "It's not that I don't want people at school to know about us."

"Really? I don't."

"Okay, sweet, me neither." He laughed and passed me the hoagie. "It just seems like a lot right now, you know?"

"For sure. Plus, even if we just go as friends…"

"People talk."

"And those people talk to other people who talk to more people and babababababa."

"Exactly. *Bababababa.* Like, I wanna know who knows."

"Yeah…" I could feel a bug in my shorts and jumped up to shake it out. "Ma knows."

Bash sat up. *"Really?"*

"Yeah. I mean, she's not bouncing around saying the words *'My son is a gay'* but she keeps coming up to my room. To talk. She always asks about you. Us."

"Huh. Does she approve?"

"Oh, you'd know if she didn't."

Bash nodded. I think he was pleased he passed the test.

I was still shaking my legs and shorts when he spoke with a mouth full of hoagie. "Del knows too."

I stopped shake-dancing. The bug could wait. "Whoa."

"Right?"

"Does he…*approve?*"

"Of me? Sure."

"Of me."

"Nah, Del hates your hairy ass."

We laughed because Del has made it clear he prefers me to Bash. I felt the invading bug somewhere around my hip and jumped back into action.

"Just take your shorts off."

"No!"

"Why?"

"I know your tricks, Villeda."

"It's a silly rule."

"*Silly?*" I made a clear and hard rule after Halloween that we would keep the ditch a dick-free zone. It was good for reading, eating, and talking but Mother Nature (and any possible wandering Moorestownians) didn't need to see our bare asses. "The ditch is sacred ground."

At the end of the battle, I discovered the bug was an ant. He was a worthy adversary and died somewhere around my waistband. I joined Bash on the incline and finished off the hoagie. He brushed some grass out of my hair and I put it back in his.

"Hey. I was thinking 'bout telling Ronny. And Phil. The band."

"About...oh. About you?"

"I thought it might be something they should know. I think I want to tell them about me."

Bash sat up on his elbows. Really considered it. I knew he wouldn't be leaping at the idea but I'd run the numbers in my head. His numbers. And I knew I had a fifty-fifty shot at him being okay with the concept. Even if I was only outing myself, Phil and Ronny would inevitably connect the dots. But Phil's on the team and Ronny's no gossip. They wouldn't spread my shit. Our shit. Also, biggest plus, those two don't talk to anyone they hate and that's just about everyone in this one-horse town.

"I wanted to ask first. If you'd be okay with that. It's okay if you're not, I just wanted to run it by you first."

Bash shrugged. "I mean...it's your...you know, *journey*. Or whatever. You don't need my permission, Dro."

"I think I do though. I do." I got up on my elbows too. "My journey's your journey, man. My shit's your shit, that's what I signed up for."

Bash stared up at the canopy above us. Shielding us and the ditch from the rest of the world. Our little island in the stream.

He smiled. "I like Phil. And Ronny. I like seeing you with them. It's like they're the people you would've found if you weren't...you know."

"Trapped in a linebacker's body? Cursed with tree trunk legs? Built like I live on top of a beanstalk?"

"I was gonna say *'sporty'* but go off."

I snorted laughing. And he let out those machine-gun cackles. He took my face and gave it a kiss. One on each cheek then a quickie on the lips.

"They deserve to know. You deserve to tell your people."

I rubbed my forehead on his. "I'll make sure they don't give you too much shit."

"I don't know if that's possible. They shit on everything."

*"Everything All the Time."*

I smiled and put my head in his lap. He scratched my back

and we just breathed for a minute. He smiled down at me. Devious. Plotting.

I laughed. "That's a weird face." He nodded. "...Why the weird face?"

"'Cause."

"'Cause?"

"'Cause I still owe you a date."

When the day of the legendary first date arrived, I'd concocted this whole game plan. A strategy on how to maneuver about the minefield that is my home without my brothers or dad or any rogue child asking questions. Asking what I was up to. Why I was getting all dolled up. It involved distraction, diversion, there was a point where I considered setting a fire, but it was all for nothing. An hour out, I left my room to snag a pair of dress socks from Raph but found the house was completely empty.

I poked my head down the stairs. "HEY!"

It echoed. "HEY! WHO'S HOME?!"

Nothing. That was weird. That never happened. Not a scream nor shout nor ESPN highlight blared from the first floor.

"HEY, THERE'S A FIRE UP—"

A hand slapped my shoulder. Ma hurried by me, a bundle of clothes in her arms. "Stop hollering, we're on a time crunch."

She was heading up my stairs before I could ask a follow-up. "Where is everyone?"

"Out. You gonna shave?"

"Wha...why would—"

She laid out a nice white button-up on my bed and some

dress pants. "Alessandro, you are not going out looking like some college freshman slob, shave your fucking face."

Ma hung a very handsome sports coat on my desk. It looked like my dad's from fifty pounds and twenty years ago. She busted out a lint roller and gave the coat a focus she usually saves for open houses or Tax Day.

"Your dad's on-site all day, won't be home till after dinner. I got him to let Gio help him out, drove GJ to his buddy's, and Raph took the little ones to the Funplex. Place's half-off all month. Who knew?"

I gotta admit, I was a little speechless. "So...we got the house to ourselves?"

Ma stopped rolling and smiled at me. "If a boy's gonna take my son on his very first date, that boy's gonna ring the goddamn doorbell. None of that end-of-the-driveway shit you two've been doing."

I didn't have time to tear up. But I found time to hug her first.

Growing up, watching the movies for boys not like me, I learned to expect certain things out of a first date. I'd have to drive to a girl's house and have an awkwardly stern conversation with her father. He would ask me about sports and the weather, all with the weird subtext that I was not to fuck his precious property. She'd come down the stairs slowly and I'd say something cheesy like:

*"Wow. You look beautiful."*

Her mom would take a picture and her dad would tell me to have her home by eight. We would see a movie, maybe something scary, and I would hold her hand somewhere around Act 2. We'd walk in a park, maybe grab an ice cream cone, and I'd kiss her under a tree.

But my life wasn't a movie. There was no roadmap for this shit. I had no idea how to follow the rules of a first date because they never made rules for boys like me. Boys like me just had to wing it.

I was waiting by the door but I let him ring the bell anyway. I'd texted him ahead of time that we wouldn't have to sneak around tonight and he was just as excited as me. After the second ring, I opened the door and we just stared at each other. Took in each other's efforts. Ma had put me in about five different outfits before settling back on my dad's black sports coat. I'd obliged and shaved for her but I really despise my face bare. I look like a giant baby. Plus, it grows back in seconds like *The Santa Clause* so what's the point?

I'm glad I listened to Ma though. Just for the look on his face.

Bash was wearing a sweater and khakis. He must've bought them just for the night 'cause his closet is sponsored by Under Armour. I'd never seen him like that, with his long hair all styled. He looked like the man he'd become soon. I was looking at Villanova Bash. He rubbed my bare cheek. He'd never seen my face without hair and it was like he needed to touch it. Register this new part of my body. He stopped, realizing where we were, but I grabbed his hand. Put it back on me and smiled. Took him in again.

I couldn't stop myself from saying it. "Wow. You look beautiful."

Bash rubbed his thumb on my cheek and kissed me.

I heard Ma from inside. "Okay, Birthday Boy, you owe me a picture."

On instinct, Bash dropped his hand. She was standing by the stairs, holding a camera. I groaned. "Ma, c'mon, we're gonna be late."

We were truly pushing time on our reservation but I really just wanted to give Bash an excuse. Maybe myself one too. Ma was holding the family camera, after all. And while I'd love a picture to remember that moment, we were treading in unknown waters. Because I'd found a path back to my mother. You could even say I'm on the way to forgiving her. But I could only see that path once she started talking to me. Once she apologized, made an effort. The path to the rest of my family is harder to see. My brothers and father still feel like something to outmaneuver. A problem to overcome. A wrong not so easy to forgive. And I couldn't shake the feeling that something as simple as a picture in my foyer could turn into evidence under our roof.

"Use my phone." Bash was walking over to Ma before I could overthink the moment to death. "It'll just be for us. You know?"

Ma smiled and took his phone. She understood what he was really saying. "Good idea, Sebastian. You look very handsome tonight."

"Thank you, Mrs. Miceli."

I joined Bash by the steps and stood by his side. We smiled and Ma took a few.

"Aww, so sweet. You look like the *best* of friends." She waved at us to get closer. "Now, look like you like each other, damn it."

I sighed and Bash laughed. He grabbed my arm and put it around his shoulder. I did him one better and moved it around his waist. Ma gave us the thumbs-up. "Better. Handsome boys."

Ma took a few, really getting us at all angles. After about a minute, she scrolled through her handiwork. I think she was getting choked up.

"*Ma.*"

"Shut up, Dro, I'm fucking human."

We all laughed. Bash took his phone back and Ma saw us off. She got us into Birdie and watched from the porch as we started in on Mile One of our driveway. I kept an eye on her from the rearview and I don't think she ever stopped smiling.

Bash noticed. "She seems good."

I slipped my hand into his as my farmhouse faded into nowhere. "Yeah. She's in our corner."

The path back to my family might be hard to make out in the dark. But for the first time in a long time, I had hope. Because my mom could stop the earth on its axis if she really tried. That's just the kind of person she is. She's always trying. And now she was trying for me.

We went to Rossi's, this fancy Italian place I'd only ever been when my grandparents were in town. It's a bit of a drive, a few towns over, which really made it special. No one would know us there. We could be anyone.

Dominic Natoli and his partner Daniel Branch flashed their legitimate Michigan IDs to the waiter and enjoyed a bottle of red with their steaks. Local restaurateur Dominic Natoli was a bit of an oenophile and knew how to order off-menu. Eight-time gold medalist Daniel Branch had a big Olympics

in the morning so he made sure to carbo-load on compli-
mentary bread. Danny and Dom were a winning pair. They
referred to each other as "my partner" without any hesita-
tion and housed twenty-five rescue dogs in their Philadel-
phian brownstone.

I chuckled at the idea of a future with Bash. He was still
inspecting his fake. "Told you they'd work, *Mr. Natoli.*"

I snapped back to reality and sipped my wine. "I think the
waiter pitied us, *Mr. Branch.*"

He laughed and put the card away. "You know... I was
thinking 'bout actually changing it. For real. Taking Del's
name."

"*Villeda* no mas? Por qué?"

He shrugged and cut up his steak. "I don't remember my
mom as Simone Villeda. She was Mrs. Branch. Married to
Mr. Branch. It just feels right. Should've done it years ago."

"*Bash Branch.*" I admired the sentiment but the name
sounded iffy in my mouth.

He shook his head. "*Sebastian.* Sebastian Branch."

That felt better. It felt right, moving forward. That outfit,
the hair, his smile. That was Sebastian Branch.

"A strong biblical name. *Salute.*" We clinked our glasses
and drank. We'd already killed our first bottle. "I'm still calling you Bash though."

"Fair. I like that though. It's like how Del and Luce call
me Seb. You'll call me Bash. Nova peeps'll call me Sebastian.
Different names for different chapters."

Different chapters. That's a good way of putting it. How
I was feeling. I was someone in the middle of Bash's story.

One day, I'd be someone he used to know. Important but past tense.

"Dro? What's up?"

I shook my head. "...I coulda known you my whole life, Bash." Bash stopped drinking. "You were right across town. We could've had years. We could've...we could've had more than a chapter, you know? I just... I wish we had more time."

I thought about Ma in my attic. All that time we wasted never talking. How much better our family could've been if we just figured our shit out earlier. So much wasted time. That noise in my stomach and my chest pounded against my skin and everything just seemed pointless all of the sudden. Why should I enjoy what won't last? What's a first date without a future?

"Hey." Bash put his hand in mine. "At least we got this part right."

I was standing by a bonfire with him again. Nine months ago. At the beginning of this road. Watching a party devolve into a blur. My words echoed in my head.

*"It was supposed to be more than this, right? This part of our lives? Sometimes I feel like I did this part wrong."*

I closed my hand around Bash's. Not Daniel's, not Sebastian's, Bash's hand. This person who knew me. Who heard me. Who I didn't want to let go.

"I don't want to stop, Bash."

Bash smiled. Like the answer to all this unknown was so simple. "Then we won't."

I chuckled. "What, we just stay at this table for the rest of our lives?"

"We have phones. Weekends. I have a car."

"Long distance?"

"Why not?"

"'Cause it doesn't work. It'll ruin it."

"Says who?"

"Says everybody. Kids at school. My brothers. Every movie ever."

Bash just shrugged. So simply. "I've never seen a movie about guys like us."

There are no movies about guys like us. There are no rules for guys like us. No precedent. No data. Without a roadmap, we had no idea what might happen next. And maybe that wasn't a bad thing. Maybe it could be better than the movies.

I smiled. "It's a long shot."

He smiled. "We've always been lucky."

If anyone could make long distance work, it's a runner.

We kissed in the parking lot and I couldn't stop. Wouldn't. Didn't have to. The stereo blared Ronny's demo the entire drive, windows down, and I never let go of his hand. Never stopped singing. We didn't have to stop. We could try. We would try for each other. That's all I wanted. Someone to try with me.

The noise in my chest poured out the open window, screaming Green Day and blink-182 all over the turnpike. Bash screamed along with me, our noises in harmony. We must've looked stupid, but we forgot to notice. We let our voices tear into the night air. Because this noise can't stay inside. That's not what it's for. Bash taught me that. People needed to hear it. They were going to hear it.

They were gonna hear me.

# bash

*field*

Birdie flew across the highway. Her reds and yellows lit up the night.

"It was you."

She flew past an unremarkable diner off the turnpike. Girls in gowns and boys with loose ties sat on their cars and ate burgers. A hard girl with soft hands kissed her date between bites. A loud boy hooted and hollered for his buddies.

"Nah, it was you."

She flew through a quiet neighborhood with tall, similar houses. Past a kid taking out the trash and a band playing in their garage.

"You gave me an opening."

By the dark windows of a school and the chain-link of a track field.

"Bullshit."

By the farmhouse at the end of the world. The lights on, never sleeping.

"You made a face."

Past the duplex with one porch. A mother getting home from work chatting with a father on his way out.

"So? You kissed me."

She parked in her field under a sky full of stars.

"Because you gave me a face!"

Her reds and yellows guided our hands in the dirt. A new patch, far from the corn, where something could grow.

Sandro patted the earth down and his hands echoed across the farmland. "You said, *'Man, I love sandwiches'* and you smiled."

"A smile's not a face. I smile."

"You don't. Not like that."

"Still. You made the first move." I emptied a water bottle on the mounds and he inspected the remaining seed. "Apple?"

"We'd know if it was an apple, though, right?"

"Maybe watermelon."

"I hate watermelon. Too much work."

"Ridiculous."

I washed his hands with my second bottle and he washed mine. He dried his palms on my sweater and we walked back to Birdie.

"Mom wouldn't have given me watermelon. She hated it too."

"It's not an aggressive fruit. What's there to hate?"

"She thought it was a waste of time. And *you're* an aggressive fruit."

"I handed you that. Don't be proud."

I turned Birdie off and we hopped up into her truck bed. Opened our whiskey/Coke and settled into our pillows. He pulled the quilt over us and I found my spot under his arm.

I could see the mounds from the truck and I wondered how many gifts I had left from her. How much my mom still had to teach me.

"I think I would've told her. About us. Me."

"Really?"

"She probably knew before I did."

I listened for the highway. Something my mom would do. She thought the sounds of the traffic echoing across the field were like waves. Growing up, she told me there was an ocean on the other side of the trees. I just needed to listen for it.

"I used to cry a lot. At night. She'd take me for these long drives in Birdie to calm me down. We'd always end up here. In her truck. In our field."

"That picture on your nightstand."

"Yeah. She'd run her hands through my hair and talk to me. Always made me feel safe."

He sipped from the bottle. Sandro had perfected the ratio of whiskey to Coke. I was just happy I didn't have to pretend to like beer anymore. I took the bottle and drank.

"I think she'd be real proud of you, Bash. I wish I knew her."

I capped the bottle. "She would've *loved* you."

"Why?"

"She was a sucker for boys. Said men are their best when they're little. Before the world gets to them."

I rubbed my bracelet and could feel her. Watching me. Always watching me.

"After she died, I wasn't happy with who I was. I forgot the kind of person she wanted me to be. That I wanted to be. And you reminded me. She would've loved you for that."

Somewhere along the road, somewhere on our trail, something changed for me. It was different. I was different. It's like I got a second chance to become a person. As if I'd made all the right choices these past four years and was allowed to be a better Bash. And that's all I ever wanted. To be better than I was.

I won the competition with myself.

Sandro dropped the remaining seed into my jacket pocket and rubbed my chest. "How long you think they'll take to grow?"

"We have to find out what they are first."

"What about when we're gone?"

"Del will check in on them."

"What if they die?"

"We'll try again."

"What if we die?"

"Then we don't have to worry about it."

"What if…" He stopped. I could feel his worry. He would always worry. That's just who he is. One of the thousands of things I get to know about him. "I say that a lot. *What if?*"

"Not too much. It's no *anywho*."

"*Anywho?*"

"You didn't know? You've got a few catchphrases, baby boy."

"I do not. You're just around me too much."

"No, I just pay attention."

He chuckled. "You know, I thought this year would be easy. Had it all mapped out. I'd get my cast off, go to every fifth party I'm invited to, and moonwalk my way to graduation."

"That's a very Sandro approach."

"I hate variables. *What-ifs*. I like knowing what happens next."

"I know what happens next."

"How?"

"Well, I'm psychic."

"Oh, you never mentioned."

"You don't know me at all, Miceli."

We laughed. He almost spit up the drink.

"Shit. So, what happens? What's next?"

I grabbed his big, hairy hand and put up his index finger. "June. We graduate. Go to Six Flags. See too many movies and grill every Friday."

I put up another finger. "July. We live on the beach. Get tattoos, maybe I pierce my nipple, and we shoot some Roman candles off at Wildwood."

"Fuck you. AC or bust, bitch."

He smiled. I raised another finger. "Then August. We go camping with Del, maybe Lucy invites us to her dad's place in the Poconos."

"Then we move away."

I could feel a shake come and go in his hand. I raised another finger. "September. I drive you and help you unpack. You repay the favor. We talk on the phone. I tell you about my roommate's weird-smelling microwave. You join a shitty a capella group."

He laughed and raised the last finger himself. "October. I start riding a bike everywhere and some sorority chick gives you HPV."

His smile made me smile. I raised my own finger. "November. Thanksgiving break. We come back."

"And Christmas. And winter break."

"Yeah."

"That's a long time."

"Maybe. Maybe it'll go quick."

"And you won't forget about me?"

I laughed. I thought he was joking. His face was serious. "Sandro."

Forget him? Forget Sandro?

I took off my prayer bracelet and slid it onto his wrist.

I could never forget Sandro Miceli.

He smiled. Leaned forward and unclasped his chain. It was cold on my neck, but his hands were warm. I'd given him my warmth, I think.

I rubbed his shaved cheek. "And we'll always talk."

"Yeah?"

"'Course."

"Good. We talk well."

"I've noticed."

"But what if we run out of things to talk about?"

I shrugged. "We'll start over. From the beginning."

"From the top?"

"And we'll see where it goes."

He nodded. "We'll see."

I laughed. "We'll see."

I felt the edges of his smile. The best thing in my life. Those dimples and lines. I could spend all night touching that smile. He took my hand and kissed it. We got close and stared at the stars. He ran his hands through my hair and I closed my eyes. Safe. Quiet.

The air was warm and I could feel summer coming. Sandro and I would have a summer together. What came next would come but summer would live again.

My ear against Sandro, I could hear summer's heartbeat.

In our field, I could hear the ocean.

★ ★ ★ ★ ★

# acknowledgments

To my mom for all the early talks.
To my dad for all the late ones.
To my sister for everything she taught me.
To my brother for everything I like about myself.
To my grandmother for Skylark.

To my friends from Jersey. I wish I met you sooner.
To my friends in Monteagle. I'll see you next summer.

To every teacher who told me I could do better.
To Ms. Morgan for taking the time to show me how.

To every kid who's cried in their car between classes.
To every kid who's stayed up for the Oscars.
To every kid who can't find the words yet.

And to Kirsten Dunst. Underrated.

To everything, all the time.
I love you, I love you, I love you all.